BOUND

BOUND

SINNERS AND SAINTS
BOOK THREE

KATHY LOCKHEART

Editor: Susan Staudinger
Proofreader: Jovana Shirley, Unforeseen Editing, www.unforeseenediting.com

Cover design:
Model cover design: © By Hang Le
Photographer: Wanderer Photographer
Discreet Cover: Wild Love Designs

ISBN:
ebook: 978-1-955017-61-9
Paperback Cover: 978-1-955017-65-7

Published by Rosewood Literary Press

BLURB

"Marry me or watch your company burn." That's how Axel Pierce—my biggest rival and brother's best friend—proposed our fake engagement.

Some call him a corporate shark.

I call him the devil in a three-piece suit.

Too bad he kisses like an angel and touches me like he means it.

Now every staged dinner feels like foreplay. Every public appearance tests our control. And every night I'm left asking:

Is this elaborate charade really about saving our companies ... **Or is there something else he's trying to claim?**

From international & Amazon Top 25 best-selling author Kathy Lockheart, BOUND is a fake engagement, billionaire, brother's best friend romance with enemies-to-lovers banter, a prank war, and a dangerously possessive alpha hero.

✔ *Fake Engagement with Forbidden Chemistry*
✔ *"Who Hurt You?" Vibes*
✔ *"Touch Her and Die" Energy*
✔ *Jealous, Obsessive, Protective Billionaire Hero*
✔ *Forced Proximity & Slow-Burn Tension*
✔ *Banter & Spice*

Stand-alone. Binge-worthy HEA.

AUTHOR'S NOTE

BOUND contains content that might be triggering for some readers. For a full list of triggers, please visit my website at Kathy-Lockheart (dot) com.

To all of us who have lost ourselves in the comparison game. May this story guide us back to the truth: we were always enough, always worthy, always whole.

1

POV: YOU ACCIDENTALLY TRIGGERED THE SOCIAL MEDIA APOCALYPSE AND NOW YOU HAVE TO FAKE DATE SATAN HIMSELF. 😈 💕 #LITERALLYDATINGTHEDEVIL

DAKOTA

"Marry me or watch your company burn."

Axel Pierce was a corporate shark, notorious playboy, and (most unfortunately) my brother's best friend. He stood across from me in his sleek home office, his jaw clenched so tight, I could practically hear his molars grinding.

I didn't sit in the chair he'd undoubtedly expected me to take. Instead, I planted both palms on his precious desk and leaned forward, invading his personal space until I could count the flecks of gold in his annoyingly perfect blue eyes.

"I'd rather perform surgery on myself with a rusty spoon than marry you," I replied, matching his intensity with my sweetest smile.

He didn't back down. Of course he didn't. Instead, he leaned forward, too, close enough that I caught a whiff of his ridiculously expensive cologne. Sandalwood and something that screamed of decadence that probably tasted as good as Axel looked.

"Trust me, Sunshine, I'd rather watch that gruesome spectacle. But thanks to what you did, I've got three hundred employees who need paychecks, and when your brother finally gets out of prison, he'll have nothing but the money he invested in this company. So, congratulations."

Okay. There was a lot to unpack there. First of all, my guilt over how this would affect everyone else. I swallowed it. I'd torture myself with that particular emotion later, during my regularly scheduled three a.m. mental hamster-wheel sessions. Second of all, the guilt that my brother, Knox, had invested in Axel's business. Knox. Who hopefully would make parole soon and would need that money to survive. Third of all, and evidently most importantly according to my emotions, was: how dare he put this all on me?

"What I did?" I balked. "You're the one who can't keep it in your pants. Maybe if you had an ounce of self-control, we wouldn't be having this delightful little chat."

"Self-control?" He stalked around the desk, each step deliberate, predatory. God, why did he have to move like that? Like every muscle had been personally choreographed to make me notice. "You want to lecture me about control? After you posted a photo of me with the caption: *When you forget you're at a CHARITY gala*?"

"How many times do I have to say it? I didn't mean to post it publicly. It was supposed to go to my private stories for friends only!"

"Your drunken mistake is now my very sober problem." He raked an angry hand through his dark hair, messing up the perfect style in a way that was unfairly attractive.

Stop. Noticing. His. Hair.

"Our problem," I corrected, jabbing a finger into his chest. Big mistake. The solid wall of muscle beneath his tailored shirt sent electricity buzzing through me, and when his eyes dropped to where my finger pressed against him, something shifted in the air between us. Something dangerous and entirely unwanted.

His gaze met mine again, darker now, more intense. "Why were you taking pictures of me with another woman in the first place, Dakota?"

Because seeing you with your hands on someone else made me want to throw things, and that terrifies me more than this fake engagement ever could.

"I thought it was unprofessional," I claimed.

"So you say." His eyes narrowed. "But why would you care who I was flirting with?"

"Like I said, I was drunk." Not totally a lie. I was three vodka sodas deep when I'd seen him with his hand on that woman's lower back, whispering in her ear while she laughed with her hand on his chest. "And in case you've forgotten, I deleted it as soon as I realized my mistake."

"After it went viral!"

"I still don't understand why it went viral. You've been a playboy for years. Who knew the public had finally set a limit on your ... recreational activities?"

A vein pulsed in his temple. "My recreational activities?"

"Oh, I'm sorry. What's the preferred terminology? Your conquests? Your rotation? Your—"

"Enough!" The sharp command sliced through our standoff. Rebecca Winters, our PR crisis manager (yes, that's a thing, and, yes, we apparently now had one. The best in the country, no less) stepped forward from where she'd been standing silently in the corner, her leather portfolio hitting the desk with practiced precision. "This isn't helping, and for the fifth time, you won't actually get married."

I'd almost forgotten she was in the room, standing like some designer-clad sphinx, judging our every word through calculating eyes.

"The reason the public didn't like this particular display," Rebecca continued, her red-soled heels clicking against the hardwood floor as she approached, "was because that woman is Victoria Webb. Senator Stephen Webb's wife. As in the Senator Webb who's planning to run for president. America's golden-boy politician with his perfect wife. Both beloved by millions."

She pulled out her tablet and turned it toward us. "You essentially posted a photo of a notorious playboy in what looks like an intimate moment with America's sweetheart. At the exact moment her husband was inside, giving a speech about family values."

"How was I supposed to know that?" Axel growled.

"The ten-carat diamond ring on her finger might have been a clue," Rebecca replied, one perfectly arched eyebrow raised. "Or perhaps the fact that her face is on every political magazine cover in the country."

I bit back a smile. *Score one for the PR guru.*

"She came on to me," Axel insisted. "If I had known she was married or who she was, I would've walked away immediately." He glanced at me, his expression shifting to something almost vulnerable before hardening again. "I might date frequently, but I don't cheat. I don't need to. There are plenty of willing single women out there."

Something in his tone, the raw honesty perhaps, made our eyes lock for a heartbeat too long. I caught a glimpse of something beneath the anger, something that looked almost like hurt. Like maybe my assumption had wounded him more than his pride.

Well, shit. That's ... unexpected.

"Either way, the image looks like you two were caught having an affair." Rebecca reached into her portfolio and pulled out a stack of printed papers, spreading them across Axel's desk like evidence at a crime scene. "This is what we're dealing with."

My stomach dropped as I read the headlines and comments:

HOMEWRECKER CEO CAUGHT RED-HANDED

This predator needs to be stopped. Going after a senator's wife? Disgusting.

JEALOUS INFLUENCER ATTACKS VICTORIA WEBB

Dakota Fox is everything wrong with social media. Slut-shaming another woman? Cancel her.

Rebecca pulled out her phone next. "Your follower count, Dakota." The number was dropping in real time. The follower count tied to Dakota Fox, the carefully curated persona I'd built. My legal name was Dakota Blackwood, but that distinction didn't matter now. "You've lost two hundred thousand in the last twelve hours. Your engagement rate has tanked from eight percent to two percent.

She swiped to another screen. "And this email came in twenty minutes ago from your pending brand deal."

I watched the color drain from my own reflection in the phone screen as I read: *Given recent events, we're reconsidering our partnership ...*

Then she turned to Axel with another screen on her device. "Your potential investors sent variations of this."

The email was short and brutal: *We cannot be associated with this scandal. Unless immediate action is taken, we'll be forced to withdraw our funding.*

"Cancel culture isn't just coming for you; it's already here," Rebecca said quietly.

Mine, I could handle. Maybe even deserved it after what I'd accidentally done. But that wasn't why I was entertaining this ludicrous proposal.

It was my family. They'd spent their life fortune (and then some) on legal fees after my brother, Knox, was arrested in college. All these years later, that financial hole still hung over their heads like a thunderstorm, one lightning strike away from foreclosure. As if my honest, hardworking, and nonviolent parents hadn't suffered enough, watching their only son—who'd won Most Likely to Rescue Kittens from Trees in junior high—get convicted of murder.

The upcoming brand deal I was on the verge of securing was my family's lifeline. Mid six figures. With promises for more. The contract was practically signed when I got drunk and ... well, you know the rest.

What is wrong with me? Sure, I was drunk. And, yes, I had feelings I didn't want to explore about the man currently glaring at me like I'd personally ruined his life. But still. Why had I been so vindictive that night to take that photo and attempt to send it to my friends with some immature caption?

"Allow me to be clear about what's at stake," Rebecca continued, her voice cutting through my spiral. "Without that investment, Axel's company is done."

"Why is your company on the verge of collapse?" I interrupted, genuinely surprised.

Axel Pierce was the definition of success. His pretentious penthouse, his ostentatious custom suits that practically whispered, *I'm better than you*, in Italian, his air of untouchable confidence. None of it suggested a man whose empire was crumbling.

The look he shot me could have frozen champagne mid-pour. "If those are the terms, I'm walking away now," he said to Rebecca.

Interesting. Whatever had his company teetering on the edge was clearly personal. And off-limits. But the way his shoulders tensed, the way his fingers drummed against his thigh—a nervous tell I remembered from years ago—told me this was killing him.

"Fine, keep your secrets," I said. "But mystery and evasion aren't exactly selling points for this whole fake relationship thing."

Something flickered in his expression, but it was gone before I could analyze it.

And as it did, guilt swelled in my stomach. "I'm sorry," I said quietly, meeting his eyes. "I am really sorry, Axel. I never meant to cause you harm. I'd never hurt you, or anyone, on purpose. But that doesn't change the fact that I did hurt you and jeopardized your business."

He studied me for a long moment, and for a second, I saw the old, kinder Axel. Then his walls slammed back up. "Intent doesn't fix the damage."

"I know. Which is why I'm here."

"You're here because you have an obligation to fix this."

Irritation crawled up my neck, mixing with that familiar heat he always managed to provoke. "Maybe, next time, don't practically grope the future First Lady at a charity gala!"

"Maybe, next time, stop eye-fucking me from across the room."

My jaw slammed to the ground. The audacity! The delusion! The absolutely correct assessment that I'd rather die than admit! "Eye-fucking?" I laughed, but it came out sharp and breathless. "Get over yourself, Axel. You think every woman wants you, don't you?"

The slow, predatory smile that spread across his face told me everything.

YEP. He absolutely does.

And worse, when he looked at me like that, like I was the only woman in the room worth pursuing, my traitorous body came alive.

"News flash: you're not the sun in everyone's solar system, Axel."

"You came here because you have no choice. There's a difference."

"This is why this will never work." I gestured between us, trying to ignore how even arguing with him felt like sexual tension disguised as combat. "We can't stop tearing each other apart!"

Rebecca cleared her throat loudly. "I've been watching this performance for twenty minutes, and I need to know: what the hell is really going on between you two? This isn't just about some photo. There's history here."

Axel and I fell silent, caught.

"Yes, Axel. Why do we despise each other?" I arched an eyebrow, challenging him to answer for his mysterious personality transplant all those years ago. The night he went from treating me like I mattered to acting like I was something stuck to his shoe.

"It's the way it's always been," he said flatly.

Secret-keeping coward.

No, it hadn't. Once upon a time, he'd been sweet. Walking me to my car when I visited Knox. Texting to check I got home safe. Then, poof, overnight transformation into King Dick. No explanation. No warning. Just started treating me like I'd personally murdered his puppy.

The rejection still stung like a bitch, especially because half our fights felt like foreplay. The kind that made my pulse do stupid, traitorous things. He'd weaponized flirtation, turned every interaction into a war zone, where I never knew if he wanted to kiss me or kill me. So, I'd learned to give as good as I got. When he went low, I went for the jugular. Was it healthy? No. Was it satisfying? Hell yes.

But the worst part was that, despite EVERYTHING, I was still irrevocably, pathetically, catastrophically attracted to him. My body was a traitor, and my hormones were mutinous little bastards.

"Look," Rebecca said, her voice softer now. "Whatever happened between you two, there's clearly passion there. The same fire that makes you want to strangle each other? That's exactly what we need to sell this relationship, so I need to know you can both put whatever happened behind you long enough to save your careers."

"We can handle it," I said finally, even though every instinct screamed at me to run.

"Good." Rebecca pulled out another document. "The story is simple. You've been secretly dating for months."

"Months?" My eyes did that cartoon thing where they practically boinged out on springs. "He's constantly photographed with different women."

"Not since he's been working on his deal. He hasn't posted a public image with anyone for over ten weeks."

"Ten weeks." My eyebrows practically achieved liftoff. "That's, like ... what? Three decades in Axel years?"

She pursed her lips, but continued, "So, the story is, the photo was taken during a lovers' quarrel. Axel was trying to make you jealous, not knowing who Victoria was. You reacted like any woman in love would."

The word *love* in connection with Axel made something twist inside. I couldn't tell if it was the twisty sensation you got before you barfed or … nope. Never mind.

"I'll stage everything. Restaurant sightings, hand-holding, the works. Eventually, an engagement to prove how serious you are."

The thought of him slipping a ring onto my finger made me want to cut it off preemptively.

"I'd be lying to my followers," I protested. "They trust me."

"Please. Every post of yours is curated within an inch of its life," Axel shot back. "You probably have spreadsheets for your spreadsheets. Don't pretend you're serving them unfiltered reality when you spend twenty minutes finding the perfect angle for your morning latte."

"Planning content is different from outright lying," I protested, though his words hit uncomfortably close to home.

"You can never believe what you see on social media anyway," he said. "People's lives are always different than what they portray online."

Well, that wasn't ominous at all. Should I be checking his browser history for how to spot catfish *or* trust issues support groups*?*

"What if the public realizes it's fake?" I wondered.

"Then your careers are over," Rebecca said bluntly. "So, you'd better make it convincing. Starting tonight. Go home and pack your things, Dakota."

My eyes widened. "What?"

"You're about to be engaged. You live together."

The room suddenly felt twenty degrees hotter. Living with Axel Pierce? Seeing him first thing in the morning with his hair messed up and his guard down? Watching him pour coffee in whatever he wore to bed? (Please let him wear something to bed.)

I opened my mouth to object, but Rebecca was already packing up. "This is your only option. Take it or leave everything to burn."

I sank back into my chair, meeting Axel's gaze. He looked

equal parts brooding and amused, like he knew exactly what sharing close quarters would do to me.

"Fine. Get me that rusty spoon," I said.

His mouth twitched, and for a moment, I saw a flash of the old Axel again. Naturally, he replaced it with antagonism. "Buckle up, Sunshine."

I rose to my feet, gathering what remained of my dignity. If Axel Pierce wanted to pretend to love me, to resurrect that intoxicating charm he'd perfected years ago, I'd make damn sure he regretted every second of it.

"I might have to appear nice to you in public, but so help me, in private, I'll make sure this is just as miserable for you as it is for me."

His eyes locked with mine, and when he smiled, it was pure sin. "I'm counting on it."

The promise in his voice sent heat racing through me, and I realized with growing horror that this fake engagement might not be the worst part of this arrangement.

The worst was how part of me—the delusional, clearly-in-need-of-help part—was looking forward to it.

2

SINNERS AND SAINTS GROUP CHAT

AXEL

*Jace: Dude, WTF? You're moving in with a woman? YOU? *head exploding emoji**

Blake: Did you lose a bet? Get blackmailed? Suffer a traumatic brain injury?

Ryker: Wait, WHAT?

Jace: Scarlett just told me. She's already making a Pinterest board for housewarming gifts.

Blake: This is the kind of thing you tell your best friends about. IN PERSON. With scotch.

Ryker: You're moving in with someone? What's next, matching Christmas sweaters?

Jace: Not just anyone ... Knox's sister.

*Ryker: *skull emoji* Seriously? I thought you two hated each other with the fire of a thousand suns. Didn't she once call you Satan's disappointment of a son?*

Blake: And didn't you retaliate by putting her number on Craigslist as someone selling a "gently used hot tub" for $50?

*Ryker: Does Knox know? He might bust out of prison just to kick your ass. *laughing emoji**

Me: It's temporary. And fake.

Ryker: The hell does that even mean? How does one FAKE move in with someone?

Jace: Are you going to fake argue about who left fake dishes in the fake sink?

Me: Long story. Shouldn't put it in writing.

Ryker: You shouldn't put it in WRITING? Should I start gathering bail money?

*Jace: We have something more urgent. We've all been volun-told to help Dakota move into Axel's place tomorrow. *annoyed emoji**

Ryker: AGAIN? My back still has PTSD from Tessa's bookcase.

Jace: Did you know there's this revolutionary service called MOVERS? People show up with a truck, do all the work, and you just cut a check.

Blake: But then we'd miss the joy of watching Axel and Dakota try not to murder each other while handling fragile objects.

Me: You don't have to go.

Jace: Scarlett says otherwise.

Me: If you guys aren't going to listen to me, then go text yourselves in your own damn chat.

Ryker: Where's the carefree Axel who once convinced an entire bar he was the heir to a maple syrup empire? That guy was fun. This guy sounds like he needs fiber supplements.

Me: He's currently pissed off about a PR crisis that someone else created.

Blake: Dude, you really know how to pick 'em. Of all the women at that gala, you had to flirt with America's sweetheart.

Me: Fuck all the way off and keep going.

Jace: If this is Axel's attitude, Blake, bring your medical bag tomorrow. We might need sedatives.

Me: I won't be there. Dakota's moving circus is hers alone.

Blake: You don't know Tessa and Scarlett very well if you think this is optional. They're like the Mafia, but with better outfits and more efficient methods of torture.

Me: You've got to be kidding me.

Ryker: They'll probably make you wear a World's Best Fake Boyfriend T-shirt while you move boxes.

Jace: See you tomorrow at 9. Bring coffee. And donuts. And leave the attitude at home.

Blake: [GIF of person being dragged away, screaming, "NOOOO!"]

Jace: Anyone taking bets on how long before Dakota and Axel try to kill each other? I've got $50 on before lunch.

Ryker: $100 says Axel cracks first.

Blake: You're on. Dakota's got hidden depths. My money's on her.

Me: I hate all of you.

*Jace: Love you too, bro. *kissing emoji**

3

BREAKING: LOCAL WOMAN DISCOVERS HER NEMESIS ENJOYS MAKING HER BLOOD BOIL, AND SHE'S … KIND OF INTO IT? 💧🔥 #PLOTTWISTALERT

DAKOTA

Moving day.

No two words had ever sounded more ominous. I could practically see Axel Pierce twirling an invisible mustache, savoring my impending misery like a fine wine. Living with him? I'd rather sleep on a bed of nails. No. Scratch that. I'd rather sleep on a bed of nails in a room full of screaming toddlers while someone played bagpipes directly into my ear.

Last night, I'd hunched over my laptop until three in the morning, the blue light burning my retinas as I desperately searched for a way out of this PR nightmare. My fingers had flown across the keyboard like they were trying to escape my hands as I researched every scandal from the past decade, hunting for an alternative solution. I'd even started drafting a public apology before remembering Rebecca's warning she'd given us before she left: "Many times, an apology becomes a bigger scandal than the original event."

The irony wasn't lost on me. One accidental post, a single vindictive moment of weakness, and now I was being sentenced to live with the very man I'd been avoiding for years. The universe was definitely lounging on a cosmic couch right now, watching me flounder with a giant bowl of buttered popcorn and a smirk.

After my night of research yielded nothing but bloodshot eyes, I'd moved to the next phase of what had to be grief: acceptance. I could do this. I had to. Besides, how bad could living with Axel Pierce actually be?

Don't answer that, brain.

If Axel and I could form a truce, things might go smoother. Yesterday, he'd rejected my apology with the emotional warmth of an iceberg, but I couldn't blame him.

Could I? *Could I?????*

No. I was the one that got us into this mess. The least I could do was be nice to him, so the next time I saw him, I was going to approach him with another heartfelt apology, this one sincere and not rushed. I'd promise to do whatever it took to make this right. Surely, he'd accept that.

We'd both had a night to digest this impossible situation, so today, calmer heads would prevail and all that. Maybe he'd accept a temporary ceasefire, at least until we got ourselves out of this mess.

The alternative—continuing our yearslong tradition of verbal throat-slashing—would make the next ... however long even more unbearable.

My doorbell rang, the cheerful ding-dong sounding more like a funeral dirge: *dun, dun, dun!!!!*

I took a deep breath, my fingers fidgeting with the hem of my oversized sweater. *You've got this, Dakota.*

And it would help, having Scarlett here with me today. She and I'd become best work friends at my old marketing job and stayed close friends since. I'd called and asked her to help with some boxes, and she'd graciously agreed. Maybe she'd have insights about Axel.

While I hadn't spent much time with him in years, Scarlett had started dating Jace, Knox and Axel's friend, so perhaps she'd spent more time with him. Perhaps she might have picked up something useful. Some magical idea that would get Axel Pierce to stop being so pissed at me.

I swung open the door and physically recoiled.

"Thought you could use the hands," Scarlett explained, gesturing toward the unexpected crowd behind her.

A lot of people stood in the hallway outside my apartment. My brother's four friends, the ones who'd been there the night of his arrest: Blake, with his arm wrapped possessively around his fiancée, Tessa; Jace, his hand placed at the small of Scarlett's back; Ryker, my brother's criminal attorney, working on his parole hearings; a woman I'd never seen before; and, because the universe clearly wasn't done tormenting me, Axel Pierce.

His blue gaze hit me like a slap, sending heat racing through my body. Not just heat, but electricity. The kind that made every nerve ending stand at attention. God, why did he have to look at me like that? Like he was cataloging every detail, filing it away for later examination.

Damn him for being so criminally gorgeous. Those ridiculous muscles pushed against his Henley like they had somewhere important to be, decorated with tattoos that I absolutely had not spent way too much time fantasizing about years ago. Dark hair, smoldering eyes that should come with a warning label, and stubble that probably violated several public decency laws. When he walked into a room, every woman's brain short-circuited. Including mine, unfortunately.

"This is Faith," Scarlett said, motioning toward the unfamiliar woman, "Blake's sister. Faith, this is Dakota."

The woman offered a forced smile. Something about her screamed wounded bird, though whether from shyness or deeper pain, I couldn't tell. But I recognized that look. The careful wariness of someone who'd been hurt before and wasn't eager for a repeat performance.

"Come in," I said, stepping back and opening the door wider. The group flowed into my small home like water breaching a dam while the heat of Axel glided over my skin as he passed. "I appreciate you all helping, but truly, I don't have enough to warrant this many people."

"It'll go faster this way," Axel said curtly. But there was something in his tone, a roughness that suggested he wasn't as unaffected as he pretended to be.

His gaze swept around my living room, taking in the peeling paint, the water stains on the ceiling, the ancient carpet worn thin in high-traffic areas. He let out a low whistle. "Wow. Your place is—"

"Cosmetically challenged but affordable," I finished, narrowing my eyes to slits.

"That's one way to put it." His mouth quirked.

My spine straightened. Sure, the walls had seen better days, the countertops were stained, the cabinets were dinged and dented, and the linoleum floor was curling up at the edges like it was trying to escape, but pointing it out was just plain rude.

"It's functional." I lifted my chin. "Not all of us can live in penthouses with marble countertops and toilets that probably play Mozart when you sit on them."

"Handel actually," he deadpanned, and for a second—just a second—I saw a flash of the old Axel. The one who used to make me laugh. But then the humor vanished, replaced by something darker. "Thought you had a social media empire." His eyes locked with mine. "At least that's what you show online. Successful businesswoman and all that."

Okay ... apparently, his animosity had only intensified overnight. And now we had several people watching our exchange like it was center court at Wimbledon. If he thought that would make me back down, he had another thing coming.

"First of all," I said, keeping my voice deliberately calm, even as my toes curled in frustration, "success is relative. Second, it's my job to exude professionalism online. Image is everything and all that. And third—"

"Three bullet points? Should I get a pen and paper?" Axel interrupted.

Do not smack Axel Pierce. Do not smack Axel Pierce. Do not think about what that mouth could do. Focus, Dakota.

"I poured all my earnings into my parents' business to save it." My voice was miraculously steady despite the volcano of emotions threatening to erupt.

Something flickered across his face. A shadow of surprise, perhaps even something like respect, but it vanished so quickly, I might have imagined it.

"Where do you want us to start?" Scarlett asked, her hand on my arm, pulling me from my Axel-induced haze. Because that's what this man did to me. He trapped me in a fog of unwanted feelings, all swirling together like a lethal cocktail. The Long Island iced tea of emotions: potent, confusing, and guaranteed to leave you with a hangover.

"Um." I blinked, forcing myself to focus on anything but how Axel's jeans hung perfectly on his hips. "Those boxes, those boxes, and those boxes are marked for my bedroom."

"We don't have room for all of those." Axel's tone was flat.

"I need my clothes."

"Pack less. I'm sure you'll survive. Pick the three boxes that are most important to you."

"Three?" My voice rose despite my best efforts. "That's basically living out of a suitcase."

"Exactly." Something rolled across his features. "We're going to sell this godforsaken story to the public as quickly as possible so we can both move on with our lives."

Heat crept up my spine. "In the meantime, I need clothes to wear. Toiletries. I need my equipment for my social media business."

"If you won't pick three, I will."

He stepped toward my stack of boxes with purpose, but I stepped in front of him, blocking his path, my palm landing on his chest before I thought better of it. Just to stop him, nothing more, but the solid heat of him made me freeze for half a second too long.

His attention dropped to my hand, then snapped back to my face. "Careful, Sunshine."

"Dude," Blake said, breaking whatever spell had fallen over us, "why did you call us all over here to help her move if she's only bringing three boxes?"

"I didn't call you guys." Axel's jaw clenched as he stepped back from me like I'd burned him. "Scarlett did."

"Right," Scarlett shot back, "because we're moving her into your house. Moving implies lots of boxes, lots of things."

"Axel," I cut in, my words a question but my tone razor-sharp, "can I talk to you?"

Of course he wanted to say no. I could see it in his stubbornness and those cobalt specks of anger swirling through his irises. Maybe he even wanted to tell me to go to hell, but his buddies were practically boring holes into his skull with glowers, and we both knew he was trapped.

Did I wait for his official answer? Nope. I turned on my heel and stalked toward my bedroom, my heart doing some ridiculous victory dance when I heard his heavy footsteps following behind me. Make no mistake. The sound was reluctant. Angry. Which both thrilled me that I won, yet also made nerves take flight at the prospect of being alone with him.

Once inside my bedroom, I shut the door firmly and turned to face him, crossing my arms over my chest. The room suddenly felt too small, the air too thick, with him standing there, taking up all the oxygen.

His gaze swept over my room, taking in the rumpled bed, the fairy lights strung across the headboard, the stack of romance novels on my nightstand. Then his eyes landed on something that made my face burst into flames: the bright purple vibrator I'd forgotten to put away, sitting boldly on my bedside table like a neon sign screaming, *DAKOTA HAS NEEDS.*

His eyebrows shot up, and when his gaze found mine again, it was molten. "Interesting decor choice."

"Don't start," I hissed, snatching a paperback from the pile and dropping it over the offending object like that could erase it from existence. I thought only one woman was coming today, and it was to grab the boxes out front. Not in here.

"Start what?" Axel challenged. "Talking? Or Picturing?" The way he said it, the way his eyes traveled over me like he was imagining exactly what that picture entailed, made my whole body flush hot.

"Look." I softened my voice. "I know I apologized yesterday, but after we've both had a night to think about this, I want to do it again."

Axel crossed his arms over his chest, mirroring my stance. I tried—and failed spectacularly—not to notice how his forearms flexed with the movement, tattoos shifting like living art, designed specifically to drive women insane.

Shame his entire vibe had gone subzero. He'd transformed into a literal iceberg. And not the sexy, mysterious kind. More like the kind that would've looked at the *Titanic* and thought, *Great. Now I have to deal with THIS disaster.*

"You done?" Two words. Curt and clipped.

I curled my fingers into my palms. "I've apologized. Twice now."

"Slow clap." His sarcasm might have been cute, if I didn't picture my fist colliding with his teeth over it.

I closed the distance between us in three furious strides, my finger jabbing toward his chest. "Let the record show that you're the one being unreasonable here. I can't physically go back into a time machine and undo that post. I know you're angry about that, but this?" I motioned between us. "This is extra, even for you, and if you think I'll tolerate it because I made one mistake, you have another thing coming, Axel Pierce."

He had the audacity to cock his head, and his eyes dropped to where my finger pressed against his chest. "You're touching me, Sunshine. *Again.*"

But I didn't move my hand. Couldn't.

He caught my wrist, his thumb pressing against my racing pulse. "You should know better than to play with fire."

His grip tightened for a fraction of a second, his eyes going dark. Then he released me like I was radioactive, stepping back.

"You're unbelievable," I breathed. *Wow. Great comeback, Dakota. Bet that'll make him shake in his designer shoes.*

"So are you, Sunshine." His eyes met mine again, and something fundamentally shifted in the air between us. Something that made my skin feel too tight and my heart race for all the wrong reasons. "Now let's get your shit so you can move in and we can get this whole thing over with."

Fantastic. Nothing said *good life choices* quite like moving into the lair of a man who called me Sunshine like it was a curse word.

What could possibly go wrong?

4

WHEN HE SAYS, "WELCOME TO YOUR BATTLEFIELD." #FAKERELATIONSHIPGOALS

AXEL

"Dude, you were being a dick," Ryker said, his lawyer voice in full effect.

"Certified asshole," Jace agreed, eyeing me from the driver's seat of his Mercedes.

"I knew you and Dakota had some kind of rivalry going," Blake said. "You made that crystal clear when Jace was in the hospital."

Christ. Just thinking about that whole nightmare made my stomach clench. Jace getting attacked, all of us camping out in those horrible hospital chairs, wondering if he was going to make it. Thank God for Scarlett swooping in like some kind of secret superwoman with a high-heeled weapon, or we might have lost him.

And then, because the universe had a sick sense of timing, guess who decided to show up the day Jace was getting discharged? Dakota. Of course she did. If I'd had any clue that Scarlett and Dakota were buddies, maybe I would have braced myself, but no. Instead, everyone got a front-row seat to what I was sure looked like the world's most awkward soap-opera showdown.

"But that felt more like … I don't know … competitive or something? This?" Blake shook his head. "This felt like you were aiming for her jugular. What's the deal with you two anyway?"

Yeah. Wasn't getting into that. "I wasn't that bad," I argued.

"You told her she'd have to live out of a suitcase," Ryker shot back, eyebrows raised. "That's nuclear."

The four of us had piled into Jace's prized car while the women followed in a moving vehicle Scarlett had rented earlier. The temporary reprieve from Dakota should have been a relief. Instead, I was trapped in a metal box with three human lie detectors who knew me too damn well.

"Thanks to her, I'm being forced into the one thing I despise the most. Every staged photo, every fake smile … it's everything I swore I'd never become." The words tasted bitter. Like the water my mother used to pour down the sink before company came over, replacing her personal bottle with vodka. Perfect tumbler. Perfect lies.

And now, I'd have to lie all over again.

I'd spent half the night staring at the ceiling, trying to convince myself to just let it all collapse. If it were only me getting screwed over, I'd have torched everything and walked away without looking back. My wealth, my reputation. Fine.

But as I'd explained to Dakota, it wasn't just me. Knox had scraped together every dollar he had and thrown it at my start-up. Not because he expected some massive return, but because he believed in what we were building. That money was supposed to be his safety net when he got out. His only shot at starting over. And the stubborn guy was too proud to take charity from any of us.

Knox wasn't the only one depending on this company either. After watching him navigate the system, seeing how society discarded anyone labeled imperfect, I'd built something to bridge that gap. Phoenix Construction wasn't just another building company. We specialized in large-scale commercial renovations and infrastructure projects, but our workforce was primarily people coming out of the system. We'd land contracts to renovate office buildings, restore historic properties, and build affordable housing developments. The construction industry was perfect because it offered real skills, decent wages, and companies were starting to care about hiring practices that looked good in their ESG reports.

We also provided job placement, housing assistance, addiction counseling, and comprehensive reentry services for people leaving prison. But the core business kept the lights on: we bid on multi-million-dollar contracts and delivered quality work. Our crews learned everything from electrical to plumbing to project management. The social mission attracted clients who wanted to feel good about their vendor choices, but we won contracts because we did excellent work at competitive prices. We were one of the few companies that actually hired people with records, and those that we couldn't take on, we didn't stop until we found somewhere they'd get hired.

Most people walked out of prison with nothing. Empty pockets, empty promises. The lucky ones found a halfway house. The really lucky ones had family who would still claim them. But most would be back inside within six months.

If Phoenix Construction failed (by the way, I was not about to explain to Dakota how, why, and who had stolen clients, resulting in massive cash flow challenges), hundreds of employees would lose their jobs, and thousands more would lose their support system, their housing, their hope. All because I couldn't swallow my pride and play pretend.

So, yeah, I had to become everything I hated. "This whole charade ... Dakota's Instagram-perfect bullshit, the fake smiles, the public performance ..."

I could see it all again. My mother at the country club, lipstick pristine, laughing at someone's joke while her hand trembled around the stem of her water glass. The tremor she'd blame on too much coffee. The way she'd grip my shoulder in the parking lot afterward, nails digging in, whispering, "Not a word to your father," about the flask I'd seen her tuck behind the tennis trophies.

"That performance killed my mom. And now I'm supposed to be the leading man in that same goddamn show. So, forgive me if I'm not thrilled about becoming everything I swore I'd never be."

Blake let out a long breath. "Look, man, I get it. We all put on masks sometimes." He shifted, his voice getting that serious edge it took on when he was about to drop some uncomfortable truth. "But Dakota's not your mother. She's not crafting some perfect facade to hide the fact that she's falling apart. She's building a brand, running a company. It's performance, yeah, but it's not the same kind of performance that killed your mom."

The words hit harder than I expected.

"And staying this angry? Painting every woman who posts a pretty picture with the same brush?" Blake shook his head. "That's not honoring your mother's memory, man. That's just guaranteeing you'll spend the rest of your life pushing away anyone who might actually matter."

I stared out the window at the Chicago skyline. The glass towers reflected the morning sun, all gleaming with promise and potential. Just like Dakota's eyes when she'd apologized. Twice.

Shit. My past wasn't her fault. And, I reminded myself, this was Knox's little sister. The same sweet girl I'd met before Knox had gone away to prison.

Luckily, the guys dropped the subject, and we drove the rest of the way in merciful silence. When we reached my penthouse, I held the elevator doors open for Dakota with exaggerated chivalry.

As I did, I arched an eyebrow at the guys, as if to say, *See? I'm holding the door open. Happy?*

Dakota stepped past me, her floral scent wrapping around me like a deliberate attack on my self-control while her eyes swept across my space. Yesterday, during that disaster of a PR meeting, she'd barely spared my place a glance. Too busy plotting damage control or my death to notice the exposed brick walls or the vintage leather furniture I'd spent months hunting down.

But now, she was drinking it all in like she was memorizing every detail. Taking inventory of what would become her temporary prison. And mine. The way her gaze lingered on the floor-to-ceiling windows, traced the lines of my custom bookshelves, assessed the artwork I'd chosen with care ... it made something lodge behind my sternum.

I shouldn't give a damn what she thought. This was my sanctuary, where every piece meant something, told a story, reflected who I actually was beneath all the corporate bullshit.

So, why was I holding my breath, waiting for her verdict like some desperate teenager showing off his bedroom?

"It's pretty," she said simply, without artifice or agenda.

The fact that I loved those two words flooded me with light and frustration at once. Which was exactly what I'd been afraid of. Having her here, in my space, breathing my air, touching my things, watching her pad around in whatever she wore to bed ... it was going to be so much harder than I'd convinced myself it would be. And if she kept being ... kind, considerate, human, I wasn't sure I could hold on to this protective rage.

The anger was the only thing standing between me and complete emotional annihilation.

"Follow me," I said, my voice clipped.

She obeyed, trailing behind me as I opened the bedroom door and gestured toward the master suite. The king-sized bed dominated the room with all gray colors. Gray bedspread, darker gray pillows. I liked gray. Gray was safe. Black and white and all that. I crossed to the dresser and opened the top left drawer.

"You can put your stuff in here."

Her eyebrows furrowed. "You mean, in the dresser?"

"I mean, in this drawer."

"I only get *one* drawer?" The beginnings of outrage simmered in her tone.

"I only have one bedroom."

Crimson exploded on her cheeks as the implication hit her. Those freckles that dusted her nose and cheeks became more pronounced against the flush, and I tried—and failed—not to notice.

"This is a penthouse. Don't penthouses have, like, multiple bedrooms?"

"This one has two. One of them is my office." I kept my voice deliberately flat.

"Why didn't you mention this yesterday?" Her voice rose an octave. "I'm not sleeping in the same room with you."

"Don't flatter yourself, Sunshine. I'm not sleeping in the same room with you either." I leaned against the dresser. "I'll sleep in here, and you'll sleep in the office." Because giving her my room would be the first crack in a dam I'd spent years building. One small kindness would lead to another, and another, until I forgot why keeping my distance was the only thing keeping us both safe.

Her attention swept to the door, then back to me. "But the office doesn't have a bed."

"It will by tonight." The only reason I'd ordered the most comfortable mattress they had was because I didn't want to listen to her complain. And the only reason I got three varieties of comforters was because that office could go from cold to hot easily. Had nothing to do with wanting her to sleep well. Nothing at all.

She swallowed, and I tried not to track the movement of her throat. "Look, I know this isn't ideal, but I need more than one drawer. You have to be reasonable here."

"Do I?" I stepped closer, enjoying the flash of uncertainty in her eyes. Except it wasn't uncertainty. It was something else. A flicker of heat that made my pulse kick up. The same heat I'd seen when she'd put her hand on my chest.

She drew in a sharp breath through her nose, which was

another thing I'd always found inexplicably appealing about her. The way she squared up for a fight, no matter the odds. "Yes, you do. Like it or not, we're stuck in this situation, and the more you fight with me, the worse you're making it."

"Thanks for the TED Talk," I quipped.

"I need more than one drawer," she repeated.

"This is all I can spare. You can keep the rest in your boxes."

Now her chest puffed up with indignation, and it took everything I had not to let my gaze drift down. She dropped the box she'd been holding and marched up to me, glaring with all the fury she could muster. Her tiny hands balled into fists at her sides.

It took everything I had not to let my lip curl up at how adorable she looked when she was angry. All fire and defiance, packed into a tiny frame of righteous fury.

God, she was so damn sexy. She barely came up to my shoulder—five-five to my six-two—but she had a presence that made up for it. Strawberry blonde hair caught the light, and freckles scattered across her fair skin like someone had flicked a paintbrush. She was toned in that yoga-instructor way, all lean strength, and those eyelashes... I'd spent weeks convinced they were fake before I'd gotten close enough to confirm they weren't.

"Let's not do what we've always done, Axel."

"What's that, Sunshine?"

"Fight. Argue."

I forced a smirk. "You think I'm going to go easy on you?"

"So, that's how it's going to be?"

"What'd you think? I'd roll out the red carpet? As if pretending to be engaged to you wasn't bad enough, now you're going to infest my home."

"Infest." Her eyes narrowed to slits. "Wow. Nice word choice."

"Get used to it." I leaned closer, close enough to see the flecks of light green in her hazel eyes.

"Last chance," she warned, lifting her chin. "I'm offering a truce. We both stop being mean to each other and muddle through this."

"Or?" I raised an eyebrow, genuinely curious where she was going with this.

Based on the faltering of her expression, she hadn't thought this far ahead. But Dakota Blackwood had always been quick on her feet. She straightened her spine, trying to appear taller and sharpened her tone.

"Or we go to war."

For one dangerous moment, I let myself imagine choosing door number one. Calling a truce. Letting her in, even just a little. But I couldn't risk it.

I leaned down, trying not to notice the faint smell of roses in her hair or the fullness of her lips. "Welcome to your battlefield, Sunshine."

5

FUN FACT: FAMILY DINNERS HIT DIFFERENT WHEN YOU'RE HIDING A FAKE ENGAGEMENT. 🤭💍 #UNIVERSEHASENTEREDTHECHAT

DAKOTA

"Welcome to your battlefield."

Damn Axel Pierce to the deepest circle of hell.

I swear, he got OFF on making me squirm. But whatever. At least I got to escape him for a couple of hours, spending time with two people who made this whole ordeal worth it.

Then, it was back to my own personal prison. My first night with Axel Peirce ... and our first public appearance.

Was it too late to fake my own death and start a new life in another country?

The crunch of gravel under my tires matched the grinding in my chest as I spotted her.

Mom sat hunched at the base of her weatherworn ramp, wrestling with a splintered board and a toolbox that had seen better decades. The wood was soft with rot in places, the grain dark, where water had seeped in winter after winter.

My chest squeezed. Here she was, fixing things herself because they couldn't afford to hire anyone. The ramp's two-by-fours were a patchwork of lumber: some gray and aged, others newer pine and still yellow. Each replacement done as boards failed, one crisis at a time.

"Mom, what are you doing out here?" I grabbed the grocery bag from my back seat, my voice artificially light.

The concrete walk beneath my feet was webbed with cracks, dandelions forcing their way through, like the yard had given up the fight, and as I got closer, I noticed how rust bloomed orange across the hinges of the toolbox. Inside, I could see the mismatched collection: screws in three different sizes, rattling loose, and a hammer with electrical tape around the split handle.

"Oh, this old thing." She gestured at the ramp with forced casualness. "It's bowing again. Don't want your father falling through when he takes the trash out."

When he takes the trash out. Not when she needs to use it. Always worried about everyone else, never herself.

I knelt beside her wheelchair, taking the wooden board from her lap. The surface was rough, splintering under my palm, and I could feel where she'd tried to sand it smooth with what looked like an old piece of sandpaper, worn down to the backing.

With the brand deal, I could install custom permanent ramps. Everywhere she needed them. Hell, I could renovate this entire house so she never had to struggle again. Replace the gutters hanging crooked from the roofline, fix the porch light that had been dark for months, get rid of the duct tape holding the mailbox together.

"Something wrong, sweetheart?"

I forced a smile. "Nothing. Just thinking about work."

She evaluated me, the way only a mom could, sensing something was wrong that I wouldn't talk about.

"You know ... you always try to make everything seem perfect. But sometimes I wonder if you forget it's okay for things to just be real."

Real. The word lodged in my throat like a stone. Real wasn't marketable. Real didn't pay the bills or house repairs or the thousand small emergencies that seemed to multiply every month. Real was the luxury I couldn't afford.

I pushed at the warped board with my fingers, trying to force it back into place. The wood splintered without warning, slicing pain across my palm as a jagged edge caught skin and tore. Blood welled instantly, bright red against pale flesh.

"Dakota?" Mom's voice sharpened with concern.

I curled my fingers into a fist, trapping the blood inside, and shoved my hand behind my back. "Just a splinter. No big deal." The smile I gave her was practiced, perfect. The same one I used for every sponsored post. "Board's in place at least. I'm going to find some tweezers to get the splinter out."

She studied me, that mother's radar pinging, but I kept the smile steady. Kept my bleeding hand hidden.

"You sure you're all right?"

"Perfect," I said, kissing her forehead. "You coming inside?"

"I'll be in shortly." Her eyes narrowed at another board.

Inside, I quickly cleaned the wound, thankful an oversized Band-Aid covered the cut. Then I washed my hands again and pulled ingredients for chicken piccata—Dad's favorite—and got to work, making lunch. It wasn't long before the front door opened and he shuffled inside with a bakery bag.

"There's my girl." His smile was genuine despite everything, and I hugged him tight, breathing in his familiar scent of discount aftershave. My injured hand throbbed against his back, but I didn't let go.

"French bread?" I asked, nodding at the bag.

"And chocolates for your mother." He pulled out a small heart-shaped box.

The tenderness of it made my eyes burn.

As I set the table, I spotted them. A stack of unopened envelopes marked *FINAL NOTICE* in aggressive red lettering, hastily shoved beneath a kitchen towel, like that would make them disappear.

My stomach dropped to my shoes.

Forty-five minutes later, as we sat around our dining room table, Knox's empty chair loomed like a ghost. My hand pulsed under the table, the Band-Aid starting to feel damp with blood I prayed they wouldn't see.

"So," Mom started, probably trying to lighten the mood. "Dating anyone?"

"No," I answered immediately. Although, at some point, I'd probably have to tell them about the Axel thing, right?

Predictably, Mom's lips pursed. "It's been ages since Mathew moved away."

Mathew. I swear Mom was just as upset by our breakup as I had been.

But she shouldn't be focused on me; she should be focused on that stack of final notices on the counter. My attention flicked over to them again, and my father tracked my gaze.

"We're ... exploring our options for the house."

My fork clattered to my plate. "What do you mean, options?"

They exchanged that look. The one married couples perfected after thirty years, where entire conversations took place in a glance.

"We love this house," Mom said softly. "All your childhood memories are here. Knox's room ... but if we downsize—"

"No." The word shot out sharper than I meant for it to, but honestly, downsize? This was already a tiny place. You didn't get smaller than this. "You're not selling this house."

"Sweetheart." Dad's voice turned gentle. "We have to be realistic."

God, I knew they'd been in trouble. Knew foreclosure was a discussion point, but it had been for years. I guess I didn't realize it was here. Now. Knocking on the front door.

The stakes just got raised. We needed to sell this love story. Fast.

If I didn't come up with the money to backpay the mortgage, it was game over.

Guess it was a good thing that in just a few hours, Axel and I would be launching Operation Convince Everyone We're Soulmates While Actively Plotting Each Other's Demise. Nothing says true love like barely suppressed homicidal tendencies.

6

POV: YOU'RE TRAPPED IN A FAKE ENGAGEMENT WITH A MAN WHO LOOKS LIKE A CALVIN KLEIN AD IN GRAY SWEATPANTS. #SENDHELPANDSELFCONTROL

DAKOTA

Five hundred and seventy-three likes on last night's post. Ouch. Definitely worse than my usual numbers, and half the comments section looked like a dumpster fire, but it could be worse.

I scrolled through the mess, bracing myself for more digital daggers, when a familiar username caught my eye. BlushBabe123 had left her usual comment, gushing about how "gorgeous" I looked and throwing around way too many heart-eye emojis.

At least someone still thought I hung the moon. She'd been one of my most consistent followers since I started. Always first to like, always ready with the compliments. Rain or shine, PR scandal or not, there she was. A little over the top? Yes, I'd argue that commenting, *You look stunning in yellow. It brings out your eyes, just like that sundress you wore four months ago*, constitutes as over the top. But in a world where people dropped you faster than last season's trends, that kind of loyalty was … nice.

One less thing to worry about, I guess.

I'd already taken the photo with my artisan ceramic mug with the tasteful speckles, not the chipped mug I actually preferred, positioned just right with the morning light. Everything in frame conveyed casual morning elegance I'd post tomorrow. Everything out of frame screamed temporary exile.

I'd set up my lighting equipment in the corner of Axel's office, arranging the portable ring light and diffuser to hide the twin bed that might as well have had *unwelcome visitor* carved into its headboard.

Now came the real work. I pulled up the image on my laptop, studying my expression in the photo. My genuine smile—the one I'd captured mid-laugh at something ridiculous on my phone—looked too real. Too unguarded. My eyes crinkled at the corners, and there was something vulnerable in the tilt of my head.

I clicked through to the next shot. This one was better. Practiced. The smile that said *effortlessly happy* without actually revealing anything.

You're selling aspiration, not fraud, I reminded myself as I prepared to replace the real smile with the safer one. *Keep posting like nothing's wrong. Tonight's the exclusive that turns this disaster into opportunity.*

The acid in my stomach churned at the thought, but I swallowed it down. Again.

"What are you doing?" The deep voice from the doorway made me jolt.

My heart slammed against my ribs as I spun around to find Axel leaning against the doorframe, arms crossed over his chest, hair still damp from the shower. Dark strands fell across his forehead in a way I'd never seen. The water separated them into points, one piece curling slightly at his temple. It was unsettling how much I wanted to reach up and brush it back. Like he needed yet another thing to make him look like the sexiest man alive.

"Jesus." My hand flew to my chest. "Knock much?"

But he wasn't looking at me. His cerulean eyes were fixed on my laptop screen, and something in his expression made my stomach drop. His jaw clenched, the muscle actually jumping beneath the stubble that darkened his face and made that sharp line even more pronounced. The tendons in his forearms flexed as his grip tightened on his biceps while I caught the clean scent of his soap, something that shouldn't have been distracting but absolutely was.

"This is my home." His voice came out rough, and when his gaze finally met mine, there was something cold in it.

"And this is the corner you designated me to," I countered, gesturing to the sad little ten-by-ten space he'd graciously allowed me to occupy. "My very own Dakota detention center."

He pushed off the doorframe and moved into the room. "You were switching them."

"Switching what?"

"The photos." He stopped a few feet away, and I hated how his white T-shirt clung to his still-damp chest, how his gray sweatpants hung low on his hips. How, even angry, he looked unfairly attractive. "I watched you. You had a real smile, and you were about to replace it with ..." He gestured at the screen with something like revulsion. "That."

Heat crawled up my neck. "It's called editing. Every influencer does it."

"I know what it's called." Something flickered across his features. Pain maybe or memory. His hands curled into fists at his sides. "I'm asking why you do it."

"Because the real one wasn't good enough." The words came out defensive.

"Wasn't good enough," he repeated slowly, like he was tasting something bitter. "Or wasn't fake enough?"

My spine stiffened. "You don't know anything about my business."

"I know plenty about faking it for an audience." His voice dropped, went rough. "I know what it looks like when someone performs their whole life. When everything is curated and calculated and hollow."

The venom in that last word made me blink. This wasn't just generic disapproval. This was personal.

"Why do you even care?" I stood, closing my laptop with more force than necessary, the cut beneath my bandaged hand biting. "What does it matter to you if I edit my photos or swap out smiles or stage my entire feed?"

His eyes flashed. "Because I promised your brother I'd keep an eye on you."

"Oh, please." I let out a harsh laugh. "You've barely spoken to me in years. If you're so concerned about Knox's little sister, you've been doing a terrible job."

"I don't need to talk to you to keep an eye on you."

The admission landed between us like a grenade.

I took a step toward him, pulse hammering. "You follow my social media."

"It invades my feed," he protested.

"You can block it." Another step. "Mute it. Scroll past. But you don't."

A cord of tension stood out in his neck. "Someone needs to watch when you're about to do something catastrophically stupid."

"Or maybe"—I closed more distance, had to tilt my head back to hold his gaze—"you just like watching."

The air between us crackled, charged. His eyes darkened, dropped to my mouth for a fraction of a second before snapping back up.

"Careful, Sunshine."

"Of what?" I was close enough now to smell his soap even more and feel the heat radiating off his skin. "The truth?"

"You wouldn't know the truth if it bit you." But his voice had gone low, rough. Dangerous. "You're too busy performing."

"And you're too busy judging me for it." My heart was racing, and I couldn't tell if it was anger or something else entirely.

He moved closer, and suddenly, the desk was at my back, the

wall of his chest in front. "Every single post. Every caption. Every carefully curated moment. It's all pretending, Dakota."

"It's my job."

His hand came up to rest on the desk beside my hip, caging me in. "One day, you're going to forget where the performance ends and you begin."

My breath caught. The way he was looking at me, like he could see straight through every filter, every carefully constructed facade, made something in my chest ache.

"You don't know me," I whispered.

"I know you better than you think." His other hand braced on my opposite side, trapping me completely. His face was inches from mine now, and the intensity in his eyes made my knees weak. "I know you switched mugs because the real one you wanted—the one you have lined up in the cabinet for tomorrow—probably wasn't pretty enough. I know you set up your lighting to hide the bed you'll be sleeping on."

Each word hit like an arrow finding its mark.

"And I know"—his voice dropped even lower—"that right now, you're looking at me like you want to do something that has nothing to do with strangling me."

My mouth went dry. Heat pooled low in my belly as his gaze drifted to my lips and stayed there.

"You're infuriating," I managed, but it came out breathy.

"So are you." His thumb traced along the desk, close enough to my hip that I felt the ghost of movement. "But you're going to need to hide that anger tonight. When I touch you. When I hold your hand. When I whisper in your ear."

"I know the script."

"Do you?" He leaned in, his mouth close enough that I felt his breath against my skin. "Because when I put my hand on the small of your back tonight, when I brush your hair behind your ear, when I look at you like you're the only woman in the room, you can't flinch away. You can't look at me like I'm the enemy."

"That's going to require Oscar-worthy acting."

"Is it?" His hand came up to trace the line of my jaw, featherlight but burning. "Because right now, Sunshine, you're looking at me like you want something entirely different than an Oscar."

Every nerve ending in my body was screaming. The tension was so thick, I could barely breathe, and for one wild moment, I thought he might actually kiss me.

Instead, I pressed my palm against his chest to push him away, to regain some space, some sanity, but the movement sent a sharp bolt of pain through my injured hand.

I couldn't stop the small gasp, the involuntary wince.

Axel froze. And for a heartbeat, something that looked like hurt flashed across his face. He jerked back immediately, putting several feet between us.

Then his gaze dropped to where I was cradling my hand against my chest, and his entire demeanor shifted. The hurt vanished, replaced by something sharp and focused. In two strides, he closed the distance again, but this time, there was nothing seductive about it.

"Let me see." It wasn't a question.

"It's fine."

"Dakota." My name came out like gravel. "Let. Me. See."

The intensity in his voice made me hesitate, then slowly extend my hand. The beige bandage I'd wrapped this morning had a small spot of red seeping through.

His fingers were surprisingly gentle as he took my wrist, turning my hand over to examine it. The muscle in his jaw moved again, but this time, it wasn't disgust. It was something else entirely.

"What happened?" The question came out quiet.

"It's nothing. I just—"

"What. Happened?" His eyes snapped up to mine, and the protective fury there stole my breath. His thumb brushed carefully over my wrist, just below the bandage, and the tenderness of the gesture clashed so violently with the storm in his expression that I couldn't form words.

"Did someone do this to you?"

The raw concern in his voice, the way his hands held mine like I was something precious and breakable, sent my heart into overdrive for an entirely different reason than before.

And I realized, staring up into those blazing blue eyes, that Axel wasn't just dangerous to my sanity.

He was dangerous to every wall I'd ever built.

7

HE'S CLEANING MY WOUND AND CASUALLY THREATENING TO WHAT NOW? #REDFLAGORMARRIAGEMATERIAL

DAKOTA

"I'm fine," I said, trying to tug my wrist free.

But Axel didn't let go. Didn't even acknowledge my protest. He just started walking, practically dragging me down the hallway toward his bathroom, his grip firm but careful around my injury.

"Axel, it's barely bleeding. Most people wouldn't even have noticed—"

"I'm not most people." He pushed open the bathroom door and guided me inside with a hand on my lower back that sent an unwanted jolt down my spine.

The bathroom was all dark tile and brushed nickel fixtures. Masculine. Clean. Almost aggressively impersonal. No photos, no clutter, nothing that said anyone actually lived here. The air was still humid from his shower, warm and close, carrying that Sandalwood scent that was distinctly him.

The shower. Jesus. Minutes ago, he'd been naked in this very room, water running over—

I shook the thought away as he released me, dropping to one knee to open the cabinet under the sink.

I blinked at what I saw. Everything had a place. First aid kit front and center, toiletries lined up with military precision, spare towels folded in perfect thirds. Not the chaotic jumble of half-empty bottles and forgotten products I'd expected from a bachelor. Not many people had probably seen under Axel Pierce's bathroom sink; it felt strangely intimate, this glimpse of how he organized his private space. How he kept everything controlled, contained.

He emerged with the first aid kit and slapped it onto the counter with enough force to make the contents rattle, the sharp sound echoing off the tile.

"You know, this is completely unnecessary. It's just a scratch."

"A scratch that made you gasp in pain." His jaw was still tight, that muscle jumping again beneath the stubble. "I'll ask one more time. Did someone do that to you?"

The intensity in his voice made my stomach flip. "Yes."

His eyes flared, something dangerous sparking in their depths.

I rolled mine. "Me. I did it to myself."

He stared at me for a long moment, those sapphire eyes searching my face like he was trying to detect any hint of a lie. Then he exhaled roughly and ran a hand through his dark hair, mussing it in a way that should not have been attractive but absolutely was.

"How?" The word came out clipped.

"Um, a board. I was helping my mom with something."

He didn't respond. Just kept watching me with that unnerving focus while he moved to the sink and turned on the water. I tried not to stare at the tattoos that decorated his forearms. The ink shifted and flexed as he lathered antibacterial soap between his palms, washing with the kind of methodical care that suggested he was trying to calm himself down.

God, those hands. Long fingers. Strong but elegant. The same hands that had caged me against the desk, that had traced my jaw with devastating gentleness.

The same hands that had held me like I might break.

"Why?" I asked, more to distract myself from the direction of my thoughts than anything else.

"Why what?" He dried his hands on a towel, movements controlled. Precise.

"Why do you care if someone hurt me?"

Axel opened the first aid kit without looking at me. "Because if someone hurt you, that would have been the end of him."

The casual violence in his tone shouldn't have sent heat pooling low in my belly. It really shouldn't have.

But it did.

"You're serious," I breathed.

"Completely." He turned to face me, and the look in his eyes made my breath catch. "Now give me your hand."

I hesitated, suddenly aware that letting him touch me again felt dangerous for reasons that had nothing to do with the cut.

"Dakota." My name was a command. A plea. "Please."

That single word—*please*—coming from Axel's mouth, undid something in me. I extended my hand slowly, watching as he took my wrist with a gentleness that seemed impossible from someone so clearly furious.

His fingers were warm against my skin as he carefully peeled away the bandage. The adhesive pulled slightly, and I bit my lip against the sting.

"Sorry," he murmured, and the unexpected apology made my heart do something stupid in my chest.

When the bandage came free, he studied the cut with an intensity that made me feel exposed. It wasn't that bad, honestly. A clean slice across my palm, less than two inches long.

His fingers tightened around the discarded bandage, crumpling it into a tight ball. "We should call Blake to look at this."

Blake was an ER doctor who tended to actual life-threatening injuries. "It's a scratch," I protested.

His ocean-colored gaze snapped to mine. "How many bandages have you bled through?"

"Two, but only because I didn't let it clot properly. See?" I tried to sound dismissive. "It's not bleeding anymore. It's just a flesh wound."

"Just a flesh wound," he repeated flatly. Then, before I could argue further, he turned on the tap and guided my hand under the water.

The spray hit the cut, and I hissed softly. Axel's thumb stroked the inside of my wrist. Once, twice, in silent apology, and I forgot how to breathe.

"Tell me if I'm hurting you," he said quietly.

I nodded, not trusting my voice.

He worked in silence, one hand cradling mine while the other carefully cleaned around the wound. The antibacterial soap stung, but I barely noticed. I was too focused on the furrow between his brows, the way his lips pressed together in concentration, the surprising tenderness in every movement.

No one had ever taken care of me like this. Like I was something precious. Like my pain mattered.

"Why are you being so ..." *Nice. Kind.* "Careful?"

His hands stilled for a moment. "Would you prefer I be rough?"

"I'd prefer you be consistent." I tried to inject some levity into my tone, but it came out softer than intended. "Five minutes ago, you were tearing apart my entire life philosophy. Now you're playing doctor."

"Maybe I contain multitudes."

"Or maybe you're just confusing."

He pressed his lips together like he was fighting back a grin. "Probably that."

He turned off the water and reached for a fresh, clean towel, patting my hand dry with the same maddening gentleness. His fingers lingered against my skin longer than necessary, and when I looked up, I found him already watching me.

For a heartbeat, I thought he might say something real. Something that explained why he'd gone from disgusted by my curated life to furious that I was hurt. Something that would make sense of the way he was looking at me right now, like I was a puzzle he couldn't solve but desperately wanted to.

Instead, he cleared his throat and reached for the antibiotic ointment.

"This might sting," he warned.

It did, but barely. I was too distracted by the feel of his fingertip spreading the cream across my palm, the warmth of his other hand still cradling my wrist, the way he bent slightly closer to see better.

He applied the bandage with the same careful precision, smoothing down the edges, checking twice that it was secure. Then he just ... held my hand. His thumb traced an absent pattern across my wrist, right where my pulse hammered against his skin.

"There," he said finally, but he didn't let go.

Neither did I.

We stood there in the quiet bathroom, his hand wrapped around mine, both of us breathing a little too fast. His eyes were dark, pupils blown wide, his gaze drifting to my mouth.

This was dangerous. This moment, this man, the way my entire body was leaning toward him like he had his own gravitational pull.

Don't, I warned myself. *Don't read into this.*

"Why are you doing this?" The question came out more defensive than I intended.

He blinked, and something shuttered in his expression. His hand loosened around mine, and I felt the loss of his warmth like a physical ache.

"You're Knox's little sister." He stepped back to throw away the old bandage and used supplies. "If you're hurt on my watch, I'm going to take care of it."

The words landed like ice water dumping over the fire of a teenage fantasy.

Knox's little sister.

Right. Of course. That's all this was. An obligation. A responsibility he'd shouldered because of my brother, not because of me.

I'd known that. I knew that. So, why did hearing him say it out loud feel like something sharp twisting between my ribs?

Because for a second there—with his thumb tracing patterns on my wrist, with the way he'd looked at me—I'd been stupid enough to let my guard slip. To almost believe this intensity, this care, had something to do with Dakota and not just Knox's little sister, who'd gotten herself hurt on his watch.

God, I was an idiot.

"Right," I managed, pulling my hand back and cradling it against my chest. My newly bandaged, carefully tended, obligatory hand. "Of course. Knox."

I turned toward the door before the humiliation could fully register on my face.

"Dakota—"

"Thanks for the bandage," I said, proud of how steady my voice sounded despite the tightness in my throat. "I should get ready for tonight."

I left the bathroom before he could say anything else. Before I could do something truly pathetic.

Like ask him why he'd touched me so carefully if I was just a responsibility.

Why he'd looked at me like that if this was only about Knox.

Why I'd been dangerously close to believing, just for one stupid moment, that maybe I was more than an obligation to him.

8

WHEN I BASICALLY FAKED AN ORGASM OVER DESSERT. THEN HE KISSED ME LIKE HE KNEW. 💕 #KISSEDBYTHEDEVIL

DAKOTA

God help me. Tonight was going to suck donkey balls.

I studied my reflection one last time, mentally calculating how much my appearance would have cost if all these products hadn't been given to me in exchange for social media posts. Two hundred for the hair. Three fifty for the makeup. Another sixty for the false eyelashes that made my eyes look innocent. The exact opposite of how I felt. All to convince strangers I was in love with Satan's favorite intern.

That's all he was. Those moments, or whatever the hell you might call them, in the bathroom and the one before it in the office meant nothing. In fact, they weren't even moments. They were glitches. Malfunctions in the matrix.

You are not a needy teen, desperate for his attention, Dakota. So, do not let him have the power. You hate Axel, Dakota. Hate. Hate. HATE!

Then why did I put on my most devastating dress?

The ruby-red fabric hugged every curve like it was painted on. No. It wasn't to impress him; it was strategic. A woman going to war needed armor, and mine came with a push-up bra and five-inch Louboutins that click-clacked like walking the plank on the way to the living room.

I rounded the corner into the foyer and froze.

Damn. Double damn. Triple damn with a cherry of F-my-life on top.

Axel Pierce stood with his back to me, tailored shoulders broad enough to fill out that suit like a movie star. When he turned, those piercing cobalt eyes hit me like a car accident. His jaw, shadowed with dangerous stubble, tightened when he saw me.

The man had no right to look so gorgeous. Tall, with perfectly tousled dark hair and a personality like a paper shredder. A really hot paper shredder. The kind that made you want to feed it important documents just to watch it work.

Heat radiated through my body as his gaze traveled from my face to my stilettos and back up slowly, memorizing every inch. When his eyes met mine again, something dark and hungry flickered before he masked it.

"You look almost tolerable when you're not talking, Sunshine," he drawled.

See? If you needed proof there were no moments in the office or bathroom, there you have it, ladies and gentlemen. We were right back where we started. Safe ground. The familiar territory of mutual loathing.

Good. That's exactly where I wanted us.

I forced my lips into a smile with too many teeth. "And you clean up surprisingly well for someone with the personality of a cactus."

"Enough, you two." Rebecca stepped forward, all business. "Three influencers will be positioned near you tonight with fifteen million followers between them. They think they scored prime reservations, but every seat was strategically placed. One of them is Paul Hargon; he can make or break this. You'll apologize publicly; Axel will forgive you."

My apology. The idea of groveling to him publicly tasted like throw-up.

"Hear that, Sunshine?" His eyebrows shot up. "Apologize. Loud and fucking clear."

I glared while he smirked.

"And you'll seal the night with a kiss authentic enough to convince those influencers you've been doing it for months."

My stomach dropped. "A kiss?" I choked. "I'd rather cut my lips off."

"You think kissing you is any less repulsive to me?" Axel snarled. "I'd rather kiss a blender. While it's running."

"Then help me here." I gestured wildly. "We can sell the whole couple-making-up narrative without my enduring his mouth on mine. We can hold hands and pretend the touch doesn't feel like acid. But a kiss? I can't pull that off. Not with him."

"We agreed to do everything she said."

I gripped my hips hard enough to leave marks. It was that or punch his perfectly structured face. "You're just saying that because making me squirm brings you joy."

His lips quirked up. Case. In. Point.

"Dry your panties, Sunshine. It's a fake kiss. Kissing you will feel like kissing a corpse."

"Kissing you will feel like kissing an insect."

"We don't have time for this." Rebecca's expression was pinched. "Is kissing each other really so bad, you'd rather lose everything?"

Yes, I thought savagely, even as images flashed through my mind: my mother's wheelchair ramp, the unpaid bills on their counter.

I swallowed the word and glared at Axel instead.

"Good." She pointed a finger at us. "Stay. On. Script."

. . .

Twenty minutes later, we arrived at the restaurant in electric silence.

Per Rebecca's script, I waited for Axel to open my door. When he extended his hand with practiced gallantry, I stared at his fingers like they might infect me.

"Come on, Sunshine."

The transformation in his voice stopped my heart. Gone was the cutting edge, replaced by something warm that slid over my skin like expensive wine. His entire demeanor had shifted. Blue eyes softened from glacial to summer skies, posture curving toward me instead of away.

When our hands connected, a shiver started in my palm and rippled inward, setting off tiny earthquakes in my chest. As he helped me from the car, his other hand settled on my lower back, fingers splaying wide, the touch burning through the thin fabric in the worst and best way.

He leaned down, breath warm against my ear. "Wipe that deer-in-headlights look off your face, Sunshine. Remember, you're seasoned at tricking people into thinking your life is perfect."

So much for the loving-boyfriend transformation. Seriously. Jekyll and Hyde had nothing on Axel Pierce.

His barb landed precisely, but when he pulled away, his expression was adoring for any watching eyes.

I motioned for him to bend down, letting my smile stay bright and affectionate. "Pretending my life is perfect and pretending I can stand you are entirely different skill sets," I murmured, letting my lips brush his ear. "One requires a filter. The other requires a frontal lobotomy."

His responding wink nearly stopped my heart. Not because it was charming—which, maddeningly, it was—but because of how effortlessly he slipped between personas. Axel Pierce, asswad by day, Oscar-worthy actor by night.

Minutes later, we were seated, intimate lighting casting

everyone golden. I immediately spotted our targets: three influencers at the nearest tables, phones out, attention seemingly fixed elsewhere but clearly locked on us.

I recognized Paul Hargon instantly. Gossip turned into a multimillion-dollar empire.

"I'm glad we're doing this," Axel cooed, right on script.

Suddenly, anxiety crashed over me. *What if I screw this up? Forget my lines?*

Axel's fingers brushed my hand, eyes locking on mine with an unspoken message: *Breathe. We've got this.*

The genuine concern caught me off guard. Strange how quickly enemies became conspirators when survival was at stake.

"You look beautiful," he continued flawlessly. "You've always looked stunning in red."

His gaze tracked down my neckline before returning to my eyes. Hopefully noticed by our audience. But beneath the performance, I caught genuine appreciation that sent unwelcome heat pooling low in my abdomen.

Traitorous body. We were supposed to be a united front against him.

Okay. Time for the main event.

"Axel," I began, projecting just enough to be overheard. "I'm sorry about what I did."

His expression softened unexpectedly, and for an eerie moment, we seemed to slip back in time before Knox's arrest, before everything shattered.

Axel nodded encouragingly, one eyebrow lifting slightly. *You're doing fine. Keep going.*

The unexpected tenderness in his gaze made my throat tight, but I pushed through the feeling, desperate to maintain my emotional distance.

"When we broke up that night," I continued, "I was so hurt, I acted in a way I normally never would. I should never have taken that picture of you with that woman. And I never should've posted it online." I drew a steadying breath, aware of Paul angling his phone toward us. "I didn't mean to share it publicly. I thought it was my private story. But that doesn't excuse taking the photo. I'm really sorry."

At least that part was true. Maybe my express ticket to hell would be downgraded to economy.

"I was flirting with her to make you jealous," Axel delivered with such sincerity, I almost believed him. "I was upset you broke up with me. Being immature and a complete jackass. I'm sorry." He paused. "And for the record, I didn't know who she was or that she was married. I'd have picked a more believable target."

Axel reached across and took my hand.

The contact sent shock waves through my system. Especially when his thumb traced slow circles on my skin and he was looking at me like I was the only person in the room.

There was something mesmerizing about this version of Axel: attentive, loving, genuine. Some hidden part of me wondered what it would be like if this wasn't an act.

"I love you," he said with such conviction, my heart nearly squealed.

"I love you too," I managed, finding myself tracing circles on his skin.

"Come back to me," he urged, voice dropping intimately. "I know you're scared of being hurt again. But I swear, Dakota, I would never hurt you."

This is just an act, I reminded myself. He'll go back to being a dick in ... 3 ... 2 ... 1 ...

Following Rebecca's directions, Axel moved my chair beside his, thighs touching, skin burning through fabric. He draped his arm around me, pulling me closer until I felt his body heat, while he began playing with the ends of my hair.

My defenses were crumbling, and I hated it. Hated how good his touch felt, how much I wanted this tenderness to be real. But I'd already learned this lesson today: Axel could switch from caring to cold in a heartbeat. And seeing his performance made me wonder if he got off on tugging my emotions around.

Well, he wasn't the only one who could play games. If he thought I'd just melt into him like some swooning damsel, he had another thing coming.

I leaned in like I was sharing something precious, speaking low so only he could hear me. "Your smile looks like you're being held at gunpoint."

We laughed together, perfectly synchronized.

"Your laugh sounds like a car alarm," he whispered back.

"Your cologne smells like a midlife crisis."

His thumb traced circles on my hand ... intimate for our audience, but I felt the pressure increase slightly. "And your perfume smells like desperation."

"At least I don't reek of commitment phobia and hair mousse."

"The hair mousse is organic," he murmured tenderly, gazing into my eyes.

"So is compost."

He pulled me closer, his voice warm for show. "Your acting is almost convincing. Did you practice in the mirror?"

"Not as much as you practiced your devoted-boyfriend face. Though I'd work on the eye twitch. It's giving more *medical emergency* than *madly in love*."

"That's just my natural reaction to being near you," he quipped.

"It's actually impressive how delusional you are about your appeal."

"The only delusion here is you thinking that dress makes you look innocent."

"Better than looking like I just stepped out of a cologne commercial no one asked for."

"And yet you can't stop staring."

I cooed sweetly, bringing his hand to my cheek like it was precious, "Your eyes have been glued to my cleavage since we arrived, but sure, I'm the one staring."

He drew in a slow breath through his nose, nostrils flaring. Score one for Dakota.

We gazed at each other with practiced adoration that hid mutual fantasies of attempted murder.

The waiter appeared with our salads, and Axel transitioned smoothly into more public conversation, but his eyes promised our banter wasn't over.

For now, we kept up the dual conversation: sweet words for our audience, cutting remarks for each other. It was almost fun, in a twisted way. Like we'd found the one thing we were actually good at together: mutually assured destruction with a smile.

When our entrées arrived, I cut into my steak and tried not to let my disappointment show.

"How is it?" Axel asked, his boyfriend voice back in place.

"It looks delicious." If you were a vampire.

His attention snapped to my plate, and something shifted in his expression. The playful antagonism vanished, replaced by genuine concern. "You ordered it well done."

"It's fine."

"It's not." He raised his hand for the waiter, voice firm. "She ordered this well done. This is medium rare."

"It's really not a problem."

"Undercooked meat makes you nauseous."

I blinked, genuinely surprised. That detail came from years ago—before Knox's arrest, when I'd gagged at a pink burger at some summer barbecue. The fact that Axel remembered such an insignificant thing about me was more disorienting than anything else that had happened tonight.

He doesn't need that detail for our charade. The influencers can't possibly know my meat preferences.

So, why did he do it?

The waiter apologized profusely and whisked my plate away, leaving me staring at Axel with something that felt unexpectedly close to softness.

"Thank you," I said quietly. Because, hello, I wasn't a total bitch. I could thank him *and* hate him. Multitasking was my specialty.

Something vulnerable flickered across his features before he looked away. "Don't mention it."

The wall between us cracked, just slightly, and suddenly, I didn't have another cutting remark ready. Not when the energy had shifted into something uncertain.

When my correctly cooked steak returned, we fell into a different kind of silence. Not hostile, but hyperaware. Of every glance, every accidental brush of hands, every breath.

After, dessert arrived with a decadent chocolate creation that looked sinful, and when I took a bite, a small moan escaped before I could stop it.

Heat flooded my cheeks. *God, did I really just...*

Axel's entire body went still at the sound. His fork actually stopped midway to his mouth, hovering there like he'd forgotten how eating worked.

I caught a drop of chocolate sauce on my finger, and for a split second I wanted to disappear into the floor. But then I saw how he was looking at me—frozen, transfixed—and something shifted. If one accidental sound had done that to him ...

A thrill ran through me. The embarrassment transformed into something else entirely, something that made me feel bold. Dangerous, even.

I slowly brought my finger to my mouth, reminding myself that the faster I sold this charade, the faster I could escape. Get away from whatever this was... this heat coiling in my stomach that had nothing to do with hatred and everything to do with the way he was watching me.

My tongue darted out to clean the chocolate off. Deliberately. Seductively.

Those eyes fixed on my lips. He didn't blink. Not once. An eternity passed between us, suspended in chocolate and heat and this dangerous game I was suddenly winning.

I licked another drop from my bottom lip, slow enough to watch his pupils dilate, to see his chest forget to rise and fall.

He wasn't breathing. I'd actually made Axel forget to breathe.

The smart thing would be to stop here. Pull back. I'd already sold the performance.

But something reckless unfurled in my chest. A need to see how far I could push this, to know what would happen if I shattered that legendary control completely. *For the act,* I lied to myself, even as fire burned low in my belly. *I'm supposed to be his girlfriend. This is what couples do.*

I dipped my finger into the chocolate sauce again, but this time I leaned closer, extending it toward his mouth. "Want a taste?"

He hesitated—because of course he did—but the show must go on.

When he leaned forward, I let my fingers linger at his lips, wiping away the chocolate with a touch that lasted a heartbeat too long. His lips were impossibly soft. Warm. The slight dampness of his breath ghosted across my fingertips, and when his mouth parted, I felt the heat of him.

I should have pulled back.

But his fingers had already closed around my wrist. Firm and inescapable. Those dark eyes locked onto mine with something that might have been a warning. Or a promise.

He wrapped his lips around my finger and dragged his tongue along my skin, cleaning the chocolate with devastating, methodical precision.

Holy. Freaking. Shit.

The sensation shot straight through my core. My breath caught audibly, and from the dark satisfaction in his eyes, he knew exactly what he'd done to me. The bastard had just weaponized dessert.

"Delicious," he murmured, releasing my finger.

My thighs clenched.

Our chests rose and fell in perfect synchronization while the space between us thrummed with unspoken desire we were both pretending didn't exist.

Sell this faster. Escape him faster.

The mantra repeated in my head, but my body wasn't listening to logic anymore. My body had apparently decided to stage a coup against my brain.

"We should really sell this," I heard myself whisper, and somehow, my hand was sliding under the table, landing on his knee. For show. Totally just for show.

His eyes flashed. "Should we?"

"Rebecca said to make it believable." My fingers trailed higher, along the inside of his thigh. "The influencers need to see we can't keep our hands off each other."

His hand shot down to grab my wrist, but he didn't push me away. Didn't stop my upward progress. "Dakota."

"What?" I let my other hand rest on his chest, leaning in close so anyone watching would see intimacy. "Isn't this what we're supposed to do?"

"You're playing with fire, Sunshine."

My hand inched higher, and when I felt the hard evidence of his arousal pressed against his fabric, I kept my hand on the outskirts. Careful not to disrespect him in that way, but, man, the primal satisfaction of realizing what I was doing to him flooded through me.

I was affecting Axel Pierce. Mr. Unflappable. Mr. I Don't Do Feelings. And it was intoxicating.

Maybe some part of me wanted to see him unravel. Wanted to know I could affect him the way he affected me.

When I nuzzled his neck, letting my lips brush the sensitive spot below his ear, a low growl rumbled in his chest.

"You'd better stop, Sunshine," he warned. But his free hand cupped the back of my head, fingers tangling in my hair possessively.

"Is that what you really want?" I challenged, voice barely a whisper.

"Yes," he claimed, but he looked like he wanted to unzip his pants and plunge my open mouth onto his waiting lap.

"Your body doesn't seem to agree with your objections."

His lips brushed my ear. "You're telling me if I dip my fingers in your panties right now, they won't come back glistening?"

Mother of …

Heat exploded through my core. My thighs began to throb with an ache that had nothing to do with performance and everything to do with the vivid, devastating image his words painted in my mind.

"I …" My voice came out breathless, and I hated how transparent I was in this moment.

"That's what I thought." His thumb stroked along my jawline, satisfaction evident in his gaze. "Don't start something you're not willing to finish."

The energy between us crackled with forbidden potential, and the way Axel was looking at me made me wonder if he might actually slide those hands over my body right here in the restaurant.

I pulled back, but Axel's gaze remained locked on me, something fundamental having shifted between us. A shift I refused to acknowledge as anything more than physical chemistry. Inconvenient, unwanted, and absolutely meaningless.

Throughout the remainder of dessert, we maintained our performance, laughing at each other's jokes, exchanging tender glances, my hand occasionally finding his arm or chest in rehearsed affection. But every casual touch now felt charged with the memory of his tongue on my finger, his words in my ear, the evidence of his desire.

My phone buzzed.

Rebecca: You're doing GREAT. They took the bait. Keep it up.

Our eyes met. We were succeeding. So, why did victory taste so complicated?

Another buzz:

Rebecca: Don't forget the kiss.

Well, shit.

Earlier tonight, kissing Axel had seemed revolting. Now I dreaded it for an entirely different reason: what if it wasn't as revolting as I needed it to be?

My heart slammed against my ribs. All the heat and chemistry of the evening crashed into this single moment. No more delays. No more pretending this wasn't about to happen.

Our gazes locked, and I saw my own conflict mirrored in his eyes.

Without a word, his hand cupped my cheek, thumb tracing my skin with tender slowness. He tilted his head. Paused, giving me one last chance to back out.

I didn't. Because apparently, I had a death wish. Or a really specific type of masochism.

Time suspended itself in that breathless moment before impact, his face hovering over mine while I felt the heat of his breath, the pulse of anticipation.

Every thought scattered the instant his mouth found mine.

His lips were warm and absolutely devastating. At first, I could pretend that this was just for show, just for the audience because his mouth moved against mine with such careful restraint. Almost tentative. Like he was holding himself back by sheer force of will.

I should have been relieved by his control. Should have appreciated the safety of it.

Instead, I found myself pressing closer, chasing something I couldn't name, and that's when everything shifted.

Without thinking, I grasped the back of his head, fingers tangling in his hair, pulling him closer, not because our script demanded it, but because my body suddenly, desperately needed more of him.

His response was immediate and fierce. His hand slid from my cheek to the nape of my neck, angling my head to deepen the kiss. The other arm wrapped around my waist, pulling me as close as our seated position would allow.

When his tongue swept across my lower lip, seeking entrance, one coherent thought managed to surface through the haze: *We never discussed boundaries. We never talked about using tongue.*

But then his tongue was sliding against mine in a caress that obliterated every rational thought, and I couldn't bring myself to care about boundaries or scripts or anything except the taste of him flooding my senses. Wine and chocolate and something uniquely, intoxicatingly him.

My mouth opened for him completely, and the kiss transformed into something consuming. Something that felt far too real.

Maybe I was reading too much into it, but he was kissing me like he had been imagining this for years, like this fake engagement gave him the excuse to finally claim what he had been dreaming of. I could feel it in the desperation of his fingers tangling through my hair, drawing me closer as he gently tilted my head back for better access, deepening our kiss. I could hear it in the soft moans rumbling from deep in his throat. And I could sense it in the way our bodies pulled toward each other like we were magnetized, bound by some invisible force.

I had always wondered, in our ongoing rivalry, how much of it might have been misplaced passion. Now I knew: all of it.

Axel wanted this. Wanted us. I could feel it in every desperate touch, every hungry kiss. All these years of verbal sparring, of pushing and provoking—it had all been leading here. To this explosion of undeniable chemistry that neither of us could fake or fight anymore.

And God, that felt freeing. Like we'd been holding our breath for years and could finally exhale. Finally be honest about what had always simmered between us.

Because this had to mean something to him. It had to. I wasn't just some random girl. I'd known him for years, been through trauma and hell with him. He'd been by my side even when I pushed him away.

In this moment, something had shifted permanently between us. And I desperately hoped I wasn't the only one who felt it.

My hands moved of their own accord—one fisting in his shirt, the other still tangled in his hair—and I felt his grip tighten on my waist as if he wanted to pull me into his lap right here. His tongue moved against mine with devastating skill, each stroke sending liquid heat cascading through my body.

A small sound escaped my throat—something between a gasp and a moan—and I felt him tense, his fingers flexing against me possessively.

The restaurant vanished. The influencers, Rebecca's instructions, our entire charade ... all of it evaporated under the intensity of sensation. There was only the solid warmth of him, the scratch of his stubble against my skin.

My free hand slid up to cup his jaw, feeling the racing pulse in his neck, and his response was to kiss me deeper, hungrier, like he was trying to consume me whole. Like, if this was the only chance he was going to get, he was going to make it count.

This was insane. This was supposed to be fake. A performance. But nothing about the way my body was responding felt remotely like pretending.

The kiss grew more desperate, more urgent. His hand slid up my back, fingers spreading wide, and I arched into him. The heat between us was building toward something dangerous, something that definitely wasn't restaurant-appropriate, something that felt seconds away from combusting into—

Axel pulled back.

The abrupt loss of contact felt like being plunged into ice water.

We were both breathing hard, his forehead resting against mine, his hand still cupped around the nape of my neck. My fingers were still twisted in his hair and his shirt, and I could feel the thundering of his heart against my palm on his chest.

For one suspended moment, we just stared at each other. The question hung between us, unspoken but deafening: *What the hell just happened?*

But before I could even get my bearings, he cleared his throat and extracted himself from my grip, the cool air rushing in where his warmth had been.

"There," he said, voice rougher than usual, not quite meeting my eyes. "I think that sold it."

The dismissal hit like a slap with the world's most gigantic hand.

Knox's little sister, I reminded myself bitterly. That's all I'd ever be to him.

"Right," I managed, proud when my voice didn't shake. "Good work."

My phone buzzed.

Rebecca: PERFECT! They're eating it up. You two are trending!

Success. We'd done it. Sold the story. Convinced the influencers.

So, why did victory taste like ashes?

"I need to use the ladies' room." I stood on legs that felt unsteady.

I didn't wait for his response. Didn't look back. Just focused on putting one foot in front of the other, navigating through the restaurant with my phone clutched like a lifeline.

Inside the bathroom, I pressed my back against the cool tile wall and touched my trembling fingers to my lips, still burning from his kiss.

This is good, I told myself firmly. *We sold it. That's all that matters.*

Relief unwound some of the tension as I realized maybe we could actually pull this off. Save our companies. Save my family.

My body's reaction was just biology. Chemistry. It didn't mean anything. It couldn't mean anything.

Even if he'd kissed me like he was drowning and I was air.

Even if I'd kissed him back like my life depended on it.

Even if, for those few devastating moments, I'd forgotten we were supposed to be pretending.

I mean, honestly, with my business already in danger, what

did I have to lose by continuing with this charade? Other than my dignity and sanity. I could do this.

Pushing off the wall, I straightened my dress and squared my shoulders before exiting.

Only to collide with a man's chest.

I looked up, and when I met those familiar brown eyes, my heart forgot how to beat.

9

FUN FACT: ENCOUNTERS WITH EXES SHOULD COME WITH A WARNING LABEL. ⚠️💕 #PUBLICSERVICEANNOUNCEMENT

DAKOTA

"Mathew?"

My ex was here?

If I wasn't so consumed with shock, maybe I would have sensed the weight of familiar blue eyes burning into me from across the restaurant. Maybe I would have remembered that I wasn't supposed to be having intimate moments with other men tonight.

"Dakota?" Mathew's voice glided over my skin and engulfed me in an invisible hug.

I couldn't believe I was standing here in front of him. Everything seemed to freeze in place. Even the dust particles in the air, dancing through the light like they had been present in our love story.

A relationship that, arguably, wasn't supposed to end.

After just three months together, we were talking engagement rings and imagining what our future babies might look like.

And then ... he was gone.

I thought I'd never see him again, but now here he was, rocking my entire world by simply breathing the same air as me.

Those charismatic eyes swept over my body, like he was in shock that he'd bumped into me. The good kind of shock, the best kind of shock, and slowly, his light illuminated like a light bulb, turning up the brightness, his mouth slanting up.

It wasn't until this very moment that I realized I hadn't moved, I hadn't even blinked, for Chriminy's sake. But in my defense, I had zero idea of what to say to him.

What do you say when your ex suddenly reappears? Do you tell him how many nights you had spent staring at the ceiling, your cheeks burning from salty tears? Wondering if you had made the biggest mistake of your life?

But where was that feeling now? I'd expected my heart to leap. To feel that old familiar rush. Instead, there was just ... shock. And underneath it, a strange emptiness where all that love used to live.

"Wow." His eyebrows shot up as his intoxicating gaze glided over my red dress. "You look beautiful."

I should feel something. Anything. The flutter I used to get when he looked at me like that. But it wasn't there.

I smiled anyway. "What are you doing here?"

"I got back three weeks ago."

I know. I saw online.

He sighed, shoving his hands into his pockets. "New job."

"I didn't think you'd come back to this country."

"As it turns out," he continued, his eyes searching mine for something, "being a world away from the people who matter isn't something I want for the rest of my life."

The people who matter.

I waited for my heart to respond. Waited for that surge of hope, of vindication. He came back. This was supposed to be the moment I'd dreamed about.

So, why did I feel nothing?

"Plus," he said, his voice dropping to that tone that used to make me surrender every defense, "I was hoping to see you."

If he really wanted to see me, he could have called and left me a message that he'd moved back. I would have been there in a heartbeat, and he damn well knew it.

Or would I have? The thought surprised me.

"I've missed you," he continued, taking a step closer.

Breathe, Dakota. Breathe.

But it wasn't his words threatening to overwhelm me. It was the confusion. The complete absence of the feelings I'd expected to flood back the moment I saw him again.

Had I cried it all away? Was that even possible? To love someone so completely and then just ... not?

"Your job," I managed. "Did you leave it?"

"Another firm made me an offer in Chicago." His smile turned rueful. "I'm joining as part of an investment committee here for potential buyouts or growth capital injections."

Finance lingo.

"Can we talk?" he asked, his eyes never leaving mine.

Seriously? He had been in town for three weeks and had made no effort to contact me. If we hadn't literally bumped into each other, maybe he never would.

"If you wanted to talk to me, you know my phone number," I said, keeping my voice gentle but firm.

He grabbed the back of his neck. "You didn't take my calls when I moved away. Figured you wouldn't answer after everything." *Everything*. Such a simple word for such a complicated history. "Plus, I assumed you hated me for what I did."

A flash of anger surged through me. Finally, something I could actually feel. "I never hated you, Mathew. I understood your choice. But it was a choice."

He nodded, a shadow passing over his face. "I regretted it from the second I made it."

I waited for my heart to leap. For validation. For joy.

"I didn't want to leave you, Dakota." His voice grew thick with emotion. "I almost didn't get on that plane. I almost turned right around and came back. I almost quit more times than I can count just to come home to see you."

These were the words I'd fantasized about hearing. The declaration I'd imagined a thousand times during those long, lonely nights after he left.

So why did they feel like they were bouncing off glass?

I took a step back, folding my arms across my stomach in the defensive posture I'd adopted when I'd been mourning what we'd lost. But now it felt more like protection from my own confusion than from him.

"It turns out," he continued, "having the career of your dreams means nothing if you can't share it with the woman you love."

"... the woman you love." Present tense.

"I've been writing a speech." He looked sheepish.

"A speech?" I arched an eyebrow.

"That's why I haven't called yet," he said. "I kept thinking I needed to find the perfect words first. Every time I picked up the phone, I'd freeze. What could I possibly say?" He let out a self-deprecating laugh. "Turns out, there's no perfect way to say *I screwed up the best thing in my life.*"

I could see the sincerity in his eyes, the regret, the longing, the suffering.

And I felt ... empty. Confused. Lost.

What was wrong with me? This man had been everything. The love of my life. The one I'd mourned for months.

Somewhere in that mourning, had I let him go completely?

"I never should've left, Dakota."

I kept my voice controlled, guarded. "It was the opportunity of a lifetime."

"Leaving you was the biggest mistake of my life," he continued. "I don't deserve for you to give me the time of day after what I did, but is there any way you'd consider having dinner with me? Where we could talk? Really talk?"

I swallowed, the memories suffocating me.

How fate had thrown our love story a curveball, disguised as a business opportunity on the other side of the world for Mathew.

It's not like he made the decision lightly; at first, he had actually turned it down. But the guilt of knowing that he, like me, had worked his whole life to build something from the bottom up and was giving it up for me after dating for just three months ... well, that was too much for me to take.

I'd been terrified that, someday, he might resent me for it. So, I insisted he take it. If love was meant to be, set him free and all that.

Free. A four-letter word that had sliced my soul into chunks.

Now here he was, looking at me like I was still his everything, saying all the words I'd once dreamed of hearing.

"Will you have dinner with me?" he asked, motioning to a table behind him. "I can tell my brother and his fiancée to scram. We haven't ordered yet."

For one dizzying moment, I let myself imagine saying yes. Maybe if I talked to him, all the feelings would come back? Maybe I just needed time for the shock to wear off. Maybe the love was still there, just buried under confusion and surprise.

I opened my mouth, not even sure what I was about to say. Maybe yes. Maybe I needed to figure out what had happened to all those feelings. Maybe—

"Don't even think about it, Sunshine." Axel appeared, sliding a possessive hand around my waist, glaring at Mathew.

10

WHEN YOUR FAKE BOYFRIEND AND REAL EX ARE ABOUT TO THROW HANDS IN A 5-STAR RESTAURANT. 🥊🍽️ #CLASSYVIBES

DAKOTA

Mathew's eyes narrowed as he registered the arm around my waist, his gaze whipping from my face to Axel's. The silence stretched as he waited for me to say something—anything—but my mind had gone completely blank, too overwhelmed to process basic human speech. When I didn't speak, alarm flashed in Mathew's eyes at Axel's possessiveness.

His expression turned guarded. "Dakota, are you okay?"

"You lost the right to ask that question"—Axel's fingers tightened on my hip—"the moment you left her."

"That's really none of your business." Mathew's voice was dark, cutting. His eyes darted between me and Axel, confusion clouding his features. "Dakota, what the hell is going on?"

Of course he was confused. Mathew knew my history with Axel Pierce. Knew I'd spent years complaining about my brother's insufferable best friend. Knew what he looked like, thanks to Mom whipping out photo albums. Yet here Axel was, arm wrapped around me like he owned me.

"Dakota, is he bothering you?" Mathew stepped closer.

Axel's chest rumbled with amusement against my side. "You don't get to act like a hero now."

"What the hell is that supposed to mean?"

"Means you broke her heart." Axel's voice dropped to a dangerous purr. "You left. And you missed your chance with her."

Something in Axel's tone transcended mere animosity toward Mathew. It was almost as if … he was genuinely angry at Mathew for breaking my heart. But that couldn't be right. Axel Pierce wouldn't give two craps if my heart was broken. Hell, he'd probably celebrate it with champagne.

I was about to ask Axel how he knew any of this, but the answer hit me like a slap: Knox. Of course it was Knox.

I visited my brother regularly, and, sure, I kept some things from him, like how dire Mom and Dad's financial situation was these days, because that would just send him into protective overdrive from behind bars. But everything else? I told Knox most everything. Including the whole Mathew disaster. The dating, the heartbreak, the spectacular way it all went to hell.

And Knox, being Knox, probably couldn't keep his mouth shut about his little sister getting her heart stomped on. Especially not to Axel, who visited him too.

God, I was an idiot for not putting this together sooner. My brother was the most protective person on the planet. Of course he'd vent to his best friend about some guy who hurt me.

"Axel," I started. "That's enough."

"So, you're with him now?" Mathew's eyebrows slammed together, disgust and shock raging through his tone.

My pulse quickened. This was where the carefully constructed PR narrative could fall apart. "Er …"

"I think you should answer that again, Sunshine." Axel's warning was velvet-wrapped steel as his eyes locked with mine, reminding me of our agreement, of everything at stake.

"Don't talk to her like that." Mathew took another step forward.

A slow, predatory smile spread across Axel's face. "Still trying to look like a hero, eh?"

"Guys, stop." I glanced nervously around the hallway. "People are starting to look at us."

The hostess at the front was watching with undisguised interest. A couple waiting for the restroom whispered behind their hands.

"She's a grown woman," Mathew growled. "If she wants to talk to me, you can't stop her."

Axel's eyebrow arched with dangerous amusement. "Can't I?"

Mathew appeared to weigh his next words. "Are you okay, Dakota? Is he hurting you?" Mathew growled in a tone that suggested he was hoping I would give him the green light to take Axel outside and beat him up. Because that was another thing about Mathew. He had put his career ahead of our love story, but he would annihilate anyone who hurt me.

Under different circumstances, that might be romantic. Under these circumstances, it created a giant problem.

Axel threw his head back and laughed. "You would love that, wouldn't you? Painting *me* as the villain."

"You are a villain," Mathew spat.

"I guess the villain gets the girl then." Axel's thumb traced a small, deliberate circle on my hip. A gesture Mathew very much noticed.

"Dakota, you're seriously with him?" The hurt in Mathew's eyes was almost unbearable.

Words failed me. Months of imagining what I'd say if I ever saw Mathew again, and now I was speechless.

"Why?" Mathew sounded like he was trying not to vomit. "He's a total asshole. He will never treat you right."

"If treating her right includes breaking her heart by abandoning her ..."

"Shut the fuck up." Mathew's voice was dangerously low.

Axel's mouth quirked up. "You stand here, pretending you

care about her, but how much could you really care if you left her?"

Mathew lunged forward, and I instinctively stepped between them, one hand on each of their chests. Under my palm, I could feel Axel's heart beating steadily, confidently, while Mathew's raced like a trapped animal's.

"Axel, we have eyes on us," I reminded him through gritted teeth. "One of those influencers is looking at us."

Twenty feet away, one had her phone raised, too far to hear but definitely recording.

"How long have you been with him?" Jealousy snaked through Mathew's voice, his fingers twitching at his sides.

"Axel, I think we should go." I pushed his chest, desperate to calm the situation.

Axel allowed his mouth to curl higher on one side, looking almost triumphant. "Come on, Sunshine. Let's go *home*."

The word *home* landed like a grenade.

Mathew's face fell, his complexion ashen. "You live together?"

My gaze darted around the space, and then I lowered my voice. "Look, Mathew. I can't talk about this now, but trust me, there's more than meets the eye." I tried to telegraph a message with my eyes, one I couldn't speak aloud without blowing everything up.

He studied my face, trying to decipher my meaning.

"You need to stay away from her," Axel warned.

"The only time I'll stay away from her is if she tells me herself."

Axel tried to push forward again, but he halted at my palm. "Tell him, Sunshine. Tell him to never contact you again."

Never again? The audacity hit me like a knee to my ribs. Our arrangement was temporary, not a lifetime sentence. Nothing in our carefully scripted agreement gave Axel Pierce the right to intimidate Mathew, to draw lines in the sand about my future, let alone issue ultimatums like he actually had a say in my life!

Rage flushed through my body. "Don't tell me what to do," I snapped.

"He left you, Sunshine."

"This really isn't your concern," I replied.

"Isn't it?" Axel raised an eyebrow, his voice dropping. "You're with me now. I would say that damn well makes it my concern."

I gritted my teeth and lowered my tone to a furious whisper. "You don't give a shit—"

"Careful, Sunshine." His warning was soft but clear.

The influencer was closer now, definitely recording, maybe even live streaming. I had no idea if she could hear us, but our body language—me caught between two men leaning aggressively toward each other—screamed love triangle.

A love triangle was not part of our carefully constructed PR narrative. Neither was a public fistfight.

"I have to go," I said apologetically to Mathew, my heart twisting at the prospect of leaving him here, thinking I was deeply in love with Axel. It was bad enough that this fake relationship required me to lie to my followers. But lie to Mathew? That wasn't something I was comfortable with. Wasn't something I signed up for.

"She'll never love you the way she loves me," Mathew warned.

Something predatory shifted in Axel's expression. "Says the boyfriend who abandoned her for some career opportunity."

Mathew's face paled, but his eyes hardened with resolve. "Well, I'm back now. I came back to win her over. Now that I know she's in the arms of a monster, I'll fight even harder for her. If only to save her from you."

11

WHEN YOUR FAKE FIANCÉ HAS ANGER MANAGEMENT ISSUES AND A POCKETKNIFE. 😳🔪 #REDFLAGSORGREENFLAGS

AXEL

"You complete and utter jackass!" Dakota's voice sliced through the car for the seventeenth time. "Do you have any idea what you've done?"

Like she was the only one having a bad night here.

I kept my eyes on the road, my molars grinding together.

The photos from tonight were probably already online. The ones that showed a perfect couple having a perfect dinner, perfect smiles for the cameras. Each staged moment had felt like swallowing glass. Every time we attempted to look more in love, I'd thought of my mother, who used to play the perfect wife at public functions while, inside, her world was crumbling.

Those weren't the only photos taken tonight though. I'd seen the influencers' phones come out when Dakota's ex showed up, their eyes lighting up like they'd struck gold. Perhaps they'd publish images of our altercation with Mathew instead. The real moments, messy and raw and human. It would make my soul feel better, but would destroy everything we'd worked for.

"Mathew is none of your business," she continued, staring out the window now. "Our history is none of your business."

Dakota Blackwood might look like a collectible doll—petite with those delicate wrists that seemed like they'd snap in a strong breeze—but, Christ, the woman could weaponize words better than the dictionary.

And I was giving her plenty of ammunition tonight.

"He's a dick."

"And what does that make you?" she countered.

The man who's been watching you for years. The man who felt things in my office, in my bathroom while cleaning your wound, and tonight when I kissed you that I never intended to. And was so shocked by it, I did the only thing I could: move safely back into rivals territory.

"You embarrassed me!" Dakota waited while I simply stared out the godforsaken windshield. "Hello? Are you listening to me?"

I wasn't listening. Not really. I was too busy replaying the image that had burned itself into my retinas: Dakota talking to Mathew like he was her sun. The way she tilted her head, exposing the curve of her neck.

In fairness, I had no idea how much Dakota liked or loved Mathew, but that wasn't the point. The point was, why did seeing her with him bother me so much? When I spotted them together tonight, why did it feel like a rock slammed into my chest?

I had told myself over the years that the only reason I followed Dakota online was to keep tabs on her. You know, she was Knox's sister and all that, so it stood to reason I should watch out for her since he was in prison and couldn't do it himself.

That's what I kept telling myself when I had seen her and Mathew's romance play out on social media. Post by nauseating post. I'd done some digging on Mathew then, and something about him didn't sit well. The guy was always too perfect, smiling too wide, walking and talking too smoothly in those videos. It was like he was doing it all for show or something.

But seeing him today, I wasn't so sure it was his douchey

personality that bothered me. In fact, something different from brotherly protection wound around me like barbed wire.

Something that felt dangerously close to jealousy.

I cycled through excuses like a man desperate for an alibi. It was probably just this fake relationship messing with my head. After all, as far as anyone was concerned, Dakota was supposed to be mine. While we knew it was fake, Mathew didn't. Having the nerve to continue talking to her like that, tugging at her heartstrings when she was supposed to be mine ... that had to be what intensified my emotions.

Or maybe the explanation was even more basic. Dakota Blackwood was stunning. A prize for any man that cared about beauty. She was gorgeous from head to toe, and she didn't even need the beautiful hair and makeup or designer outfits to make her look that way. Back before everything had gone to hell with Knox's trial, I had seen her plenty of times in sweatpants and a messy bun, no makeup. Perfectly imperfect.

And of course, there was the simplest explanation: the brotherly protector in me had latched on to the fact that Mathew had broken her heart.

How dare he?!

Dakota Blackwood might be infuriating to me, but she was kind and compassionate. So compassionate, in fact, that she lived in that shithole place because she was helping her parents financially. That knowledge spread guilt through my system like a disease because I should've helped them more through the years. Should have checked on them as much as I'd checked on Dakota.

But back to the point. How dare Mathew treat her like she was expendable? How dare he leave her? Take her for granted and mistreat her?

What a prick.

When the valet had let me have my keys to find my own car under the veil of walking off my anger, I couldn't pass up the temptation. I'd seen his penis mobile parked three spots down.

The blue one I'd seen in his egotistical social media posts, same plates as before he'd abandoned Dakota for temptation overseas.

The responsible adult in me—admittedly a very tiny, malnourished part of my brain—suggested I walk away. The rest of me retrieved my pocketknife from my center console.

The knife slid into the first tire with ease, the sound of it deflating surprisingly satisfying. *Psssssht.* The sweet sound of inconveniencing the man who'd shattered her. In short order, all four fell victim to my blade because I'm nothing if not thorough in my vindictiveness.

I stood up, dusting off my knees, and pocketed my knife with the satisfaction of a job well done. Petty? Absolutely. Juvenile? One hundred percent. But imagining Mathew's face when he discovered his precious compensation mobile sitting on four flats would be worth whatever karma had in store for me. It was the least he deserved after how he'd mistreated Dakota.

The irony wasn't lost on me—what a douchebag I was being to her. Even now, on the car ride home. But this was different. We weren't really together. I wasn't the guy she'd opened her heart to, the one she'd trusted with her vulnerability.

I wasn't supposed to be her safe place. Mathew was.

So, why, when I watched her storm out of my car and into the penthouse's building, did I want to be?

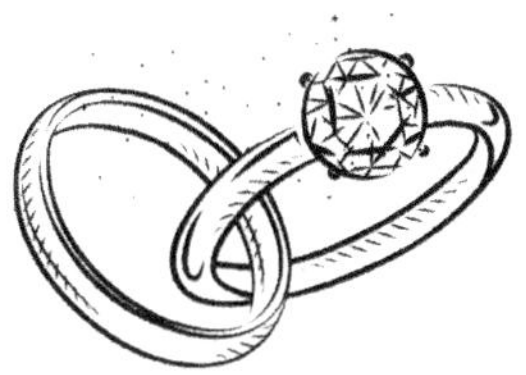

12

WHEN YOU THREATEN HIM WITH A GOOD TIME AND HE SMIRKS LIKE THAT'S EXACTLY WHAT HE WANTED. 😏 #SOYOUSTARTPLOTTING

DAKOTA

"Hey. We need to talk," Rebecca said the millisecond I walked through the door.

"I'm sorry, Rebecca, now's not a good time," I said, managing to keep my voice soft.

Look, was I confused about my feelings for Mathew? Yes. Obviously. Where I'd expected a volcano of love and warmth was an empty, echoing chamber. But A) that was probably just shock. And B) Even if it wasn't—even if my feelings for Mathew had shriveled up and died somewhere between his leaving and today—Axel didn't know that. For all he knew, I was seconds away from throwing myself into Mathew's arms. For all he knew, this was my one shot at fixing the love of my life, at mending something that had torn me apart for months.

He'd stolen that choice from me.

This—whatever this arrangement was between us—didn't give him the right to play puppet master with my life. I would never insert myself between him and anyone.

But apparently, he thought he owned me now. Thought he could just ... what? Make my choices for me?

Axel, who had always been an ass to me. ALWAYS. This wasn't just about that post's photo disaster. His animosity predated any of that, and I had officially reached my limit.

I couldn't think about selling our ridiculous fake love story with the man I least wanted to share oxygen with right now. I needed to calm down before I did something stupid, like cut holes in the crotches of all his underwear.

My mouth kicked up on one side at the thought. Not a terrible idea actually. Maybe I'd start with his silk boxers. He definitely seemed like a silk-boxers kind of guy. Pretentious bastard.

The elevator doors slid open, and there stood my archnemesis, hands shoved casually in his pockets like he hadn't just potentially torpedoed my life.

"Sunshine," he cooed, his voice dripping with fake sweetness.

"Don't *Sunshine* me! Do you have any idea what you've done?" I snapped.

"You can't be seen talking to another guy," Axel answered with the condescending tone of someone explaining basic math to a kindergartner.

"That's not what this is, and you know it."

"Isn't it?" His eyebrow arched.

I narrowed my eyes at him. "There were a million ways to ask me to stop talking to Mathew. Discreet ways. You wanted to humiliate him."

"And what if I did?" He shrugged like we were discussing a coffee preference instead of my love life.

"You probably ruined my shot at getting back together with Mathew."

"You want to get back together with him?" Axel spewed.

Well, that's not the point.

When I didn't answer, his lips went thin, his fingers pulling out of his pockets and twitching at his sides like they were itching to punch something. Or someone. Preferably Mathew's face, if I had to guess.

"Why in the world would you ever give that dickhead a second chance?"

"That's not your concern."

"I disagree."

"You're my fake fiancé. Nothing more. Stay. Out. Of. My. Life," I spat, enunciating each word.

"He left you. You deserve better than him."

"Like you care. The only thing you care about is making me miserable. Well, two can play at that game, Axel." *And, honey, I'm about to become a professional.*

"What the hell is that supposed to mean?"

I don't know. But I needed to reclaim some semblance of power and control here. The words had tumbled out before my brain had formulated an actual threat. *File that under Things to Figure Out Later.* Right next to How to Survive Fake Dating Satan Himself.

"Did you see how he was acting tonight?" Axel stepped forward, closing the distance between us. "He leaned into the altercation, Dakota. He was practically marking his territory like a dog."

I suppose I should've been upset by Mathew's behavior, but I wasn't. The truth was, it was healing in a way. The man who never fought for me was finally fighting for me, in more ways than one.

"Hey!" Rebecca clapped her hands like a teacher who was breaking up a playground fight. "You two can argue all you want later. But right now, we are going to debrief." She turned her screen. "Is this the guy you're fighting about?"

It was a photo of the altercation.

Axel snarled, "She was canoodling with her ex-boyfriend."

Canoodling. Who even says canoodling anymore? *What is he, eighty?*

I tried to murder Axel with my glower. "Ratting me out? Seriously? What are you, twelve?"

"He's your *ex*?" Rebecca shrieked. "Someone got a video! No audio, thank God, but the body language ... do I need to state the obvious here, Dakota?"

"I wasn't canoodling. I ran into him and had a cordial conversation."

"That wasn't part of the plan," she chided.

"I didn't plan to run into him."

"You should've walked away."

"I will sell this ridiculous love story to save my parents, but let me be clear about my boundaries. I will not hurt relationships in the process."

"Relationship?" Her eyebrows shot up so fast, they might have achieved orbit. "So, you *do* want a relationship with this guy?"

"It was written all over her face," Axel accused, the smug satisfaction in his voice making me want to throw something at his perfect teeth.

"Why are you doing this?" I stormed over to him, jabbing my finger at his chest. "My conversation with Mathew wasn't even on anyone's radar until you decided to butt in. That was bad enough, but then you come here and tattle on me like we're in third grade? What's next, Axel? Going to tell my mommy I stayed up past my bedtime?"

"My business is on the line, Sunshine." He caught my finger mid-jab. Why did his hands have to be so warm? *Stupid, attractive villain hands.* And why did my stupid ribs get all squirmy with delight at the contact? Did they NOT experience that fight? "Rebecca needs to know exactly what happened if she has any hope of salvaging my reputation after your little reunion tour."

"That's all you care about, isn't it?" I accused, yanking my finger back.

"Should I care about something else?"

I opened my mouth to argue, but suddenly forgot where the hell I was going with that. I shook my head, mentally cursing the effect his proximity had on my ability to form coherent sentences.

"Let's just have the debrief and get this over with." I stepped back.

"You cannot be seen with your ex-boyfriend," Rebecca said. Her tone suggested that violating this rule would result in my immediate execution.

"Fine. If I want to see him, I'll make sure it's somewhere private."

She shook her head like I'd suggested we rob a bank. "We cannot take that chance. If you're seen with an ex-boyfriend, it will call the authenticity of your relationship with Axel into question."

"I wouldn't do something stupid like kiss Mathew," I assured her. Maybe I should have confided in her how confused and empty I was feeling for Mathew, but that was so not happening right now.

"It doesn't matter. We can't risk it. You cannot see him," she said.

"What if I told him the truth? About the fake engagement? Then he'd understand why I can't see him, and—"

"Absolutely not." Rebecca's voice cut through the air. "Ex-boyfriends are off-limits for confidential information. Period."

"But Mathew's not like that. He wouldn't—"

"Dakota." Rebecca's tone turned gentle but firm. "I've seen what happens when jilted ex-lovers get their hands on information like this. It doesn't matter how much you trust him or how good your relationship ended. Jealousy makes people do things they never thought they were capable of. One angry moment, one too many drinks, one argument about why you chose Axel over him—real or fake—and suddenly, your secret is trending on social media."

I wanted to argue, to defend Mathew, but something in Rebecca's expression stopped me. She'd clearly seen this scenario play out before.

"Besides," she continued, "think about it from Mathew's perspective. You're asking him to keep quiet about information that could destroy the man you're supposedly choosing over him. That's not fair to put on anyone, especially someone who still has feelings for you."

My stomach sank because she was right. Mathew did still have feelings for me. And asking him to protect Axel's reputation would be cruel.

But so was lying to him.

I wasn't sure how I felt about Mathew. But I did know that I *wanted* to want him back. If I had enough time to process everything, I bet my feelings for him could come back. And then I'd have the life I'd dreamed of with him.

But now ... because I hadn't sacrificed enough for this fake engagement, I'd lose any hope of exploring a possible reconciliation with the only man I'd ever loved?

It seemed my whole life had been one series of sacrifices after another: helping my family through their ordeal with my brother, spending a tremendous amount of time helping them with repairs because they didn't have the money to hire someone to do it, and now enduring the animosity of my enemy to try to save us all from my mistake. And now they were asking me to give up the one thing—the ONE!—that had once mattered most to my heart?

It wasn't fair. For once, I just wanted to be selfish. Put myself first.

But I couldn't. And you know what? A better daughter would never have these self-pitying feelings. A better daughter would do whatever it took to save her family, period.

"Look, the faster we sell the story, the faster you can get out of it. And then once you're out of it, you're free to do whatever you want," Rebecca said.

"How long will that take?"

"It takes as long as it takes."

The most unhelpful answer in the history of unhelpful answers.

But what if Mathew moved on before then? I couldn't tell

him to wait around for me, could I? My throat swelled at the realization that I might lose Mathew forever. Before I even knew what I wanted.

"Then Axel can't date anyone either." The declaration didn't make me feel as better as I'd hoped.

"He can't," Rebecca agreed, nodding.

A look of panic settled across Axel's face, like someone had just told him Christmas was canceled. "I can have a woman over to my penthouse. Discreetly."

"A booty call?" I glared at him.

"A man has needs." He spread his hands like it was the most reasonable thing in the world.

"Then you're the neediest man I've ever met," I said, thinking of all the Instagram posts I'd seen of him with a different woman on his arm in every photo. I had nothing against a lifestyle of free love and all that, but that wasn't the point.

If I couldn't see Mathew to keep this story alive, then Axel couldn't see anyone either.

"Any woman I call over would be very discreet," he assured.

Oh, how noble of him. Discreet booty calls. What a gentleman.

"If I can't meet Mathew, you can't have some rando come over for a hookup."

"She's right." Rebecca crossed her arms. "No women."

"Are you kidding me right now?"

Boy, look at that raging case of panic.

"Axel Pierce, Chicago's biggest playboy, unable to get some ass," I quipped. "Must be hard. Literally and figuratively."

Jeez. I had left the neighborhood of Bratty and entered Bitchville without stopping for directions. I needed to get it together, but something about Axel Pierce made my normal self-control (and evidently kindness) evaporate like ice on hot pavement. His seething resentment infected me like a virus, making me want to hurt him like he did me. It was a vicious cycle—his contempt feeding my hostility, which fed his contempt.

Honestly, of all the people in Chicago—hell, on the entire planet—why did karma decide to shackle me to him?

"What can I say," Axel sneered. "I'm an ass man."

"I just threw up in my mouth a little."

"Now"—Rebecca rubbed her thighs like she was warming up for a marathon—"as we move forward, it will be very important that you and Axel know each other very well. Your homework assignment is to learn personal details about each other that will increase your credibility as a couple."

"I can google him," I assured her. I'd already done that, if I was being honest. Not because I cared, obviously. Just ... research.

"You need to learn everything about each other. What are your fears? Goals? What's something in your past that shaped who you are today? The things that couples know about each other."

Oh, hell to the no. Hard pass.

"We don't need to know all of that information to sell this love story." Because, fine, I would rather put my arm around Axel's hip than divulge any personal information to him. At least physical contact was temporary. Emotional vulnerability was forever.

"At some point, you are going to be giving interviews, and you two will be prepared for them." Rebecca pointed her finger at us like a mother scolding unruly toddlers. "Got it?"

So, let me process this fresh hell for a moment. Now, not only did I have to endure these fake romantic dates with Axel, not only was I evidently going to have to give interviews—which, let's be clear, made me break out in hives at the thought of some nosy reporter asking me questions about a relationship I wanted nothing to do with—but in order to be prepared for that, I had to divulge extremely personal information about myself? To *him*?

I wanted to argue. I wanted to fight tooth and nail. I even considered calling this whole thing off because this was too much. Too extreme.

But I pictured Mom with that wooden board strung across

her lap, and I imagined how many broken boards she would endure if I didn't get this together.

"Fine," I said, my voice flat. "But for the record, this whole thing is making me miserable."

Axel walked up to me, towering over me like the human skyscraper he was. Probably wanting to intimidate me with his size and muscles, but I held my ground. Raised my chin and squared my shoulders.

"Trust me, Sunshine," he said, his voice a dark silk activating something inside me, "there's nothing you could do to make me more miserable than I am right now."

I met his gaze without flinching, a slow smile spreading across my face. "Challenge accepted."

Apparently, I had a petty side to me. And she was about to come out and play.

13

SINNERS AND SAINTS GROUP CHAT

AXEL

Ryker: Axel, care to explain this masterpiece? [Sends image of Axel face-to-face with Mathew.]

Jace: For someone faking a relationship, you look REALLY possessive. That vein in your forehead is doing overtime, dude.

Blake: Tessa has explained to me that possessive, jealous heroes are—and I quote—"hot as hell." She also said you look like you're about to commit a homicide, which is apparently "peak book-boyfriend energy."

Me: Will you jackasses shut up? That assclown was harassing Dakota.

*Blake: Assclown. *eye roll emoji* I see college really refined your vocabulary.*

Ryker: Define "harassing" because it looks like he has hearts over his eyes, looking at her. Meanwhile, you look like you're calculating where to hide his body.

Jace: But wait, there's more. I assume this is your handiwork? Found her ex tagged in this: [Sends image someone took of Mathew, looking furiously at his four flat tires, under a meme of "Does your car ride low? Does it flatten to and fro?"]

Me: Ryker told me not to put confessions in writing.

Blake: Jace, you owe me $50. I told you it was him.

Jace: Thanks a lot, Axel. I bet against your jealous spiraling.

Me: I'm not jealous.

Ryker: [Sends screenshot of legal definition of jealousy with Axel's photo attached.]

Blake: [Resends images of flat tires.] What was that? I couldn't hear you over the sound of her ex-boyfriend's tires deflating.

Ryker: Fun fact: fake fiancés don't typically vandalize their fake girlfriend's ex's property. Just a legal observation.

Blake: Same. I've seen less dramatic meltdowns in the ER. And I once had a guy who superglued his hand to his ex's car.

Ryker: [Renames the group chat to Tire Slasher Support Group.]

Blake: Tessa says jealous heroes who slash tires are romance-novel gold. You're basically a walking book boyfriend now.

Me: For the last time, this engagement is FAKE. F-A-K-E.

Jace: Fake fiancés don't risk felony charges over some random guy talking to their fake girlfriend. Just a business observation.

Ryker: Careful, brother. Your worst nightmare might be coming true: catching actual feelings.

Me: Are you three done psychoanalyzing my life?

Ryker: Oh, we're just getting started. This fake relationship drama is better than Netflix.

Blake: Knox is going to lose his shit when he finds out his sister turned our playboy into a tire-slashing Romeo.

Ryker: [Sends GIF of man eating popcorn with huge grin.] This is me watching your "fake" relationship unfold.

Jace: Should we start a betting pool on when he admits he's falling for her?

Blake: I give it two weeks.

Ryker: One week, tops. Did you SEE his murder face in that photo?

Jace: Three days. He's already shopping for more tire-slashing equipment on Amazon.

Me: I hate all of you.
*Blake: Love you too, tire slasher. *kissing emoji**

14

WHEN YOUR GIRLS' NIGHT TURNS INTO A MASTERCLASS IN PSYCHOLOGICAL WARFARE. 🍷 #REVENGESERVEDHOT

DAKOTA

"Challenge accepted?" A soft chuckle escaped Faith's lips. "You said, 'Challenge accepted'? What exactly did you mean by that?"

"I have no idea," I admitted, already feeling the pleasant buzz from the wine spreading through my veins. "But it was either say something to get under his skin or flat-out punch him in the throat, and I decided physical assault would probably violate the terms and conditions of this ridiculous charade."

God, I was so glad she came early to our girls' night so I could confide all of this to her: Mathew, our breakup, and how he'd come back fighting for me, only to have Axel act like a complete ass. Blake's sister, Faith, didn't know me like Scarlett and Tessa did, so I felt less pressure to be ... well, a decent human being.

I didn't want to be decent right now. After what Axel did last night, I wanted to be petty. With a capital P. Maybe all caps: PETTY.

While we waited for Tessa and Scarlett to arrive, Faith and I sat at Axel's obscenely expensive dining room table, some wood monstrosity that probably required seven men to assemble up here. Floor-to-ceiling windows stretched behind us, showcasing a view of the city most people only saw from rooftops, and the chandelier overhead was all geometric crystal and brushed bronze, the kind of fixture you'd see in a design magazine. Beautiful and cold.

He had everything. The classic elegance, the space, the view. He didn't need to try and control my life too.

Faith poured us both more wine, and I took a sip, grateful I'd invited them over to commiserate.

Okay, fine, I invited the girls over to talk me out of doing something stupid. Because after Rebecca and Axel left, I'd paced by the elevator door, beyond tempted to run to Mathew and tell him what was going on.

"Why do you hate the idea of doing the whole get-to-know-you talk?" Faith cocked her head.

"Axel already knows enough about me," I argued. "He was there to witness my family's downfall firsthand and saw me at my most broken in the courthouse." Something I hated more than the smell of rotten eggs. "Plus, he already holds the key to my most painful secret: that my brother is a convicted killer." I'd mentioned that little tidbit to Faith, too, and I could tell Faith was just waiting to press me on that for information. "That secret could destroy my brand if anyone found out. The last thing I want to do is pretend to love someone who has the power to ruin everything."

"Maybe what you hate isn't Axel," Faith said quietly. "Maybe what you hate is how he makes you feel when you're around him."

"Which is?"

"Like you can't hide."

This time, I glared, but it was to pretend her words didn't bounce around in my head.

She smirked. "Okay, but answer me this." She swirled the ruby liquid in her glass thoughtfully. "Why does he seem so angry at you?"

"The photo."

"No, it's more than that." She examined me like I was a puzzle missing pieces. "Trust me, after growing up in the foster care system, you become really good at reading people. It's a survival skill."

There was something behind those words that I wanted to explore, a shadow that darkened her eyes momentarily, making me wonder, *What had made reading people a matter of survival for her?* But I didn't know her well enough to push on that particular door.

"What's the history of you two?" Faith asked. "Because the sexual tension between you guys could power a small city."

"Sexual tension?" I feigned shock. "We hate each other."

"Uh-huh. Sure." Faith's smirk said she wasn't buying it. "Spill. Because my imagination is running wild right now."

I sighed, regretting this conversation. "When my brother, Knox, was in college, I used to visit him all the time. Enter tall, dark, and absolutely impossible."

"Mysterious backstory. I'm here for it."

"I felt something between us right away. All those stolen glances, finding excuses to bump into each other. You know, the usual *I'm totally not staring at you* dance."

Faith leaned forward. "Classic lovers setup. Continue."

"But then one weekend, like someone flipped a switch, Axel didn't just push me away; he shoved. Hard." The memory still stung, even buzzed on wine. "At first, I kept asking myself, what happened? I replayed everything, looking for clues. Had I said something? Done something? We'd had the best time together just days before. When I couldn't figure it out, I mustered the courage to ask him."

"What did Mr. Tall, Dark, and Brooding say when you confronted him?"

"And I quote, 'Nothing happened, Sunshine. Whatever you thought was going on between us, you thought wrong.' "

Faith winced. "Ouch. That's some premium-grade rejection right there."

"Right? And that was the first time he used that stupid nickname, which made it ten times worse. Like, thanks for the emotional whiplash, wrapped in fake affection." I took another sip. "When my eyes welled up, his whole body deflated like he wanted to take it back. But I left before he had the chance to apologize because ... screw him, you know?"

"So, he basically led you on and then slammed the door in your face."

"Maybe. Or maybe I imagined the whole thing." I shrugged, hating how uncertain I still sounded. "Either way, I decided if he was going to be a complete ass, I'd be one right back. I'd never been mean to anyone before, but with him, I would literally rehearse my insults in the shower."

Faith snorted. "Please tell me you didn't use index cards."

I grinned despite myself. "I'd deliver these carefully crafted verbal daggers with total fake confidence, and he'd just—"

"What?"

"Smirk. Then get right in my space, close enough that I had to crane my neck to glare at his ridiculously sexy face, and he'd say something like, 'Did you practice that in the mirror, Sunshine?' " My cheeks heated at the memory of how he knew me so well, even back then. "The infuriating part was how he'd get this look in his eyes, like he was enjoying every second of our little battles."

"Girl." Faith set down her glass. "He was definitely into you fighting back."

"That's what made it worse! Every time I'd launch into one of my prepared attacks, he'd stalk across the room like he owned the place, invade my personal space, and then do that thing where he'd run his thumb across his bottom lip while smirking down at me. It was like he was weaponizing his own mouth."

Faith bit her lip to keep from smiling. "Sounds to me like he looked forward to your jabs as much as you liked rehearsing them."

"Yeah, well, then Knox got arrested, and everything changed." The lightness in my voice dimmed. "My whole world imploded.

One day at the courthouse, Axel saw me shaking and tried to comfort me. But I was so raw, so angry at everything, I told him he was the last person I'd ever want comfort from."

"Ouch."

"I know. I was a mess. Before Knox's arrest, my biggest problem was decoding mixed signals from my brother's hot friend. After? I just wanted to get through each day without completely falling apart." I twisted my wineglass. "Axel tried reaching out after Knox went to prison, but I shut him down every time. Instead of spending those last free months really being with my brother, I'd wasted all my mental energy obsessing over someone who apparently didn't want anything to do with me."

Faith reached over and squeezed my hand. "You were young and had no idea your brother was about to go to prison. Cut yourself some slack."

"I guess. But now here we are, years later, and I still don't know if what I felt back then from Axel was real or just wishful thinking." I laughed, but it came out hollow. "And somehow, that's still the story of my life with Axel Pierce. Never knowing what's real and what's fake."

Faith's eyes gleamed with mischief. "Well, fake engagement or not, one thing's crystal clear: that man is still very much affected by you."

"Did you not hear the part about how rude he was?" I challenged.

"You want my opinion? The guy likes you. With a capital L. Maybe he was jealous when he saw your ex."

Something unwelcome settled into my chest. Something that felt like a pang. I knew Axel's reputation with women. He never stayed with anyone, never committed, which was a fact Knox once warned me about when he saw us eye-flirting. Opening the idea that he might like me risked not only professional devastation—because, hello, he'd probably find some way to use it against me and it'd ruin my brand—but also, I wouldn't survive that kind of personal destruction of his rejection.

My heart had already been through too much.

I took another long sip of my wine, welcoming the increasing fuzziness to my muscles.

"It doesn't matter why he's being this rude," I decided. "I guess I could've handled that. But him sabotaging my chance with Mathew?" I hadn't told Faith about my confusing feelings for Mathew because here was the headline: Axel's behavior probably burned a real bridge for a fake relationship. "I want to hit him back where it hurts."

My eyes went wide at my own words.

"Sorry," I said quickly. "I assure you, I'm not normally a vindictive person. I'm usually the one telling people to turn the other cheek and be the bigger person. I'm basically a walking Hallmark card most days."

Faith waved her hand dismissively. "I'm big on revenge. People say to take the high road and all that, but that is totally overrated. It feels so much better to just get revenge."

The casual way she said it made me laugh. There was something so refreshingly straightforward about her philosophy. "I've never really thought to do that. My revenge game is tragically underdeveloped."

"You should try it out. Trust me, it feels amazing." She leaned forward, her voice dropping conspiratorially. "One time, I was in a foster family that had this older brother who was a total assclown. I get the whole *angry at being in the foster care situation* thing, but he decided to make me his personal target. He used to do things like smash my lunch so it was all crushed by the time I wanted to eat it. Or steal the laces from my shoes. Anything to cause chaos. And before you ask, no, it was not a crush thing," she added firmly. "The guy just used me as a punching bag for his anger."

The casual way she dismissed what sounded like genuine bullying made me wonder what other worse things she'd experienced that made this seem minor in comparison.

"What did you do?" I asked, curious now.

Faith took a deliberate sip of wine and leaned forward with a smirk that could only be described as deliciously devious.

"So, the guy was a major jock, right? And at that point, he was in baseball season. He had this super-expensive bat that he worked all summer to save up for. The thing was shiny black, very manly." She rolled her eyes. "That particular weekend, he had a baseball tournament coming up. I went to a garage sale and found a hot-pink bat. I painted Hello Kitty all over it, and just before he left for the tournament, I replaced his manly black bat with the hot-pink Hello Kitty masterpiece."

I chuckled, the image forming vividly in my mind. "He didn't notice?"

"Had one of those gym bags that was so big, it was hidden until it was too late."

I laughed.

"It was the only bat he had to use the entire tournament," Faith said, a satisfied gleam in her eye. "The coaches wouldn't let him borrow one because they said he needed to learn responsibility. His face was the exact color of the bat by the end of the weekend."

"Okay, you really are fun." I raised my glass in a toast.

"I have my moments." She clinked her glass against mine. "You should do something like that to Axel."

"It's tempting," I admitted, the wine making the idea seem less outrageous by the second. "He either needs to talk to me about whatever I did to offend him or move on. Torturing me for the rest of my life isn't acceptable. There's a statute of limitations on grudges, and a decade definitely exceeds it."

"You might be stuck with him, but he's also stuck with you," Faith pointed out. "Trust me. Pull a prank on him or something. It'll make you feel so much better. Bonus points if it hits him in his Achilles' heel."

"His Achilles' heel is his business. As angry as I am, I would never hit him there." Even in my wine-soaked state, I knew some lines shouldn't be crossed.

"No, this has to be more fun. What else is his weak spot?"

I shrugged, sighing dramatically. "I have no idea." God, Faith came up with a Hello Kitty bat, and I couldn't think of one thing to make him mad. "He *is* upset that he can't date at least. So, I have that small victory, I guess."

She snapped her fingers, her eyes lighting up like she'd just had an epiphany. "That's it."

"What's it?"

"He's not allowed to date, right? The whole time you guys are fake together or whatever?"

"Yeah?" I tilted my head, curious where she was going with this.

"And from what you've described, this is a guy that doesn't go two days without a date."

"He'll be taking a lot of cold showers." I nodded, a grin forming on my lips at the thought.

Faith's answering smile was positively wicked.

"You're plotting," I accused, pointing at her with my wineglass. "I can practically see the cartoon light bulb above your head."

"What if the guy came home to this gorgeous girl in a scandalously clad outfit? How hard would that be for him?" Her eyes danced with mischief. "It'd be like a starving man coming home to a perfectly cooked Italian feast, smelling it all, feeling the aching hunger in his stomach, and not being allowed to have a single bite."

I laughed, the wine amplifying my amusement. "That would be hilarious. And he did say he was an 'ass man.' " I mimicked his smug tone with surprising accuracy.

Faith raised her eyebrows suggestively.

I shook my head, even as the idea took root. "I don't think I can do that." It was mean. Deliciously mean, but still mean. "Besides, he probably hates me too much to see me as anything other than the target of his mysterious pent-up aggression."

"I doubt it. And even if you're right," Faith countered, "you are warm flesh and blood of the opposite sex. And the only female that he is allowed to be near for the foreseeable future."

True ...

"I haven't missed a day of squats since before my mom's accident," I mused, a new confidence seeping into my voice. "I did them to keep my legs strong so that I could lift her in emergencies or any other situation where she needed me." The side effect of all that dedication was that I had a rock-hard ass that could probably crack walnuts. Not that I'd tried. Yet.

"Okay, here's what you do." Faith set her wine down, eyes gleaming with purpose.

Two hours and several glasses of wine later, the girls had cleared out, and I was alone in Axel's penthouse, feeling ridiculously reckless.

When the elevator doors opened, I bit back a giggle and got into position.

The sound of his footsteps came to a sudden halt.

"What. The. Actual. Fuck?"

I turned slowly, feigning surprise, and watched with immense satisfaction as Axel Pierce, Chicago's most notorious playboy, stood frozen in his tracks, his eyes wide and fixed directly on the part of my anatomy he'd so smugly declared himself a connoisseur of.

Game on, Axel.

15

FAKE FIANCÉE TIP: WHEN YOU REALIZE HIS ACHILLES' HEEL IS HORMONES, SAUNTER AROUND IN NEXT TO NOTHING. 😈 #WARFAREJUSTGOTINTERESTING

AXEL

"What the fuck are you doing?"

Dakota looked at me over her shoulder. The one still angled down toward the floor with her ass pointed right at me like a goddamn invitation. She had the audacity to bat her eyelashes.

"Yoga," she answered, voice dripping with innocence.

"At eleven thirty at night?" I growled.

She pushed herself up into what I'm pretty sure was the world's most pornographic warrior pose. The barely there tank top—and I'm being generous, calling it that—rode up to reveal miles of toned stomach. Next, her heel pulled up to her knee, forming a perfect triangle.

Putting that space between her thighs on full display, beneath a scrap of fabric barely bigger than a postage stamp.

"Couldn't sleep," she claimed, stretching her arms overhead like she was reaching for heaven while sending me straight to hell.

My dick pressed against my zipper hard enough to leave permanent damage. Her eyes tracked the movement, and a victorious smirk spread across her face like she'd just won the lottery.

"Why are you wearing that?" I clenched my fists.

"This?" She glanced down. "I was hot."

Yeah, well, now we're both burning alive.

She transitioned into downward dog—because of course she did—pressing her palms flat while her ass shot skyward like a beacon of pure temptation.

This is fine. I'm a grown man. I've survived hostile takeovers and boardroom bloodbaths. I can handle one tiny woman in ...

Jesus Christ, are those actual lace panties?

They barely covered the curve of her ass, and I could see the outline of everything that had haunted my dreams for the past decade.

"Stop." My voice came out rougher than sandpaper.

Did she stop? Hell no. Dakota Blackwood had never stopped anything fun in her life.

She pivoted slowly, deliberately, giving me a front-row view of abs that belonged in a fitness magazine and breasts that were clearly enjoying the show as much as she was.

She's doing this on purpose. She has to be. No one does yoga in Victoria's Secret sexwear unless they're planning a murder. And I'm definitely the victim.

Look away, Pierce. Look. Away.

I tried. Really, I did. But as I desperately tried to escape the room and head into the kitchen, my eyes had other plans, staying glued to the gentle curve of her waist.

CRASH.

My hip collided with the foyer table hard enough to rattle my teeth. A crystal vase wobbled dangerously.

"Everything okay over there?" She tilted her head, batting those long lashes. "You seem a little ... distracted."

My dick throbbed at the sultry rasp in her voice, then did a full-on salute when she trailed her tongue slowly along her bottom lip.

I've made grown men weep during negotiations. I will NOT be defeated by Dakota in ... holy shit, is that tank top see-through? I can see her nipples.

Which were hard. And perfectly outlined as she arched her back, reaching toward the ceiling like she was putting on a private strip show.

"I'm great," I lied through gritted teeth. The pain in my hip was nothing compared to the ache building behind my zipper.

All these years, I'd wondered what Dakota looked like with less clothes. I'd fantasized about her in my bed, bent over while I took her from behind, her whispering my name like a prayer. She was even more devastatingly beautiful than every forbidden dream combined.

"Really?" She shifted into what had to be the most obscene yoga pose ever invented. "Because the usually confident Axel Pierce looks like he's about to spontaneously combust."

Because I'm staring at the one woman I can never have. And feeling more tempted than ever before.

"I'm fine," I managed, though my claim would've landed better if my dick wasn't straining against my pants like it was trying to escape.

"So ..." She moved into warrior pose, arms stretched wide, legs slightly parted, head cocked at that perfect angle that made my brain short-circuit. "Where were you tonight? Hot date?"

"Out," I growled.

"Mmm." Her lips curved into a knowing smile. And then she had the evilness to bend again, slowly this time. "If you were with another woman, your poor fake fiancée would be devastated. What would Rebecca say?"

"I wasn't with another woman."

"But I bet you wanted to be." She shifted into cobra pose: chest pushed forward, back arched, looking like every wet dream I'd ever had. "It's got to be killing you, staring down weeks, maybe even months of celibacy. No touching." She knelt and ran her hands down her abs. "No kissing." She wet her lips again. "No hot, sweaty, all-night—"

"Stop." The word came out strangled.

"I'm just empathizing," she said, spreading her legs wider as she moved into some position that should've been illegal in twelve states. "It must be so hard, knowing you can't have any relief."

What is she doing to me?

"All's fair in love and fake engagements." She smirked, her gaze dropping to my crotch like she was cataloging exactly what her little show was doing to me.

"Do you really think it's wise to parade around my penthouse, dressed like that?"

"Like what?" The picture of innocence, if innocence wore lingerie and had a PhD in driving men insane.

"It's like holding a glass of water in front of a man dying of thirst."

Her eyebrows shot up, lips forming a perfect O of mock surprise. But I knew exactly what she was doing with that mouth. Knew exactly what would fit in that O.

"Are you saying you find me attractive, Axel Pierce?"

More than any woman who's ever existed.

"Put some goddamn clothes on," I said.

Or don't. God help me, please don't.

My phone buzzed. A welcome distraction from the Dakota Blackwood torture chamber my living room had become. I could barely focus on the screen, too mesmerized by the way she was now stretching like a cat in the sun.

Luckily—or unluckily, depending on how you looked at it—the message was like a bucket of ice water.

Ryker: We have a serious problem. I'll be there in twenty minutes.

Shit.

I looked up to find Dakota watching me, her expression shifting from playful to concerned.

"What is it?" she asked, all traces of seduction gone from her voice.

"Ryker said we have a problem."

"We, as in the fake engagement? Or we, as in you and your buddy?"

"I don't know," I admitted. "But if he's on his way at this hour, whatever it is must be bad."

16

PLOT TWIST: TURNS OUT, THERE ARE WORSE THINGS THAN FAKE DATING YOUR ENEMY. LIKE REAL DYING BECAUSE OF YOUR ENEMY. #PERSPECTIVE

DAKOTA

"Get changed before Ryker gets here," Axel barked, his voice rough as gravel.

"Sure thing." I bent down slowly and was rewarded with his sharp intake of breath. "Just need to finish my cooldown stretches."

Victory tastes so sweet.

"Dakota. Get. Up."

"Hold on." I rose inch by torturous inch, rolling my spine vertebra by vertebra. "You know what they say about proper form."

When I glanced over my shoulder, I caught him staring at my ass with an expression that looked like pure torture. His hands were clenched into fists at his sides, and I could see the exact moment he realized I'd caught him looking. The flush that crept up his neck was absolutely delicious.

The man looked like he was about to stroke out.

But then Axel did something I didn't expect. He stormed across the room in three long strides, closing the distance between us until my brain went fuzzy.

He towered over me, all six foot two of furious male, looking down like his eyes were blazing a path of possession across my barely covered skin. I'd expected his anger. Hell, I'd counted on it. I'd even expected the impressive bulge straining against his dress pants. What I didn't expect was how prominent it was or how the sight of it sent unwelcome fire engulfing the space between my thighs.

Every inch of exposed skin started tingling. My nipples peaked against the thin fabric, and I prayed he couldn't see the goose bumps racing down my arms. This was supposed to be revenge, not ... whatever the hell this electric current was.

"Do not tempt me, Sunshine."

His voice was low, dangerous, like a tiger giving its last warning before it pounced.

"I have no idea what you're talking about," I managed, though my voice came out breathier than intended. *Traitor.*

His eyes dropped to my mouth, then lower, scanning the curves barely concealed by lace and satin. When his gaze lingered on my peaked nipples, his jaw clenched so hard, I thought he might crack a tooth. The evidence of his arousal pressed more insistently against his pants, and I had to fight the urge to stare at just how affected he really was.

"You're playing with fire," Axel warned, stepping even closer. So close that if I shifted just slightly, my barely covered breasts would brush against his chest.

"Oh?" I tilted my chin up defiantly, even though my heart was hammering against my ribs. "And what exactly are you going to do about it?"

Why did I just challenge him? *What is wrong with me?*

His jaw ticced. Once. Twice. A muscle in his neck strained like he was fighting some internal war. His eyes dropped to my lips again, and I could practically see him imagining what it would feel like to crash his mouth against mine. I mean, my word, the tension between us was so thick, I could barely breathe.

"Get. Changed." His hands clenched and unclenched into fists at his sides again.

"Make me."

Did I just say that out loud? *Jesus, Dakota, what are you doing?*

Something dark and hungry flashed in his eyes. For a split second, I thought he might actually do it. Thought he might grab me, pin me against the wall, and show me exactly what kind of fire I was playing with. His gaze dropped to my lips one more time, and I swear I saw him lean forward slightly before he caught himself. The bulge in his pants was now impossible to ignore, straining against the expensive fabric in a way that made my mouth water.

Even more alarming, part of me wanted to reach out and touch it.

What in the actual hell?

It was probably just hormones. After all, I hadn't been with a man since Mathew and I had broken up.

Instead, Axel took a step back, running a hand through his perfectly styled hair. But not before I caught the way his eyes lingered on my body one last time, drinking in every curve like he was memorizing them for later.

"Put on some goddamn clothes before I do something we'll both regret."

Whoa ...

What if I didn't want to? What if I wanted to—

No, Dakota!

I stumbled backward, suddenly desperate for distance. This was Axel Pierce. My brother's best friend. My enemy.

So, why did I want to find out what those hands would feel like on my skin? Dipping beneath my bra, my panties?

I thought I'd won this prank. But suddenly, I felt like the loser as I watched him storm down the hallway. Not because he left. But because I didn't want him to. And because the way he'd looked at me, like he wanted to devour me, was now burned into my memory forever.

An unsettling feeling rocked my core, but I swallowed it. Whatever had happened between me and Axel was nothing. Hormones, fueled with wine. That was all. Him looking at me like he wanted to taste? Was just his hormones, nothing more.

I forced the thoughts out of my head and went into my room and changed into an appropriate outfit: a long-sleeved cotton T-shirt and sweatpants.

There. Crisis averted. No more tingling skin, no more traitorous thoughts about Axel's hands, and definitely no more wondering what those lips would taste like.

I was winning this internal battle. Totally in control.

Until I walked into the kitchen and found Axel leaning against the counter.

Shirtless.

Oh, for God's sake.

Apparently, he'd decided to torture me by changing out of his shirt and into ... nothing. Just low-slung sweats that highlighted the V of muscles disappearing beneath his waistband. His chest was a masterpiece of defined abs and intricate tattoos. Dark ink swirling across his shoulders and down his arms in patterns that made my fingers itch to trace them.

And, damn him, he was still semi-aroused. The outline was clearly visible through the fabric of his sweatpants, and the sight sent a fresh wave of fire through my already-overheated body.

"Subtle," I said, grabbing a water bottle from the fridge and pointedly not looking at the way his muscles shifted when he moved.

"Problem?" He cocked his head.

Oh, hell no. He wasn't winning. I'd worked too hard on that yoga stunt to lose now.

I opened the water, took a long drink, deliberately letting a few drops escape and trail down my chin to the base of my neck.

As I trailed it even lower with my finger, his eyes tracked the movement, his Adam's apple bobbing as he swallowed hard.

"No problem at all," I said sweetly, drawing the water droplet to the neckline of my shirt. "Just admiring your ... commitment to staying cool." This time, I dipped my finger into the water and slowly drew it into my mouth, wrapping my lips around my knuckle and giving off a soft groan because, seriously, if we were going to play hormone war, I was going to win.

When I pushed the finger deeper into my mouth, his nostrils flared, and I caught the way his hands gripped the edge of the counter behind him. Like he needed something to hold on to, to keep from reaching for me.

Muhahahaha.

I was totally going to go further, but before I had the chance, the elevator opened, and Ryker stormed in like a man on a mission, a manila folder clutched in his hand.

"You want the bad news or the really bad news?" Ryker asked.

His eyes swept the room, landing briefly on Axel's strategic hand placement over his sweatpants. Ryker's gaze flicked to me, then back to Axel's obvious predicament. With a look of pure annoyance, Ryker rolled his eyes and cleared his throat pointedly.

"Seriously?" he muttered under his breath.

"Whatever this is, it couldn't wait until morning?" Axel wondered. Probably needing to get into his room with a serious bottle of lotion right now.

Ryker ignored him, opening the file with the dramatic flair of a prosecutor presenting evidence. But I guess it tracked; Ryker was a criminal defense lawyer.

"That woman you were caught 'flirting' with." Ryker slapped an 8x10 photograph down in front of us. "Victoria Webb. Senator Stephen Webb's wife."

Axel squinted at the photo. "Have you heard of digital photography? It's this new concept where you can pull pictures up on your iPad instead of printing them like it's 1995."

"Her name sounded familiar to me."

"We already know this," Axel insisted. "She's married to—"

"Beyond that," Ryker continued. "So, I did some digging into her family background."

Okay? What did this have to do with Axel or me?

"Fascinating," Axel drawled. "Did you also dig up her favorite coffee order? I'm betting she's a pumpkin spice latte kind of woman."

Poor guy. Blue balls was making him super cranky.

"Do you know who Victoria Webb really is?" Ryker's voice had that edge that meant business.

Axel shrugged, the movement making his shoulder tattoo shift in a way that was definitely not distracting me. "America's sweetheart. Political wife. Future First Lady. Woman with a ten-carat ring I apparently didn't notice."

"Her uncle is Tony Romano," Ryker continued. "Now, what I've gathered here is uncorroborated testimony from an informant my colleague worked with. But it's long been suspected that Romano is organized crime."

Axel's cocky smirk faltered. "The hell you talking about?"

I felt an unexpected twist in my stomach at the thought of Axel being in actual danger.

Ryker slid another photograph across the counter. This one was of a distinguished-looking man in an expensive suit with silver hair and cold, calculating eyes. Despite the respectable appearance, something about his smile promised violence.

"Victoria's father and uncle have purposely been keeping distance, one side legitimate business, the other not so much. Meanwhile, behind the scenes, they had an arrangement in which a handpicked politician marries into the family to become their political puppet. With the help from the Romano business money, they fast-tracked Senator Webb's political career, in large part from a social media blitz campaign that quickly dubbed them the *it* couple with aspirations for the White House."

"Jesus," Axel replied.

People used social media for all sorts of things evidently. Who knew even organized crime families had tapped into it?

"Anyway, the arrangement would be a win-win for everyone. The Romano family would have control over the most powerful person in the country. But evidently, Victoria isn't being as careful as she should be."

Seriously. She shouldn't have been flirting with Axel.

"Dakota's photo is wreaking havoc on their curated image. Crime bosses don't like reporters digging into their niece's background," Ryker said. "Especially when that niece is married to a presidential candidate who's been very useful to their ... business interests."

"I didn't know she was married, let alone that she's connected to the mob," Axel protested, running a hand through his hair in frustration.

The movement made his biceps flex, and I forced myself to focus on the terrifying man in the photograph instead.

Focus, Dakota. Danger. Death. Very unsexy things.

"Doesn't matter," Ryker said. "Your scandal brought unwanted media attention to Victoria's family ties. Reporters are starting to dig into the Webb marriage, asking questions about Victoria's background and her family connections. No one in the press has picked up on the Romano connection yet; the crime family has done a good job burying it. But the thing about a scandal is that it has a news cycle. Reporters have to keep digging up fresh information, and eventually, they'll run out of readily available material. They'll start digging deeper into her background, and when that happens, they'll uncover this crime family connection. If that comes to light, his political aspirations are over, and the crime family loses their pawn who's about to move into the White House. Now, thus far, there hasn't been enough proof to make any mob ties stick legally, but public perception is a different beast."

The room fell silent, except for the hum of the refrigerator and the sound of my heart hammering against my ribs. A muscle jumped in Axel's neck as he processed the implications, and I felt that stupid twist in my stomach again.

Holy irony, Batman. Here Axel and I were, scrambling to sell a fake relationship because the woman he'd been seen flirting with was married. Only to find out we'd unknowingly exposed that Victoria's "perfect marriage" was also complete bullshit.

I could practically hear Axel's furious thoughts: *As if we needed another shining example of people crafting fairy-tale images for likes and popularity.* The real kicker? We were all living proof of how quickly that house of cards could collapse, how one misstep could turn the adoring public into a vengeful mob.

"If she has that sort of family, it would have come out eventually. Especially if her husband is running for president," I reasoned.

"Be that as it may"—Ryker drummed his fingers on the table—"that viral photo is responsible for this coming out. And I've heard rumblings from informants about payback."

Jesus.

"So, you're here to warn us that Axel is in danger?" *Why does the thought of that make me want to throw up?*

"Not just Axel." Ryker's expression was grim. "You had a role in creating this mess. And you two just went public with your relationship. As far as Tony Romano knows, you're the beloved girlfriend of the man who's threatened everything."

"But," I protested weakly, "our fake engagement is supposed to make this scandal go away. So, really, we're helping them right now."

Ryker's glare leveled me. "You think mob bosses wait around to see if PR strategies work? They handle problems before they become bigger problems. And right now, you two are problems."

17

ME: I HATE THIS FAKE RELATIONSHIP. LIFE: HERE'S A HIT MAN TO PUT THINGS INTO PERSPECTIVE. #DEATHBYROMANCE

DAKOTA

"So, good news." Axel raised his crystal tumbler of whiskey toward the men currently occupying his penthouse living room.

Blake Morrison—emergency room doctor and Tessa's fiancé—leaned against the far wall like he was posing for a medical drama. Next to him stood Jace Lockwood, CEO extraordinaire and Scarlett's boyfriend, who probably had more money than some small countries. Ryker paced the length of the windows like a caged panther while Axel and I sat on his ridiculously expensive couch, both looking like we'd been hit by a freight train.

A freight train named Tony Romano.

After Ryker had dropped his little bombshell about my fake fiancé potentially being on a crime family hit list, the guys had apparently activated their version of the Avengers. Because nothing says *crisis management* like summoning the rich, the brilliant, and the medically trained.

Rain hammered against the floor-to-ceiling windows like Mother Nature herself wanted a front-row seat to our impending doom. The storm had cast Axel's normally bright penthouse in shades of gray, all sharp shadows and cold light.

Real cozy atmosphere for discussing death threats.

"The good news," Axel repeated, swirling his whiskey as he prepared to fill in Blake and Jace on why they'd been summoned here, "is that we're trending. The dinner show worked like a charm." He paused, letting that sink in. "The bad news? We might also be featured on a Romano family hit list now."

Jace and Blake exchanged a loaded look. Both turned to stare at Ryker.

"The hell are you talking about?" Blake asked.

Oh, just that my fake engagement might get us both murdered. You know, typical day.

Ryker stopped pacing long enough to explain everything. Again. Victoria Webb. Senator Stephen Webb. The Romano crime family connections. The whole *Mafia controlling a presidential hopeful* thing that apparently wasn't covered in any PR handbook.

"Jesus, Axel." Blake ran a hand through his hair. "I always figured your love life would kill you eventually, but I assumed it'd be from an STD."

"Super helpful, Blake," Axel snarled. "Really feeling the support here."

I snorted despite myself. Probably on account of the stiff drink I'd consumed after Ryker's bomb. "At least STDs are treatable. Pretty sure there's no antibiotic for a crime-family bullet to the head."

Okay. Axel did not like my attempt at humor. Look at him going even broodier. But wait, was that concern flickering across his face? Like the idea of me with a bullet to the head actually bothered him?

I guess, in fairness, we might loathe each other, but being comfortable with a whole death thing was over the line.

"We need a plan," Ryker said, resuming his pacing.

"Like what?" Jace wondered. "I don't know jack about organized crime, but my understanding is they're pretty goddamned dangerous. And vengeful."

And here I thought, my biggest problem was pretending to be in love with my mortal enemy.

Axel shot me a look, and there was something in his expression. Something that looked almost like fear for me. For a split second, his face softened, and I caught a glimpse of the college guy who used to build bonfires in our backyard when Knox would visit from college that first year.

Then the moment passed, and his walls slammed back up.

"We need to figure out how to keep Axel safe," Ryker said. "He's most likely in danger. Dakota might be too."

Might be? Gee, that's reassuring.

"What about my private estate in Colorado?" Jace suggested. "You two could disappear for a while. Let things cool down."

Ryker shook his head. "Crime families specialize in making people disappear when there are no witnesses. Isolation just makes you sitting ducks. No crowds, no cameras, no help. You'd be harder to protect and easier to eliminate quietly."

"Perfect." Without thinking, I shifted closer to Axel, and he didn't move away. In fact, his arm stretched along the back of the couch behind me, not quite touching, but close enough that I could feel his warmth. His ... protection? "Let's just hide in a cabin and wait for the murder montage to begin."

Either I was going to crack jokes or start crying in the fetal position, and frankly, sarcasm seemed like the better option.

"What if they leave the country?" Blake jumped in. "Find some tiny town on the other side of the world. Lie low."

"Let me just google *places organized crime can't reach.*" Jace pulled out his phone with exaggerated sarcasm.

Blake glowered at him so hard, I swear I could feel the heat of it. "I'm trying to help here."

"The Romano family has international connections," Ryker said. "Same problem as Colorado. These aren't street thugs. They're a sophisticated operation with political ties."

Of course they are. Because why would anything in my life be simple?

"How do you know all this?" I asked, though I wasn't sure I wanted the answer.

"Criminal lawyer, remember? I've tangled with organized crime cases over the years. Unfortunately, I know more about them than your average person."

So, our legal counsel was basically a walking encyclopedia of organized crime. At least that helped us, right?

"Let's go to the police," I said. "That's literally what they're there for."

"No actual crime has been committed yet," Ryker replied. "This is theoretical danger."

"Yeah, I don't think, *Dear Officer, I pissed off a very bad man*, is grounds for opening a criminal investigation," Blake reasoned.

"Plus, these kinds of people have political connections," Axel added. "Senator Webb, remember? They're probably not thrilled about police involvement."

"He's right," Ryker agreed. "It'll just paint a bigger target on your backs."

Fantastic. So, our options are hide and die, or don't hide but still die. I'm sensing a theme here.

Axel's hand moved from the back of the couch to briefly touch my shoulder. Just for a second, but long enough for me to feel the heat of his palm through my shirt.

"Then we hire private security," Jace said, straightening. "I'll cover the cost. Former special ops, best in the country."

Ryker was already shaking his head. "I don't think that'll work. They can still aim a gun from a distance. Plus, that'll just escalate the threat. Crime families love a challenge, and they love it even more when people are scared of them."

"Well, this is just delightful," I muttered, appreciating it when Blake's mouth hitched up slightly.

Throwing me a bone of sarcasm to lighten the mood, he said, "If you do get shot, try to fall on your left side. Easier to repair the damage in surgery."

I smirked, feeling a small part of tension leaving my body.

Axel leaned forward. "What if I try to talk to the guy? Man to man?"

"NO." The word exploded from everyone simultaneously. Including me. The thought of Axel walking into danger made something fierce and protective rise in my chest.

Axel's gaze locked on to mine, as if he felt my desire to shield him. And liked it. But with a thinning of his lips, I could also see he'd walk into the lion's den if that's what it took to keep me safe.

Wait, why did I just think the word *me*?

"That's not man to man," Ryker said. "That's a death trap."

The room fell silent, except for the rain battering the windows. The weight of our complete and utter helplessness settled over us like a blanket made of anxiety and impending doom.

This is it. This is how I die. Not in some grand romantic gesture or heroic sacrifice, but because I took a petty revenge photo that went viral. And I'm taking Axel down with me.

The thought hit me like a sucker punch. Axel Pierce might die because of me. The man I'd spent years hating, who drove me absolutely insane, who made my blood boil with just a look ...

The idea of losing him made something crack open in my chest.

What the hell is wrong with me?

"So, we don't have any good options?" I asked. "We just sit here and wait to get whacked?"

"You said this dinner has you two trending right now? As a couple?" Jace stepped forward.

I blinked. Our stupid fake engagement seemed absolutely meaningless now. "Yeah. Why?"

Jace pulled out his phone, fingers flying over the screen. "You're not just trending. You two are everywhere right now. Every influencer and gossip site is speculating about you."

Oh good. At least I'll die famous.

"So, what, you think all those people will reveal our location and help us get shot faster?" Axel questioned with tension in his voice.

"No." Jace locked eyes with Ryker, and some kind of silent communication passed between them.

"The story might help," Ryker declared. "You need to lean into it."

I laughed because I thought it was a joke. Turns out, I was wrong. Ryker shot me a look that snapped my mouth shut.

"That's ridiculous." Axel's voice went dangerously quiet. "I'm not gallivanting all over town with staged romance dinners when some crime boss might be looking for us. It's dangerous. And for the record, I'd rather lose my business than my life. Or hers."

The casual way he included me in that statement, like my life was automatically part of his calculations now, made my heart do a cartwheel in celebration. When had that happened?

"Same," I said quickly. "We can kiss the whole fake engagement goodbye. I hate that my parents might lose their house, but they'd rather lose their house than their daughter."

Though saying it out loud twisted my stomach into knots. I didn't want them to lose their house. Especially if they were about to lose their daughter anyway.

Oh my God, was this seriously a fork in the road right now?

Thank God for survival skills. Your brain makes things feel so surreal, you don't fully feel the fear or absurdity of it all.

"If the crime family thinks you were never really interested in Victoria Webb—" Blake started.

"I doubt that'll matter," Axel cut him off.

"And the public buys it too, then it might stop the speculation about the Webb marriage," Blake continued stubbornly. "And if they stop poking around about the marriage, they won't continue hunting, and they won't find the crime family ties; the press will move on to another story."

"There's no way faking some romance makes a difference,"

Axel pressed. "If they feel we screwed them, we screwed up everything they've been working for, it won't matter."

"Unless you're actively working to undo the problem," Blake pressed.

"He's right," Ryker agreed. "A love story online that the public buys might convince the public there was never anything between Axel and the wife, and if that's true, then the happy couple can publicly reconcile, and the press backs off." He scrubbed his face, resuming his pacing. "Plus, if you two stay in the public eye ... if you manage to stay this viral, maybe even become the next *it* couple ... if you have eyes on you at all times, that makes it far harder for them to eliminate you quietly."

"You can't be serious." My voice cracked. "You think we should actually *continue* with the fake engagement?"

"I think it's your best shot."

Then perhaps we need a crime-family crisis consultant. Maybe they make those, the same as they make PR crisis managers?

"I agree with Dakota," Axel said. The fact that we were on the same side sent a strange thrill through me, even under these circumstances. "If we might have a crime family after us, we need tangible, realistic protection. Parading around at dinners and posing for influencers will just broadcast our location everywhere we go."

Finally, something we agree on. *Mark your calendars, people.*

"Crime families know how to find people hiding with fake identities in holes in the forest," Ryker said. "Trust me, them knowing your location isn't the problem. They'll find you regardless."

"Well, that's super comforting," I said flatly.

"If you stay viral, all eyes will be on you everywhere you go." Jace nodded slowly. "Witnesses. Cameras. Social media."

"Good luck killing America's new *it* couple," Blake added.

"Unless they just break into the penthouse and slit our throats while we sleep," I pointed out.

Something dark flashed across Axel's face at my words, and his hand moved another inch closer to mine. Not touching, but close enough that I could feel the tension radiating from him.

"That's not going to happen." His eyes met mine with an intensity that sent my heart into more cartwheels. "I won't let anything happen to you."

The promise in his voice, the protective edge to it, sent something warm and dangerous spiraling through my body. When had Axel Pierce started looking at me like I was something worth protecting?

"Look," Ryker said, ignoring my cheerful observation, "the more you two look obsessed with each other, the less of a threat Axel ever looked to the marriage. And that'll make the heat die down on the political couple. Win-win."

"You're speculating," Axel argued.

"You're right," Ryker admitted. "But *speculation* isn't the right word. In my line of work, I've worked with victims of organized crime families. I know them better than anyone else in this room, and they are businesspeople. You either help them or you're still a liability." He stopped pacing, fixing us with an intense stare. "There are no guarantees. But out of everything we've discussed, this is your best option."

This cannot be happening.

"Maybe we're overreacting," I suggested weakly. "I mean, we're just assuming this guy will be blood-killing angry. Maybe Tony Romano won't come after us."

Every pair of eyes in the room looked at me like I'd just suggested we all start a book club that specializes in fairy porn.

"Public visibility equals safety," Ryker said simply.

"He might be right," Jace agreed reluctantly. "I still think we should consider bodyguards. But if you two become the next *it* couple with everyone watching your every move ... that makes it harder for a hit man to operate. And harder for them to do it under the radar."

A *hit man*. How did that term belong in my life?

"So, if he kills the city's *it* couple, that's bad for business," I said.

"Exactly. Might bring even more speculation on them."

"So, you don't think we're in danger?" Hope crept into my voice.

"Oh, no." Ryker's frown was grim. "I think you two are completely screwed."

"Don't sugarcoat it or anything," Axel muttered.

Well, at least he's honest.

"But even if Tony Romano is fuming," Ryker continued, "there's one thing he absolutely won't want: the investigation and heat that would come from taking out an *it* couple."

"I love how you discuss murder investigations like Sunday brunch plans," I said. "Not disturbing at all."

"When a beloved, famous couple gets murdered, the media scrutiny is relentless. That means the investigation puts massive pressure on his organization." Ryker's eyes were deadly serious. "At the end of the day, he's a businessman who weighs risks and opportunities. I have to believe that rationality will win."

"Have to believe? As in we're still guessing." Axel pinched the bridge of his nose.

"We don't know anything for sure," Ryker admitted. "But out of all your options, your best shot at staying safe is selling this fake engagement like your lives depend on it."

"There has to be another way," Axel pushed.

"You can't just sell the engagement," Ryker continued. "You have to become the *it* couple that everyone follows and talks about. And you need to change the narrative about Axel flirting with Victoria Webb. If you sell this as a love story where you were never pursuing Victoria, the PR crisis effectively goes away, and her husband's PR team will smooth the wrinkles of any portion of her flirting long before the press digs into criminal family ties. If you can manage that, hopefully, the Romano family will lose interest."

Hopefully. Our heartbeats depended on *hopefully*.

The room fell silent again. Rain continued its assault on the windows, and I could practically hear everyone's minds racing.

Well, nothing says romance like mortal terror.

Thunder cracked overhead, and I had the distinct feeling our fake engagement was about to become a lot more complicated than either of us had bargained for.

18

WHEN SHE LOOKS AT YOU LIKE SHE'S ALREADY PLOTTING YOUR DEMISE AND YOU'RE WEIRDLY EXCITED ABOUT IT. 💀 #REDFLAGATTRACTION

AXEL

Was pranking Dakota a good idea or a bad idea?

Hopefully a good one.

Two nights ago, everything changed. The moment we learned about the danger, I caught something in Dakota's eyes, just for a second. Terror, quickly buried under her usual confidence.

Yesterday only confirmed what I'd seen. We'd had another scripted public appearance as the happy couple, this time lunch at some trendy bistro. Dakota played her part perfectly, smiling at all the right moments, but I knew her tells. She was quieter than normal, picking at her salad instead of devouring it. Every few minutes, her gaze would drift to the entrance or sweep across the other tables, those beautiful eyes just a little too watchful. When our server appeared suddenly at her elbow with the check, her fingers tightened on her water glass.

Back home, where she should have relaxed, she still seemed on edge. I noticed her checking her phone obsessively, standing by the window a beat too long. When I accidentally bumped into her in the bathroom doorway while she was brushing her teeth, she flinched. Just slightly, but enough for me to notice.

I'd been racking my brain all night trying to figure out how to make it better. Talking about the danger would only make it worse, force her to acknowledge the fear she was working so hard to hide. What Dakota needed was to laugh, to forget for a while, to feel normal again. The only thing I could think to do was lighten her mood.

Maybe a prank would accomplish that? After all, the last time I'd seen her genuinely smile was when she'd pranked me with her public display of—let's call it what it was—soft-core porn disguised as yoga.

I smirked, remembering those batting eyelashes as she pretended she didn't know exactly what she was doing in that barely there tank and panties. If we'd just entered some sort of prank war, I doubted anything would ever top her using my libido as a weapon of mass destruction.

God, that ass. The way she'd bent over, giving me a perfect view of curves that had haunted my dreams for the past two nights. The memory alone was enough to make me shift uncomfortably in my chair.

Before Ryker had dropped the world's coldest shower in our lap, I'd been imagining burying myself in—

Nope. Not going there again.

Point was, I had to give it to her. Dakota had a wicked sense of humor. At the prospect of losing her business and being forced into a fake engagement with someone she hated, she didn't curl into a ball and cry like many people would.

In fact, she'd never even cried after Ryker warned us our lives might be in danger. Not once. Which was strong as hell.

Add that to the things I definitely shouldn't admire about Dakota Blackwood.

Another shocking thing about the cold slap of fear from a possible danger was how it lowered my anger wall toward Dakota. You know, the one that kept me so busy, mentally cataloging how right I was and how wrong she was for curating her perfect online image? Yeah. Turns out, realizing my best friend's little sister might be in danger made me hate what she did at least ten percent less.

Okay, maybe twenty.

In fact, Blake's words from moving day had been echoing through my head ever since.

"We all put on masks sometimes. But Dakota's not your mother. She's not crafting some perfect facade to hide the fact that she's falling apart. She's building a brand, running a company. It's performance, yeah, but it's not the same kind of performance that killed your mom."

And she was different, wasn't she? In my time with Dakota, it was becoming clearer that she didn't normally outright lie to people. Not like this fake-engagement situation anyway. And let's remember, she wasn't thrilled about that either. Hell, she'd explicitly said she hated lying to her followers. She wasn't lying the way my mother had. Dakota was simply showing the best version of herself, the one she felt safe with showing, I guess.

But why did she think that's all people would accept?

Ugh!

See? This kind of thought was exactly what I was avoiding today. I still loathed Dakota Blackwood. I did. So what if she was funny and sexy and apparently made of titanium? That didn't change my feelings.

My animosity was still there, buried under all this ... whatever this was. And I'd hold on to it like a life preserver—that was for damn sure.

She was just Knox's sister. That was all. He wasn't here to protect her, so it fell on me to watch out for my best friend's little sister. As soon as this blew over, we'd go back to hating each other.

Wait. Go back to? *Present tense, Pierce. Present tense.*

I do not like Dakota Blackwood. I do not like her in a vest. I do not like her goddess-like chest.

I wasn't going to slip into non-loathing territory just because we were in danger. Being in danger didn't change the fundamental dynamics of our relationship.

So I wanted to make her a little less scared. So what? It was basic human decency. Contrary to popular opinion—specifically her opinion—I wasn't a complete raging asshole.

Plus, she freaking deserved this prank, that evil little vixen. How dare she give me the blue balls from hell?

Dakota's coffee maker gurgled to life, right on schedule. The thing was programmed to go off at the ass crack of dawn so the princess's coffee was ready when she emerged from her beauty sleep. Because God help the person who had to deal with her before she'd had her caffeine fix.

If there was one thing I'd learned from sharing mornings with Dakota, it was that the woman was usually grumpier than a wet cat when she first woke up.

I suspected it was because she spent half the night working on her business, but whatever. She had her perfect coffee maker scheduled to brew the perfect blend, designed to suck that bad attitude right out of her and replace it with liquid humanity.

Next to her coffee maker sat her perfect little container of sugar, complete with a neat label because Dakota labeled everything.

The fun thing about sugar? It looks exactly like salt.

I slid the sugar container back into place, checking to make sure it didn't look conspicuous. Then I moved on to the kitchen clocks: stove, microwave, and counter. I fast-forwarded all of them by exactly twenty-seven minutes.

Let's see how Princess Punctual handles being "late."

I settled into my usual seat at the table, scrolling through morning news on my phone, when the queen herself emerged at the exact same time she had yesterday. Down to the minute.

And, damn, she looked good. Her hair was tousled from sleep, falling in soft waves around her shoulders. No makeup, just smooth skin that practically glowed in the morning light streaming through the windows.

"Morning, Sunshine."

When she glared at me, I couldn't contain my smirk. That

was, until my traitorous eyes went on an unauthorized scouting mission all over her body. They cataloged how her gray cotton shorts hugged her hips like they were painted on, how her tank top with no bra showcased her toned abs and the curve of her breasts. The thin cotton did absolutely nothing to hide the fact that she was cold, her nipples clearly visible through the material.

"Stop staring at me," she grumbled, padding to the cabinet to retrieve her mug.

And the way she said it, all husky and rough from sleep, sent heat shooting straight to my groin.

"Don't flatter yourself." But damn if the woman didn't look hot in nothing but cotton and a bad attitude. Like some kind of sexy, grumpy goddess who'd just rolled out of bed.

The thought of her actually rolling out of *my* bed, all warm and sleepy and naked, hit me like an ice-bucket challenge. I shifted in my chair, grateful the table hid my body's immediate and enthusiastic response to that particular mental image.

She reached for the cabinet where she kept her favorite mug. The one with the little cat on it. The one I'd moved to the *top* shelf this morning as part of my multi-pronged prank strategy.

"Where's my ..."

Her frustrated eyes narrowed at it, and then with a huff, she stretched up on her tiptoes, trying to reach the higher shelf. And as she did, two things became apparent:

First, her tank top rode up to reveal skin on her lower back that made me lose complete focus. I had to clear my throat to remind myself to pay attention. Second, it was clear I'd moved the mug too high for her to reach.

Like a whipped puppy, I found myself standing up.

"Here, let me." I was up and behind her before I could think twice, my chest pressing against her back as I reached over her head for the mug. My other hand automatically settled on her hip.

The contact sent lava coursing through my body, and any doubt she felt it, too, was answered when she went completely still beneath my touch. Hell, we both stilled. To the point that I could feel the rise and fall of her breathing.

We were alone. No cameras, no audience, no reason to sell anything to anyone. But here I was, touching her like it was the most natural thing in the world.

The hand on her hip seemed to have developed a mind of its own, my thumb tracing small circles through the thin cotton. The movement was unconscious and instinctive, like I'd done it a thousand times before. Like some part of me had memorized the shape of her without my permission.

That thought stopped me cold, as if I'd stepped off a cliff I hadn't seen coming.

I jerked back, nearly knocking over the mug as I set it down, putting distance between us before I could think too hard about how much I didn't want to.

"There you go."

The tension stretched between us, thick and charged, until she finally moved to the side to make her coffee and I retreated to my seat, trying to pretend my hands weren't almost shaking.

And that my mouth wasn't hitching up, savoring every inch of her body. And sass.

Thankfully, her supreme resting grumpy face reminded me to get my head out of the gutter and back into the game.

She poured her coffee and got to work, adding what I knew was an insane amount of "sugar" to the liquid.

Oh, this is going to be so good.

I watched her measure out not one, not two, but three heaping spoonfuls of salt. My inner twelve-year-old was practically cackling with glee.

"We're not going to suddenly be nice to each other just because your stupid move put us in danger," she said, not looking at me as she stirred with mechanical precision.

"Back to blaming me for your mistakes, I see." I had to bite the inside of my cheek to keep from grinning. "I think there's a term for that." I snapped my fingers. "Narcissism."

This time, she full-on glowered at me as she retrieved oat milk from the refrigerator. The woman was a creature of absolute habit. Always the same amount of milk, always stirred clockwise exactly seven times. When she bent over to put the carton back, I caught a glimpse of smooth thigh and had to grip my phone tighter to keep from making some kind of embarrassing noise.

Any second now ...

"Stop. Staring."

"Wow," I managed. "You're even grumpier than yesterday, and that's saying something."

She stirred the mug's contents with enough force to create a tiny whirlpool, simultaneously attempting to slice my face open with her stare.

Come on, Dakota. Just one little sip.

Look at her. The way she was concentrating on stirring her coffee, her tongue darting out slightly to wet her lips. My groin liked that a little too much.

"You look like a bear who got woken up from hibernation early and wants to commit mass murder for revenge."

"Screw you, Pierce."

There's my girl.

The way she said my name, all venom and heat, shouldn't have been sexy. But somehow, when Dakota told me to go to hell, it sounded like an invitation.

"Maybe you should go back to bed," I suggested, leaning back in my chair. "Sleep off the jerk hangover."

The image of her going back to bed—specifically my bed—flashed through my mind again. Of me following her there, pinning her against the mattress, showing her exactly how much her grumpy morning attitude affected me.

"Gosh, you are just the funniest man I've ever heard in my life." She sat down across from me. "I'll be out of your hair within the hour."

That got my attention.

"I thought you were staying home to film content today."

"Change of plans. I'm squeezing something in before that. I have to leave in—" Her eyes landed on the clock and flew open wide. She shot out of her chair like she'd been launched from a cannon. "What the hell?"

The sudden movement made the hem of her shorts ride up, revealing a strip of toned thigh that I wanted to trace with my tongue. *Focus, Pierce. Focus on the prank, not on how badly you want to taste her skin.*

"Problem, Sunshine?"

Her mouth dropped open. "I didn't hit snooze. I came out as soon as my alarm went off."

"Late for a meeting?"

"I'm going to visit Knox today."

I set my phone down, suddenly serious. "You're going to the prison?"

"Damn it, I had my whole day planned out down to the minute." She ran a hand through her messy hair, and I tried not to notice how the gesture made her breasts swell.

The way she moved, all frustrated energy and unconscious sensuality, was driving me insane. I wanted to grab her wrist, pull her closer, show her exactly what kind of trouble that restless energy could get her into.

"Why are you going to visit Knox?"

"He's my brother."

"I'm aware. I meant, why today?" It was obvious this was last minute, and Dakota Blackwood didn't do last-minute anything.

She sank back into her seat, seeming to accept the loss of twenty-seven minutes in her perfectly calibrated schedule. I could practically see her mentally reshuffling everything to accommodate this "mistake."

"If we're about to become an *it* couple with people following us around, I really don't want them trailing me to the penitentiary."

She raised her cup for her first sip—*finally, sweet vindication*—but before it reached her lips, realization dawned on me.

"Your followers don't know your real name is Dakota Blackwood. Or that Knox is your brother. In prison for murder."

She paused, cup halfway to her mouth, staring at the dark liquid.

No! So close! Drink the damn coffee, woman.

But watching her lips part slightly as she prepared to take that sip was making it extremely hard to focus on this prank. I found myself imagining those lips on my skin, wondering what sounds she'd make if I—

Stop. Just stop.

"If we're about to become famous, for lack of a better word, I can't risk them connecting the dots and following me there."

Right. This whole fake engagement would be pointless if her business tanked anyway.

"I'm coming with you."

Damn it. She lowered the cup again. Still no sip. My masterpiece was getting cold.

This is torture. Pure, exquisite torture.

"No."

"Look, hopefully, Ryker's blowing this whole thing out of proportion. But until we know for sure, I don't want you going anywhere alone."

Dakota went still at the protective undertone in my voice. That warmth shooting from her eyes hit me like a direct punch to the solar plexus.

Oh, come on. Now is not the time for a moment. Drink. The. Coffee.

Seconds later, she shook off whatever that moment was with a small clearing of her throat.

"I'll see if Ryker can go with me; today's the day he normally visits Knox. But let's be clear: it's not because you told me so. Although, thank you for caring enough."

Uh-oh. She was being sweet.

And then—Lord help me—she actually smiled. A real smile

that reached all the way to her eyes and made something dangerous flutter in my chest.

She even tilted her head and added, "You know, it's moments like these that make me remember it hasn't always been an ocean of animosity between us. Once upon a time, I actually thought you were nice."

Shit.

Dakota had just let a genuinely happy moment slip between us. Her voice hadn't held a trace of sarcasm; she was being authentically nice to me.

And of course she chose this exact moment to finally, finally raise that mug to her lips.

Oh no. Oh, this is bad. This is very bad.

I opened my mouth to warn her—

Too late.

She took a huge gulp of what was essentially saltwater with a caffeine chaser. Her eyes bugged out like a cartoon character, and she spat the liquid out in a volcanic explosion of disgust as she shot to her feet.

"WHAT THE HELL?"

Panting, Dakota stared into her mug like it had personally betrayed her. Her chest rose and fell rapidly, and I couldn't help but notice how the quick breathing made her breasts strain against her shirt.

Then her gaze snapped to my face, and I tried—really tried—to hide my laughter. But the moment of kindness we'd just shared didn't erase a decade of hostility, and frankly, her expression was priceless.

Her eyes narrowed into laser-focused slits, and she glanced at the clocks again, the pieces clicking into place with almost-audible precision.

"You're dead, Pierce."

But instead of looking murderous, something shifted in her expression. A slow, wicked smile spread across her lips. The kind that promised trouble of the most delicious variety.

"Actually, no. Death would be too easy." She set the mug down and crossed her arms, the movement pushing her breasts up in a way she knew would demand my attention. *Dammit.* I shifted the bulge in my pants. "I'm going to get you back so good, you won't know what hit you."

Well, shit. The prank had definitely worked. All the fear and anxiety I'd seen winding through her shoulders two nights ago had evaporated into pure, focused determination to make my life interesting.

I just had the sinking feeling I'd started something I couldn't finish.

Something that looked suspiciously like ... fun.

And the way she was looking at me right now, like she was already plotting her revenge and enjoying every second of it?

I was so screwed. And weirdly ... I couldn't wait to see what she'd come up with.

19

MEET MY BROTHER: FORMER FROG RESCUER, CURRENT CONVICTED MURDERER. CHARACTER DEVELOPMENT TOOK A DARK TURN. #FAMILYSECRETS

DAKOTA

"Thank you for taking me." I stared out the window, watching asphalt blur beneath our tires.

"I'm heading there anyway. Next parole hearing prep." Ryker's knuckles went white against the steering wheel, his lean, tattooed muscles in his forearms flexing beneath his fitted black shirt. "You can talk to him first though."

That was nice of him.

"Saw some of your posts from lunch yesterday," Ryker said. "For what it's worth, you guys are doing a good job of selling your story."

Ugh. That lunch that we'd muddled through, despite learning about a possible threat the day before. Like the dinner facade, we'd looked happy. Naturally, it was before his stupid prank this morning, but still. We'd touched hands. (I pretended it did not affect me. Couldn't. Wouldn't.) He pulled my chair out, and we laughed and smiled like a couple in love.

Puke.

It seemed to work though. Public speculation was taking off. Comments rolling into my feed that had nothing to do with products and all about this secret relationship that was being posted by others.

Operation Play Coy About It would end soon, Rebecca had warned. Then it was on to the next phase.

"It seems to be heading in the right direction," I agreed.

Ryker turned off the main road, steering us toward the penitentiary that loomed in the distance.

"I'm glad they finally opened that new parking lot," I said, watching the familiar route unfold. "When I used to visit Knox, I had to do street parking and got, like, three parking tickets." I nibbled my lip, remembering the frustration. "Weirdest thing though. When I went online to pay them, they were all dismissed due to clerical error." I glanced at Ryker. "You wouldn't know anything about that, would you?"

"No," he said, but he wouldn't meet my eyes.

I studied his profile. Ryker was a criminal lawyer. He probably had tabs on the days I visited. Maybe he'd made those tickets go away?

"And one time, my car even broke down right outside the prison," I continued. "When the tow truck guy showed up, he said it was free of charge." I waited for his reaction. "You wouldn't know anything about that either, would you?"

Again, no eye contact. No response.

"Hmm." I turned back to the window, then remembered something else. "Oh, and every year on my birthday, I get this gorgeous bouquet of gardenias delivered to my place. Anonymous. I always suspected it was Knox organizing it somehow since he can't be here for the big events." I looked at Ryker again. "Pretty sure the only person he could organize that through would be you. Do you arrange that too?"

This time, Ryker did meet my eyes, his response matter-of-fact. "No. The flowers are not from Knox. At least, not that I'm aware of."

"Really?" That surprised me.

"Have you asked Knox about it?" Ryker questioned.

Typical nonanswer.

"He denies doing it," I said.

And, really, I didn't want Knox to be doing those things for me. The guy had to worry about surviving, and it's not like he made money in the penitentiary. So, how he was doing that, I had no idea, but if it wasn't Knox, then who?

"You know," I started, "I don't think I've ever properly thanked you." I studied his profile. He had a sharp jaw, the kind of focused intensity that probably served him well in courtrooms. "For everything you're doing for Knox. For ... staying."

Knox's college friend. A guy who became a criminal defense attorney. I wondered if that career decision was rooted in the trauma of seeing his friend hauled off to prison. You go to college to study and maybe play beer pong, not watch one of your closest friends get hauled off in cuffs.

"The day Knox was arrested ..." Ryker's voice caught. "It's like watching innocence die. You're young, think the world's your oyster, that life just keeps getting better and better."

The prison loomed ahead, all concrete and razor wire. A monument to broken dreams.

"I know plenty of people go through hell," he continued. "Blake and Faith survived a dark side of the foster system. But watching Knox get convicted of murder?" He shook his head. "Nothing compares to that."

He pulled into a parking space between a rusted Honda and a pickup truck held together by duct tape. The visitors lot told its own story of families scraping together gas money to see their locked-up loved ones.

I twisted my fingers until they ached. "I hate talking about it."

"Hard to face what someone's done." His voice gentled. "But your brother's still a good man, Dakota."

Right. A good man who happened to have killed someone.

Before the arrest, Knox had been the golden boy. All-American kid from an all-American family, clawing our way toward upper-middle-class respectability. We weren't the Cleavers, but we weren't the cautionary tale either.

Normal families don't breed killers.

Or so I'd thought.

"It's hard for you to see him," Ryker realized, walking beside me toward the first checkpoint.

The prison stretched before us. Gray walls topped with coils of razor wire that caught the sun like broken glass. Beyond those walls, the yard sprawled with inmates and guards, whose rifles glinted from watchtowers. The air smelled like industrial disinfectant and something else. Fear maybe.

"Every time I see him ..." I swallowed hard. "Something breaks inside me."

Because I still saw him at seven, thunder-crashing through the hallway in his Hot Wheels pajamas, hair sticking up in twelve directions as he dove for the Christmas tree. His small hands would tear through wrapping paper.

Then there was the summer he turned nine and declared himself the official Frog Relocation Specialist. Every Saturday, he'd spend an extra hour and a half moving every single frog out of the mower's path before starting his lawn duty. Dad would find him crouched in the grass, cupping some tiny creature in his palms, whispering reassurances as he carried it to safety by the pond.

"They're just trying to live their lives, Dakota," Knox had said. "They don't deserve to die because I need to cut grass."

Now that same compassionate boy sat behind bars, shoulders broad with muscle he'd built to survive, ink crawling up his arms, telling stories I didn't want to know. The shell he'd grown was thick enough to stop bullets.

"At least it's not maximum security," Ryker reminded me, pulling me back to the present. "If he'd been sent to one of those places ..."

He didn't finish. Didn't need to.

The first metal detector beeped as we passed through. A guard with dead eyes and coffee breath waved us forward. Next came the pat-down, the surrender of our IDs, the slow shuffle through corridors that echoed with the slam of distant doors.

"How much longer will he be in here?" I asked as we waited for the final clearance.

Ryker's lips thinned. "I'm working on it."

"He hasn't seen his daughter in years."

She'd been born when he was still in high school. Unplanned, but never unwanted. In fact, after she arrived, she became his everything. He'd matured overnight, stepping up immediately and building his whole future around her. College wasn't about finding himself or partying; it was about creating a life stable enough to support a family. Because that was Knox. Every decision filtered through how it would affect the people he loved.

When he got arrested, his ex had been understanding. Theoretically committed to maintaining Knox's relationship with their daughter.

Until she wasn't.

"It scares me," I admitted, voice dropping to a whisper as we approached the visiting room. "He's getting harder. More hopeless. What if he does something stupid because he thinks he has nothing left to lose?"

"I know."

Ryker didn't sugarcoat it, and I was grateful. We both saw Knox slipping away, the boy who'd saved frogs disappearing beneath layers of survival instinct and prison politics.

"He spent a week in solitary not that long ago for fighting."

"Word is, he's not someone you want to cross," Ryker agreed.

The visiting room doors opened with a mechanical groan. Fluorescent lights buzzed overhead, casting sickly shadows across plastic chairs and metal tables bolted to the floor. The smell hit me: Fear. Sweat. And desperation.

"If he doesn't make parole ..." I couldn't finish the sentence.

"Have you talked to him about this?"

"He shuts me down every time." My voice cracked. "I think

he's in pure survival mode. So, now I try to just ... bring some light. I can't imagine living every day, wondering if someone's going to shank you in the shower or jump you in the yard."

Ryker looked at me thoughtfully. "You're a good sister."

"No." The word came out sharp. "I'm hiding him from my followers like he's some shameful secret."

"Is he?"

The question hung between us like a blade.

No. But ... "I wish I understood what happened," I whispered. "It's like this dark crater in our family history. We dance around it, never speak of it, but it poisons everything. Mom and Dad are drowning financially from legal fees." Fees that added up when they couldn't let this go, when they paid for lawyer after lawyer in a bathtub of denial.

From what I understood, Ryker was working on Knox's case pro bono. He'd started his own independent law firm, which enabled him to take on Knox's case without charging him, but that came after all the debt.

"Their health is shot from stress," I continued. "It's like Knox dropped a nuclear bomb, and we're all still living in the fallout."

"You're angry with him." Not a question. Ryker could read the tension radiating from every muscle in my body.

"Of course I'm angry!" The words exploded out of me. "I'm furious that he killed someone, that some family lost their son because of him. I'm angry about what it did to us. The sleepless nights, the reporters camping on our lawn, watching Mom age ten years in ten months. And Mom's accident never would have happened if he hadn't gotten convicted."

"Knox is still a good man."

"That's a hell of a thing to say about a convicted murderer."

"But you know it's true."

I did. God help me, I did.

"He never told me why he did it," I said quietly.

"Do you need that? For closure?"

"I need to understand how the boy who wouldn't hurt a frog

could ..." I shook my head. "There's something he's not saying. I see it in his eyes. This weight he's carrying. Like the real story is eating him alive."

Ryker met my eyes and gave me an almost-imperceptible nod, a silent acknowledgment that my suspicions were right.

And it freaking gutted me.

We entered the visiting room, and there he was.

Knox rose from his chair when he spotted me, his protective gaze sweeping the room, cataloging threats and potential problems. Even here, even with me, he couldn't let his guard down.

"Dakota." His voice was different now. Rougher. But when he wrapped his arms around me, I caught a glimpse of the boy who used to rescue frogs.

"No touching," a guard barked.

That incited a terrifying glare from my brother.

"Hey, Knox." I pulled back to study his face, searching for traces of the brother I remembered.

His eyes were the same storm gray they'd always been.

"Sit down, sis. We need to talk."

20

APPARENTLY, PRISON GOSSIP TRAVELS FASTER THAN BREAKING NEWS, AND MY BROTHER HAS OPINIONS. 📺 #PRISONTMZ

DAKOTA

"Tell me it's not true." Knox's voice boomed through the visiting room chatter like a grenade. His hands were flat on the metal table between us, and I could see the tension rippling through his forearms. "Tell me you're not dating Axel."

Well, hello to you too, brother dearest.

"How did you—"

"Inmates have nothing better to do than sit around, gossiping like old ladies at a church social." He leaned back in his chair, and I caught a middle-aged woman at the next table over stealing a glance at him. *Again.*

Seriously? Even in prison orange, my brother apparently had game.

Objectively speaking, Knox was ridiculously good-looking. Athletic build that even the shapeless uniform couldn't hide, muscles that spoke of hours in the prison gym, and a face that belonged on magazine covers rather than mug shots. His hair was buzzed shorter on the sides but longer on top in that perfectly messy way that probably took him all of thirty seconds but looked like he'd stepped out of a salon.

"Did you really think I wouldn't find out?" he continued.

"It's ... complicated."

"Complicated." His eyebrows shot up. "He's my best friend. You're my sister. It's not exactly rocket science why I might have an opinion about this."

I shifted in the uncomfortable plastic chair. "Well, you don't have to worry about it. It's fake."

Knox went perfectly still. "Fake?" The word came out like he was tasting something bitter. "The hell does that mean?"

I gave him the CliffsNotes version (sans *Romano family, hit man* fears), watching his expression grow darker with each word. When I finished, he was quiet for a long moment, studying me with those sharp eyes that had always seen too much.

"So, you fake moved in with him too?"

"It's temporary."

"Jesus, Dakota." He scrubbed a hand over his face. "I'm surprised he agreed to this. A fake relationship with you, of all people."

"Gee, thanks, Knox. Really feeling the brotherly love here."

His mouth quirked up on one side with the same lopsided grin that used to get him out of trouble when we were kids. "I didn't mean it like that."

"Oh, please. Enlighten me. How exactly did you mean it?"

"You're sort of the antithesis of everything he stands for."

I blinked at him. "And that was supposed to make me feel better than your first comment?"

Knox threw his head back and laughed—really laughed—and for a split second, I saw the seven-year-old boy in Hot Wheels pajamas who used to build blanket forts with me. The sound hit me square in the chest, a mixture of joy and pain so sharp, I had to swallow hard against it.

God, I missed that laugh.

"Your conversational skills are really going to need some work when you reenter society," I said.

"Let's hope that's sooner rather than later." The humor faded from his face, replaced by something heavier.

My stomach twisted. We both knew the parole board had been problematic.

Knox cleared his throat. "Look, I just meant that with Axel's past ... you should know it's going to be hell for him."

"It's not exactly a cakewalk for me either."

"But you don't know about the skeletons in his closet."

The way he said it made my skin crawl. "Skeletons?"

"And you, Dakota? You're a walking reminder of everything that's painful to him."

Well, that's dark as hell.

"Wow." I sat back in my chair. "Way to make a girl feel special."

"I'm not trying to hurt your feelings. I'm trying to prepare you."

"For what exactly?"

"For the fact that this arrangement is going to cost him more than you know."

The weight of his words settled over me like a lead blanket. Instantly, I wondered what he meant and considered pressing him on it. But I knew Knox; he'd send me a warning, sure. But he'd never tell me his best friend's secrets.

"Well, like I said, it's temporary and fake. We just need to convince people, and then we can go back to avoiding each other."

Knox's expression shifted, became almost pitying. "The truth always comes out, Dakota. The only choice is whether it's on your terms."

If only you knew how close to home that hits, big brother.

I was hiding more than just my fake relationship. I was hiding my entire identity, my past, the fact that my perfect influencer life was as manufactured as everything else about me.

"Anyway," I said, desperate to change the subject, "I don't know how you can stand Axel. He's such an ass."

Knox tilted his head, and I could practically see the gears turning. "You realize how ironic that is, right? He's a respectable CEO. I'm an inmate, convicted of murder." He paused, letting that sink in. "Yet apparently, I'm the good guy in your book."

Shit. He had a point.

"I hate it when you're logical," I muttered. "It's very unsettling."

That earned me another laugh, smaller this time but genuine. It transported me back to summer afternoons at the park, racing down slides and Knox always winning. Except when some kid tried to cut in front of me. Then Knox would appear at my shoulder, my fierce protector, ready to take on anyone who dared mess with his little sister.

"None of this Axel drama matters anyway," I said, waving a dismissive hand.

"Like hell it doesn't."

"These are silly problems compared to your real-world issues." My gaze swept the visiting room, taking in the other inmates who looked like they could snap someone's neck for getting their coffee order wrong. "I worry about you every day you're in here."

"How are Mom and Dad?"

Typical Knox. Always deflecting, always worried about everyone but himself.

"They're fine." The lie came easily. "I still have dinner with them every week."

"And the house?"

"Great." Another lie.

Knox and I resumed talking about safer topics until the guard called time. Too soon. Always too soon.

"I miss you, Knox," I said, the words catching in my throat.

He studied my face. "Why are you getting all sappy on me?"

Because what if this is the last time I see you? What if some Mafia asshole decides I'm too much trouble and puts a bullet in my head?

Not that I told him that layer of it. He didn't need to worry about me more than he already did.

"I love you," I said instead, needing him to know how I felt. "No matter what you did or why you did it, I love you."

Knox's eyes tightened. "You want to tell me what's really going on?"

Several heads turned in our direction, and I felt the weight of curious stares.

"Nothing," I said quickly. "I just don't tell you that enough." My gaze swept the room again, noting all the big, scary men in orange jumpsuits. "Sometimes, I get afraid that you'll ..." I couldn't finish the sentence.

"Get killed?" His voice was matter-of-fact.

I shrugged because, suddenly, I couldn't speak around the lump in my throat.

It was selfish, wanting him safe when he'd taken someone else's life. But that was the thing about Knox. He'd probably take his secrets to the grave.

And something told me there was far more to his story than any of us would ever know.

I stood, motioning for Ryker to take my seat. "You two need to finish your parole prep," I said firmly. "That's what you're here for."

I could see the questions written all over Knox's face. He was probably debating whether to grill me again, but I wasn't giving him the chance.

After, I said goodbye to my brother, casting him one last look over my shoulder.

I'd been an unexpected visitor to him today.

Little did I know, I was about to have one of my own ...

21

WHEN YOU KISS YOUR EX AND YOUR FAKE BOYFRIEND LOOKS LIKE HE WANTS TO COMMIT ACTUAL MURDER. #MIXEDSIGNALS

DAKOTA

"What are you doing here?" I asked.

"How did you know where I lived? Who let you up here?" Axel's voice could've cut glass.

I didn't tell Axel that the guards had called me and said Mathew was here and I'd cleared him. I'd been so shocked that it wasn't until Mathew was already riding up the elevator that common sense had kicked in.

"Axel, it's fine. I've got this." I placed a hand on his arm, feeling the tension coiled beneath his expensive shirt.

Mathew's lips curved into that infuriating smirk I remembered too well. "What are you now, Rapunzel? Does he keep you locked up in this tower?"

"Not helping, Mathew."

"Get out of my penthouse." Axel's nostrils flared.

"I'm not in your penthouse." Mathew's tone was deceptively casual. "I'm in *here* to talk to her." He gestured toward the inside of the elevator.

"Get out of my building." Axel hit the elevator button, trying to send it down to the lobby.

Mathew's eyebrow shot up with theatrical surprise, keeping his hand on the door so it couldn't close. "Oh, you own the whole building now? Moving up in the world, aren't we?"

This wasn't like Mathew. The Mathew I knew was the guy who helped old ladies with their groceries and apologized when other people bumped into him. He wasn't one to poke sleeping bears with sticks. The fact that he was doing it now, for me, sent an unwelcome flutter through my chest.

"It's fine, Axel." I shot him a look that said, *Please don't make this worse.* "I've got this."

"You know the rules, Dakota."

"Rules?" Mathew repeated. "He gives you rules?"

My stomach dropped. "It's not like that—"

"Then what is it like, Dakota?" Mathew's voice softened, and suddenly, I was melting under those warm eyes.

Focus. You can do this. "Look, you can't be here."

"You heard the lady. Leave." Axel crossed his arms.

If I had any shot of getting Mathew to walk away without causing a scene, Axel was systematically destroying it with every word.

"Axel, will you give us a minute? Please?"

"I don't want him in my home."

I shot him a look that said, *It's here or downstairs in the lobby. The lobby runs the risk of someone seeing us.*

Axel's fingers flexed at his sides, his control hanging by a thread. "Make it quick," he bit out. "We have dinner reservations."

With one final glare that promised Mathew a slow, painful death, Axel disappeared into the depths of his penthouse.

"He keeps you on a short leash." Mathew's eyes swept over me like he was cataloging changes. "I don't like it."

"Mathew, why did you come here?" I wrapped my arms around myself, suddenly feeling exposed in my silk blouse and pencil skirt.

"You haven't been returning my calls."

"I can't see you."

Hurt flickered across his features. "I know I made a huge mistake, leaving you. But please ... just have coffee with me. One cup. Thirty minutes."

My throat felt like sandpaper. "I can't."

His jaw worked from side to side. "Look, I'm not asking you to cheat on the guy." His attention flicked toward the hallway where Axel had vanished. "I just ..." He grabbed the back of his neck, a gesture so familiar, it made my chest hurt. "Dakota, I love you. I made the biggest mistake of my life, and I just want a chance to make this right."

My mouth opened, but no words came out.

He stepped closer. "I can tell you still have feelings for me."

No. I don't know how I feel yet. More importantly, it wouldn't matter if I did.

"Tell me you love him," Mathew said quietly, "and I'll walk away."

Just say it. Three little words: I love Axel.

But the lie stuck in my throat like concrete. Mathew knew me too well, could read every micro-expression, every tell. We'd spent too long learning each other's secrets.

And despite all that had happened between us, I didn't have it in me to lie to him. Not about being in love with Axel at least.

I should though. To save his heart. A better person would.

"I don't know what's going on," he said, his voice dropping to that gentle tone that used to talk me down from panic attacks. "But I can tell you don't want this. And that makes me worried about you. More invested in making sure you're okay."

Crap. So, the more he could read this lie, the more he'd come barging into my life, threatening everything. *File that under Fantastic Complications of Epic Proportions.*

"I'm fine."

"You're not." His eyes burned with protective fury. "Is he hurting you?"

"No." The word came out too fast, too sharp.

Mathew didn't look convinced. His gaze swept over me, searching for evidence of injuries, I guess.

"Dakota, if he lays one finger on you—"

"He doesn't." *This isn't real. None of this is real.*

"Then what's going on?"

"Nothing. I'm in a relationship with Axel now." The words felt like glass lies and betrayal in my mouth.

"Then why am I having such a hard time believing that?"

"Because you're seeing what you want to see," I lied, hating myself for it. But my parents needed me to pull this off, and I seriously didn't want a Mafia bullet in my head for not selling this story.

Mathew stepped even closer and brought his hand up to cup my cheek, just like he always used to do.

Just like he'd cupped my cheek the first night he told me he loved me. Just like he'd cupped my cheek that time in the rain when he kissed me like a man coming back from war.

Only this time, the warmth I'd once felt wasn't there.

"I love you." Mathew leaned down so quickly, I didn't have time to react. His lips crashed into mine. They were urgent, demanding, desperate.

I pressed my palms against his chest and pushed back, gasping. "Mathew—"

"It's okay. You don't need to say anything." He pressed a gentle kiss to my forehead, gazing over my shoulder. And when he did, his expression morphed into something that looked almost like satisfaction.

I turned around and found Axel standing in the hallway, his face carved from stone.

Axel's eyes moved from Mathew's hands still tangled in my hair, to my swollen lips, to the guilty flush I could feel burning across my cheeks.

He'd seen everything.

"Come on," Axel grumbled, voice flat as roadkill. "We need to get ready."

Crap. I knew he'd be pissed at the complication, but it felt like his anger had another level to it. One I couldn't place.

I said goodbye to Mathew and then swallowed my dignity as Axel and I posed for our first public photo that I'd post on my account, going *officially* public with our romance. Not just *oh, we've been caught by other people* public.

Cuddling into his arms by the window felt like snuggling up to a very attractive, very pissed-off glacier. We smiled and gazed out at the city, two lovebirds lost in ... well, lies mostly.

It felt stranger than our dinner charade. Stranger than lunch. Probably because minutes ago, I'd been kissing another man, and now I was pretending to be madly in love with the human equivalent of a thundercloud.

As soon as I clicked a few shots, Axel muttered, "Good?"

I reviewed them, my thumb swiping through images of us looking disgustingly happy. "I can edit them to make them look even—"

"Don't care."

Excuse me?

I held my phone tighter, knuckles going white.

"I know you didn't like Mathew being here—"

"You got that damn straight."

"But stop acting like this was preplanned or something. I didn't know he was stopping by."

"You still let him in."

"I'm sorry." But honestly, why the hell was he *this* mad?

"Not okay."

I took a deep breath. "I realize he's not welcome in your home, but you don't have to be *this* mean to me about it."

Axel stepped into my space because of course he did. Probably knew that having him this close made me feel even more confused about my feelings for Mathew because instead of imagining Mathew's hands on me, I was very much wondering what Axel Pierce would feel like, pinning me against this very wall.

Traitorous body.

"Post the damn photo and be done with it."

I clenched my jaw so hard, I'm surprised my teeth didn't crack. "Try that again. This time with less venom and more basic human decency."

"Don't lecture me about manners when you were just making out with another guy in my foyer." The words came out sharp enough to cut glass. "But sure, let's pretend this is about my tone."

Okay, you know what? I needed this. I needed to remember that Axel was hot and cold. Because before this moment, the way he was glaring at me like I was an offensive stain in his home, I'd almost forgotten that I'd promised to get back at him for that coffee prank.

I smiled sweetly. The kind of smile that should've come with a warning label.

"You're absolutely right," I purred, already plotting.

He narrowed his eyes at me. I could tell he was officially worried.

And he should be.

22

FAKE FIANCÉE TIP: MAKE SURE YOUR VANDALISM IS TECHNICALLY JUST INCONVENIENCE, NOT A FELONY. 🚗 #LEGALLYPETTY

DAKOTA

Okay, look. I didn't slash Axel's tires.

Technically.

All I did was slowly let the air out of each one, carefully, so as not to damage his precious rims. Vandalism wasn't exactly my style. I preferred psychological warfare. And after the way Axel had been treating me? The salt in my coffee? Fast-forwarding all the clocks to give me a panic attack? His hostile treatment after Mathew stopped by?

What. A. Dick.

I stood back to admire my handiwork. His prized Mercedes—the sleek black S-Class he probably polished every Sunday like it was a religious ritual—sat deflated in the underground parking garage like a very expensive, very sad balloon animal. All four tires kissed the concrete with a pathetic wheeze of finality.

Beautiful.

The harsh fluorescent lights overhead cast shadows that made the whole thing look even more dramatic. The once-aggressive stance of the vehicle now resembled a sulking teenager, its chrome grille practically pouting against the floor.

The garage smelled like old tires and concrete dust, with that particular underground parking musk that never quite goes away, and somewhere in the distance, a car alarm chirped twice and went silent.

I'd left the valve caps arranged in a neat little row on the hood. A professional courtesy, really. The kind of thoughtful touch that would make him even angrier.

Then I frowned. What if Mr. Penthouse Living had one of those portable air compressors tucked away somewhere?

Nah. This was a guy who probably paid people to change his light bulbs.

Dusting off my hands, I grinned. Phase one: complete.

Time for phase two.

I pulled out my phone and dialed the number to the person I'd been conversing with earlier.

"Sparkle Car Rentals," a man answered.

"Hello. This is Dakota again. I just want to make sure that car will be here right on time." I smiled at their response. "Great. Thank you!"

Twenty minutes later, I was perched at the kitchen island, scrolling through my phone like I hadn't just orchestrated the most satisfying revenge plot of the century. When Axel strode in, all sharp angles and predatory grace, it took every ounce of self-control not to cackle like a Disney villain.

He was dressed for his investor meeting in a charcoal suit that hugged his shoulders and tapered perfectly to his narrow waist. The crisp white shirt underneath was open at the collar, revealing a tantalizing glimpse of the tattoos I knew sprawled across his chest. He looked like sin, wrapped in Italian wool, and my traitorous body responded accordingly.

"Trying to make your pathetic life look perfect again?" he snarled, nodding at my phone.

Yeah. The whole kiss with Mathew had turned up his iceberg status.

I didn't look up. "You really need new material, Axel. That insult was stale the second time you used it."

He grabbed his keys from the counter, all business. "Stay here. Don't go out. Don't talk to Mathew."

Oh boy. The smidgen of guilt I'd felt earlier? Yeah, that was officially dead and buried.

"Good luck today, darling." I flashed him my most innocent smile.

His eyes narrowed. "What are you up to?"

"What could I possibly be up to?" I blinked at him with wide-eyed innocence.

"So help me, Dakota, if you do anything to jeopardize this meeting ..." Even when he was threatening me, his voice did things to me that it absolutely shouldn't.

"I would never do that." Not technically a lie. I wouldn't ruin his meeting. I'd just ... bedazzle his commute.

"I'm serious. If you—"

"Relax." I stood, deliberately slow, letting my body stretch in a way that I knew would draw his attention. Sure enough, his eyes tracked the movement, lingering on the curve of my hips in my fitted jeans before snapping back to my face. "Actually, I went out of my way to help you today."

"What the hell does that mean?"

"Well, unfortunately, your tires are flat."

If looks could kill, I'd be six feet under. Steam was practically radiating from his ears.

"But"—I held up a finger—"don't panic. I knew how important this meeting was, so I took the liberty of arranging a rental car. Used that emergency credit card you keep in the kitchen drawer." I patted his chest, letting my palm linger against the solid warmth of him for just a beat too long, until his heart thundered beneath my hand. While I worked massively hard to pretend mine wasn't mirroring his. "You're welcome."

"You did *what*?"

"The rental guy is waiting downstairs by your parking spot.

Just needs to see your driver's license and a signature." I checked my phone again, barely containing my glee. The way Axel was staring at me, like he was caught between strangling me and doing something much more interesting with his hands, was almost as satisfying as the prank itself. "You should probably hurry. Traffic's going to be murder."

Axel stepped closer into my space, his presence overwhelming. The silence between us vibrated with something that was part fury, part something much more dangerous. "If you're playing games ..."

I stepped closer, too, refusing to be intimidated, until my breasts pressed against his chest with each breath I took. "Go ahead. Finish that threat."

I dare you.

We stared at each other, trapped in a silent battle of wills. It felt like if either of us flinched, something would happen, but what that something was, I wasn't sure. Based on the look on his face, he could scream at me or slam his mouth against mine.

For a moment, I thought he might actually do it. Thought he might grab me, pin me against the counter, and show me exactly what happened when I pushed him too far. The thought sent liquid fire rushing through my veins.

But eventually, he was the one to take a step back, though his eyes never left mine.

"Good luck today, honey." I rolled up onto the balls of my feet and even offered a friendly wave.

23

POV: WHEN CHICAGO'S BIGGEST PLAYBOY GETS CAUGHT IN … WAIT, WHAT IS THAT? 🐱 #VEHICULARHUMILIATION

AXEL

"What the actual fuck?"

I stared at the carnage in front of me, my brain struggling to process the level of petty genius Dakota had just unleashed.

All four tires on my Mercedes had their air let out, and the caps were arranged neatly on my hood. Which meant … she'd staged this whole thing.

Diabolical. Brilliant.

I was going to murder her.

But that wasn't even the worst part. Oh, no. Standing next to what I could only assume was my "rental car" was a guy with a clipboard, grinning.

The car—and I use that term loosely—looked like Barbie, Hello Kitty, and a five-year-old girl's fever dream had a three-way and spawned this … abomination.

Hot pink. Gradient paint job. Glitter. A fucking convertible with what appeared to be whiskers made of black wire protruding from a kitten nose on the front bumper. Googly eyes stared at me from the hood like some demented cartoon character, and I'd bet my left kidney there was a tail attached to the back.

This wasn't a car. This was vehicular humiliation.

"Mr. Pierce?" Clipboard Guy approached, all smiles and sunshine. His T-shirt read *Sparkle Car Rentals. Fun Rental Cars for a Fun Price!* in Comic Sans font because of course it did.

"I can't take this car."

A pause. Like he was legitimately surprised by my pushback.

"Actually, it's one of my most popular models." He said this like it was a selling point. Like normal human beings regularly chose to drive around in a motorized stuffed animal.

"I need something else. Something that's not ... a hot-pink kitty."

He scrolled through his phone with the urgency of a sloth. "I've got a ladybug or a cow available, but they'll take at least an hour to get here—"

"No. No animals. I need a normal car with a normal paint job."

Okay, now he looked annoyed. "Yeah, that's not exactly what my company does, man."

Of course it's not.

"Forget it." I yanked out my phone. "I'll get a rideshare."

God. Dammit. Forty-two minutes for the closest ride. The next app? Even worse. I checked my watch, like I'd have magically factored in an extra forty-two minutes into my commute. Shit.

"I'll take a taxi," I declared.

Clipboard Guy was already walking away. "They take forever to flag down in this neighborhood."

Crap. He was right, and we both knew it.

"Any chance you have a portable tire inflator in that thing?" *Please say yes. Please say yes.*

"No."

Dakota. Fucking. Blackwood. I will haunt you from the grave.

"How were you getting back?" I challenged. He'd obviously driven the cat car here.

"My coworker. But he won't be here for at least 30 minutes."

Shit!

"Good luck."

"Wait!" The word tasted like defeat. "Let me borrow your tires."

He stopped. Turned. Stared at me like I'd suggested we sacrifice a goat. "Pardon?"

"Your tires. I'll pay to borrow them. Just need to swap them onto my car for one meeting, and then I'll bring them right back."

In the awkward silent seconds that passed, I realized just how ridiculous I'd sounded. Even I knew it wouldn't work, but I guess when faced with a Kitty Mobile, one panics.

"First of all," he said slowly, "these tires won't fit your rims. Second, I don't carry tire-changing equipment. Third, if you're too impatient for a rideshare, how long do you think changing four tires will take?"

Dammit. All. To. Hell.

"You could call AAA," he offered helpfully. "But they'll take longer than a taxi."

My heart hammered against my ribs as I checked my watch. The meeting started in twenty minutes.

"I'll give you everything in my wallet to drive me to the restaurant." Maybe if I wasn't the one driving, it would be less humiliating. Maybe I could hide in the back seat. Lay down, below window level.

His expression shifted from reluctantly helpful to offended. "I'm not a chauffeur."

I pulled out my wallet, flashing the cash like some desperate asshole. "$150."

His lips thinned. "I'm a business owner, not a driver."

He's the owner of this ridiculous business, and I'm basically calling his baby ugly.

The guilt hit me then, sharp and unexpected. Here I was, the penthouse-living Mercedes owner, throwing money at problems like some entitled prick. If he only knew I'd clawed my way up from nothing, maybe he wouldn't be so determined to humble me right now.

"Please." The word scraped my throat raw.

He shook his head. "If your meeting's so important, take the car."

My jaw clenched so hard, I feared jawbone damage.

The bastard had me cornered, and he knew it.

"Fine!" I said. "I'll take the cat on wheels."

Maybe I could hide inside Chicago traffic. Park far from the restaurant. Sprint the last few blocks. Maintain some shred of dignity.

I signed the papers with more force than necessary, my signature looking like an angry scribble.

As I pulled out of the garage, there she was. Dakota. Standing on the sidewalk instead of the penthouse, waving at me with that shit-eating grin plastered across her face.

Our eyes met across the distance.

And she—she—had the absolute audacity to blow me a kiss.

My blood pressure nearly exploded my heart right then and there, and it didn't recover either. Any hope of blending into traffic died a spectacular death the moment I hit the street.

In a sea of sensible grays, blacks, and whites, my hot-pink nightmare strutted down Michigan Avenue like a neon billboard advertising my humiliation. The convertible top, naturally, wouldn't close, leaving me completely exposed to the pointing, laughing, phone-wielding masses.

Pedestrians doubled over with laughter. Drivers honked. Not in anger, but in amusement. Someone actually applauded as I crawled through a yellow light.

I wanted to disappear. I wanted to sink through the pink leather seats and emerge somewhere far, far away. Preferably somewhere Dakota had never been born.

Things got exponentially worse when some jackass in a pickup cut me off, and I instinctively hit the horn.

MEOW.

The sound that emerged wasn't the sharp blast of a normal car horn. It was a loud, obnoxious cat sound that echoed off the surrounding buildings like an audio announcement of my shame.

The pickup driver nearly swerved into a parked car; he was laughing so hard.

Blood roared in my ears as I inched closer to the restaurant, my hands gripping the steering wheel like it was Dakota's neck. But the absolute worst moment—the cherry on top of this shit sundae—came when I was stuck behind a delivery van, waiting to turn right.

Because when I glanced over at The Blackstone's outdoor seating area, positioned right there on the sidewalk next to traffic, I locked eyes with two very familiar faces.

No.

No, no, no, no, no.

Of course the executives were sitting outside. Of course they had front-row seats to my vehicular humiliation. The very men who controlled the funds that could rescue my business from its cash flow disaster with one healthy investment.

Their gazes swept over the hot-pink monstrosity, taking in the whiskers, the googly eyes, the fuzzy (yep) tail on the back, the sheer impossibility of what they were seeing.

Then, because this day couldn't get any worse, they burst out laughing. Not polite chuckles. Not suppressed snickers. Full-blown, tears-streaming, can't-breathe laughter.

Frank Prescott, CEO of Prescott Industries, was literally holding his side. Carl Chen was wiping tears from his eyes.

I sat there in my pink prison, trapped by traffic, while the two people who held my company's future in their hands watched me inch past in what could only be described as a motorized cat toy.

And as I did, one thought beat through my anger:

I'm going to kill Dakota.

24

WHEN YOU THOUGHT THE CAT MOBILE WAS AWFUL. UNTIL THE MYSTERIOUS GUEST ARRIVES. 🐱➡️💀 #PLOTTWISTUNWANTED

AXEL

"Nice car," Frank said, that smirk still plastered across his face as he stood to shake my hand.

I forced a smile, wondering if they could see my molars grinding to dust. *Dakota, you beautiful, diabolical vixen.*

"My fiancée is a prankster." Fiancée. Shit. I was supposed to still call her my girlfriend until we'd officially and publicly become engaged. *Thanks, Dakota, for making me slip.*

I shook Carl's hand and settled into my chair, immediately surprised to see a fourth place setting. Menu. Water glass. The works.

What the hell?

This was supposed to be just the three of us. If Dakota had somehow orchestrated a way to crash this meeting, I'd figure out some creative form of revenge that would make today's stunt look like child's play.

"Your fiancée did that?" Carl's eyebrows shot toward his hairline.

"I'm sure she assumed no one would see it," I lied smoothly.

Dakota, I'm coming for you.

"How did she manage to trap you in a ... was that a bunny car?"

"Kitty," I corrected, taking a steadying sip of water.

"A kitty car," Frank repeated, like he was testing the words. "I didn't even know such things existed."

"They're probably for special occasions. Bachelorette parties, tourists." *Why am I defending the world's most ridiculous business model?*

"But how'd she get you to actually drive it?"

I set down my water before I crushed the glass. "It's a long story." I placed the napkin on my lap. And folded my hands in front of me so I wouldn't punch the table. "We like to prank each other."

"Prank wars?" Carl leaned forward, intrigued.

I shrugged. "Keeps things interesting. Though I'll admit, this one wasn't my favorite."

The two men exchanged a look and burst into laughter. The kind of genuine, belly-deep laughter that should have made me feel relieved they believed my story.

Instead, my ego clawed up my throat like a rabid animal.

"Well, this sounds like a woman I'd like to meet," Frank declared.

"Indeed," Carl added, wiping his eyes.

Great. My business meeting had officially become the Dakota Fan Club meeting. I had a few choice words about that woman. None of which were appropriate for polite company.

"Of course," I said carefully. But when they exchanged another meaningful look, unease prickled down my spine. "Someday."

"I have to say, I've really enjoyed watching you two together online," Frank admitted. "It's refreshing to see young love in action."

I managed another sip of water, hoping my smile looked

genuine. Part of it was real, the relief that our charade was working, that we were controlling the narrative. But the lying about who we were in public versus private? That part made my stomach churn.

"Truthfully," Carl said, steepling his fingers like a judge about to deliver a verdict, "after that incident with the photo of you and that political wife, we had some serious reservations." He paused, letting that land. "But seeing you with Dakota ... well, who hasn't had a heated lovers' quarrel—am I right?"

"Exactly." I forced the word out, my eyes drifting again to that mysterious fourth chair.

"So, you two are the real deal?" Frank's tone went flat, all business.

What a loaded question. "Of course."

"Good." Frank's chuckle held zero humor. "Because my PR team raised an interesting possibility: that you two might be staging this whole thing to clean up your mess."

Anxiety slammed into my chest like a freight train. "Really?" I kept my voice shocked, innocent, as if to say, *Who in the world would do such a thing?*

Me, apparently. I'm exactly the kind of hypocrite who would do such a thing.

The irony wasn't lost on me. Here I was, pretending to be something I wasn't, just like my parents had done all those years. I opened my mouth, tempted to come clean. To tell them that my personal life had no bearing on my business skills, that I had a track record worth their investment, that we were all human beings capable of mistakes.

But I couldn't. Not with everyone else in the cross fire.

So, I smiled and cleared my throat. "That's ... quite an imagination they have."

"We like what Dakota's done for your image," Carl continued. "And by extension, your business's image. Stability is important to us."

"Naturally, we'd like to meet her," Frank added. "See you two together with our own eyes."

The way he leaned forward slightly, holding my gaze like a silent warning, told me everything I needed to know.

Translation: we had to sell them on our love story or watch my deal die. The problem? Their radar was up. They were actively hunting for cracks in our facade, and one slip—just one—would destroy everything.

"That sounds perfect," I said. "How about you come to my place? Dakota and I can cook dinner for you." *Shit. I'll have to clear out my office, make it look like she actually lives in my bedroom.* "Or better yet"—I backtracked—"we could go to Dakota's favorite restaurant—"

"Your place." Carl's tone brooked no argument. "Next Friday."

I swallowed my pride, my ego, and what remained of my moral compass. "Looking forward to it."

Crap.

Selling our love story through carefully curated social media posts was one thing. Having two sharp-eyed businessmen poking around our lives, asking pointed questions, looking for tells? That was a whole different level of terrifying.

And it wasn't just my ass on the line. Knox trusted me to protect his sister, and despite the fact that Dakota was currently driving me insane, I wasn't about to let her family pay the price.

"Oh, one more thing," Frank said casually. "We'd like you to meet the newest member of our team. He'll be joining us for dinner next Friday too."

My blood turned to ice as a familiar figure approached our table, hands casually slung in his pockets and that infuriating smirk working across his face like he owned the world.

No. Goddamned. Way.

"Axel," Frank said cheerfully, "meet Mathew."

Are you kidding me?

Of all the people who could have a hand in my deal, my future, my company's survival, it had to be Dakota's ex. The same Mathew who'd been pissing on his fire hydrant, trying to win her back, kissing her in my own damn foyer while I looked on like some jealous stalker.

The universe had officially declared war on me.

"Mathew." I stood, extending my hand with what I hoped passed for professional courtesy. "It's good to see you again."

"Indeed."

As Mathew and I shook and released hands, Frank and Carl exchanged a look.

"You two know each other?"

"We only recently met," I admitted. "It turns out, he used to date Dakota."

The older gentlemen exchanged another look.

"We had quite the memorable introduction," Mathew said. "Had some car trouble that same night actually." His gaze locked on mine. "Funny how these things happen."

My prospective business investors looked between us, sensing undercurrents they couldn't quite identify.

"Car trouble?" Carl asked.

"Oh, just some vandalism in the parking lot," Mathew said with a casual shrug, never breaking eye contact with me. "You know how it is downtown. Sometimes, people get ... territorial."

I had to soften my eyes to make it less obvious I was glaring at him.

"That's unfortunate," I said evenly. "I hope you got it sorted out."

"Eventually." Mathew's smile sharpened. "Though I have to admit, it's fascinating what some people will do when they feel ... threatened."

"City violence, eh?" I gave him a shrug of my own.

If Frank or Carl suspected any of Mathew's implications, they didn't show it. They seemed too intrigued by the fact that Mathew was Dakota's ex.

"Well," Frank said, "this dinner just got a lot more interesting, now didn't it?"

Mathew's eyes glittered with something that made my blood pressure spike into dangerous territory.

You want a war, motherfucker?

You've got one.

25

TIRE SLASHER SUPPORT GROUP CHAT

AXEL

Blake: Axel, nice ride, man. [Sends picture of Axel looking murderous in the pink kitty mobile.]

Me: Where the hell did you get that?

Blake: Dude, you're Chicago's biggest playboy, driving a pink car covered in cartoon cats. You really think women wouldn't snap photos and post them online?

Me: THEM??? As in several?

Jace: [Sends meme of Axel driving.] Forbes hottest CEO meets Hello Kitty's nightmare.

Ryker: What the hell happened? Did you join the circus?

Blake: Did you lose a bet or something?

Me: I don't want to talk about it.

*Blake: What's the matter? Cat got your tongue? *lol emoji**

*Me: *middle finger emoji**

Ryker: OMG, I just saw another video. The horn MEOWED. I'm dead. RIP me. Here lies Ryker, dead from laughing too hard. [Sends GIF of a person laughing so hard, they spit out a drink.]

Jace: Did they not have something more masculine? Like a My Little Pony mobile? Or a Barbie Dream Car?

Me: You guys are getting on my last nerve.

Ryker: [Renames the group chat to Axel's Pink Pussy Wagon Support Group.]

Me: I'm leaving this group chat.

Jace: Not until you tell us who did this. Because we KNOW this wasn't voluntary. Did a business rival force you into automotive humiliation?

Blake: Was it a hostile takeover? "Sign here or drive the kitty car"? Did they threaten to release your browser history?

Ryker: Are we sure he wasn't kidnapped? This feels like a hostage situation. Honk the MEOW horn twice if you need rescue.

Me: Fuck off. And it was Dakota. I'm going to kill her.

*Jace: *laugh out loud emoji**

Ryker: [Sends GIF of a person laughing so hard, they fall to the ground.]

Me: I'm glad you guys are getting a big kick out of this.

Blake: Come on. Even you have to admit this is hilarious. Chicago's biggest playboy, reduced to a meowing hot-PINK vehicle.

Me: Yeah, my investors thought it was really funny too.

Jace: Oh my God, they saw this? Please tell me you got a video of their reaction.

Me: I'm going to strangle her when I get home.

*Ryker: With what? Your sparkly pink steering wheel cover? *laughing emoji**

Jace: Ten bucks says he secretly loves it.

Me: I hate all of you. And her. Especially her.

Ryker: Sure you do, Pink Panther. Sure you do.

26

WILL HE MARRY, KISS, OR KILL ME? I'M LEANING TOWARD OPTION 3. 💍💀 #ENGAGEMENTTHREAT

DAKOTA

When the familiar hum of the elevator sounded, letting me know that Axel was almost home, close enough to the penthouse floor that I could hear his impending arrival, my heart fluttered wildly in my chest. I could only imagine the wrath I would face with him after what I had done with the kitty mobile.

But, my God, seeing the hot, sexy-AF businessman in a custom-tailored suit, driving out of the garage in that hot-pink (did I mention it had sparkles?) kitty-cat mobile? Priceless. Worth every ounce of whatever I was about to face.

The question was, what version of Axel was I going to get? The silent treatment? Or total volcanic explosion?

Please be volcanic. Please be volcanic.

Not that I'd planned this prank to get my hormones all twisted up. My traitorous body just had a thing for Axel's controlled fury. The way his jaw ticced, how his voice dropped to that sultry octave that made my knees forget how to function properly.

File that under Deeply Unhealthy Thoughts, Dakota.

Dear Diary,

You know how Mathew is everything that I thought I ever wanted in a man? Safe, predictable?

Vanilla, some part of my mind shouted.

Well, apparently, there's some dark corner of my psyche that craves watching Axel lose his composure. That gets off on poking the beast until—

The elevator doors slid open.

Holy hell.

His eyes locked on to mine with the intensity of a lightning strike. Furious didn't begin to cover it. This was molten rage, wrapped in a custom-tailored suit, and, God help me, it was gorgeous.

"You're dead, Sunshine."

I painted a fresh streak on my toenail of a defiant shade of crimson red, going for the picture of innocence. "Rough day at the office, honey?"

He stalked over, snatched the nail polish bottle from my grip, screwed the cap on, and slammed it onto the coffee table. The sudden contact when his fingers brushed mine sent electricity shooting up my arm. Especially when he loomed over me, all brooding alpha energy and expensive cologne.

Focus, Dakota. Do not think about how good he smells.

"Do you have any idea what I just went through?"

"A scenic drive through the city?"

"You think you're funny."

I stood, the distance between us a dangerously low three feet. Which absolutely did not send my heart ricocheting around my rib cage like a pinball. Nope. Not at all.

That's when his gaze dropped, just for a split second, taking in my tiny sleep shorts and formfitting tank top. I watched him try not to look, watched him fail spectacularly, and felt a surge of feminine power.

"Picturing Chicago's biggest playboy, cruising around in a glittery hot-pink kitty mobile?" I tilted my head, all fake sweetness. "Yeah, that's comedy gold. The internet seems to agree."

I gestured toward my phone on the coffee table, and his eyes followed the movement before snapping back to mine. A cord of tension stood out in his neck, and when he spoke, his voice had dropped to that low register that made my pulse skip.

"You're going to pay for this." He stepped closer, invading my space until I could feel the heat radiating off his body. "And so help me, if my tires are actually ruined, you'll be even sorrier."

I gulped. *Oh shit.* Maybe I went too far. My stomach dropped, my pulse spiking.

I tried to hide it all with a straightening of my spine and arching of my brow. But his lips quirked up slightly, and he was clearly aware that he made me nervous. And, damn it all to hell, he loved every minute of it.

He probably also loved that from this point forward, I would be haunted with anxiety of how he would get back at me. More salt in my coffee? Doubtful. I had gone nuclear with the kitty mobile; chances were he would go nuclear as well.

I couldn't decide if that thrilled me or terrified me.

Clearly, I should have thought this out more.

What terrified me even more though was how much my body was currently aware of his. His tailored suit clung to his skin like it was kissing it, and as he moved, I could see his muscles flexing beneath his shirt. It definitely didn't help when he shrugged his jacket off, tossed it on the chair, then began loosening his tie. All while staring. Right. At. Me.

This time, when I gulped, it was because I wondered ...

"What are you going to do, spank me?" The words left my mouth when the grouping of brain cells that filtered inappropriate thoughts from escaping my lips went on strike.

His pupils dilated as his gaze raked over my body like he was seriously considering it. Like he was imagining exactly how he'd bend me over his knee, how my skin would feel under his palm.

"You'd like that, wouldn't you, Sunshine?"

Yes. "No."

He slipped his tie off completely, letting the silk fall to the floor. "Is that what this is about? You like getting me all worked up?"

How could he flip from furious to seductive in the span of thirty seconds? It was like sexual whiplash.

"No." It was only a half lie.

He saw right through me. Again. Moving closer, he tucked a strand of hair behind my ear. Though his fingers barely grazed my skin, the feel of his touch sent shock waves through my entire system. Instead of pulling away, his hand lingered, his knuckles tracing the line of my jaw with devastating gentleness.

"Liar," he growled, his voice rough with desire. His thumb moved to brush across my bottom lip, and I couldn't stop the soft gasp that escaped. And I swear, my tongue acted of its own accord when it had the brazenness to sweep out and lick his salty skin.

Holy. Hell.

His eyes all about exploded with hunger, and between my frantic *what in the hell are you doing, Dakota* thoughts, I could feel my heart racing. Fire traveling down my stomach to the space between my thighs.

"You're going to pay for what you did to me, Sunshine."

His thumb was still on my lip, and without thinking, I parted them slightly, inviting his thumb inside. His eyes darkened to midnight.

Especially as I wrapped my lips around him and sucked on the tip.

Look at his Adam's apple bobbing for dear life.

Did I want him to push me down? Take me right here and now? My body certainly believed so.

Jesus.

Get your head on straight. This is war, not foreplay.

With massive effort, Axel stepped back, my mouth cool in the absence of his thumb. I tried to focus on his words rather than wondering what other parts of his body would feel like in my mouth ...

"Now ..." He pulled something out of his pocket. A small

velvet box. Grabbing my other hand—which made me gasp, thanks to the shock and electric current that charged through my skin at his contact—he slammed it into my palm. "Wear this."

Swallowing my desire, I opened the box. A five-carat diamond ring stared back at me, all elegant perfection and serious money.

"Congratulations, Sunshine. We're officially engaged."

Anger flared, hot and immediate. I snapped the box shut.

"This isn't how we're supposed to get engaged. We had this all planned out—"

"That was before you sent me through downtown Chicago in a rolling cat."

"What does that have to do with this?" My voice pitched higher. "We have a very specific PR script—"

"The purpose of which was to save my deal. Your little stunt? Those executives saw me driving that thing."

Oh shit. I bit my lip to keep from laughing, but he tracked my movement. His face hardened to stone.

"I told them my fiancée likes to prank me. Which was probably for the best. I doubt they'd buy that someone I'm supposedly *dating* would be stupid enough to pull a stunt like that on someone she's desperately trying to win over."

My jaw fell open. "Win? Like you're some kind of prize?" I gestured between us, my voice dripping with disdain. "I have news for you, Axel Pierce. The only thing bigger than your ego is your ... your ..."

Come on, brain. Work with me here.

"Cat got your tongue, Sunshine?" His smirk was absolutely infuriating. He stepped closer again, close enough that I had to tilt my head back to maintain eye contact. Close enough that when I breathed deeply, my chest almost brushed his.

"You don't get to change our story," I said through gritted teeth. "We have a plan—"

"God, you really hate when anything happens that you haven't color-coded and scheduled in advance, don't you?"

I balled my free hand into a fist, but before I could do something stupid, like punch him in his esophagus, his fingers wrapped around my wrist.

"Easy, Sunshine," he murmured, his thumb finding my pulse point and pressing gently.

I knew he could feel how fast my heart was racing, knew he was aware of exactly what his touch was doing to me.

"If we're moving up the engagement timeline, fine, but we can't just—"

"The executive team thinks we're already engaged. It's done, Sunshine. Deal with it." He stepped back, coldness lingering on my skin as he worked his cuffs with infuriating calm. "And wear the damn ring."

God. Damn. It.

My head was spinning, trying to find a way to buy time, to go back to our plan. "It probably won't fit."

"Oh, it will. I made sure of it."

"How do you know my ring size?"

"I pay attention to details when it comes to you, Sunshine."

Something in his tone made me go very still. There was an intensity there, a hint of something deeper that made my chest warm.

"Now"—he rolled up his sleeves, all business again—"get comfortable because, tonight, we're learning everything about each other. Next Friday, those executives are coming here. They're suspicious of our relationship, and we're going to convince them that what's between us is real."

He paused, drawing out the silence like torture.

"Oh, and, Sunshine? Guess who just joined their team."

I waited.

"Your ex."

I followed him into the kitchen, my bare feet padding against the cold floor. "What do you mean, Mathew's part of—"

"What is *that*?" Axel stopped dead in his tracks.

I followed his gaze to the crystal vase on the counter. "The flowers you sent me. What do you mean about Mathew—"

"I didn't send you flowers."

Oh. "Maybe they're from Mathew then?"

Axel turned to face me, his expression dark. "*Black* roses?"

I shrugged. "Figured you were being all dramatic and ordered some kind of dramatic delivery—"

"I didn't."

Okay ...

"Who cares about the flowers? Tell me about Mathew! He's working with them now?"

But Axel wasn't listening. His entire demeanor shifted like our fake engagement didn't matter right now, like he sensed something I didn't. "Did you read the note?"

I frowned, moving closer to the expensive-looking vase. "I didn't see one."

The tiny card was tucked deep among the black petals. I'd been so distracted, worrying about Axel's reaction to my prank, that I'd missed it completely.

Axel plucked it from the flowers.

"What does it say?" I asked.

He handed it to me without a word.

To the lovely couple. You messed with the wrong person.

27

DEATH THREATS MAKE HIM GO ALL PROTECTIVE, AND I'M TRYING TO NOT FIND IT ATTRACTIVE. 🥀 💀 #MIXEDPRIORITIES

DAKOTA

Ryker's hand gripped my shoulder. "I'll make some calls and figure out what's going on, okay?"

"Please don't tell Knox about this." My stare was undoubtedly pleading.

Ryker exchanged a look with Axel, but after a few seconds, he pressed his lips together and nodded. "If that's what you want."

"It is."

We sat in Axel's living room, which had once again descended into chaos with all of his found family. Blake stood against the opposite wall, his arm draped around Tessa. Jace lounged by the window, his hand possessively resting on Scarlett's hip. Axel paced like a caged panther, fresh scotch in hand, his shirtsleeves rolled up to expose those annoyingly distracting forearms. Ryker sat beside me, and Faith perched on the chair to my right.

At a time like this, it was really nice to have friends that were like family. People who would drop everything and rush over at the whisper of a problem. It made everything feel less terrifying.

"Maybe we're jumping to conclusions?" I suggested, voice

pitched higher than I'd like. "I mean, our romance went public, so maybe this is some creepy fan or something?"

The guys exchanged one of those loaded male looks.

Okaaayyy, we'll file that under Not Reassuring.

"I've had some followers that are ... overly enthusiastic," I admitted. And that was putting it kindly. "If I'm being honest, I do get some creep vibes from followers sometimes."

A fresh look of alarm washed over Axel's face. "Anyone in particular?"

"There's this one girl, BlushBabe123, that is always the first to comment on my posts. At first, I was thrilled because it helps the algorithms, but over time, I couldn't help but wonder how she has that much time to invest in one influencer. And her comments are ..." I wobbled my head. "Overeager."

Axel shot a glare to Ryker, who seemed to digest this possibility.

"Maybe she did this. Or some other follower." Maybe it wasn't the Romano crime family, who knew how to tie concrete anchors to your feet.

"It's possible," Ryker said, but his tone suggested he thought unicorns were more likely. "Have you ever had a fan send you something like this before?"

"Follower," I corrected. "And no."

"Has she or anyone else threatened you in any way?"

"Well ... no."

"Nothing's impossible." Ryker was careful with his words and even more careful with his tone. "But this is anger. Not adoration."

Fair ... but where does the life of an obsessed stalker begin?

"Crime families tend to have a flair for dramatics," Ryker added. "Black roses have surfaced in some of their activities before."

Activities. Right. Because *murders* would've been too harsh of a word for polite company.

"So, you honestly think the Romano family is going to come after Axel and me?" I asked.

Was I in denial, thinking that was overkill?

Ugh. No pun intended.

"Let's just take this one step at a time." Ryker's lawyer voice kicked in.

It dawned on me that Ryker was pretty damn good in a crisis. It also dawned on me that while his primary reason for being here had been to see the message and roses with his own eyes, to reconcile them against organized crime cases he'd worked in the past, he'd quickly developed a secondary purpose: his attention sweeping over Faith like she was a beacon of light in a room of darkness.

If Faith realized he was staring, she gave no indication. But I noticed. Hard not to when the man looked like he'd been struck by lightning.

Even with everything we were going through, I couldn't help but feel joy, watching my brother's friends find happiness, one by one. Which made me wonder. Why hadn't Ryker found it yet? The guy was selfless to a fault. He stood by Knox's side, spent God knows how many hours each year working on Knox's parole hearings, probably sacrificing his nights and weekends, and he never so much as asked for a thank-you.

What if all those hours had been stealing him away from having a life of his own?

"I think it might be best if you guys stay here, stay inside, until I can figure out what's going on," Ryker added, his protective hand finding my shoulder again.

"I can't stay inside." The words tumbled out. "I have to meet with folks from my brand deal, and I have weekly dinners with my parents."

"Can't you reschedule?" Jace suggested.

"To when?" When would this be over? "When the crime family decides they're done sending us horticultural threats?"

Axel's attention laser-focused on me. "Maybe you can meet with your brand people here."

I blinked. "You never let anyone in your penthouse." I gestured around at the room currently full of people. "Except for close friends."

"For your safety, I'll happily make an exception." His stare deepened, voice dropping. For a moment, everyone else fell away, and it felt like Axel would bend every one of his sacred rules just to keep me safe.

"As for your family," he continued gently, "I'm sure they could understand you missing one dinner."

My shoulders shrank. "I can miss *one* dinner, but I can't miss them in perpetuity. My dad and I need to tackle his broken bathroom faucet. It's been on the schedule for weeks. If we don't fix it, we'll get behind on fixing the drain, and then that'll put us behind on the next project."

Everyone exchanged glances. Great. Now I sound like a crazy person with a home-repair obsession.

"My parents' house has seen better days," I explained. "That's why I have to meet with this brand agency. The deal isn't for me; it's for my parents. They spent a fortune on lawyers, trying to get appeals." Before Ryker eventually took over.

Jace looked genuinely shocked. Having inherited a fortune, he'd generously funded the original lawyers for Knox's trial. But clearly, Knox had never told him about the lawyers that came after. How could he? Mom and Dad had kept most of that from Knox, too, and I could only assume if Ryker knew from court records or something, he kept it to himself on the grounds of attorney-client confidentiality. Besides, by the time Ryker had become my brother's lawyer, those sharks who'd siphoned the funds were long gone, so Ryker telling everyone my parents had been taken for a ride would have done nothing but embarrass them.

Axel, on the other hand, was clearly surprised by this. His

brows furrowed. "Knox pled guilty. There'd be no need for lawyers after that."

"I know." The words tasted like scam artists. "I think my parents were in denial. And unfortunately, when desperate people ask for help, even if that help is doomed, there are still people out there who are willing to take their money. My parents got taken advantage of. People took their savings, but of course there was no shot of getting Knox out of prison. Now their house is falling apart." *And they might lose it.* But I kept that fun fact to myself.

Looks were exchanged around the room.

"Let me make some calls," Jace said, already reaching for his phone. "I know great contractors."

"Hello? I'm in construction; I can organize a crew," Axel added.

I held up my palm. "I appreciate it, but my dad is nothing if not stubbornly independent. My parents grew up doing everything themselves, and they will not accept a handout from anyone. A daughter coming over to get her hands dirty is one thing. But some wealthy guy sending an army of contractors?" I shook my head. "He won't even let them past the front door. But seriously, thank you. It means the world."

Poor Jace looked like I'd just told him his credit cards had been canceled. This was what he was used to: fixing things with a phone call. And I was crippling his superpower.

"Okay, here's what I'm going to do," Jace said, already typing. "I've got a bodyguard who can be discreet. He can follow you from a distance. It's not ideal. I'd rather put you in a suit of armor or lock you in a tower, but it's better than you guys being alone. Plus, we need to document everything. Every moment you two are together needs to be photographed and posted. The more viral you become, the safer you are."

I could have argued. The independent-to-a-fault gene ran strong in our family. But the truth was, those flowers did scare me. Just a little.

And that didn't make me weak, thank you very much. It

made me *aware,* the same way an animal was aware there was a lion nearby.

"Maybe we should postpone the wedding," Tessa suggested quietly.

She and Blake were engaged, with their wedding coming up fast.

"You're absolutely not doing that," I declared, pointing at her for emphasis.

"Why are you guys getting married so quickly again?" Jace smirked, earning a death glare from Blake.

"Because we're madly in love and want to start our life together," Blake said through gritted teeth.

"You're a wedding planner," Scarlett said to Tessa. "Don't you want the wedding of the century?"

"I already have the wedding of the century." Tessa looked at Blake like he was a hero, walking away from an explosion in slow motion. "Because I'm marrying *him.*"

Axel made a gagging sound. "I will never get used to seeing Blake all lovey-dovey. I miss his grumpy, brooding ass. You're changing him for the worse, Tessa."

She beamed, and Blake glowered at Jace. "What are you smiling about? You're turning all goofy too, cowboy."

"He only goes riding with me occasionally." Scarlett laced her fingers through Jace's.

"Still." Axel shook his head. "Seeing Jace Lockwood on a horse ... it's massively disturbing."

"You'll see," Jace said, making googly eyes at Scarlett. "When you fall in love, it softens you. For the better."

Both Blake and Jace looked directly at me. *Oh, hell no.*

Did everyone here think Axel and I were destined to wind up together? Did they miss the memo about our relationship being built on hostility and prank wars?

It made me feel things I didn't want to, made me feel like I was under a spotlight I wanted no part of. My throat ran dry.

"I'm going to grab some water," I announced, pushing off the couch before anyone could read too much into my sudden need for hydration.

"You okay?" Faith appeared in the kitchen, moving with that silent grace of hers.

I smiled. "I'm fine. But it's sweet of you to check."

She walked over to the black roses and cocked her head at them. In a totally casual voice that didn't hint at all that Axel and I might be in mortal danger, she asked, "How do you think they make them black? Some kind of dye?"

I blinked, and then I couldn't help but smirk. "Really good question."

"Can you even imagine?" She leaned against the counter. "Some big, bad crime boss in a flower shop? Picking out roses? Like, do you think organized crime has their own preferred vendor? Maybe sometimes, they send black roses. Other times, they hide a dead fish inside a bouquet. You know, *sleeping with the fishes* and all that."

I was genuinely smiling now. God, I appreciated her coming in here and trying to make me laugh. Everyone else was being so heavy about this.

"We should ask Ryker what other 'flair for dramatics' crime families used," I said.

"Maybe a chalk outline outside your front door."

"A box of snakes. Dyed black, of course."

"Ooh, or maybe they send you a fake lottery ticket. Really mess with your emotions."

I snorted. "A singing telegram, but it's just someone dressed as the Grim Reaper."

"They order you a pizza, but when you open the box, it's just a photo of you sleeping."

"Okay, that one's actually terrifying." I laughed.

Faith smirked. "They're so dramatic though, right? Like, just send a text like normal people."

I smiled wider and let a small silence pass. "Thank you for

this. Everyone else is so freaked out. I needed to see the humor in it, or I'd explode. Not many people could pull that off."

She shrugged. "I'm used to living under the threat of danger."

I stilled. The casual way she said it, like discussing the weather, sent chills down my back. "What does that mean?"

Her gaze snapped to mine, widening when she realized I wasn't taking this as casually as she'd intended.

"Oh, we're not doing that." She jumped up and sat on the counter, waving her hand dismissively.

"Doing what?"

"That thing where you might have just gotten an actual death threat from a crime family, and you're turning it into worrying about me. I'm fine. Trust me, I've been dealing with darkness and skeletons since I was a little girl. I'm good."

It broke my heart to think of all the darkness she must have endured. I knew a little about her background from Blake. How their parents died in a car accident when they were young, how she'd almost been killed by her foster father, and how they were separated in the foster system. But I sensed there were even more layers of pain she kept buried deep.

Why did I get the impression that Faith was always scanning doors and windows, looking for signs of trouble? Always checking the shadows for threats?

"Look, I know we haven't known each other long, but if you ever need anything ..." I trailed off, letting the offer hang in the air.

Her smile didn't reach her eyes. The urge to hug her and demand answers was so intense, it took everything I had to hold back. But I sensed that if I pushed too hard, she'd run.

Her body language screamed, *Change the subject.*

"Axel hasn't taken his eyes off you," she said, pretending our moment of vulnerability hadn't happened.

I didn't want to let her off the hook that easily, but I could see the walls slamming back into place. "He's just worried."

"Those weren't worried eyes." Faith's tone turned knowing.

"Those were more *if anything happens to her, I'll burn the world to the ground* eyes."

"You're wrong. He still blames me for this whole PR mess. Probably blames me for this too." I gestured toward the vase.

"Those are not blaming eyes. Those are protective eyes."

I glanced into the living room and found that Axel was, in fact, looking at me with an intensity that made my stomach flip.

"I'm his best friend's sister. He feels obligated to keep me safe. If he doesn't, Knox will probably murder him when he gets out."

I winced, realizing I'd said that so casually.

Faith's head tilted. "Your brother really is in prison for murder?"

"He is."

"Wrongfully imprisoned?"

I shook my head. "He pled guilty."

"People plead guilty for all sorts of reasons," she suggested.

"Well, in this case, he pled guilty because he did it," I clarified. "This is the part where a lot of people get all self-righteous and awkwardly tiptoe out of the room. Won't hold it against you if you do that."

To my surprise, she raised an eyebrow like she was raising chips in a poker match. "I was taken away from my brother when he killed someone right in front of me. Splattered brain matter on the wall and everything. And I appreciated it." Holy shit. "So, listen when I say, I'd never judge whatever your brother did because I learned at an early age, things are never black and white."

What the hell? Tessa had implied Faith and Blake had a traumatic past. But Jesus.

"Do you mind if I ask who he killed?" she asked too casually. I'd argue most people couldn't pull off the *who did your brother murder* question with such normalcy.

I blinked, having to work hard to stop myself from asking a million questions. "Maybe someday, when this is all behind us, we can get into Knox's whole story. But honestly, I don't even know the whole story. He bottled up secrets and kept them locked away in that prison cell."

"But you never turned your back on him."

I chewed my thumbnail. "He's family."

Faith patted my arm with a clear change-of-subject tone. "Well, in any case, I don't think Axel's looking at you because you're his best friend's sister."

My cheeks burned. "My ex-boyfriend wants me back," I reminded her, as if saying it out loud would make her stop talking about Axel.

She paused. "Okay, but let me ask you this: is there any part of you that likes Axel?"

"He drives me crazy."

"That's not what I asked."

"He calls me Sunshine, and I don't even know why."

Her lips tilted up. "Have you asked him?"

"No, because I don't care why he calls me Sunshine."

Faith laughed. "Your body language disagrees with literally everything you just said."

"My body language is naive."

"Well, I guess that solves that then. My radar must be really off because when I'm around you two, I pick up all sorts of vibes."

With that, Faith hopped down from the counter, patted my arm, and said, "You get any other creepy Mafia threats, send me a picture. We can make a scrapbook of them."

Smiling, I watched her leave the kitchen.

Later, after everyone left, I retreated to my room with a book, trying to lose myself in someone else's problems, but a soft knock interrupted my escape.

"Come in."

Axel stood in the doorway, wearing light sweats hanging low on his hips and a white T-shirt that clung to the planes of his chest. His feet were bare, hair slightly mussed, like he'd been running his hands through it, maybe working up the courage to come to my room.

My ovaries took notice. *Traitors.*

"I'd like you to sleep in my bed."

I blinked, certain I'd heard him wrong. "I'm sorry, what?"

"I just ..." He scrubbed the side of his face. "I can't sleep with you all the way across the hall. If someone broke into this penthouse ..."

"This place is a fortress," I reminded him.

"There's no such thing, Sunshine. Someone with skills can get into anywhere."

Well, let's file that under Comforting Things That Will Cause Me Sleepless Nights in Perpetuity.

"I'm fine," I said.

He didn't budge. Instead, he swiped his thumb across his lower lip while I tried not to trace the movement, something coiling tight in my stomach.

Axel stepped into my room and sat on the edge of my makeshift bed.

"Okay, look. There's a word I'm about to use, and I don't use it very often. If ever." He paused, then said it. "Please."

Wow. Faith must have been right. You don't worry about someone like this unless you care about them. I wasn't expecting the swirls of light and heat stretching through my body at the thought of Axel Pierce liking me.

"You're scared," I realized.

"Those flowers concerned me."

Maybe Faith was right. Maybe I was feeling something for Axel.

"I'm fine. Really." I turned back to my book and flipped on the reading light. "If you wouldn't mind getting the lights on your way out?"

Axel studied me for a long moment, and I could feel his gaze like a physical touch.

Eventually, he stood. But instead of leaving, he walked to the wall and flipped off the overhead lights, leaving only the soft glow of my bedside lamp.

Then he sank to the ground, his back against the wall.

"What are you doing?" I managed.

"You wanted the lights off." His voice was rough, different. "But I'm not leaving."

In the dim light, his eyes found mine. "Go to sleep, Sunshine. I'll be right here."

Oh, we're definitely not sleeping now.

With all these confusing feelings circling around us, I officially wondered how in the world I was going to get through the next stage in our fake engagement: the dreaded get-to-know-you session. You know, finding out everything about each other that couples are supposed to know, so we could pass any scrutiny with the dinner from hell coming up.

How was I supposed to reveal my deepest secrets to a man who already saw too much? And worse ... how was I going to survive learning his?

Especially now that our lives literally depended on selling this love story.

28

WHEN HE THREATENS YOU WITH ORGASMS AND YOU'RE TRYING TO REMEMBER WHY THAT'S A BAD THING. 🔥 #EMPTYTHREATS

DAKOTA

I had no clue Axel was about to find out my favorite sexual position was TBD. I think it was the worst way this possibly could have gone.

I suppose drinking wine in advance of having to do this thing was a bad idea, but it was the only way I was getting through Operation Get to Know You. My goal? Survive this interrogation as fast as possible, then get to bed and forget Axel Pierce had learned things about me I never wanted to tell him.

Funny. Back when I had first met him, all those years ago, I had dreamed about getting the chance to sit across from Axel and learn everything about him. I wanted to reach my fingers into his brain and find out every secret, every hidden fantasy, every fact. He was like a puzzle I wanted to assemble, all thousand pieces, one at a time, and each one I wanted to savor.

Fast-forward to right now. The thought of learning about him didn't bother me. It was the thought of exposing parts of myself to him that had me all sorts of anxious.

The fire crackled in his living room fireplace, casting dancing shadows across the walls. I was curled up on one end of his ridiculously expensive leather couch, wineglass in hand, while he sat on the opposite end like we were in some kind of standoff. Which, let's be honest, we were.

Axel was dressed in a black T-shirt that accentuated his muscles, flattened along his frustratingly flat abs, and gray sweats that not only showed off his legs, but notably ... well, what was between them.

I mean, wow. *Focus, Dakota. Wine. Drink more wine.*

"Okay. Ready for this?" he asked.

Not really.

We'd pivoted and posted our stupid *Yay! We're engaged!* photo online and were once again "spotted" at dinner together. Looking lost in love. To follow that, we stopped by a place for dessert. More in love. To my equal parts pleasure and horror, it seemed to be working. The public seemed to be buying it, and as Rebecca predicted, they were thirsting for more. More us. More of the backstory.

And my brand deal wasn't officially dead anymore. The rep "loved" what she was seeing online, citing how authentic our "flawed" love story was. #Irony. I just had to keep it up, I guess, but that was about to get a whole lot harder. And riskier because the reps at that brand deal had somehow sniffed out this dinner from hell and snagged an invite. I bet my money it was Rebecca's doing, but I couldn't blame her for helping me, now could I?

In any case, if each of our public events and subsequent posts had been like football games, the Super Bowl was looming ahead of us. A live event, where we'd have to think on the fly, make sure our story was airtight and impenetrable.

God. Help. Us.

Thus us sitting here now.

"You're my brother's best friend. You know me." I pushed back, taking a generous gulp of my cabernet.

"First of all, you're guarded as hell. Second, you were a completely different person back then. And third?" His eyes narrowed. "You've hated me ever since."

"I don't hate you." I took another sip. *Liquid courage, don't fail me now.*

His gaze remained locked on mine, and for a heartbeat, I thought it actually mattered to him that I didn't hate him. *(By the way, why exactly did I admit that again?)* And, hello, was it just me, or was he trying to see straight into my soul right now? But then he cleared his throat and chucked whatever moment we'd just had aside.

"Right. Let's start with something easy. When we first met."

I glared at him over my wineglass. "We already know this information. We need to fill in the gaps between then and now."

"One of the first questions couples get asked is how they met," Axel said, settling back against the couch cushions like he had all the time in the world.

"Yeah, well, we're not a normal couple. We met forever ago, and we're just now engaged. Because apparently, I have terrible judgment." I gestured with my wineglass for emphasis.

"And we need a story about that timeline." He leaned forward, the firelight playing across his features. "We need to romanticize our first meeting. Make it sound like there was something there we didn't act on. Sexual tension we ignored."

Oh, there was tension all right. "Okay, fine. Let's get this over with." I drained half my glass.

"Tell me about the first time you saw me, and I'll tell you about the first time I saw you."

The memory warmed my cheeks despite my best efforts. *Great. Now I'm blushing.* "I came to visit Knox in college. First year, you were his roommate."

"And when you walked in and saw me, you thought ...?"

I thought you were the hottest guy I'd ever seen in my life. You were sprawled across your bed in a white T-shirt and gray athletic shorts, no shoes, scrolling through your phone like you owned the world. Which, let's be honest, you probably thought you did.

"I don't remember. You were just some random dude on a bed." I took another gulp of wine.

"Liar." His lips curved into that infuriating smirk. "You practically tripped over your own feet when you saw me."

"That was a loose floorboard."

"In a carpeted room?"

"Very loose carpet," I claimed.

He bit back a smile and got back to the script. "Our eyes locked, and right then, we both knew something. Felt something. But neither of us would admit it."

My heart did this stupid little flutter. *Wait, is he ...?*

"That's what we tell them," he added, gesturing dismissively.

Ouch. Right in the ego. "Got it. Moving on." I reached for the bottle on the coffee table.

When I leaned forward to pour more wine, my shirt gaped slightly at the neckline. I caught Axel's eyes dropping for just a second before snapping back up.

"Did you just check out my cleavage?"

"I was looking at your necklace."

"I'm not wearing a necklace."

"I was looking at where a necklace would be."

"Mmhmm. Very believable. Your eyes just happened to take the scenic route back to my face?"

"There was traffic."

Why did I love that he was looking at me like that?

"Keep going with the story," he insisted.

"We sat down, talked briefly, and ..." *The way you looked at me sent butterflies exploding through my entire body. I was suddenly self-conscious about everything: my hair, my voice, the way I was sitting.* "I remember thinking you had the warmest smile I'd ever seen." *What he doesn't know? That smile part wasn't made up. Confessing it under the guise of fake engagement prep feels weirdly liberating.*

He stared at me for several long seconds before clearing his throat.

"My turn." Axel's voice dropped lower, and the firelight made his eyes look almost golden. "I took one look at you and was thunderstruck. Thought I'd laid eyes on an angel. After you left, Knox smacked my shoulder and told me I better not even think about going near you."

I smiled despite myself, swirling my newly refilled wine. *Fun to imagine, but Knox never mentioned that, so clearly, that part of the story was a ruse.*

Or was it? The way he said it ... there was something in his voice. Something that made me wonder if maybe, just maybe, that part was real too.

"We need to leave Knox out of this," I reminded him. "My followers don't know we're related."

"Right. Friend of my friend then."

"Now we need to explain the hostility." I leaned forward, wine making me bolder, and didn't miss how his eyes tracked the movement. "Anyone who's around us knows we haven't gotten along in forever. How do we explain that?"

Axel's jaw tightened. "We don't. You were off-limits. Forbidden. End of story."

"Except it's not the end of the story." Frustration bubbled up, aided by the alcohol. "You used to be nice to me when I first visited. Then it was like a switch flipped, and you became a complete ass."

"If you think that's being an ass, you have no idea what life can throw at you, Sunshine."

"See? What does that even mean? You're so cryptic." I stood up, pacing in front of the fireplace. "I'm supposed to be your fiancée. Shouldn't I know what goes on in that twisted brain of yours?"

"That's not how relationships work."

"That's exactly how it works. And, we can't skip this part!" I gestured wildly with my wineglass. *Oops.* A few drops spilled onto the hardwoods, inciting a glower from Axel. The man looked like I'd just personally murdered his entire family. Over three drops of wine. His eye twitched, and I swear I could hear his soul leaving his body. God forbid anyone disrespect his precious Brazilian rosewood or whatever tree died for these floors. I squatted down and slurped it up with my finger. Was it just me, or was he watching my finger with an inappropriate amount of intensity as it trailed along my tongue?

"You know I have paper towels, right?"

"Where's the fun in that?" I said, maintaining eye contact as I licked my finger clean.

"You're doing that on purpose."

"Doing what?" I asked innocently. "Being environmentally conscious? Reduce, reuse, recycle."

"That's not what recycling means."

"I'm recycling the wine. Through my mouth. Very eco-friendly."

He shifted in his seat. His eyes darkened, tracking a drop of wine I'd missed at the corner of my mouth. For a moment, we just stared at each other, the air between us crackling with something dangerous. Something that made me want to spill more wine just to see what he'd do about it.

I cleared my throat. "Anyway, you being mean to me for YEARS is a massive plot hole in our story."

"You were mean right back to me."

"Yeah, that's what happens when someone's a complete dick to you for no reason."

His lips thinned. "Like I said. Forbidden. Off-limits."

"Bullshit." I gestured again, this time without spilling crimson. "You're mean to me specifically. I've seen you with other people. You're charming, funny, somewhat likable. Your special brand of jackassery is reserved just for me. And I deserve to know why."

Something flickered across his face. His Adam's apple bobbed, fingers twitching at his sides. For just a second, I saw something raw there. Something vulnerable. But instead of answering, he just cleared his throat. "Next subject. Why did we start dating now?"

Oh, hell no. "You can't have it both ways. You can't tell me we have to know everything about each other and then shut down the most important part of our story."

"We'll navigate around it." His voice was clipped.

"Like that time in college, when you navigated making a fake dating profile for me?"

"That was helpful. I set your age preference to sixty-plus to help you find someone mature," he quipped.

"My bio said I collected ceramic frogs and believed the moon landing was fake."

"You got twelve matches. Thirteen if you count the guy who wanted to start a conspiracy podcast with you."

"That's not the point, Axel. And let's stay on topic."

"Fine. Here's what I've been thinking about our timeline. We reconnected when Jace was in the hospital. That's true; there are witnesses. We helped him get back home. Also true. But instead of our usual verbal sparring match and you being an absolute—"

"Choose your next words very carefully, Pierce."

"Pain in my ass, we actually talked. Reconnected. Something sparked."

"And we kept it secret because ...?" I snapped my fingers, nearly spilling my wine again. "Oh! I know. Because I figured your nice-guy routine had a shelf life and you'd go back to being a complete jackass."

His glare was soooooo satisfying.

"Fine." I rolled my eyes and plopped back down on the couch, this time closer to his end than before. Close enough that I could see the way his muscles tensed when I settled next to him. "I made the decision to keep it private."

"Why you and not me?"

"Because I'm a strong, independent woman running my own business. I carefully curate my image, and dating Chicago's biggest playboy wasn't exactly on-brand for me." I took another sip. *Nailed it.*

His tightened face told me he was less than thrilled with my assessment. "Adorable. Now let's talk about the important shit. Goals, dreams, life plans. Do we want kids? Where will we live?"

"This is going to be impossible to remember." And, hello, now that I thought about it, drinking was a terrible idea; it'd make memory recall even harder. The problem? I was already buzzed, and buzzed me wasn't very responsible.

"Then stick to the truth. Pretend I'm not the guy you hate. Do you want kids?"

The question caught me off guard. *This suddenly feels way too intimate.* Sharing hopes and dreams with Axel Pierce, my sworn enemy? But I had to sell this.

"I want three kids. And it would be amazing if two of them were twins." I took a nervous gulp.

The way he looked at me then, his gaze lingering on my stomach like he could picture me round with his children, sent heat flooding through my entire body.

When he finally spoke, his voice was rough with genuine curiosity. "Why twins?"

I considered this, swirling my wine. "I've always been fascinated by them. Two little babies, two toddlers running around, looking similar ... it's the cutest thing in the world."

The way he looked at me then, like this was the most interesting thing he'd ever heard, made my chest warm.

This is getting hard, these lines blurring between fake and real. Even harder are the feelings this conjured up, wishing that moments like these were the real ones.

Dangerous territory, Dakota.

But also ... nice territory. When was the last time someone had looked at me like that? Like I was fascinating?

"What about you?" I cleared my throat and took another sip. "Kids?"

"No." Axel said it so fast, it was like a gunshot to my soul.

"Wow, don't sugarcoat it or anything. Tell me how you really feel."

"I just did."

"What if someone asks why your fiancée wants three kids and you want negative three?"

"Negative three?"

"That's the vibe you're giving off. Like you'd return other people's kids if you could."

Why did I care that he didn't want children? I suppose it was because having kids wasn't something I was willing to sacrifice, and maybe that small part of my brain that wondered if we could ever possibly work out realized now there was no way we ever could.

"Why don't you want kids?" I pressed.

"Not everyone wants kids."

"Right, but why? I'm supposed to be your fiancée. If I want three and you want zero, how did we resolve that? What was the compromise?" I drained my glass again.

His shoulders went rigid. "Families are overrated."

Oh. "I take it, yours was a nightmare?"

"I don't like talking about it."

"Bet this get-to-know-you session really sucks for you then," I quipped.

He sent a fresh glower my way.

"What if someone asks about it and I don't know? That'll blow our entire cover."

He held my stare for a long moment, and I sensed whatever happened to him as a kid was what made him think families were doomed. Was that why he was a playboy whose only real relationship attachments were the men he'd bonded with in college?

And suddenly, I wasn't just curious for the sake of our fake relationship. I wanted to know what had hurt him so badly.

"Asking about my childhood scars is a bit deep for the moment," he decided. "For now, tell me a fact about yourself that most people don't know."

Should I let him off the hook? I wanted to press more. In fact, the less he wanted to talk about it, the more I sensed was behind it. Especially when I replayed Knox's words when I'd visited him in prison. What had my brother said? I was the antithesis of everything Axel stood for? Was that why he hated me?

"I hate true crime documentaries," I answered. "Can't change the channel fast enough."

Fun fact. Want to know what happens to a family when one of them gets convicted of homicide? It wasn't one of those *trauma makes us stronger* situations. Mom and Dad became withdrawn. Depressed. Any TV show highlighting someone else's hell didn't make for popcorn-worthy television.

Understanding settled over his features. "Is that why you like to be in control all the time?" Axel wondered.

Wow. Leave it to Axel to see right through me and land his target on something even Mathew hadn't figured out.

"Life was totally normal," I said quietly. "I was getting a haircut the day everything changed. My biggest choice in life was bangs or no bangs." I picked at my wineglass again. "And then I find out my brother's been arrested for murder. So, yeah, that made everything feel out of control. Gave me anxiety attacks."

He studied me like the idea truly bothered him, like he had to push the pain of my hurting aside to have a shot at focusing again. Then he nodded gently. "If you control everything, you feel like something like that can't happen again."

"It's irrational."

"It's understandable."

Okay, that was ... unexpectedly kind.

He looked at me like understanding this part of me answered a puzzle piece he'd been desperate to understand for years. And something inside me softened. Just a little. Because for the first time in forever, someone got it. Got me.

This was dangerous. I was starting to feel ... connected to him. And then, as if that wasn't enough of a glimpse into my soul, he shifted forward and asked a doozy.

"Why did you fall in love with Mathew?"

There was something in his tone: hurt mixed with astonishment, like I'd chosen Mathew over him. *Which is ridiculous because we were never an option.* The wine was clearly going to my head.

"Mathew's kind. Smart. He wants the same things I do. He made me feel like I mattered." I took a large gulp for courage. "Plus, he can reach things on high shelves."

His lips curled. "That's your criteria? *I* can reach high shelves."

"You also reach new levels of jackassery daily, so it's a mixed bag."

"Until he left you."

My body went rigid. "You're not exactly the authority on treating people well. Your longest relationship is with your gym membership."

"At least I'm committed to something."

"Your abs don't count as a personality, Axel."

"He's not good enough for you." The words came out possessive in a way that made my pulse react.

"Mathew's a good guy." I swirled my glass.

"We have different definitions of *good guy*."

"You're not one to lecture on what makes a good person. Let's get back to this." I set my wineglass down so I could cross my arms over my stomach.

Axel studied me for a moment, and I could practically see him deciding to rescue me from the Mathew feelings-fest. His eyes lit up with mischief.

"You know what? You're right. Let's stick to the easy stuff." He leaned back, all swagger and false innocence. "Favorite sexual position."

Heat exploded across my cheeks. When he noticed my blush, his resulting smirk made me want to murder him. I reached for the wine bottle again. *Definitely need more alcohol for this.*

"I'm never answering that. No one would ever ask that."

"Men will ask me."

"Business guys? I highly doubt that. What kind of business

dinners are you attending? *Great quarterly reports, Johnson. By the way, how does your fiancée like to—*"

"You'd be surprised what comes up after the third martini."

"Then maybe drink less at these dinners."

"Where's the fun in that?"

I leveled him with a glower.

"Not all men are gentlemen. We have interviews, dinners. What if I meet someone who's been with you and I get it wrong?"

My neck warmed, and I saw his eyes track the flush spreading down my throat. "That won't happen. Unlike you, Mathew is a gentleman and would never talk about me that way."

"Well, we have many interviews and fake dinners and whatnot. Who knows who will show up? All it takes is one guy from your past for our story to implode. Just tell me."

"No." My cheeks were on fire. I chewed my thumbnail, wineglass forgotten.

"You only do that when you're nervous," he noted. *Great. He sees right through me at the worst possible time.* "Why does talking about sex make you nervous?"

"It doesn't."

"Liar." He leaned forward, the firelight making him look dangerously handsome. "Are you a freak in the bedroom?"

"No."

That's when I saw it: the exact moment everything clicked. The reason I said *Mathew* would never talk about me that way. Not *none of my exes.* Not *anyone I'd ever dated.* Just Mathew. Axel's expression shifted from confusion to understanding and then something deeper.

"You've *only* been with Mathew." Luckily, his tone was soft and not antagonistic or humorous at all. At least that was something.

"I know that's hard for you to understand, but not all of us have a revolving door to our bedroom. Some of us have standards."

He cocked his head, studying me with an intensity that made

me feel naked. "Why is he the only one you've ever been with? You're a gorgeous woman in her thirties. Surely, men have thrown themselves at you. In fact, I saw it in college. Thought about breaking a jaw over it on more than one occasion."

Holy crap, there was a lot to unpack with that. He found me gorgeous? He wanted to break someone's jaw for hitting on me? And most of all, he was genuinely curious about my decisions? Not judging me for them?

The confession hung in the expanse of his living room, and for a moment, I forgot we were supposed to be enemies. This felt like ... intimate conversation. Real conversation. The kind I'd imagined having with him all those years ago.

"My parents raised me with strict values. That was saved for marriage."

He chewed the inside of his cheek. "And since they're already worried Knox is going to hell, you tried to be extra good to compensate."

Stop seeing through me!

"Why didn't you save yourself for marriage then? I mean, why wait that long just to ... not follow through with it?" His tone wasn't condescending; it was careful, soft.

"Because I loved him."

Something dark settled over his features. He scrubbed his face, looked away, then snapped his attention back to me with an edge. "Did he pressure you?"

"I'm in my thirties. It's understandable that a guy in a serious relationship wants intimacy."

"That's a yes."

"No. We talked about it and realized that we either would date for years without intimacy or get married before we were ready. We mutually agreed to a compromise."

Why am I sharing this with my nemesis? And why does he look like he's plotting Mathew's fall from a bridge? But also ... why does it feel so natural to tell him these things? Like he actually cares about the answers?

"I don't regret it," I said quickly, looking down at my hands.

"Do you regret waiting as long as you did?" Again, his tone was kind, curious.

And for a minute, just a minute, I wondered if he was asking because he wanted to know.

"Maybe," I admitted.

"Is that why you were so pissed the night you took that picture of me? Seeing me with yet another woman?"

I sighed. *Axel is like a human lie detector.* I suppose I could have avoided the answer, but honestly, with him knowing I'd only ever been with Mathew, what was the point?

"Maybe I was jealous of how free you are with your sexuality," I said. "You don't care what people think; you just go for what makes you happy. Meanwhile, I've spent my whole life trying to be what people want me to be."

That tasted bitter, but there it was.

Something shifted in his expression. Surprise, maybe even understanding. For a moment, the air between us felt different. Less hostile. Almost ... tender.

We weren't supposed to be connecting like this. This wasn't part of the plan. But here we were, sharing pieces of ourselves we'd never shared with anyone else.

Then something dark and dangerous flashed in his eyes. When he spoke, his voice was deceptively calm. The kind of calm that comes before someone punches a wall.

"You saved that part of yourself for three decades because it meant something to you. Something sacred." His knuckles went white with tension. "Please tell me that asshole at least made it worth it. Tell me he made you feel like the fucking goddess you are. Tell me he worshipped you the way you deserved."

Goddess? Axel saw me as a goddess?

Heat crawled up my neck. "He was ... fine." I took a massive gulp of wine.

Axel's head snapped back like I'd slapped him. "Fine?"

"I'm not discussing this."

"Fine isn't exactly a glowing review, Sunshine."

"This is a complete violation of Mathew's privacy. I'm not telling you how he was in bed."

"You don't have to." He stilled, massaging his hands. "I can see it written all over your face. He never made you lose control, did he? Never had you screaming his name or seeing stars."

I opened my mouth to argue, but the lie wouldn't come. *Damn him for being right.*

"Jesus Christ, Dakota." He ran a hand through his hair, looking genuinely tortured. "You waited all that time for *fine*?"

Something about the way he said it, like it personally offended him, like my disappointing sex life was somehow his problem to solve, made heat pool low in my stomach.

The silence stretched between us, heavy with everything I wasn't saying. His breathing had changed, gone deeper, and when I looked up from my glass again, his eyes were practically black with something that looked like fury. Or hunger. Maybe both.

"You have no idea what you've been missing," he said, standing slowly. The predatory way he moved toward me made my pulse race.

I stayed curled on the couch as he towered over me, bracing one hand on the back cushions and planting the other on the armrest, caging me in. His eyes darkened as they roamed over my body, and suddenly, the air in the room felt too hot to breathe.

This wasn't supposed to happen. We were supposed to stay enemies. Safe in our animosity. But somewhere between the wine and the confessions and the firelight, something had shifted. Something that made my entire body hum with awareness.

"Let me paint you a picture of what you deserve, Sunshine." His voice was rough velvet, his face inches from mine. "You deserve someone who memorizes every single thing that makes you gasp. Someone who learns your body like a symphony and plays it perfectly every time. You deserve to feel worshipped, cherished, absolutely wrecked in the best possible way."

His eyes burned into mine. "If I touched you, you'd see stars.

You'd feel my tongue between your thighs, until you screamed my name. Then I'd sink so deep inside you, you'd forget your own."

Holy shit.

"I'd pull your hair. Pin your hands above your head. Make you feel powerful and vulnerable at the same time. There would be nothing ordinary about it. Nothing *fine* about it." His eyes burned into mine. "You deserve someone who has you grabbing the sheets and begging for things you didn't even know you wanted. Someone who takes their time with you. Hours, Dakota, until you're shaking and can't form coherent sentences."

I swallowed.

"You deserve passion that leaves marks on your soul, not just your body. The kind that has you daydreaming in meetings and blushing at random memories. You deserve someone who looks at you like you're their personal religion." His voice dropped to a growl. "And when you finally fall apart, completely undone, I'd put you back together just to do it all over again. As many times as you could take it."

I became hyperaware of every inch separating us. Heat bloomed beneath my skin. A slow burn that started in my chest and radiated outward until even my fingertips tingled.

His eyes held mine captive. There was something in his gaze that made my pulse stutter. The breadth of his shoulders, the corded strength in his forearms, the way he seemed to fill the entire room without moving ... it all pressed against me like a physical weight. I couldn't look away. Couldn't do anything but feel the overwhelming presence of him.

"That's what you've been missing, Sunshine. That's what you deserve."

Suddenly, his phone rang, shattering the moment.

He stepped back, waiting several seconds before, finally, with his eyes still locked on me, he answered. "Pierce."

I sat there, trembling, wondering what the hell had just happened.

And more importantly, what might happen next.

29

PSA: NEVER UNDERESTIMATE THE POWER OF GIRLS' NIGHT TO COMPLETELY DESTROY YOUR DENIAL. #TRUTHSERUM

DAKOTA

"He stayed there all night?" Faith's eyes practically sparkled as she abandoned her ribbon-tying duties, a slow grin spreading across her face as I recounted how Axel had been worried enough the other night to sleep on my floor.

That was *before* our get-to-know-you session.

I hadn't told them about that session yet. That was ... well, still processing through my mind like one of those computer spin wheel things. Especially the last part, where he threatened me with orgasms. The way his voice had dropped to that dark, velvety register, how he'd caged me against the couch, the promises he'd made about what he'd do to my body ... it all kept replaying in my head like some kind of erotic highlight reel that I couldn't turn off. I mean, my God, who the hell wraps threats of sexuality in a ribbon of silk? I figured my needs would pass with a good night's sleep. But nope.

Now, every time I saw Axel, I was imagining what he'd said. What he wanted to do to me. How his hands would feel on my skin, his mouth between my thighs, the weight of him above me as he—

"Hello?" Faith said. "You there?"

"Sorry. Yeah, he stayed on the floor all night."

"Did he climb into bed with you?" Scarlett waggled her eyebrows while stuffing heart-shaped candies into a mesh bag with unnecessary enthusiasm.

"God, no. He just ..." I fumbled with a QR code sticker, my cheeks heating up. "He stayed on the floor. Against the wall. Like some kind of ... floor guardian."

Smooth, Dakota. Really sold that one.

"Uh-huh." Tessa paused mid-ribbon curl, fixing me with that knowing look that made me want to crawl under the table. "You have to admit, that doesn't sound like somebody who hates you."

"*Hate* is a strong word," I mumbled, focusing intently on matching thank-you notes to names. Anything to avoid their laser-focused stares.

Tessa and Blake's penthouse dining room had been transformed into wedding-favor central. The table practically groaned under the weight of supplies: ribbons in every shade of blush, little drawstring bags that seemed to multiply when I wasn't looking, and Tessa's handwritten thank-you notes that made me feel like a terrible friend for never writing actual letters.

The music from Tessa's wedding playlist—some acoustic love song that was way too on the nose—filled the momentary silence as all three girls exchanged looks. The kind of looks that said they were about to gang up on me.

"Okay, I'm calling BS," Scarlett announced. "You know exactly what we're talking about."

"Tell me you didn't see the way he looked at you when he thought you might be in danger." Tessa's voice had that gentle but persistent quality that meant she wasn't letting this go.

"Like the world was about to end," Faith added.

Okay, so maybe I noticed. Maybe when Axel's face went all hard and protective, something in my chest did this weird fluttery thing that I'm definitely not ready to analyze.

"It's just a temporary truce," I claimed. "I'm sure, deep down, he's still pissed about the hot-pink kitty mobile."

"Seems to me you two are enjoying each other's company." Scarlett's grin turned positively wicked. "Your penthouse is filled with sexual tension."

My hands froze mid–candy drop. *Well, crap. Was it that obvious?*

"Attraction isn't the same thing as affection," I said weakly.

"Says the girl who had a guy literally sleep on her floor just to make sure she was safe." Faith's voice was gentle, but her words hit like tiny arrows straight to my chest.

The heat that flooded my cheeks could have powered the entire penthouse. Even I couldn't deny how much Axel's protectiveness had meant to me. All this time, I'd felt like I had to be the strong one for my family, the one who held everything together. But Axel had just ... stayed. Without being asked. Without expecting anything.

I shook my head, trying to dislodge the dangerous thoughts taking root. "I should want Mathew."

The words hung in the air like a confession I hadn't meant to make.

Scarlett's hands stilled on her bag stuffing. "Did you catch that, girls?"

"Sure did," Faith said, her voice singsong.

"Loud and clear," Tessa added with a knowing smile.

"Catch what?" I glanced around the table, but their expressions told me I'd walked straight into a trap.

"You said *should*. You *should* want Mathew," Faith pointed out.

Crap.

"Poor choice of words," I claimed, but my voice lacked conviction.

"Admit it." Scarlett leaned forward like she was about to solve the mystery of the century. "Somewhere along the way, you've started to like Axel. A lot. Maybe even more than you ever liked Mathew."

The accusation hit too close to home, sending panic skittering through my chest. Because it was true. Somewhere between the pranks and the protection and the way he looked at me like I was the most fascinating puzzle he'd ever encountered, I'd started to fall for him. Hard.

"Axel isn't right for me," I said quickly, the words tumbling out like a well-rehearsed defense. "He doesn't want kids. He's basically a man-child. He's immature, and he lives to drive me insane."

And he makes me explore things about myself I never wanted to before. And he remembers how I like my coffee. And when he thought I might be in danger, he looked like he'd burn the world down to keep me safe. And if I ever did sleep with him, I know he'd dote on my every sexual desire.

"Anyone else hearing all that protesting?" Tessa asked.

"Crystal clear," Faith confirmed.

Desperate to deflect, I pointed at Faith. "Says the girl who was looking at Ryker the other day like he was walking in slow motion in an action movie."

Faith's cheeks pinked. "Did not."

"Oh my God." Scarlett threw her hands up, scattering ribbon everywhere. "Isn't it hilarious how we deny what's completely obvious to everyone else?"

"Fine, he's hot," Faith admitted, waving a hand dismissively. "So I have functioning eyeballs. Sue me."

"Those weren't *that guy is hot* looks you two were exchanging," I pressed, grateful to have the spotlight off my own romantic disaster. "Those were *I want to climb you like a tree* looks."

"Ryker's a good guy," Tessa said softly, and something in her tone made us all pause. She would know. Not only because she was his sister, but also, from what I'd heard, Ryker had kept Blake out of prison after he'd ended the life of the man who'd attacked Tessa. Self-defense, but still. "And he's single."

"Not interested." But Faith's voice had lost its playful edge.

"Why?" Scarlett asked, her tone gentler now. "By your own admission, he's gorgeous. You two clearly have chemistry. So, why not give him a shot?"

The change in Faith was immediate and heartbreaking. Her face fell, all the laughter and lightness draining away like someone had flipped a switch. When she spoke, it was so soft, I almost couldn't hear her. "Trust me, if he really knew about my past, he'd run in the opposite direction."

It broke my heart, hearing her pain. I wanted to ask her what happened. What made her believe that a wonderful guy wouldn't ever be interested in someone like her.

"Faith ..." I started.

She waved me off with a brightness that was clearly forced. "This is supposed to be fun wedding prep day. Let's keep it that way."

Just like that, her mask slipped back into place. But knowing it was a mask made it even sadder, realizing how much practice she must have had, hiding her pain from the world. From everyone ...

I wanted to know Faith's story. Blake's little sister. A beautiful woman who deserved happiness.

"So," Faith said, her voice determinedly cheerful as she redirected the conversation with calculated precision, "Mathew or Axel?"

I blinked. "What?"

"Who do you want more? Mathew or Axel?"

The question hit me harder than I wanted it to, making my stomach twist into knots. Because suddenly, with startling clarity, I knew the answer. And it terrified me. Mathew was safe, predictable, everything I thought I wanted. But Axel? Axel made me feel like I was on fire, like I was truly alive for the first time in years.

"Aren't you supposed to meet Mathew later?" Tessa asked.

I'd texted Mathew, asking to meet. Somewhere private

though. Couldn't risk being seen together. His place made the most sense since Axel would probably have an aneurysm if Mathew showed up at the penthouse again. Originally, I'd asked to meet so I could ask him to stop texting me, but now ... now I had a different message.

"I am." The words felt like an ominous weather forecast. *Prediction: Tornado warning. Seek shelter immediately.* Because I was about to permanently close the door on a good man for someone who might never be able to give me what I wanted.

"What are you going to say to him?" Tessa questioned.

For a long moment, I just sat there, surrounded by wedding favors and the ghost of romantic music, while my romantic world shifted beneath my feet. Because all those moments with Axel—the banter, the pranks, the way he made me feel alive and challenged and completely myself—they'd been building to something. To this.

I looked up at my friends, who were watching me with a mixture of anticipation and sympathy.

"I know what I need to say to Mathew," I said quietly.

And I suspected he wouldn't take it well.

30

WARNING: DISASTER OF EPIC PROPORTIONS LIES JUST BEYOND THIS DOOR. 🚪 💀 #SHOULDHAVESTAYEDHOME

DAKOTA

"Dakota." Mathew's smile lit up his entire foyer as he stood with the door open, looking as handsome as ever.

A pang hit my chest, realizing how much effort he'd put into his appearance. Brand-new gray pants that hugged his hips just right. Black shirt that matched his belt and shoes. All of this for me.

Well, this is going to suck.

"Mathew ..."

Before I could finish, he enveloped me in a hug. Pressed against the warmth of his chest, I closed my eyes and tried to breathe through the aching burn searing through my ribs.

You're doing the right thing, I told myself for the hundredth time since making this decision.

Three months ago, all I wanted was Mathew, but something had shifted. When I first saw him at the restaurant, the shock had overwhelmed my system, like an infection had finally found its antibiotic. Then Mathew started fighting for me. And being desired by the person who'd left you? That shit can cloud your judgment.

But as the days passed, something became painfully clear. I only *thought* I'd been in love with Mathew. Looking back, I had been in love with the idea of being in love with him, with being swept off of my feet by a man who seemingly checked all of my boxes.

Had he never left, maybe we would've gotten engaged. Married. Had babies. The whole Pinterest board dream.

But that wasn't my path.

Everything happens for a reason, they say. Maybe Mathew leaving had been the shock my heart needed. Because if he was the one, I wouldn't catch myself looking at Axel the way I did. I wouldn't feel that flutter every time I heard the penthouse elevator. I wouldn't have felt that heat when he pressed me against the couch or that liquid desire pooling low in my belly when he described what he'd do to me if he ever got me in his bed.

"Come in." He stepped back.

"It's nice." I smiled, glancing around. Clean, modern, contemporary furniture in blues and grays that reminded me of sailboats. Very *I shop on Michigan Avenue and have my life together.*

"You like it?" God, the hope in his voice. The way his shoulders relaxed slightly as he shoved his hands into his pockets, looking at me like my opinion was everything.

Aaaand cue the guilt spiral in three, two, one ...

"I do. It's impressive."

His smile faltered slightly, as if he sensed my distress, but he quickly hitched it back up. "Let me get you a drink."

I followed him into his kitchen, my throat suddenly feeling like I'd been chewing cotton balls.

"Have to be honest," he started, filling a glass with ice and water. "I was surprised to get your invitation to meet."

The tone in his voice told me that my calling had made his entire day. Too bad I was about to take that happiness and light it on fire.

He handed me the glass. "Thank you for coming over."

He studied me then, once again registering my anxiety. Because apparently, my poker face needed work.

"What's wrong?"

"Mathew, we need to talk."

His attention flicked to the diamond ring on my finger, and his expression turned to stone. "You're staying with him."

Not a question. An accusation, wrapped in disappointment, with a side of barely contained rage.

Taking a sip of water, I geared up for my rehearsed speech. Earlier, I'd outlined it, practiced it in the mirror, even worked on my facial expressions. But standing here now, all that rehearsal went out the window like confetti in a tornado.

"Things changed after you left," I managed.

"I came back for you."

"I wish you would've visited first before you uprooted your entire life."

"Dakota." When he stepped forward, I looked up at him, my heartbeat suddenly auditioning for a death metal band. "You don't have to do this. I can tell you're confused. You can take more time ..."

"I don't want you waiting for me."

"Waiting for you is my decision. And I would wait a hundred years for you to come back to me, Dakota. Look, I know you're engaged, but—"

"Even if I wasn't," I interrupted.

Shock registered on his face, followed by a flash of anger. "He's gotten inside your head."

Well, that was a bit condescending.

"This is me and my decision alone." *Stay strong, Dakota. You've got this.* "I want you to find someone who will make you happy."

"I already have." His tone had gone ice cold.

"I'm sorry." I handed him the glass. "I came here to say goodbye."

For a moment, I thought he might throw the glass across the room. Instead, Mathew set it on the counter and crossed his arms, staring at me like I was a confused child who needed her head cleared by an adult. "You're still mad at me for leaving you."

"This isn't about you leaving."

"Tell me you don't love me." He cupped my cheek. His palm was warm, but it wasn't electric. Not like Axel's touch.

"Mathew." I pressed my hand on top of his, looking into his eyes. "I will always care about you. But you need to understand that—"

His lips crashed into mine.

I gasped from the shock and tried to pull back. But his grip was unyielding. He wasn't being mean, but he was desperate. I could feel it in the strength of his kiss, the way his fingers threaded through my hair like he was trying to keep me locked in this moment.

I pressed both hands against his shoulders and pushed back.

"I love you, Dakota. I'm not letting you go."

Something about the way he'd said it sent warning bells clanging in my head. "I'm not a collectible, Mathew."

"You're my wife. You just don't know it yet."

And there it was. Some people would probably hear those words and find them romantic. Hell, maybe I would have a few months ago. But hearing the authority in his voice, seeing that possessive look in his eyes? I didn't find anything romantic about it at all.

In fact, seemingly mundane moments were replaying in my mind like a highlight reel I definitely didn't want to watch. How, when I'd get ready for dinner with him, he had strong opinions about which dress I wore. What color eye shadow. At the time, I thought it was adorable, having a boyfriend who wanted to help me get ready.

He liked our outfits to be coordinated. Always.

And that time we went grocery shopping when I was in jeans

and flip-flops and he ran into an old work buddy, he seemed ... annoyed. Had made a comment about me not wearing makeup. In public. To get groceries.

"You know what your problem is?" he said, his tone shifting to something colder. "You've forgotten what made you special. The perfectly polished Dakota. That's who I fell in love with. This person"—he gestured toward me, now wearing jeans and a T-shirt—"isn't the real you. You're confused."

How did I not see this before? Mathew started dating me when my social media persona had taken off. The one who always looked perfect online. He liked the curated me. The fake me.

While Axel liked the real me. Messy hair, no-makeup me.

"I don't think you like who I actually am," I said slowly, the realization hitting me like a bus I should have seen coming. "I think you only liked it when I looked perfect."

"Who doesn't like perfection? You're beautiful with your makeup on and your hair done. Why wouldn't you want to show that off?"

"But that's just for the camera, Mathew. When the lights go down, I'm just an ordinary person. You know that."

A look crossed his face. Something cold. Dismissive. "I was giving you a compliment."

"You're saying that the best part about me is the version of myself that I put online."

He didn't deny it.

Which felt like someone had just ripped the ground out from under me. All those times I'd felt insecure about not being perfect enough, about whether people would still love me if they saw the real me? Mathew had just confirmed my worst nightmare. For him, I wasn't enough just as I was. I was only lovable when I was performing. When I looked like I belonged in a magazine instead of, you know, real life.

I felt sick to my stomach. Couldn't breathe. Needed to run until my muscles screamed for relief.

"That isn't me, Mathew. That's just a persona."

"Of course it's you."

"What, you want me to be some kind of trophy wife?"

"You say that like it's a bad thing. Having a beautiful wife on my arm that I enjoy showing off should flatter you."

"Should it?" The words felt like someone had taken sandpaper to my heart. "I'm not an accessory, Mathew. I'm a human being. I'm smart and hardworking and college-educated. I help my family. I built a business from nothing. My hair and makeup don't define who I am."

"You defined yourself that way."

His words were like a slap that left me reeling.

"I'm more than just arm candy, Mathew." Damn these tears threatening to break.

"You should take it as a compliment."

"Oh, yes, I feel extremely complimented, having my intelligence, work ethic, life goals, and contribution to society boiled down to having the perfect shade of lipstick."

"You're getting exhausting. Maybe you should get some rest."

The condescension in his voice made me want to throw something. Preferably at his head.

And just like that, I could see my entire future with him laid out like a road map to misery. "This is how it would be between us, isn't it? You'd want me to be the perfect version of me all the time. The Instagram version. Never the real me."

"That *is* the real you."

I could feel the air leave my lungs. Standing here with Mathew was like getting a preview of my own personal hell.

"It's over, Mathew."

"I don't believe you really want him," he said flatly.

Damn it. He needed to accept this was over. If he didn't, he'd keep trying to win me back. Plus, he might blow our cover.

"Let me make this perfectly clear." I loaded the words into my gun and fired. "It's over between us. There's nothing you can say to change my mind."

His chest swelled like he was preparing for battle. "You don't love him," he accused.

"This isn't about Axel."

"This is me you're talking to, Dakota. Me. I know you." He pointed a finger toward me like he was casting some kind of spell. "Whatever he's done to manipulate you—"

"Being with him is my choice. You need to accept that."

He cocked his head, studying me like I was a specimen under a microscope. "You know what I think? I think your relationship with him is bullshit. I don't know why you're doing it, but I don't buy it."

Adrenaline surged through my system like I'd just chugged five energy drinks. *Shit, shit, shit.*

For Axel's sake, for my parents' sake, for Knox's and everyone's job at Axel's company's sake, I knew what I needed to do. And I hated myself for it.

"I'm. Not. In. Love. With. You." I kept my tone strong even though, inside, I felt like I was crumbling into a million tiny pieces.

When he huffed, when his face darkened like a storm cloud, I could tell my words finally landed their mark.

"Well," he said, voice dripping with enough venom to kill a small village, "I don't believe you. Maybe I should share my suspicions with my new bosses."

Wow. That wasn't love. That was punishment, wrapped in a pretty bow. "Threatening me? Really, Mathew? I thought that was beneath you."

Apparently, I was wrong about a lot of things.

"As you should know, my bosses only want to proceed with Axel's deal if your relationship with him is real."

"Well, they'll get to see it firsthand when they come over for dinner." *Keep it cool, Dakota. Don't let him see you sweat.*

"Yes. This dinner will be very interesting, won't it?" There it was again, that warning drumming through his words, his glare. How badly I'd misjudged him.

How dare he? How dare he reduce me to makeup and hair spray? How dare he not take no for an answer? That was controlling with a capital C.

"To think, I felt bad for you," I snarled. "But you're mean and vindictive. Looks like I dodged a bullet when you left."

"You dodged a bullet?" His laugh was sharp, cruel, like broken glass. "Some might say you're a pathetic nobody who uses social media to try to make yourself into something big. But deep down, you know you're worthless."

The words hit like psychological bombs.

"Your brother is a convicted murderer, Dakota. You share his DNA. If anyone saw the real you—the broken, damaged girl behind all that online perfection—they wouldn't want anything to do with you."

The shock hit first. So paralyzing and absolute that my muscles locked and my throat closed. Every word I might have said died before it could form. I stood there, frozen, while his words carved through the air between us.

Then came the anger, white hot and fierce. How dare he? How DARE he speak to me like this, use the insecurities I'd trusted him with as ammunition? We'd had something good once. Or so I'd thought. And, hello, he was the one who'd left, not me. He was the one who'd walked away and shattered everything we'd built.

But right behind the anger, rushing in like a flood I couldn't hold back, came the pain. Unimaginable, soul-deep pain. Because this wasn't just any insult from any person. This was someone who'd seen all of me: the scared girl who worried her brother's crimes made her unlovable, the perfectionist who feared she was only valuable when she had it all together, the daughter who carried shame she didn't earn. I'd let him see the rawest, most vulnerable parts of myself, the parts I kept hidden from the world. And now he was using those very vulnerabilities to slice through my soul.

A stronger person wouldn't give him that power. Would

simply look at him like the trash he evidently was and walk away, unscathed. But my heart? My heart was absolutely shattering. Because when someone you once loved weaponizes your deepest wounds, it doesn't just hurt; it shatters the illusion that love and safety can coexist, that vulnerability is ever anything but a loaded gun you hand to someone and pray they never pull the trigger.

It felt like a sledgehammer had just shattered me into a thousand pieces.

Breathe, I ordered myself. *He's wrong. He has to be.*

But these words weren't random. They were too specific. Too calculated. He'd found my deepest wound and twisted the knife with surgical precision. Every insecurity I'd ever had about being loved for who I really was, every fear that I was only valuable if I projected an air of perfection, he'd just weaponized them all.

Why couldn't I just order my heart to stop hurting from someone who didn't deserve it? Rationally, I knew he didn't deserve my heartbreak. But the pain was still there, carving through my chest like it was trying to make a permanent home.

And in that moment, it made me realize how much I respected Axel. Say what you want about his antics, but at least he was up front and honest. He would never have done this to me. Because Axel, despite all of his flaws, wouldn't have used my vulnerabilities against me just to watch me bleed.

"You can go screw yourself," I managed.

The tears were coming whether I wanted them or not. My heart was replaying all the times Mathew had held me close to his chest, had been my safe haven in a storm. To realize it was never real, to realize I'd been living in a storm all along... it broke me in ways I didn't even know were possible.

"See you Friday, Dakota."

I looked at the man I'd once loved with everything I had, then ran out of his apartment. I made it to the sidewalk before I broke down crying. For the first time in as long as I could remember, I let myself completely fall apart.

I'd had two goals, talking to Mathew today: End things. And do it in a way he'd back off and go on with his life.

Instead, I'd just made everything a hundred times worse.

God help me, this dinner was going to be a disaster of epic proportions.

31

UPDATE: TURNS OUT, I'M CAPABLE OF GRAPHIC VIOLENCE WHEN IT COMES TO SOMEONE HURTING HER. 🔥 #PROTECTIVEMODEUNLOCKED

AXEL

I knew something was wrong before she even entered the room. The sound of her knock lacked any energy or enthusiasm, almost painful in its sadness.

And then she appeared in my office, the room that doubled as her bedroom. She didn't even have to knock, which was another tell.

To anyone else, she might look okay, but I could see everything. The deflation of her entire being, like someone had punctured a hole and let all the fight leak out. Her posture was slumped, eyes cast down, the fire completely drained from them. The telltale signs were all there: residual puffiness, reddened lids.

She'd been crying.

Fuck. Time came to a standstill. I'd never seen Dakota cry. Not since the trial at least. She was the strongest woman I'd ever met, the kind who'd probably tell Death to go fuck itself if it showed up at an inconvenient time.

"What's wrong?" I shot to my feet and crossed the room, cupping her cheek before I could stop myself. "Did something happen? Did someone hurt you?"

"No." She stepped back like my touch burned her.

My fingers itched at my sides, desperately trying to understand what the hell could have happened. The sight of her body curling in on itself, like she was in too much pain to even stand up straight, felt like a chainsaw cutting me in half.

"What is it, Dakota? Are your parents okay? Is Knox—"

"They're fine," she assured me, twisting her fingers together. She cleared her throat, and I could see the conscious decision she made to project strength. But her voice came out weak and brittle.

Someone broke my Sunshine.

The thought hit me like a military tank. When had I started thinking of her as mine? When had her pain become something that could literally bring me to my knees?

"I have a proposition," she announced.

A proposition? This wasn't a woman wanting to negotiate; this was a broken animal that had been kicked while down. My fists clenched. *Who the fuck did this to her?*

"What is it, Sunshine?" It took everything I had not to pull her against my chest and wrap my arms around her until whatever was hurting her couldn't reach her anymore.

I hated how small her voice sounded. "I'll give you whatever you want. And in exchange, I ask for one night. Oscar-winning performance. A couple so in love that we make every other person jealous."

What the hell?

Someone got to her. Were they convinced she was lying about us? Whatever the reason, by the looks of it, they'd verbally destroyed her. And that took a lot. Which meant whoever had done this must have stooped low. Must have known exactly how to hit her where it hurt most.

"I need us to sell us to somebody in my inner circle. So we have to be extremely believable at our dinner."

"Your inner circle," I repeated.

"My ex-boyfriend."

"Mathew?" I nearly choked on his name. "We already knew he was going to be here."

"I know but ..." Her lip quivered, and fresh rage shot through my veins like boiling water.

"Dakota, what happened?"

She swallowed hard. "I went over there to tell him we would never get back together. I didn't want him to wait for me. But he won't take no for an answer. He's determined to prove we're fake."

Still, something else had changed. Something that had crushed her.

"What did he say to you?"

She shook her head. "Doesn't matter."

"Like hell it doesn't."

"The point is, he was angry, and I could be wrong, but I don't think he'll let me go until he knows we're real."

She's scared of him, I realized. Maybe not physically, but emotionally.

"He's controlling," I deduced. When I saw the look on her face, I added, "He's acted this way before."

She squared her shoulders, trying to find some of that Dakota fire. "There were a couple of moments I was concerned he might have been more controlling and possessive than I felt comfortable with."

Possessive and controlling. A dangerous combination for someone infatuated with her.

I narrowed my eyes. "Did he ever lay hands on you?"

"No."

"Did you ever worry he might?"

She opened her mouth, then snapped it shut.

Mother. Fucker. "Elaborate." The word came out like a growl.

She looked like she was debating whether to answer, but I stood there, making it clear I wasn't going anywhere until she did. I didn't want to be possessive or controlling like him, but her safety meant more to me than anything else, and I needed to know what I was dealing with.

What type of insect I was about to crush into dust.

"The last couple of times we argued before he left, he got in my space until I backed down. Literally backed away from him." Her voice was barely above a whisper. "It felt like ... like if I said the wrong thing, his hand would've just ... flown up."

I cracked my knuckles, the sound sharp in the quiet room.

"But I convinced myself I'd misread it. And for the record, he didn't lay a hand on me," she assured quickly. "I just ... I need to do something big and final to make him go away. For good."

"Announcing you were engaged didn't do the trick?"

"Would we be having this conversation if it did?"

Fair point. "And he's convinced we're fake. Is there something specific that's tipping him off?"

She considered this for a moment, biting her lip. "I think in his mind, there's no way some other man can 'win' me," she said, using air quotes. "The fact that I'm the one who ended it is incomprehensible to his ego." She pressed a hand to her forehead. "Why do we look past red flags in relationships?"

I swallowed about a dozen things I wanted to say. I wanted to find Mathew right now and beat his face until he was unrecognizable.

I didn't give a damn about my deal anymore.

What I cared about was her.

But she'd just come out of a relationship with a jealous, possessive asshole who never took her feelings into consideration. I needed her to feel like she had control.

"What do you propose?"

"Let's be a little more over the top than we planned at the dinner. I think for him, we just have to act like we're madly in love."

That won't be hard. The hard part will be not introducing my knee to his jaw until it cracks off.

"And, Axel?" she said, apparently reading my mind. "Whatever you do, please don't get into a fight with him."

"You just told me that a controlling, possessive, aggressive ex-boyfriend won't let you go. You implied you're afraid of him. If you think I won't do something about that, you're sorely mistaken."

"Please." Tears shimmered in her eyes, threatening to spill over. "Please do this for me."

Shit. What do you do when two competing desires go head-to-head? On one hand, I'd give Dakota anything she ever asked for. Anything that made her life happier, easier. Especially if it meant so much that her eyes filled with tears.

But those tears were put there by that prick of an ex-boyfriend. And in my book, that deserved one hell of a beating.

I studied her face. Really looked at her. Beneath the pain, beneath the deflation, I could see something else.

"What aren't you telling me?" I asked softly.

She bit her lip. "He threatened to call his bosses. Tell them our relationship is fake."

Manipulative bastard. Now I understood. This wasn't just about him not accepting rejection. This was about control. Power. He was holding our careers hostage to get what he wanted.

Mine, I no longer cared about. Hers, on the other hand ...

I moved closer, close enough that she had to tilt her head back to look at me. "Dakota, I'd burn my entire deal to the ground before I'd let anyone hurt you."

Her eyes widened slightly. "Axel—"

"I'm serious." I reached up, tucking a strand of hair behind her ear. "Screw these investors. Screw the money. You're more important."

For a moment, something flickered in her eyes. Something that looked almost like hope. Like maybe she was starting to believe that someone might actually put her first for once.

"But we're not going to let it come to that," I continued. "We're going to go to this dinner, and we're going to put on the performance of our lives. We're going to make him believe we're so disgustingly in love that he'll have no choice but to back off."

"And you won't hit him?"

I was quiet for a long moment. "I won't hit him unless he gives me a reason to. But if he so much as raises his voice to you, if he makes you feel even slightly uncomfortable ..." I let the threat hang in the air.

She wiped a stray tear. "What if I told you that seeing you get protective over me is maybe the sexiest thing I've ever witnessed?"

Jesus. My heart damn near stopped. "Then I'd say you have terrible taste in what's sexy."

"I have excellent taste actually." The ghost of a smile played at her lips. "For instance, I find it very attractive when a man respects my wishes."

She's trying to manipulate me with flirtation, and damn if it isn't working.

"You're playing dirty, Sunshine."

She smiled, and for the first time since she'd walked in, she looked like my Dakota again. Still hurt, still fragile, but with a spark of that fire I'd fallen for.

Fallen for. When had that happened?

How about right this minute? When she wrapped her arms around me and buried her cheek against my chest like I was her safe haven. When I returned the embrace and kissed the top of her head.

"All right," I said finally, "I'll attempt to behave." During this dinner. But when this was all behind us, if she thought I'd let Mathew go without consequences, she didn't know me. "But I want something in return."

"What?" She pulled back, the absence of her making me feel cold.

"After we've convinced your asshole ex that we're madly in love, you and I are going to have a conversation about what this really is between us."

Her breath hitched. "Axel ..."

"Because, Sunshine, what I'm feeling right now? The way seeing you hurt makes me want to tear the world apart? That's not fake. And I don't think what you're feeling is fake either."

I'd been thinking about Dakota's online persona lately. The perfect image wasn't deceit or vanity. It was armor. Protection. She wasn't my mother, choosing image over getting help; she was choosing survival while she figured out how to trust again. And I could love her enough to let her heal at her own pace, mask and all.

She stared up at me, lips parted, and for a moment, I thought she might admit it. Might finally say what we'd both been dancing around.

Instead, she whispered, "One night. That's all I'm asking for."

One night to convince her ex we're in love. Easy enough, considering my heart was falling hard and fast for her.

"Then let's go show that bastard what real love looks like."

But even as I said it, I was already planning. Mathew was about to learn that when it came to protecting Dakota, I didn't play fair.

And if he so much as made her shed one more tear ...

Well, some promises were meant to be broken.

I waited for her to leave my office. Only then did I open my phone and see an ominous text waiting for me from an unknown number.

Your days are numbered.

32

FAKE FIANCÉE TIP: MAKE SURE YOU HAVE A SAFE WORD. #SAFETYFIRST

DAKOTA

"I've invited three major influencers to this evening's dinner," Rebecca announced, her manicured fingers flying across her phone screen without bothering to look up.

"What?" I stopped pacing mid-stride, my bare feet sliding slightly on Axel's hardwood floor.

The words took a second to register. My mind had been elsewhere. Not just replaying Mathew's harsh words, but stuck on that crawling sensation that had followed me all day. Ever since leaving my parents' house, I couldn't shake the feeling of being watched.

Which made sense actually. Jace had insisted on sending a bodyguard with me. The guy kept his distance, professional and discreet, but he was still there. Watching. That had to be why my skin kept prickling with awareness. What else could it be?

"This is supposed to be a work dinner only," I managed, forcing myself to focus on Rebecca. "Axel's business associates and the brand leaders for my deal."

"And it is. The influencers will be here too."

Oh, that's just ... fan-freaking-tastic.

"This night was already risky enough," I reminded her, probably a little too sharply. "My brand deal just got CPR after flatlining, and it can't handle another shock to the system. Axel's business associates are already side-eyeing our relationship like we're a bad Lifetime movie. Did we really need to compound the potential disaster by adding influencers to document our every potential misstep?"

Honestly.

"You both said you need to sell this story as quickly as possible." She finally glanced up, her perfectly contoured face set in that *I know better than you peasants* expression I was growing to loathe. "So we need to make each event work twice as hard."

Work twice as hard or crash twice as spectacularly?

I tugged at the hem of my oversized sweatshirt, struggling to find another branch in my argument. "You should've run that by us first. I didn't organize enough food for extra head count."

"I took care of that. Ordered catering and staff." Rebecca waved a dismissive hand. "And speaking of extra head count, I took the liberty of inviting your friends."

My jaw dropped. Literally. "Excuse me?"

Rebecca was already back to typing, her acrylic nails clicking against the screen. "It would look suspicious if influencers were invited to your dinner with only business associates attending. We need to round out the guest list to make it less obvious."

"We never agreed to drag our friends into tonight," I argued.

Rebecca stopped typing and leveled me with a glare. "We also never agreed about telling your friends about the fake engagement. You and Axel are the ones who dragged your friends into this in the first place. And we also never agreed to send Axel to a business meeting in a ridiculous pink convertible. We wouldn't even be having this dinner if it weren't for that stunt."

"Hold up." Axel pushed off from the kitchen counter, looking inconveniently good in gray sweatpants and a fitted T-shirt. His hair was doing that messy thing that probably took zero effort. "They were already suspicious before the car thing."

Something warm unfurled in my chest at his defense, but I pushed it down. "I don't want our friends to lie for us."

"Me neither." Axel's voice was firm. "Uninvite them, Rebecca."

"No can do." She didn't even look up from her phone.

I bit down on the inside of my cheek. "Then uninvite the influencers."

"It's too late for that."

"We still have two hours."

"If I suddenly canceled the influencers with this late of notice, that would raise a hell of a lot more suspicion. And by the way, make sure you're both dressed and ready to go early. I don't want them waiting."

Yes, Mom.

"I'm sure they're already suspicious." I started pacing again, my anxiety manifesting in restless energy. "I mean, why do they think they're even coming here?"

"To witness a potential business investment and the finalization of a brand deal with one of the biggest influencers in the country."

"Rebecca, you need to run all major decisions by us first." My voice was getting sharper, tension coiling in my shoulders.

"I'm doing my job," she argued, finally setting her phone down with a sharp click against the marble countertop.

"We hired you," I shot back.

She looked to Axel for support, probably expecting him to take her side, like most people did when faced with Rebecca's particular brand of confident manipulation. Instead, Axel stepped closer to me.

"You heard her." His voice carried an edge. "You work for us, not the other way around."

Holy shit. Was Axel actually taking my side? Again?

Rebecca's perfectly applied foundation couldn't hide the flush creeping up her neck. "Do you want to sell this love story or not? Because when it comes to selling this story, tonight is live TV with no chance for retakes."

Axel and I exchanged a look. One of those wordless communications that had been happening more frequently lately.

"This was supposed to be intimate, Rebecca," Axel said, running a hand through his hair. "This is spiraling out of control. With this many people at the table, do you know how many things could go wrong?"

"They won't go wrong. You two will be on your best behavior. You're madly in love." She gathered her designer purse and jacket. "You kill this dinner, guys, and you might be home free."

I felt a strange mix of relief and something else at the thought of this all being over. Something I didn't want to examine too closely.

"I have to go," Rebecca said, already typing furiously on her phone again. "You two get ready. Early," she repeated, in case we didn't catch that the first time. "If anyone shows up early, we don't need them realizing you get ready in two different rooms. Speaking of which, lock that office door so a snooper can't get in there. Make sure your stuff is in his master suite shower. And, Dakota?" She paused at the door, her smile as sharp as glass. "Don't forget to wear the ring."

I rolled my eyes as the door clicked shut behind her.

The penthouse fell into charged silence. Axel was still looking at me with that expression I couldn't quite read, and suddenly, the space between us felt heated.

"I should"—I gestured vaguely toward the bedroom—"get ready."

He nodded, but his eyes never left mine. "Dakota?"

"Yeah?"

"We've got this."

The certainty in his voice made something warm flood my system. Oddly, I felt like with Axel by my side, I was safe from the hidden dangers of tonight, no matter how irrational that sounded.

After giving him a nod, I slipped into the bedroom and took great care in transforming myself from ordinary woman to fake fiancée extraordinaire. I applied the perfect makeup that gave me a pore-less, airbrushed look, added false eyelashes, styled gentle curls in my strawberry-blonde hair, and slipped into a sapphire custom-tailored dress donated by one of Chicago's high-end designers. Looking at myself in the mirror, I tried to do a little pep talk.

"You can do this," I whispered.

After locking the office/guest bedroom door so you could only get in with the key in Axel's master suite, I emerged and entered the living room.

I swear I saw the air leave Axel's lungs.

His hungry gaze swept slowly from my face to my feet and back up again, like he was memorizing every inch. The path his eyes traveled left a fiery buzz across my skin, as if he'd actually touched me.

"You look ..." He cleared his throat, his voice rougher than usual. "Stunning."

Heat crawled up my neck. "You do too," I managed, nodding toward him.

God, did he ever.

He was wearing a suit I'd never seen before with fitted black fabric that looked like it cost more than a small island, paired with a shirt that was exactly two shades darker than my dress. Color-coordinated. Making us look like we'd stepped out of a magazine spread for "Perfect Couples Who Definitely Aren't Faking It."

Axel walked toward me, pulling a small velvet box from his pocket. The engagement ring. Right. Our little prop.

Per Rebecca's explicit instructions, I'd cleaned it earlier and left it in the box until showtime. Massive sparkles were needed for this massive fraud, evidently.

"May I?" he asked, opening the case.

The diamond caught the light, throwing rainbows across the

ceiling. I lifted my hand, wishing my skin didn't come alive every time he touched me.

With one hand, he gently gripped my wrist, his fingertip brushing against my pulse point, which was currently hammering like a hummingbird's wings. With the other, he slipped the ring onto my finger slowly.

Before it reached its final position, Axel looked up and locked eyes with me.

God help me.

Axel Pierce was the most gorgeous specimen of man I'd ever seen. Eyes that could sparkle with mischief one second and darken with heat the next, making you feel like you were the only person on planet Earth. Beautiful, full lips that would quirk up at my sarcastic jabs before spewing out equally sharp barbs right back. And that jaw. Damn, that jaw was something I could stare at for hours. Get a canvas and paint it over and over, trying to capture the way his dark stubble caught the light.

As if his model-perfect face wasn't enough, the body underneath that suit spoke to years of dedication, turning those muscles into art. The suit looked like Axel was doing it a favor by wearing it.

"You're staring, Sunshine."

I blinked, snapping back to reality. *Shit.* My jaw was literally hanging open.

"You look ..." I stepped back from this bubble of intoxication before I did something stupid. "Nice."

Nice? Really, Dakota? The man looks like sex in a designer suit and you go with nice?

His shoulders rounded as he casually slid his hands into his pockets, tilting his head to study me with those penetrating eyes.

"Nervous?" he asked.

"No," I lied.

He moved to my side, close enough that his heat wrapped around me like a warm hug. "We don't have to do this, you know."

"Yes, we do."

He sighed, staring at me with a slight frown. "You need to escape, you look at me," he said. "We end the dinner. Period."

My muscles' tension began to unwind. There was something so comforting in his words. "You're being awfully nice to me."

His eyes pierced mine, traveling a path of heat straight to my soul. He opened his mouth to say something. Something kind and warm by the looks of it. It wasn't lost on me how different everything felt right now. His protectiveness. The way he'd sided with me against Rebecca. Like something fundamental had shifted between us.

But it also wasn't lost on me that he'd never admit it out loud.

"Ice cubes," he said instead.

"What?"

"You need to escape, you say *ice cubes*. I'll kick everyone out."

I couldn't help but smile. "Ice cubes?"

He shrugged, that cocky smirk playing at the corners of his mouth. "It can be our safe word."

I snorted. "Are we becoming friends, Axel?"

"Never," he said, but his smirk betrayed him. "I still owe you for that glitter cat ride. Did you know the horn actually meowed?"

I pressed my lips together to keep from laughing. "You have to admit, that was masterful."

"I'll never admit to that." His eyes sparkled with delight. "But theoretically, it might've been the best prank I've ever witnessed."

"If all it took was a bouquet of black roses for you to be nice to me, I would've sent you some years ago," I quipped.

Something flashed across his face then. Pain maybe. Regret. The playfulness dimmed, replaced by something deeper, more vulnerable.

Wanting to ease back into lighthearted territories, I nodded toward the good lighting. "Come on. We should snap some photos of our epic romance."

I pretended snuggling up against him wasn't continuing to

spiral me into a new level of want. In fact, the more I thought about it, the more I realized there was something else about this night that was going to be hard for me: pretending to be in love with Axel.

Because it wasn't feeling like pretend anymore.

33

PSA: DON'T START DEEP CONVERSATIONS BEFORE DINNER PARTIES. YOU MIGHT LEARN SOMETHING DEVASTATING. #REGRETIMMINENT

DAKOTA

"Well, that took a lot less time than I thought," I said with surprise. Usually, my photo shoots took an eternity. Straightening every wrinkle, shifting to get different angles of lighting. But with Axel, I just ... relaxed into it. We snapped a few, and they looked great. "Sorry. Looks like we have time to kill before everyone gets here."

"Have a drink with me?"

A drink with me. He's just offering you a beverage, Dakota. This isn't a real date. Stop looking for clues that this matters as much to him as it does you.

I followed him into the kitchen, watching as he poured me a generous glass of red wine and himself an even more generous whiskey. The man had priorities. We drifted toward the living room, where the fireplace was already painting the walls in amber light, and I couldn't help but think this felt dangerously domestic.

"I know tonight's going to be brutal for you." Axel settled beside me on the couch, close enough that I swear my body could FEEL him here, even if I closed my eyes. "Remember the safe word. You say it, I evacuate everyone faster than a fire drill. No questions asked."

I smirked. "Ice cubes."

"Ice cubes."

"We could lose our deals if we do that." I took a sip of wine, letting it warm my throat. "There's actual money on the line here, Pierce."

"Sunshine." His voice dropped to that tone that made my hormones stand at attention. "Some things are infinitely more important than money."

His gaze locked with mine, as if silently ensuring I understood he was referring to me. I mattered more.

"We'll have to post most of tonight on social media," I warned, knowing how much he'd hate that.

Axel stared into his glass like it held the secrets of the universe. Or maybe like he was trying not to say something he'd regret.

I tilted my head, studying his profile. "Can I ask you something?"

His attention snapped back to me with laser focus. "Sunshine, you can ask me anything you want."

The way he said it. Like all pretenses had been stripped away. Maybe it was because in a few minutes, we'd have to perform for an audience all night long, and right now, it was just the two of us, sitting in the calm before the storm. Our storm.

Our only chance to be real. Authentic. No filters, no lies. No pretenses. I mean, my God, we were basically going into battle, where metaphorical lives could be lost. If you can't share true feelings before then, when can you?

"Why do you hate what I do for a living?" I asked.

"Never said I *hated* it."

"You didn't have to. You make it pretty obvious." I swirled my wine, watching the liquid catch the firelight. "Every time I mention work, you get this look. Like you've tasted something sour. And you said, and I quote, 'I don't like when people act one way in public and another way behind closed doors.' "

And then he'd refused to tell me what that meant, even though I could tell it was something deep. Profound. As evidenced by Knox's assessment.

Axel took a long breath, and I could practically see him wrestling with whatever he was holding back. Something big. Something that cut deep.

"Can I ask you a question first?" Axel swiped a thumb along his lower lip.

First. As in he'd finally tell me why he despised my perfectly curated online world. I wanted that answer more than my next breath because I suspected it was the key to understanding the parts of him he kept locked away from everyone else.

"Sure." I took another sip, watching him over the rim of my glass as he gathered his words.

"Why do you work so hard to make every post picture-perfect?" His tone wasn't condescending or sharp, like I expected. Instead, it was soft. Curious. Like he genuinely wanted to understand me better.

"What do you mean?" I hedged.

He tilted his head slightly, studying me with those penetrating blue eyes. "You think I don't see it? The way you use that perfect smile to cover your fear?" His voice grew quieter, more vulnerable. "I lived with a smile like that most of my life."

My breath caught. In all our years of knowing each other, Axel had never offered me more than a hint at whatever haunted his past. But here he was, sharing something raw and real and seeing me in a way that no one ever had before.

"When I first started posting, I noticed the edited ones got more engagement." I shrugged.

Axel studied me for five long seconds. "It was more than that."

Heat flooded my cheeks. How did he see through me so easily? It was like he had X-ray vision, straight to my soul.

I stared into my wine, watching the liquid swirl, like the truth I'd never told anyone that circled around my heart. Not even Scarlett knew this part. Hell, it had taken me years to figure it out myself because my perfectionism had manifested into other things long before social media came around.

After a generous gulp of liquid courage, I confessed something I'd kept buried.

"I guess … after I started building my account, I fell in love with having this online alter ego. I could control everything. My image, my story, the lighting that made me look flawless. Everything."

"You liked the control." It wasn't a question.

"God, yes." I nodded, feeling lighter already. "It was intoxicating. I could paint this picture of a perfect life because inside, my real life felt completely broken."

"Because of Knox." Another statement, delivered with surprising gentleness.

"Before Knox was arrested, my life felt … safe. Predictable. Like each year was a domino falling into the next one, pushing me toward some predetermined happy ending." I smiled, but there was no humor in it. Just painful nostalgia. "After his arrest, it was like someone grabbed the game board and hurled it at the wall. Those dominoes flew everywhere."

Axel studied me, giving me the space to gather my thoughts and continue.

"After his conviction, I became obsessed with organizing things. My closet, every drawer, every cabinet. When I ran out of physical spaces to control, I put that into school, work, and eventually, I moved online. Same perfectionism, different platform."

"Dakota …" His voice was rough.

"But it wasn't just the organization thing." I was on a roll now, years of suppressed truth spilling out. "After Knox was convicted, we lost family friends. I lost friends too. They didn't say it outright, but they stopped coming around. And when we'd bump into them at the grocery store or whatever, you could see it in their eyes. They looked at us differently. All of us. Like we were these imperfections staining the world."

I paused, remembering those looks. The way conversations would die when we walked into a room.

"I wish I could say it didn't mess with my head, but it did. For a while, I felt"—I searched for the right word—"dirty. Like I needed to scrub myself clean, but couldn't reach the stain."

He took a sip of his drink, looking part furious at those people for making me feel this way, but part enthralled, learning everything that made me tick. "So, you created a perfect online persona because you thought that was what people wanted to see."

"I figured if I wasn't perfect, I'd be cast aside. Again." I met his eyes, surprised by the fierce protectiveness I saw there. "I know logically that wasn't true, but feelings don't always listen to logic."

"Knox's actions have nothing to do with you or your family." The steel in his voice meant everything to me.

"It got worse when my parents started struggling financially. More people disappeared from our lives. It was like we were only worthy of love when everything was perfect. So, I decided to give people what they wanted to see." I took a shaky breath, surprised by how raw this felt. "I loved that control. I could edit out the days I spent crying and only show the ones where I was smiling. I could crop out the vacation disasters and only post the postcard-worthy moments. It became my way of creating the version of myself I wanted to be while editing out the parts I wanted to erase."

My eyes burned, but I blinked the tears back.

"And people responded to that," Axel realized, his voice soft. "Which reinforced the idea that you had to be perfect to be loved."

Well, damn. "I'd never thought about it like that before."

"You're wrong, Dakota." He set down his glass so he could focus all his attention on me. His gaze traveled down my body, then back to my face, searching my eyes to make sure I was paying attention to every word he said. "The real you is the perfect you. The real you is the one I want to see. I want to see your mistakes. I want to see you fall down and get back up. Hell, if accidentally posting that photo of me counts as a mistake, then I'm grateful for it. Because without that 'mistake,' I wouldn't be sitting here, having this conversation with you."

Holy hell. It felt like a barbed wire that had been wrapped around my heart broke free and my heart beat fully for the first time since Knox's arrest.

"You say that like you're actually happy I posted that image," I teased.

"What if I am?" He leaned closer, throwing his arm behind the sofa. "Because it forced us to spend time together when we normally would have avoided each other like the plague."

Axel unleashed the full power of his gaze on me, and I swore I could feel the distance between us collapsing, gravity bending around him like he had his own pull. Heat spread from my heart to places that had no business warming up during an impromptu therapy session.

I was starting to think he might be right. Maybe mistakes and imperfections were the real beauty in life. The unplanned moments that became the most precious memories of all.

Like this moment. Sitting on this couch, realizing I was falling hard and fast for a man who saw me better than I saw myself.

"That night ..." I worried my lip between my teeth, nodding. "I'd found out Mathew was back in town. And he hadn't even reached out to me."

"Mmm ..." Axel didn't seem surprised. In fact, he cocked his head. "These last few years, everything in your life was finally going according to plan. Your social media business was exploding, you left corporate America to become your own boss, and you thought you'd found the love of your life."

I groaned. "I can't believe I thought Mathew was *the one*. What was I thinking?"

"Point is, your real life was finally matching your online fantasy. But then it all came crashing down in spectacular fashion when Mathew chose his career over you. And when he came back into town without even reaching out?" He paused, letting that sink in. "That night, you felt it all: the gap between the life you wanted and the one you were actually living."

I sighed. Somehow, understanding this healed wounds inside of me that I hadn't even realized were there. Most days, I chose to believe that any pain from my past was in the past. That it didn't haunt my heart or my actions in the present, but looking back now, I could see each hurt influenced how I interpreted the world and people around me.

With a cracked lens.

His voice went soft again. "I understand you a lot better now."

I understand myself a lot better too, I thought. I now understood that my belief system had been completely backward. That I didn't have to be perfect to be loved. That Axel seemed to love everything about me. Imperfections and all.

His acceptance of my authentic self—the good, the bad, the broken—made me question everything. I mean, look at us now. With no cameras rolling, he was choosing to spend time with me. To see me. To hear me, and to challenge my belief that my worth lay in perfection.

Axel was bringing out the messy, unpredictable, authentic me. The one that liked how she looked with no makeup and messy hair and in sweats. The one that let air out of his tires and hired a pink kitty car just to get a rise out of him.

But with this newfound authenticity came a bucket of dangerous feelings. The more I tried to control the narrative, the more I risked losing this unexpected connection forming with the one person I never expected to trust.

Which forced me to confront an uncomfortable truth: What if the vulnerability I feared was actually the path to everything I ever wanted? Career success, genuine connection, love I never thought possible?

Looking back, every staged kiss for the camera felt like maybe it'd lingered too long. Every casual touch ignited feelings I couldn't script or control, to the point where I found myself both dreading and anticipating our public appearances. What started as a performance quickly blurred the lines, especially during private moments when no one was watching.

Moments that were starting to mean everything to me.

Oh God. The realization hit me like a punch to the esophagus. I wasn't just falling for him. I was already there, standing at the edge of the cliff, ready to jump.

And that's when the fear kicked in. Because Axel might be starting to know me better, but Chicago's biggest playboy had never been in an authentic relationship before. What made me think I'd be any different?

Maybe understanding him would help me figure out if I was setting myself up for heartbreak.

"You hated that I hid my imperfections," I recalled. "That all I showed was perfectionism. Why?"

Axel's entire body went rigid. "Because," he said, his voice deadly quiet, "I know what happens when the perfect image becomes more important than the person behind it." He stood abruptly, moving toward the fireplace, his back to me. "I've watched someone I loved die, trying to be perfect for the camera."

34

HE'S ABOUT TO FINALLY TELL ME SOMETHING THAT CHANGES EVERYTHING ... #WORSTTIMING

AXEL

I stared at the amber liquid in my glass, watching it catch the low light of my penthouse as I swirled it. The ice clinked against crystal—a sound that still reminded me of my mother's nervous habit of fidgeting with her jewelry when my father started yelling.

Dakota sat on the sofa, her strawberry-blonde hair falling in soft waves around her shoulders. The woman who'd driven me crazy for years was looking at me with genuine curiosity rather than the carefully curated sympathy she used for her followers. She'd asked why. Why I hated her meticulously constructed online persona so much. It was a fair question. One I'd been avoiding since this fake engagement began.

I downed the whiskey in one burning gulp, buying myself a few more seconds.

"In public, we were the perfect family." I set the empty glass down with more force than necessary. "My mom never had a hair out of place. She always had crimson-red lipstick on. Always. Never left the house without it. Not even to go to the mailbox."

Dakota remained silent, her gaze steady on mine.

"You'd never see a wrinkle in her clothes or a chip in her

nails." I pushed up the sleeve of my shirt an inch, absently tracing one of the tattoos that crawled up my forearm. Ink that had been my first act of rebellion against that perfect image.

"Everyone aspired to be like us, at least in our circle." The muscles along my spine went rigid. "They were always commenting about wishing they had this or they had that."

I sat down, put my glass on the coffee table, and put my elbows on my knees. "I hated when they said that because it made it so hard to keep my mouth shut. And that was rule number one." I tapped my finger against the coffee table. "You never showed anybody your weaknesses."

Dakota's expression softened, and she reached out like she might touch my hand, but pulled back at the last second. Smart woman. I wasn't sure I could handle her touch right now.

"Behind closed doors," I continued, my voice dropping to nearly a whisper, forcing her to lean in, "we were an absolute train wreck."

I stood abruptly, needing to move, to put distance between us. The floor-to-ceiling windows offered a view of the Chicago skyline, twinkling like a promise that never delivered. I pressed my palm against the cool glass.

"My dad cheated often and was quick to anger. My mom hated him." I stared at my reflection, superimposed over the city lights. "But most of all, they loved fighting. I think they loved fighting more than they loved me."

When I turned back, Dakota had tears in her eyes. That was the problem with real emotions. They were messy, unpredictable. Nothing like the perfect selfies we all posted.

"I was never abused," I clarified quickly, shrugging one shoulder.

"Axel ..." she started, but I cut her off with a sharp gesture.

"Aside from that," I continued, "it was a house of horrors. Broken glasses and dinner plates being thrown across the wall." I closed my eyes briefly, could still hear the crystal shatter, followed by my mother's perfect, practiced laugh when the neighbors called to check if everything was okay.

"Just a clumsy moment. Everything's fine here!"

"It's one of the reasons that when I left that all behind, I didn't care who saw me for who I really was." I ran a hand through my hair, messing it up in a way that would have horrified my mother. "I was somebody that had no interest in long-term relationships, and I wasn't going to pretend like I wanted one."

I returned to the couch, but didn't sit, instead bracing my hands on the back of it, needing the physical barrier.

"In fact, I leaned into it. Authenticity and all that, I guess." My lips curved into a bitter smile. "I never set out to create this image of myself as a playboy. I was just being young and unattached and not afraid to show the truth."

Dakota nodded slowly, understanding dawning in her eyes. "And then the next thing you knew, people were taking photos and putting them online."

"Exactly." I nodded. "Maybe it was an act of rebellion, leaning into it. Maybe I enjoyed when my parents would get upset, seeing their son destroying their perfect image."

The admission cost me, each word feeling like it was being ripped from somewhere deep and private. "Church-going, pearl-clutching, country-club perfection," I spat. "I don't know. I suppose it was a way of rebelling while also just being true to myself."

I fidgeted with my watch.

"That's why I hated the social media side of your business so much," I admitted, finally looking directly into her eyes. "Every perfect post, every flawless photo ... it reminded me of my mother's crimson lipstick. Beautiful on the surface, hiding something broken underneath."

Dakota's breath caught audibly. "You thought I was like her."

It wasn't a question, but I answered anyway.

"I did." Past tense. I let that hang between us, an admission of its own.

Her hand found mine in the space between us, her touch tentative but warm. "And now?" she whispered.

The question lingered, dangerous and full of possibility.

"Now I know you're not," I answered.

She swallowed, her shoulders relaxing like this took a tremendous weight off of them. "How did I not know this before?"

Which was fair. She was, after all, Knox's sister. And she was friends with Scarlett, who was dating Jace. Jace, someone in my inner circle, who knew my demons. But I'd been clear with the guys I considered brothers long ago that my business was my own, and it meant a lot to me that they hadn't shared my past with anyone.

"Because like you, I don't like people to see what I keep hidden."

She seemed to consider this, her beautiful eyes dancing in the orange light of the fire. I knew what she was waiting for: for me to continue with the hardest part to admit.

"My mom started drinking to cope with my father's verbal cruelty," I continued. "The constant criticism, the cutting remarks, the way he'd tear her down. I didn't see that her drinking had become an issue. Not right away at least." But I should have. "Once I did, I begged her to get help."

My stomach clenched at the memory of that night. The crystal tumbler in her trembling hand. The way her perfect lipstick had smeared slightly at the corner. The first crack in her flawless facade I'd seen in years.

"Please, Mom." My voice broke like I was still seventeen instead of a grown man. "I'll do anything. Please."

Her eyes, once the same color as mine, were now bloodshot and glassy. They darted toward the window like the neighbors might be watching. Even drunk, even falling apart, she was still performing.

"I don't want anyone to find out!" She pressed her manicured hand to her mouth like she could stuff the sound back in.

"Who gives a damn what people think, Mom? You need help!" I reached for the glass, but she clutched it tighter.

"I care!" She recoiled. "I don't want people to see me as a mess. Do you know what the neighbors would say? People at church? We're the family they aspire to be, Axel."

My heart shattered. Even now, even like this, it was about the image.

"You're not a mess, Mom. You have a disease." I tried to keep my voice gentle, but desperation bled through every word. "A treatable disease."

She laughed. Bitter, broken. "Do you know what they'd say? Poor Richard. His wife is one of those people. *They'd look at your father with pity. They'd whisper about us at church."*

"They'll see you're human, Mom. They'll be proud. I'll be proud that you took the brave step to seek help." I moved closer, close enough to smell the vodka on her breath. "Please. I need you here. I can't sit back and watch something happen to you."

"Nothing's going to happen." She reached for the bottle.

"Please," I begged, and I felt the tears start, hot and desperate. "If you're worried what people will think, we can find a discreet treatment facility. We can tell everyone you went on vacation or something. A spa retreat. Whatever story you want."

Terror filled her eyes. "They'll find out, Axel. They always do. They gossip, and someone always talks."

My chest felt like it was caving in. "And that's more important than me? Than being here for your son?"

The question suspended between us like a guillotine. She looked at me—really looked at me—for the first time in months. For a heartbeat, I thought I'd gotten through.

Then she straightened her shoulders, smoothed her hair, and became the perfect society wife again. "Axel," she chided, like I was being dramatic, like I was the problem, "nothing's going to happen."

. . .

I blinked away the memory, forcing myself back to the present, to Dakota's pain-filled face. "That was the last thing she ever said to me." My voice came out raw, scraped hollow. "Not *I love you*. Not *please forgive me for putting our public image above your needs.* Just ... 'Nothing's going to happen.' "

Dakota's hand flew to her mouth. "Axel ..."

"She got behind the wheel that night. Wrapped her car around a tree." I stared into the fire, watching the flames dance. "The police said she was doing sixty in a thirty-five zone. No skid marks. No attempt to brake."

The air seemed to thicken, heavy with unspoken understanding.

"I replay that conversation almost every day of my life. Wondering if I'd said something different, could I have saved her?"

Dakota stood and crossed to me, her hand settling on my arm. "It wasn't your fault."

"Maybe if I hadn't gone along with her compulsive need to continually live a lie ..." I let the sentence die. There was no point in finishing it.

And as the silence stretched between us again, Dakota let my profession sink even deeper into her heart, realizing something.

"I had no idea this fake engagement was this hard for you," she whispered. "No wonder you were so angry with me in the beginning."

"I was being a jackass."

"With good reason," she said, shaking her head. "I'm surprised you went along with it."

I was too. "I almost backed out on more than one occasion."

"Why didn't you?"

"My business," I reminded her. "The employees depending on keeping their jobs. As ex-cons, they'd have a damn hard time finding another. Not to mention the thousands of people they help across the country with reentry services so they can actually rebuild their lives after prison."

Dakota's eyes stayed fixed on my face, in awe and fascination. "Was your business inspired by Knox?"

I allowed several seconds to pass. "My mother died because she was too ashamed to get help for her addiction. Society told her that perfect people don't have problems like that." My voice lowered. "Meanwhile, guys like Knox get written off the moment they make one mistake. I built this company for everyone society has decided isn't worth saving."

She shifted, as if the weight of all of this was heavy on her heart. "Still, you must have hated everything about this fake engagement."

I swept a stray hair from her face, letting my fingers linger on her skin, and decided if I was being honest, then I needed to tell her the truth.

"I didn't hate the idea of spending time with you."

She smiled slightly, but then her expression fell, her eyes darting to the ground, as if she was processing something profound. It took her several seconds to say it, and when she did, her voice was low, like she was talking to herself more than me.

"This is what I'm personifying." Dakota's voice was laced with disgust. "I'm the kind of person who makes your family think they have to be perfect."

"That's not true."

"It is," she insisted. "But that's not who I want to be."

"Sunshine ..." I drew my knuckles along her jaw. Her skin was impossibly soft. "Makeup, designer dresses, and good lighting don't make you responsible for other people's choices. I'm sorry I ever made you feel like that."

I could tell she didn't agree with me, that something fundamental had shifted in her eyes, but to her strong, brave credit, she didn't belabor the point. I suspected it was because she didn't want to make this moment about *her*.

"Everyone is guilty of showing their best side for the cameras, Dakota. Some people just do it more than others."

She looked to the ground, shaking her head. "No wonder you

never wanted real relationships. After watching your parents' 'perfect' marriage destroy itself, who would want that?"

I stilled.

Tell her. I'd told her everything else, and if I was going to be honest with Dakota, I needed to come clean about this too.

Hell, I was being a hypocrite if I didn't tell her. She'd been hiding her imperfect family from the public because she thought it made her unlovable. And now I was afraid to tell her about another chapter in my imperfect past because I was scared it would drive her away.

But as I looked at her, at this beautiful woman who'd just trusted me with her deepest wounds, the words stuck in my throat.

It didn't help that Dakota took a step closer to me, that my gaze was wandering all over her face, neck, and shoulders. That with her heat this close to my skin, I was wondering what she'd do if I pressed her against the wall and kissed her all over her body.

"Dakota," I murmured.

Her eyes dropped to my mouth, then back up, and I saw my own desperate need reflected there.

"You make me want to stop being afraid of being seen," she whispered.

For the first time in my life, I was with someone who knew what it felt like to carry the burden of other people's expectations. Someone who understood the suffocating weight of always having to be perfect.

And maybe this was selfish of me, but I wanted to hold on to this moment for just a moment longer before risking it with a truth that might send her running.

I leaned closer, and she didn't pull away.

35

POV: ONE HEARTBEAT AWAY FROM THE KISS THAT COULD CHANGE EVERYTHING. #NOGOINGBACK

DAKOTA

"Dakota ..." he murmured, tucking another strand of hair behind my ear. But his knuckles lingered along my jaw, rough against my skin, while my lungs decided to forget how to function properly.

Holy shit.

His touch scorched through me in waves, and his gaze dropped to my mouth and stayed there.

One second.

Two.

Three.

And then—*holy shit*—he tilted his head, drawing achingly closer.

My brain short-circuited, rifling through a highlight reel of moments I'd been trying to ignore. The image of him sleeping with his back to the wall the night when he was worried about my safety. The way he'd admitted he'd been attracted to me all those years ago, before Knox had made me off-limits. How he'd caged me against that couch with fire in his gaze, telling me exactly what he'd do to my body and how explosive it would be. The way he'd just protected me from Rebecca's snarky comments.

But mostly, I realized in this moment that I wanted his lips on mine again. This time without influencers or cameras. Wanted to taste him, pull him closer, feel the heat of his mouth work down my neck and—

The elevator hummed to life.

Axel froze, his mouth inches from mine. His gaze snapped to the door, then back to me. We locked eyes in silent understanding. Heat and desire and disappointment swirling between us like a storm gathering strength.

What do you do when you start to fall for the guy you absolutely shouldn't want?

No. I couldn't think about that right now. Had to keep my mind sharp and focused. Because we were about to face a room full of suspicious people, and we had a story to sell.

The elevator doors opened with a soft ding, spilling the first of our guests into the foyer. Reality crashed back in, but something fundamental had shifted in those stolen moments when the world had narrowed to just us.

Axel stepped back, his professional mask sliding into place, but his eyes lingered on mine for one more heartbeat. A silent promise that we were in this together.

"Mathew." I smiled, pretending not to notice his glare. "Jennifer." One of the influencers. "It's so nice to see you."

"Are we the first to arrive?" Jennifer's eyes widened, and she checked the time. "I didn't mean to get here this early. Chicago traffic is so unpredictable."

"It's fine," I managed, though my voice sounded strained, even to my own ears.

Jennifer being early was clearly a mistake. The genuine surprise on her face said as much. But Mathew? Based on the way he stood there, hands shoved deep in his pockets, shoulders tense, this wasn't an accident. He'd planned this.

Of course he had.

We had at least twenty minutes before anyone else aside from the waitstaff would show. And they were currently confined to the kitchen. Maybe more than twenty. And suddenly, the spacious penthouse felt like it was shrinking around me.

It was strange how quickly everything could shift. Minutes ago, I'd been floating on cloud nine, wrapped in Axel's intimacy, feeling like maybe, just maybe, I was exactly where I belonged. Now, with Mathew standing in here, it felt like someone had flipped a switch.

My pulse kicked up in my throat, a trapped-bird flutter that made swallowing difficult. I forced my feet to stay planted when every instinct screamed to move as my mind painfully replayed all the awful things Mathew had said to me.

Funny how your heart can break for someone who doesn't deserve it.

"This way," Axel said, his voice cutting through the tension. "We can have some drinks while we wait for the others."

We made small talk for a couple of minutes, but Axel's worried gaze kept glancing at me, taking in my discomfort. Then he'd tighten his jaw and look at Mathew, the source of my obvious pain.

"Please"—Axel drew our guests into the dining room, the one with privacy and a magnificent view of the city—"take a seat. If you'll excuse us, Dakota and I need to attend to something."

"Oh, what a view!" Jennifer smiled, sitting down.

Mathew glared at Axel. Like he knew he was up to something.

Which, in fairness, he was ...

36

DINNER PARTY 101: FIRST ORGASMS SHOULDN'T BE WITH YOUR EX IN THE NEXT ROOM. 🔥💀 #SITUATIONALAWARENESS

DAKOTA

"Come here," Axel said.

What was he up to? Maybe pulling me aside to ensure I was okay? But the look on his face looked less reassuring and more ... well, mischievous.

He drew me to the far corner of the living room, theoretically out of sight from Jennifer and Mathew, but still. Axel pulled me closer by the hand, then wrapped his arm around my waist, tugging my chest against his.

"What are you doing?" I pressed both palms against his shoulders, desperate for distance. My heart hammered against my ribs like it was trying to escape. Or reach out and touch Axel ...

He tilted his head, genuinely surprised he had to explain. In one swift move, he pressed my back to the wall, and his palms bracketed my head, caging me in.

"Making it look real," he whispered. "And showing him what he's missing."

Oh.

"This isn't what I meant ..."

"Relax, Sunshine." The gentle smile tugging at his lips was

meant to reassure me, I guess. But his knuckles drifting down my neck were all sorts of distracting.

"No, Axel," I whispered. "I meant we should get our stories straight, maybe hold hands or something. Not ... this." I gestured frantically between us. "This is too much."

"Trust me, hand-holding isn't going to convince anyone." His knuckles dipped lower, then trailed down my side.

"But I don't want to make Mathew *jealous*," I hissed, trying to duck under his arm. "That's not who I am. I just wanted him to see I've moved on, that I'm happy—"

"Same thing." His voice was maddeningly calm.

"It's not the same thing at all." My voice came out as an angry whisper.

Axel's expression softened slightly, but he didn't move away. "You asked for my help, Dakota. Let me help you."

"Not like this." I shook my head, but even as I protested, I was acutely aware of how solid he felt, how his proximity was making my thoughts scatter. "I can't do this to Mathew. It's cruel."

"And he wasn't cruel to you?"

Er ... not the point.

"He broke your heart," Axel reminded me, his voice dropping lower. "Twice."

"That's not ..." I started to argue, but then his fingers traced along my lips, and my words died in my throat.

Oh no.

My mouth opened involuntarily, and worse, much worse, I felt my resolve crumbling like a house of cards at his touch. Case in point, a sharp breath escaped as his heat penetrated my skin and shot straight to my core.

His fingers drifted down my neck, knuckles grazing my collarbone again, this time with maddening slowness.

"I guarantee you've never had a man like me, Sunshine," he murmured, and despite every rational thought screaming at me to stop this, my body was betraying me completely.

"Axel ..." I meant it as a warning, but it came out more like a breathless plea.

"Stop thinking so much," he said, reading the war playing out on my face. "Just for once, stop being so damn noble. Pretend you're bent over my desk," he whispered against my ear. "Legs spread, arms bound behind you, like an offering."

Holy crap. Dirty talk. He was trying to disarm me with dirty talk.

And you know what? It was working.

Heat exploded across my cheeks, but his boldness was contagious. Liberating.

I trailed my palm down his chest, feeling brazen for the first time in my life. "My legs would be spread, but you'd be the one making offerings."

His eyes darkened, and a devilish smirk spread across his face. "My tongue between your thighs, making you come more times than any man ever has."

The words hung between us, heavy with promise.

"Which is how many times, Sunshine?" he challenged, evidently wanting to know what number to beat in this fantasy of ours.

I opened my mouth, but the lie stuck to my tongue. Of course he picked up on it. Axel picked up on everything.

"How many times has a guy made you come?"

Which I guess was fair. Yes, I'd lost my virginity to Mathew, but there were three other bases in the game of sexual "baseball." I'd never explicitly said I hadn't done other things with guys.

"I ..." I swallowed. "Never."

He went still. "Never?" But instead of mockery, his mouth quirked up in something almost tender.

"I just ... couldn't relax enough."

His smile widened. Not laughing at me, more like he found my confession endearing. "You're so uptight."

I shoved him playfully. "I don't trust people easily. And *that* ..."

"Coming."

Heat incinerated my cheeks. Something his eyes tracked, naturally. "It's the most intimate thing you can do with someone."

He tilted his head, his infuriatingly electric touch drifting down my neck. "Tell me, Sunshine, you think you'd be able to come for me?"

Yes. "Not a chance in hell."

His eyes electrified with something predatory. Like I'd just become his personal conquest.

And the thing was ... I didn't hate that idea. Not even a little. Especially when Axel's lips pressed just beneath my ear, drawing a line of kisses down my jaw.

Part of me screamed to push him away. Reminding myself this was fake and these feelings surfacing with each press of his lips were very much real. In fact, this was exactly what I'd been afraid of.

But my resistance drowned beneath the waters of desire when Axel's mouth met mine. I wanted to pretend in this moment that Axel wanted me as much as he was pretending he did.

When his lips parted mine, I opened for him eagerly, inviting his tongue to sweep against my own. The electricity that exploded in my mouth drew a groan from my throat, and suddenly, we were moving in perfect sync. He stepped impossibly closer, and I could feel the hard length of his desire pressing against my thigh.

I smiled against our kiss, thrilled this was affecting him too.

Threading my fingers through his hair, I anchored myself to him as our kiss deepened. And suddenly, nothing else existed in my world anymore. All the problems faded away, and the only thing that existed were Axel's lips, his hand skating down my collarbone, and then his palm pressing against my breast.

I sucked in a sharp breath, and I felt his lips curve against mine.

But then his mouth abandoned mine, trailing fresh kisses down my jaw as his hand slid to my thigh, inching the fabric of my dress up.

"What are you doing?" I hissed.

"You have no idea what I can do with my tongue."

"No," I said quickly. Even though—let's be clear—what my hormones wanted was to kick everyone out, permanently disable the elevator, and strip naked to find out exactly how skilled he was with that tongue of his. "Someone could walk in."

He sighed. "I'm not going to use my tongue right now," he clarified. Shockingly, I was more disappointed than I should have been. What the hell was wrong with me? And why was the phrase *right now* bouncing around in my head like a squealing cheerleader? "Let me talk dirty to you instead."

Oh ... that was new.

I nodded. So, he continued, kissing my neck, trailing his fingers up my leg.

"I'd lick you slow. Up and down, coming so close to where you need it that it torments you."

His hand slipped under my dress hem, rising higher to my inner thigh.

"Only after you beg do I finally take that perfect bundle of nerves into my mouth and swirl it with my tongue." His voice was pure sin. "I wonder ... what do you taste like, Sunshine?"

His fingertips played with the edge of my panties, and the pulsing between my legs became unbearable.

"And how would you take me?" I managed, the wicked part of my mind wondering aloud.

"The way I've imagined for years," he growled. "Slow at first. Sinking into you inch by delicious inch."

The way he said it implied there was a lot to take.

The throbbing between my legs intensified. Heated. And begged for mercy.

I gasped when his finger traced over the thin fabric covering my sex.

"Soaked for me, Sunshine," he whispered approvingly against my ear.

"Yes," was all I could manage, but my hips rocked forward even more, pressing more desperately against his touch.

"If you don't want me to touch your bare flesh, tell me now," he warned.

He was giving me an out, I realized. One last chance to back away before he touched me without barriers.

In response, I rocked my hips into him. I couldn't tell him no. Hell, I wanted him so badly that if I had my way, we'd abandon this dinner party and ravage each other all night.

The strange thing was, this wasn't just sexual either. I felt a connection with Axel that I hadn't felt before. I had always assumed that Chicago's biggest playboy would just take what he wanted and go. But that wasn't Axel at all. With me, he understood me, understood what I needed, understood what I wanted, even more than I did.

"No man has ever made you come?" he whispered. Possessive. Angry. Determined.

I shook my head.

The fresh hunger in his eyes made me even hotter. His finger slipped past the fabric to stroke my bare flesh.

I bit my lip to swallow my groan as he worked me with expert precision, pressing two fingers against my most sensitive spot and beginning to swirl.

Oh my God. He knew exactly what he was doing. The pressure, the motion. He knew my body better than I did.

And the thing was, unlike any other time in my life, with *him*, I relaxed into his touch.

"Dakota," he growled in my ear, "I'm going to bury my fingers in you." Holy hell. "And you're going to pretend it's me sinking deep inside you."

Good Lord.

He circled that bundle of nerves while kissing my neck, my collarbone, then worked his mouth back to mine.

Pulling back slightly, he locked eyes with me and slid two fingers deep inside, watching my head fall back against the wall, my mouth slack. His lips curved up as he pulled out slightly, then pushed deeper. My body stretched and wrapped around him, trembling in ways I'd never experienced.

"You're perfect, Sunshine," he whispered. "So tight."

He moved his fingers with skill, curling them to hit something inside me that made my hips jerk, and his mouth hitched with knowing satisfaction.

"Never felt that before, have you?"

I swallowed, shaking my head.

Then he added his thumb to that external bundle of nerves, swirling as he pumped his fingers inside me. Heat coiled in my belly as the sensation built.

Axel worked my body like he owned it. Like I was his.

And I was.

I thought about all those times I'd seen him when he was in college, how I'd dreamed of this moment: feeling him inside me, his hands on my body. All our heated exchanges over the years had carried an undercurrent that had nothing to do with hostility and everything to do with unfulfilled desire.

Now Axel was claiming me, branding me. Somehow, I knew that no matter what happened after this, I'd never be the same. I'd never settle for a man who couldn't give me *this*.

Something began to uncoil in my stomach, something I'd never felt with any other man. I gripped his shoulders suddenly, and he drew his mouth to my ear.

"Come for me, Sunshine."

His eyes locked on mine as my body shattered around him, crashing and surrendering. He moved his hand like an expert, drawing out every ripple until my muscles melted into submission. All while keeping our gazes locked with each other in what was the most intimate moment of my life.

After, he kept his fingers inside me, studying my face.

"Even better than I imagined, Sunshine."

Better than I ever did too. I mean, my word, if he was that

skilled with fingers, what could he do with his tongue? His body? I wanted to know. Needed to know.

"You've imagined this before?" I breathed.

He pushed himself deeper inside of me one last time. "Every single day since the moment I saw you."

Holy ... did he just say that?

He pulled his fingers out slowly, so slowly, my body ached with the loss of him. And then, keeping his eyes locked on mine, he drew them to his mouth. Closing his eyes with a groan.

"And you taste even better than I imagined too."

Oh. My. Word.

Only as my orgasm faded did his words anchor me back to reality. But suddenly, I wasn't sure what had just happened.

Had Axel and I surrendered to something real between us? Or was this just a moment of convenient pleasure he could enjoy with any woman? Did this hit him as deeply as it hit me?

Before I could find my voice to ask though, a flash of movement caught my eye.

Mathew stood frozen in the space between the dining room and living room, his face a mask of shock and rage. I'd forgotten all about him, I realized. In this heated moment with Axel, a heated moment that had started as a way to make Mathew jealous and escalated into something beyond sensual, I had forgotten all about the man who'd broken my heart. Chains had broken free. And my heart launched in one direction: toward Axel.

The problem was, Mathew launched in a direction of his own: toward Axel too. His fist connected with Axel's jaw with a sickening crack.

But instead of stumbling back, Axel straightened slowly, swiping his lip with his thumb, looking at Mathew with a smile that was pure predator.

"Problem, Mathew?" he drawled. "You walked away from a goddess. Now you get a front-row seat to watch someone else treat her like the treasure she actually is. Because she's mine now."

37

POV: INVESTORS ON ONE SIDE, YOUR MORTAL ENEMY ON THE OTHER, AND HER TASTE STILL ON YOUR TONGUE. #UNFINISHEDBUSINESS

AXEL

The delicious taste of Dakota lingered on my tongue. So did the rage, the burning need to beat Mathew into an unrecognizable pile of flesh. But when his fist connected with my jaw, something crystallized in that moment: a few punches wouldn't be enough. He deserved to suffer for what he'd put Dakota through.

I hoped he'd gotten a good look at her coming all over my hand.

I could tell he was seriously considering round two. Hell, I'd have let him take another swing. Would've hit him back twice as hard, obviously, but seeing that raw agony twisting his face? Priceless.

Too bad the elevator chose that exact moment to open, spilling out a fresh wave of guests and killing whatever reckoning had been building between us. The tension was still there though, crackling like the thunder of a coming storm.

This wasn't over. Not even close. But for now, we had guests to deal with. Deals to close. Business to handle.

As people filtered into the dining room, including my friends,

I glanced down at my buzzing phone. The name on the screen made me grind my molars.

AXEL'S PINK PUSSY WAGON SUPPORT GROUP CHAT

Blake: The victim of your tire slashing is here? [Sends GIF of eating popcorn.] This is better than pay-per-view.

Ryker: $50 says Axel redecorates his face by the end of the night.

Jace: You're on. He'll behave in front of important investors. Right, Axel?

Jace: Right??????

Jace: Your silence is concerning. And your murder face is showing.

Me: Don't you have something better to do? Like stay on your PI to trace down that blocked number who sent me that creepy text?

Jace: He's working on it. Still hitting dead ends. Professional job, whoever it was. Meanwhile, maybe worry about the very real threat sitting three seats away, plotting your demise.

Me: Stop texting. It looks suspicious to the influencers. Who might see your chat, by the way. Could you BE more obvious? Maybe wave some neon signs while you're at it.

Blake: For someone whose clothes are suspiciously wrinkled, you're in a bad mood. Did you get dressed in a tornado? Or were you ... busy?

Ryker: Ew. I have so many questions, but most importantly: Couldn't you wait until AFTER dinner to do whatever you did with your "fake" fiancée? Is this table a biohazard now?

Jace: Gross. I'm switching seats. I don't want your pheromones all over my salmon.

Me: Shut up. Put your phones away. And play along.

Ryker: Mathew looks like you pissed in his drink. The man is practically vibrating with rage. His eye is literally twitching. I'm counting the twitches. We're at 47.

Blake: He's been staring at you for five minutes straight WITHOUT BLINKING. It's like a really awkward nature documentary.

Jace: And here, we observe the deflated tire victim in his natural habitat, preparing to strike his unsuspecting prey with what appears to be ... a butter knife? The prey, meanwhile, is marking his territory by aggressively holding his fake fiancée's hand.

Blake: Mathew's blood pressure is visibly 180/110. I can see his carotid from here. If he doesn't stroke out, you might kill him.

Ryker: Axel, as your future lawyer, I need you to stop glaring at him like that. That demonstrates premeditation.

Blake: Pulse check: His temple vein is spelling out "murder" in Morse code.

Jace: $300 says Mathew tries to propose to Faith mid-dinner just to be petty.

Blake: Counter bet: $500 says Axel snaps the second Mathew breathes in Dakota's direction.

Ryker: Should we start a betting pool on which utensil becomes evidence first?

Me: I will murder all three of you.

Jace: Thought you already called dibs on murdering Mathew. Don't get greedy.

Ryker: Oh shit, dinner's starting. This is happening. CODE RED, CODE RED.

Blake: Someone needs to live stream this for posterity. Future generations need to know how Axel died.

Jace: Showtime, gentlemen. Place your final bets. Death by steak knife or wine bottle to the head?

Blake: May the best fake boyfriend win.

Ryker: My money's still on Axel. Fake feelings hit harder than real ones, apparently.

Jace: [Renames the group chat to The Real Housewives of Chicago: Axel's Meltdown Edition.]

Blake: [Renames the group chat to Live from the Tire Slasher vs. Flat-Tire Victim Fight.]

Me: I hate all of you.

Blake: Love you too, bro. Now smile pretty for the cameras. Mathew's in shanking range.

38

PSA: IF YOUR EX HEARD YOU GETTING ROMANTIC WITH YOUR FAKE FIANCÉE, MAKE SURE HE DOESN'T HAVE DIRT TO SHARE ... 💣 #REVENGESERVED

DAKOTA

Rebecca had transformed the space into something that belonged in a magazine spread. *Okay, I'll give her this one.* The woman knew how to sell a fantasy. The table had been extended to accommodate our ridiculous guest list: Axel and me (the happy couple), Blake, Jace, Ryker, Faith, Tessa, Scarlett, Frank and Carl from Axel's business deal, three influencers, two reps for my brand deal, and of course, Mathew. Because nothing would make us less nervous than having a massive audience for this performance.

The crisp white tablecloth cascaded to the floor like fresh snow, and the centerpiece—a cascading arrangement of white peonies and peach roses—filled the air with their sickeningly sweet perfume. Every detail screamed money and romance. The peach napkins were folded into perfect little swans. The bone china gleamed under the dining room light's warm glow, each plate positioned with military precision.

The lighting had been dimmed to that golden-hour magic that made everyone look like they'd stepped out of a skin-care commercial. Even the waiter—yes, Rebecca had hired actual staff—stood at attention in his pristine tuxedo, hands clasped behind his back like he was guarding the Crown Jewels instead of waiting to serve overpriced wine to a group of preplanned witnesses.

I ran my fingers along the stem of my wineglass, the crystal cool against my suddenly clammy palms. Everything was beautiful. Everything was perfect.

Everything is fake, I reminded myself, trying to push what happened in the living room out of my mind. Because honestly, how could I think about anything with the memory of Axel's fingers inside—

"So, why don't you tell us about how you two met?" Frank suggested, leaning back with his wine like he was settling in for story time.

I smiled, hoping it looked natural. Hoping no one else noticed the major death glares Mathew was shooting at Axel. Hoping that Axel and I hadn't ruined everything by making Mathew even more upset than he'd already been before he got here. Honestly, how could I have been so reckless?

"I actually met him when I was visiting a friend."

"But it wasn't until years later that we reconnected," Axel said smoothly, taking my hand.

The second his fingers intertwined with mine, two things happened: First, a jolt of heat shot through my skin, engulfing my chest in the best possible, albeit unexpected, way. Second, Mathew's eyes snapped to our joined hands and narrowed.

Crap. This couldn't be easy on Mathew, witnessing the love of his life with another man. Nor could it have been easy seeing whatever part of our romantic encounter he'd seen between me and Axel. Guilt clawed at me, and I wished I could pull him aside and apologize right now.

"Jace was in the hospital," Axel continued, his thumb tracing a small circle on my hand, as if to say, *Breathe. We've got this.*

"I think I read about that. You were attacked, right?" Carl asked, leaning forward with morbid curiosity.

"I was." Jace cleared his throat while even more guilt clawed through my chest. Jace didn't like talking about that day he'd been airlifted to the hospital. He'd almost died, for God's sake.

"Anyway," I continued, "we reconnected, and what can we say? Sometimes, fate takes the wheel."

Axel brought our joined hands up to brush a kiss across my knuckles.

Poor Mathew. I couldn't even shoot him an apology stare without risking everything.

"And when did you get engaged?" Frank pressed.

Axel's voice dropped to that soft tone that made my insides go liquid. "I came home one night after the day from hell. Dakota was in our kitchen, singing while she baked cookies. Off-key, I might add."

"Hey!" I protested, but I was fighting a smile. Because he was talking about a real memory, and somehow, that made this fake moment feel ... very much *not* fake.

"She was wearing this ridiculous apron with flour in her hair." His eyes found mine, and suddenly, the room felt smaller. More intimate. "I'd had the worst day, was ready to burn everything down, and then I walked into that chaos, and ... everything else just disappeared."

The sincerity in his voice was doing dangerous things to my chest cavity.

"I originally had this elaborate proposal planned," he continued, still holding my gaze like we were the only two people in the room. "Dinner at that rooftop place she loves, roses, the works. But standing there, watching her sing to cookies that were definitely going to poison us both, I realized I didn't want to wait another second."

The table had gone silent, hanging on every word.

"So, right there in the smoky kitchen, with cookies burning, I got down on one knee and asked her to spend the rest of her life creating beautiful disasters with me."

Jesus. If I didn't know better, I'd believe every word.

"And what did you say?" one of the influencers asked breathlessly.

"I said yes. Of course I'd marry him. Though I made him turn off the smoke alarm first. I have standards."

The table erupted in laughter, but Mathew's anger launched into a new stratosphere. Could everyone else see his neck going red?

Scarlett gave me an *uh-oh* look.

"When's the wedding?" Frank asked.

"We're still deciding," I said, grateful for safer ground. "We don't want to overshadow Blake and Tessa's big day."

"You two are engaged too?" Carl turned to Blake with renewed interest.

"We are." Tessa beamed.

"She's planning the whole thing herself." Blake's chest practically puffed with pride. "Every detail."

"Tessa Kincaid, as in the wedding planner?" Carl's eyebrows shot up. "I've heard great things about you. I have a niece who just got engaged. It would mean a lot to me if you would consider talking with her."

"Tessa has a three-year wait list right now," Blake interjected proudly.

"But I'd be happy to at least take a look." Tessa placed her hand on Blake's. "No guarantees I can squeeze anything in, but I'd be happy to try."

Look at our friends, winning everybody over. They were phenomenal, and they were taking the heat off our story.

And off Mathew's growing anger ...

Frank raised his glass. "Well then, to the happy couples!"

"To the happy couples!"

As everyone drank, I caught Axel's eye and silently communicated to him, *Holy shit, we might actually pull this off.*

Don't jinx it, his wink replied.

Mathew's eyes glared at my engagement ring like it was an infectious disease and then locked eyes with me.

"I'm just curious," Mathew started. To everyone else, his tone probably sounded curious, but I could hear the bite in it. "You two were rivals for years. Couldn't be in the same room without arguing. What changed?"

The businessmen leaned forward, suddenly very interested. The influencers practically had their phones out. This was exactly the kind of drama that would make great content.

Shit.

"You're right," I said slowly, buying myself time. "We did argue constantly." I glanced at Axel, who was watching me with those intense eyes. "But maybe ... maybe I was picking fights for a reason I didn't want to admit."

"Such as?" an influencer pressed eagerly.

Axel leaned back in his chair, a slow smile spreading across his face. Either he didn't sense Mathew's hostility or he enjoyed it. "She liked getting me riled up. Liked seeing the effect she could have on me."

"That's not—" I started to protest, but he cut me off.

"It's true. You'd walk into a room and immediately find something to goad me. Your eyes would light up when I'd bite back. Like you were collecting reactions."

Jesus, he's good at this. Too good. Because he was right, and we both knew it.

"And you?" one of the influencers asked breathlessly. "What was your excuse?"

"Easy," Axel said, his gaze never leaving mine. "I liked seeing the fire in her eyes when I would do something that would get under her skin. And I loved seeing her reaction. The way she'd square her shoulders and jut her chin out. She's a tiny, beautiful woman, but she has the force of a hurricane. Especially when she's angry." He paused. "It was intoxicating."

My cheeks heated.

"But that doesn't explain the rivalry," Mathew pushed, drumming his fingers on the table and cocking his head. "What started it all?"

The million-dollar question. The one Axel had never answered.

But now, with the whole table watching, with everything on the line, he looked directly at me and said, "Because when you want something so badly that it scares the hell out of you, when you're terrified you'll destroy it just by getting close ... it's easier and safer to be the villain."

My heart stopped.

Holy shit.

"Well," Frank said after a moment, clearly charmed by the whole exchange, "that's quite the love story."

"Isn't it just?" Mathew muttered, but I barely heard him.

Because Axel had just confessed that our yearslong rivalry had been because he'd *wanted* me. More than anything else in his life.

And suddenly, everything made sense. The way he'd always seemed to know exactly which buttons to push. The way his arguments with me had an edge that was missing with everyone else. The way he'd look at me sometimes, like he was seeing something no one else could.

It took serious effort for me to swallow all that down and act normally, but thankfully, I managed to do just that.

The rest of dinner flew by in a champagne-soaked blur. I found myself actually laughing, stealing glances at Axel like we were sharing the world's most delicious secret.

Mathew had gone quiet though, and I noticed he was still watching. Every time I laughed at something Axel said, every time our hands touched, I could feel his eyes tracking the movement like he was taking mental notes.

And then came the moment that made this entire charade worth every nerve-racking second.

"You know, Axel"—Carl set down his glass, his tone turning serious—"I'll be honest. I had reservations after that PR mess. But tonight? Seeing you with Dakota, the kind of people you surround yourself with ... I think the internet got it wrong." He smiled and waited for a nod from his business partner. "We'd like to move forward with the partnership."

Axel went very still beside me. Something flickered across his face, and I knew instantly what he was feeling. He did not like the discrepancy between his fake persona and his real one. He hated the juxtaposition it caused and hated even more that it was lying about his life that was landing him the deal he had earned.

Don't you dare. I squeezed his hand. *Don't you dare turn this down out of pride.*

Especially when most of this was real. The friends. The new ... friendship/relationship he and I now shared. One component, sure, was a lie, but he had built a fantastic group of people around him.

Still, I could practically see him wrestling with his conscience, so I did what any good fake fiancée would do: I saved him from himself.

"I think this calls for another toast," I said, standing before Axel could say something noble. "To my ridiculously talented fiancé." I looked directly at him, letting every ounce of sincerity I felt seep into my voice. "I'm so proud of everything that you've built, Axel. You built this business from the ground up. It was your hard work and dedication that got you here."

His eyes locked on mine, and I saw the exact moment he realized these words weren't part of our performance. They were me, speaking to him.

You deserve this. Don't you dare apologize for it.

"And to our wonderful guests," I continued. "Thank you for making tonight magical."

Because it was magical. There was no more denying that I was falling in love with Axel. No more denying these feelings or the hope that maybe there could be something real between us. All these years, I'd convinced myself he was just a player, that his coldness toward me was proof he'd never take anything seriously. But tonight proved me wrong. He'd held someone's hand like they were precious. In fact, I'd never seen him look at another woman the way he'd been looking at me all evening. Maybe I was different. Maybe I was the first person to make him want to try.

The thought sent warmth flooding through my chest. Dangerous, reckless hope that maybe I could be the one to finally crack through those walls he'd built around his heart.

"Cheers!"

As everyone drank, I noticed Mathew's posture shift. He went unnaturally still, and there was something in his expression that reminded me of a predator whose prey had just escaped. When he noticed me looking, he forced a smile, but it didn't reach his eyes.

Uh-oh.

I knew him well enough to recognize the signs. It was bad enough to witness us holding hands, showing love. But gushing over Axel? Putting him on a pedestal? Mathew had a big ego—that was for sure—and I could tell it bothered him that this love might be even deeper than anything Mathew and I had shared. More than that though, there was something possessive in the way he was looking at me. Like I was something that had been taken from him.

Mathew set his wine down with deliberate precision, straightening his napkin like he was preparing for war. When he looked up, his smile could have cut glass.

"I'm so happy for you both." His voice dripped with false sweetness. "Dakota always did deserve someone who could appreciate her ... unique qualities." The way he said *unique* made it sound like a flaw rather than a compliment. "Let's just hope Axel can actually make it down the aisle this time, hmm?"

The words hit like a bucket of ice water. The table went dead silent. Even the influencers stopped mid-giggle.

This time?

My blood turned to ice as I looked at Axel, whose face had gone completely pale.

"What the hell does Mathew mean by *this time*?"

39

DINNER PARTY RULE: IF YOU STORM OUT, DON'T LOSE CONSCIOUSNESS. #SAFETYTIP

DAKOTA

"You don't know?" Mathew practically purred, savoring whatever bomb he was about to drop. "When I found out my new company might be investing in Axel, I had a PI look into him. You know, just to be safe. Turns out, Axel's been engaged before."

The world tilted.

And Axel did not—I repeat, did not—even try to deny it.

Ladies and gentlemen, start your engines. On your mark. Get set. Explode.

"You've been engaged before?" Even I could hear the shriek in my voice. My perfectly controlled public personality would normally never do this, but was he kidding me right now? All that *we need to know everything about each other* bullshit and he'd omitted *this*?

The betrayal hit me like a cannon to the gut. On so many levels. This was the guy who'd asked me the most personal questions ever, including my favorite sexual position, for Christ's sake, and he left out basic facts, like having been engaged?

How dare he?

I guess I wasn't special at all. I was just the second one he'd gotten engaged to.

My heartbreak was on full display for everyone to see.

"Excuse me." My napkin hit the table so hard, I swear I could even hear a soft thud.

"Dakota, wait ..." Axel's voice followed me as I stormed out of the room.

But I couldn't wait. Tears were threatening to spill, and that pissed me off even more. I did not care that Axel had been engaged. Didn't. Wouldn't. If I needed any reminder that all of this was fake—FAKE—this was it.

It just sucked that somewhere between the hand-holding and heated glances tonight, my stupid heart had started to love the idea of us.

"Dakota!"

I made it three steps into the hallway before his hand caught my arm, spinning me around.

"Wait."

"Leave me alone, Axel." I jerked away from his touch.

"I can explain."

"Can you?" I crossed my arms over my chest, nails digging into my flesh. Behind us, I could hear our friends desperately trying to steer the conversation back to safer waters, but it was too late. The hurricane had already stirred up deadly waves that would capsize this entire evening.

Necks craned. The influencers were probably already typing. Maybe even recording.

I should have cared about the optics, the business deal, the whole charade falling apart. Instead, I only cared about one thing.

"How could you not tell me this?" The words scraped past the glass shards forming in my throat.

"Can you keep it down?" He glanced back toward the dining room, and that small gesture—choosing them over me, even now—sent fresh pain spiraling through my chest.

"A fiancée? Are you kidding me right now?"

"Look, we can talk about this later—"

"When were you planning to tell me about this? Ever?"

"We have company, Dakota."

"Screw the company, Axel." My voice shattered on his name, and I hated myself for it. Hated how much power he had to destroy me. "You lied to me. You let me stand there like an idiot while he, while everyone ..." A sob threatened to escape. "You humiliated me in front of a house full of people who probably knew all along."

"I didn't lie to you."

I huffed in disbelief. "Your definition of lying and my definition of lying are very different. And that should give me major pause about this whole"—I made exaggerated air quotes—" 'relationship.' "

Thank God nobody from the dining room could see that particular gesture, hidden and blocked by Axel's body.

"Look, let me just say goodbye to them, and then we can talk, okay?"

"You failed to disclose something major to me." When we were supposed to know all, if only to sell this story. Plus, "You held something back from me when I thought we'd opened up and shared our pasts."

When I let myself believe this was real. When every stolen glance, every accidental touch, every moment alone made me think I was special. That maybe, just maybe, someone like you could actually want someone like me. But you were playing a different game entirely, and I was the only one who didn't know the rules.

"Dakota, I can explain everything."

He reached for me, and I jerked back as if his touch would burn.

"Scarlett never mentioned this to me. Nobody did." A horrible thought crept in. "Am I the butt of everyone's jokes?"

"Scarlett doesn't know."

At least there was that small mercy. But surely, all the guys knew. Maybe they'd even laughed about it over drinks, how Knox's little sister was catching feelings.

"Look, the dinner is almost done. Let's just get through this and—"

"Sure, Axel. Get through your precious dinner." The words tasted like ash and betrayal. "Clearly, appearances matter more to you than ..." Than me. Than us. Than whatever I'd stupidly thought was blooming between us. "I'm leaving."

"Dakota!"

But I was already moving, my vision blurring with unshed tears. I didn't know where I was going. Didn't have a plan, didn't have a destination. All I knew was that I couldn't breathe in this suffocating penthouse, couldn't stand another second, surrounded by witnesses to my humiliation. My chest felt like it was caving in, and somewhere between the kitchen and the elevator, I realized the worst part wasn't that he'd lied.

It was that I'd let myself believe it could have been real.

"Dakota, wait." Axel's voice cut through the foyer as I stormed into the elevator.

"I just need some air," I managed, my voice sounding foreign to my own ears.

Scarlett's heels clicked rapidly across the floor. "Dakota, let me come with—"

"No." Her face crumpled at my tone, and guilt twisted with everything else churning in my stomach. "I need ... I just need a minute."

Against the protests of my friends, against Axel's tense plea to let him explain, I managed to close the elevator without any of them getting in.

The elevator felt like a tomb, carrying me down, down, down, away from the wreckage of whatever the hell I'd thought was happening between us. Stepping out of the elevator, walking through the lobby, I shoved the front doors of the building open.

The moment I stepped outside, I inhaled my first real breath in what felt like hours. The cool night air hit my lungs like salvation as I tilted my face up to the blackened sky, as if the universe itself could answer the questions tearing me apart.

How could I have been so stupid? How could I have thought—

A searing pain exploded across the right side of my skull.

Then everything went black.

40

WHEN SOMEONE HURTS THE WOMAN YOU ADORE, AND SUDDENLY, MURDER SEEMS REASONABLE. #PRIMALINSTINCTS

AXEL

"You're a fucking jackass—you know that?" I snapped.

Mathew's smirk widened. Mission accomplished, apparently.

"Axel, calm down." Blake stood up, hands raised, like he was dealing with a rabid animal. Which fair enough. I felt pretty rabid right now.

"Someone should go check on Dakota," Ryker said quietly, but no one was listening. They were all watching me, like I might spontaneously combust. Or commit capital murder.

I jabbed a finger at Mathew. "You did that shit on purpose. But you hurt her, doing it, not me."

Look at him with that arrogant smirk. I knew I was feeding right into whatever trap he'd laid, but I couldn't give a damn. The damage was already done.

"See, Frank? Carl?" Mathew turned to my business associates with theatrical concern. "I told you the guy was unpredictable."

"I'm going to check on her," Ryker said, slipping away while everyone's attention was on the testosterone showdown.

"You're an asshole, Mathew." My voice came out low. Dangerous. "If you want to hurt me, hurt me. Do not"—I stepped forward—"hurt Dakota. You leave her out of this, or so help me—"

I lunged, but Blake and Jace were suddenly in front of me like a wall of expensive suits. The influencers scattered to the far side of the room, phones probably already recording. Great. Just what I needed: my meltdown going viral.

Frank and Carl rose slowly, their disapproving eyes sweeping the chaos.

"Seems to me," Mathew drawled, "if you two really were lovebirds, she'd know all about your other fiancée."

The room went dead quiet.

Motherfucker.

"You left her." My voice was deadly quiet. "You had her, had everything, and you threw it away. And you think you can just walk back in here and claim her like she's some prize you misplaced?" The nerve. "She deserves to be with someone who knows her worth isn't something to be measured against some new job offer. Her worth is something to be cherished."

"Well, I'm back now." He shrugged like we were discussing the weather. "And I'm not leaving again. Dakota belongs with someone who understands her value."

The way he said *value* made my stomach curl. Like she was an asset to be appraised.

"You hurt her the other night," I accused. "She came to *me*. She cried on my shoulder."

"People can say things they don't mean when they're confused," Mathew said, his tone turning almost clinical. "Dakota has always been ... impressionable. She just needs the right guidance to see clearly again."

Guidance? What the hell was that supposed to mean?

"Listen to your words," I snapped, trying to lunge past my friends. "Taking no accountability for breaking her heart. It's too late to get her back. She doesn't want you anymore, and getting her upset with me won't change that."

Mathew scrubbed his cheek. This was the side of him Dakota

probably never saw before. The competitive, calculating side that would gladly destroy her if it served his purpose.

"We'll see about that." Mathew shoved his hands into his pockets and started walking toward the elevator. Casual. Taunting. "Dakota and I have a deeper connection than you realize."

Red. All I could see was red. And Dakota's face when that bombshell hit.

I was the one who put that hurt there. My lie. But Mathew? He was the one who'd loaded the gun and pulled the trigger.

"If you really cared about her, you never would've hurt her tonight," I said.

His smile was cold, calculating. "She needed to see the truth about you."

I lunged, but the boys held me back.

"That's enough." Frank and Carl were buttoning their suits, heading for the elevator. Professional disappointment radiated from them in waves.

"Careful there, Axel," Mathew warned with mock concern as the businessmen vanished from my penthouse. "Your deal isn't inked yet."

"You came here to sabotage this," Jace snarled at Mathew, shoving him away from me.

Somewhere in the back of my mind, I registered that I'd probably just blown the one shot at saving my business. But right now, I didn't give a shit. The influencers, on the other hand, made no move to leave. Of course not. This was social media gold.

#EngagementDrama.

"You're not good enough for her," I snarled.

"I was there when she built that online persona. I helped shape it. I know the real Dakota. The one who needs someone to take care of her."

The possessive way he talked about "shaping" her made my blood boil. Like she was some kind of project.

"Let me go," I snapped, shaking free of Blake's grip. I stalked to the other side of the room, shoving my hands through my hair, and glowered at Mathew. "Get the fuck out of my house."

"Gladly." His smile was all teeth. No warmth.

My boys flanked me, bodies coiled for violence. Ready to jump in if I completely lost it.

Which I was about to.

"You're lucky my friends have better judgment than me," I said through gritted teeth, "because if they weren't here, so help me God, I would beat the living shit out of you."

"My, my. Such a temper." Mathew tsked like a disappointed teacher. "This is exactly why Dakota needs protection from men like you. You know what? You guys had better watch her for bruises. I'd hate to find out you're violent toward women. Although, given your track record with women ..."

I lunged for him, slipping past my boys this time, and slammed him against the wall so hard, the picture frames rattled. My hands found his throat and squeezed until his smug smile finally disappeared.

Around me, chaos erupted. My boys tried to pry me off. The influencers and girls began screaming. But all I could hear was the sound of Mathew's ragged breathing and the blood rushing in my ears.

This was for Dakota.

This was for every tear she'd cried because of him.

This was for—

The elevator dinged.

41

LET HIM CARRY YOU IN A BLOOD-SOAKED GOWN. IT'S CALLED MAKING AN ENTRANCE. 🦇 🩸 #DRAMATICRETURN

DAKOTA

Holy shit. I just got sucker-punched in the head.

I'd seen the news about this happening all over Chicago, but I never thought I'd be the lucky victim. Turns out? It sucked even worse than I'd imagined. The good news: I didn't lose consciousness. The bad news: something split open because now a dribble of sticky, warm blood cascaded down my ear and neck.

Gross.

And as I lay here, trying to catch my bearings, I also decided that chivalry and human decency were pretty much dead. The few pedestrians in the area continued to amble by like a woman getting sucker-punched wasn't worth looking up from their screens.

Welcome to the big city, I guess.

To his credit, one dude did stop and ask if I was okay. But he didn't exactly wait for my answer. When I stumbled to my knees and mumbled, "Yes," he walked off.

Damn it to hell. In the category of Shit Nights, this one was inching its way to the very top.

Resigning myself to sitting on my ass, I brought my hand up

to check if my head was still attached. Based on how the pain was escalating, I wasn't entirely sure. Good news: the side of my head seemed intact. *Yay.* Bad news: the bleeding was worse than I thought. My entire hand was covered in blood, dripping onto the sidewalk like a crime scene.

"Jesus!" a male voice barked.

Okay, maybe I'd jumped to conclusions about chivalry being dead because, suddenly, a Good Samaritan was at my side, his arm protectively wrapping around my shoulders.

"Dakota, are you okay?"

I knew that voice. I managed to lift my eyes and met the very worried gaze staring back at me. Eyebrows pulled together, attention sweeping over my body, looking for injuries.

"Ryker?"

"The fuck happened?"

"Why are you here?"

"Are you shot?"

He touched the side of my head, and I winced.

"No. Why did you come down here? The dinner party's still going on."

"That's seriously your question right now?" His voice cracked with disbelief. "What happened to you?"

"You first."

"Are you kidding me?" he snarled. "You're hemorrhaging all over Chicago, and you're asking me why I happened to come down the elevator?"

"I'm not hemorrhaging. And yes."

His lips thinned like he couldn't believe I was holding my medical assistance hostage over something so trivial.

"You were incredibly upset and went off alone into the night when there's a potential crime family threat after you. You think I'm not going to follow you out and make sure you're okay? Jesus, I knew we should have hired security for tonight."

Well, that was ... really nice of him.

Too bad he didn't come, like, two minutes earlier. Maybe we could have snapped my attacker's dick off together. #Bonding.

"Thank you. That's very chivalrous."

And now that I was thinking about it, why was he the one who came? It stung, realizing Axel hadn't checked on me. In his defense, I'd specifically told him I needed space. But now that I knew said space came with a fist to my skull, I'd definitely changed my mind. A girl could do that. Pretty sure I'd read in a magazine article somewhere that it often happened after one got punched in the head.

"Where is Axel?"

Ryker continued examining my head, half paying attention to his answer. "Last I saw, he and Mathew were going at it."

"He ... what?"

"Looks like the bleeding's slowing, but—"

"Holy shit. As in fighting?"

"Most likely," he said absently.

"We need to get up there and stop them!"

"We should have Blake check you out."

He helped me to my feet, which turned out to be more of a process than I'd expected. Maybe that hit had destabilized my inner ear because I was all sorts of dizzy.

"Dakota?"

"Yeah?"

"I'm going to lift you up now and carry you upstairs. You're going to do that thing where you protest and tell me you can walk up there alone, but it's not happening. So, just skip it. If you want to save your fiancé from murdering Mathew, we need to get up there fast."

Well, that was one way to get a girl to go along with something.

So, I didn't resist when Ryker scooped me up bridal-style and carried me through the lobby and into the elevator.

Once we were safely inside, ascending toward what I could

only hope wasn't a murder scene, Ryker growled, "Tell me exactly what happened."

"Hell if I know. I stepped outside, something hit the side of my head, I went down."

"Did you hear a gunshot?"

"No. I think it was a fist or maybe something small and hard. A rock maybe?"

"You see anyone?"

"A guy wearing all black. He ran off."

"Fuck." His jaw tightened. "Whoever did this is lucky I didn't see him."

I eyed him. "You're a lawyer. You wouldn't hurt someone."

"Wouldn't I?"

Okaaay…

"It's against the law," I pointed out.

"Really? Hadn't learned that in my years of law school training."

I bit back a laugh, shocked that anyone could get me to feel any ounce of humor right now.

"I'm sure it's not the Romano family," I said, trying to steer us back to safer conversational territory.

"What makes you say that?"

"Aren't they supposed to be, like, ruthless? This seems really childish. Sucker-punching a woman in the head. I've seen this on the news. It's probably just some stupid kid."

"Yeah," Ryker said. "Maybe."

But he didn't fully believe that. I could tell by the way his grip tightened around me.

"I'm bleeding on your suit," I realized in horror.

"Fuck the suit, Dakota."

My eyes burned, and suddenly, I was hit with a wave of gratitude so fierce, it nearly knocked me sideways. Which, granted, wouldn't take much in my current state.

But seriously, here was Ryker. Researching crime family threats in his spare time like some kind of legal superhero.

Keeping tabs on us when we were too stubborn or distracted to keep tabs on ourselves. And when I'd stormed off into the night like a dramatic heroine in a gothic novel, he'd actually followed me.

Not because he had to. Not because anyone asked him to. But because he cared.

And now he was carrying me against his warm chest, his arms solid and protective around me, like I was something precious instead of a bleeding mess who couldn't even walk straight. The steady thrum of his heartbeat under my body was more comforting than it had any right to be.

"You know, you're a really good guy, Ryker."

"I try."

"No. Like, really good."

"If you're hitting on me, stop. Axel will cut my balls off. He's already pissed that Mathew likes you. Don't add me to his hit list."

I couldn't help but smirk. "I'm not hitting on you. I just meant ... thank you and all that."

"Anytime, Dakota."

"Ryker?"

"Hmm?"

"If you tell Knox about me getting punched, I'm afraid I'll have to be the one to cut off your balls."

He smirked. Shook his head. "You're fierce—you know that?"

If by fierce, you mean concussed and bleeding, then sure.

The elevator dinged and opened.

Revealing a red-faced Axel with his hands around Mathew's throat.

42

UPDATE: FAKE FIANCÉ IS CAPABLE OF TOSSING EX-BOYFRIEND ACROSS THE ROOM LIKE A RAG DOLL. #UTTERSATISFACTION

AXEL

What. The. Fuck?

The only thing capable of making me release Mathew's neck was the sight before me: Dakota covered in blood. It stained the side of her head like spilled wine, cascaded in a crimson waterfall down her ear and throat, and pooled onto her designer gown.

I dropped Mathew and sprinted across the foyer, scooping her from Ryker's arms. Her scent was tainted with the metallic tang of blood.

"Sunshine." My voice came out rougher than I'd ever heard it. "What the fuck happened?"

"I'm fine," she claimed, but her gaze darted between me and Mathew, as if—and you have to be shitting me here—she was more worried about the two of us fighting than whatever the hell was wrong with her.

"I can walk." She tried to release herself from my grip, but I tightened my arms around her. Her body felt too light, too fragile. Like she might dissolve if I let go.

I carried her to the leather couch, laying her down against the cream cushions. Our dinner guests gathered around the edges of my living room, their designer evening wear suddenly obscene against the backdrop of her injury.

"Axel, I assure you, I'm totally fine ..."

"She's not fine," Ryker cut through her protest. "Someone clocked her in the head. Hard enough to drop her. Found her crumpled on the concrete."

"Fuck." I had never experienced the level of fury now boiling through my blood. My fingers balled into fists, and instantly, I could feel the shift in everything. The moment where everything in my life changed, split into the before and after.

Before she was attacked. And after.

Before I took her for granted. And after I realized I couldn't survive without her.

Before someone dared touch her. And after, when I'd hunt him to the ends of the earth to make him pay for what he did.

While my mind was preoccupied with rage and concern, Blake slipped into emergency-doctor mode and knelt next to her head, his movements clinical and efficient.

"She needs stitches," Blake said. "And a CT scan."

"Stitches?" Dakota's voice pitched higher. "Can't we just use butterfly bandages?"

"Sunshine." I moved closer so I could take her hand. "You're doing whatever the doctor says."

Her lips pressed into that stubborn line I knew too well.

Jesus. Look at her, lying there on my couch. She wasn't crying. Not even after being attacked and left bleeding on concrete. With blood actively leaking from her wound, trickling down her neck to stain the silk, she looked more uncomfortable with all the attention this was bringing her than with the injury itself.

Strongest woman I'd ever met.

"Before we leave for the ER, I'd like to get gauze on the wound to control the bleeding. You have a first aid kit?" Blake eyed me.

I nodded, then sprinted down the hallway toward my bathroom. When I returned, Mathew was huddled beside her with an ice pack from my freezer.

Mathew's voice was soft. Snake-like. "Just try to stay still, Dakota. You've been through enough tonight."

My pulse pounded in my ears as I watched him lean over her, playing the concerned ex-boyfriend. Now he was trying to be the knight in shining armor when he was the one whose big mouth had caused this mess in the first place.

I stormed over to him, grabbed him by his expensive suit collar, and flung him backward across the living room like a rag doll. He hit the window with a satisfying thud.

Too bad it didn't break and send him free-falling to his death.

"What the hell—" Mathew started.

"Keep your hands off her." I took his spot, handing Blake the gauze.

Blake's glare could have frozen hell, but I didn't give a damn about his judgment.

"Did you see who did this?" I asked Dakota.

She shook her head, but worry creased her brow as she scanned the crowd of guests still watching like this was dinner theater.

She didn't need an audience.

"Everyone, out." I didn't look up from her wound. "Now."

"I'm not going anywhere until I know she's okay," Mathew declared, straightening his tie like he hadn't just been hurled across the room like a little bitch. He made the mistake of taking a step closer, so I shot to my feet and shoved him with both hands.

Jace materialized in front of me, holding me back, while Ryker moved in front of Mathew.

"She's hurt because of you. Your big mouth," I snapped.

"I told her what she deserved to know! You're the one who lied!" Mathew's voice stayed level, controlled. "And now look what's happened. She's hurt, Axel. This is what I was worried about."

"You seriously think this is how you win her back?" I snapped.

"She doesn't belong with you! Look at her. She was safe until she got involved with you."

"You son of a bitch!" I broke free from Jace long enough to crack Mathew's jaw.

"Enough!" Blake's voice boomed like a gunshot.

"Get out of my house," I snarled between pants.

Mathew touched his split lip, blood trickling down his chin. His eyes found Dakota's. "I'm going to win her back."

White-hot fury exploded behind my eyes. Every muscle in my body coiled, ready to launch across the room and drive my fist through Mathew's goddamn face. I wanted to feel his nose break under my knuckles. Wanted to wipe that smug expression off his bloodied mouth permanently. Rearrange his dental work while I was at it. Give him something to remember me by every time he smiled in the mirror.

I took a step forward, violence singing in my veins.

But then I caught sight of Dakota out of my peripheral vision. Still bleeding. Still fragile. Still *mine* to protect.

If I lost control now, if I gave in to the primal need to destroy Mathew, I'd be abandoning her when she needed me most. He'd probably get me arrested, put in jail for the night.

I forced myself to stay rooted in place, every fiber of my being screaming in protest. My hands clenched into fists so tight, my knuckles went white. The taste of copper filled my mouth from biting back the words I wanted to snarl.

Jace and Ryker flanked me, sensing how close I was to snapping, but it wasn't them holding me back anymore.

It was her.

Mathew stepped into the elevator, never breaking eye contact, that bastard's smile still plastered across his face. "I'll call you later, Dakota."

The doors closed on his smug, bloodied face, and I nearly put my fist through the wall instead.

I turned back to Dakota and froze.

Which was when I registered the fresh look of horror painted across her features. I followed her gaze to the influencers, who had their phones out. Recording every moment of what had happened, evidently.

The influencers exchanged glances, practically salivating over the drama.

Dakota's carefully curated fairy-tale image was crumbling in real time, and they were documenting every second.

43

BREAKING: SOME CONFESSIONS REQUIRE BLOOD LOSS TO UNLOCK. #PAINFULTRUTHS

DAKOTA

"Absolutely not." I gripped the doorframe as Axel bent toward me, his arms already positioning to lift me. "I can walk."

"Blake said better safe than sorry. You might get dizzy and fall."

I shot a desperate look at my supposed friends, searching for backup. Jace suddenly found the ceiling fascinating. Tessa examined her manicure like it held the secrets of the universe. Even Scarlett was avoiding eye contact.

Traitors. All of them.

If Blake hadn't rushed ahead to the ER to prep supplies, maybe I could've reasoned with him about his ridiculous no-walking decree. But, no, Dr. Blake had spoken, and apparently, everyone had decided to pledge allegiance to his medical tyranny.

Before I could voice any of this, Axel swept me up against his chest like I weighed nothing. "Arms around my neck, Sunshine."

"This is ridiculous." But my traitorous body betrayed me, arms looping around him as he carried me toward the elevator. His heart hammered against my ribs. Or maybe that was mine. "Put me down."

"No."

"Axel."

"Dakota." He hit the elevator button with his elbow, still holding me close. Too close. I could smell his cologne, mixed with copper from the blood on his suit. My blood. "Stop fighting me on this."

My mind scrambled to process what was happening. I should still be angry at Axel Pierce. He'd omission-lied to me about his fiancée after all, but in this moment, everything else felt suspended around us like unimportant dust particles.

The only thing that mattered was the way he was looking at me. The way concern leaked from his words and his gaze.

Because I could feel it: the energy between us had shifted. Something raw and primal was breaking free from whatever dam we'd built to hold it back.

The elevator ride down felt like an eternity. Neither of us spoke, but I could feel the tension radiating from his body, the careful way he held me, like I might shatter.

When we reached Jace's waiting car, he maneuvered the door open and settled into the back seat, still cradling me. "Driver, Mercy Harbor. Emergency entrance."

"I can sit normally," I said, trying to shift away. The leather seat creaked beneath us, and a sharp throb pulsed behind my temple, where the blood had started to dry, sticky and metallic against my skin.

His arms tightened. "Please." The word came out broken, his breath warm against my ear. "Just ... let me."

I stopped struggling. He guided my head to rest against his shoulder, the expensive fabric of his suit soft against my cheek. One hand stroked through my hair while the other held me secure against him, his fingers tightening slightly where they pressed against my ribs. The city lights blurred past the windows, neon blues and golds streaking like watercolors on the rain-slicked glass. I could smell his cologne mixing with the copper tang of blood, feel the rapid beat of his heart beneath my ear.

"This is my fault." His voice was rough as sandpaper, vibrating through his chest and into mine.

"What? No, Mathew's the one who—"

"If I'd told you about the engagement from the start, you never would have stormed out. You never would have gotten hurt." His hand stilled in my hair. "Seeing you bloody. Hurt." He shook his head, and his voice dropped to an octave I'd never heard before. One that ran through rivers of pain. "It cracked something in me, Sunshine."

I pulled back enough to look at his face. The raw anguish there stole my breath. "Axel ..."

"You're all that matters." His thumb traced my jawline, leaving fire in its wake. "Not the business. Not the deal. Not any of it. Just you."

The confession hung between us, heavy and charged. My heart hammered so hard, I was sure he could feel it, and his eyes—those stormy eyes that had tormented me for years—darkened to midnight as they searched mine. The air grew thick, buzzing with something inevitable and terrifying and perfect.

His thumb paused at the corner of my mouth, and I couldn't help the way my lips parted slightly, my breath catching. The muscle in his neck flexed like he was fighting some internal war.

"Don't look at me like that," he said, voice strained.

"Like what?" The words came out breathy, barely there.

"Like you want me to ..." He swallowed hard, his gaze dropping to my mouth. "God, Sunshine. You have no idea what you do to me."

Every inch of my skin felt hypersensitive, alive. Years of heated arguments, of barely controlled chemistry, of denying what simmered beneath every barbed word ... it all compressed into this single moment. The city lights painted shadowed colors across his face, and I watched, mesmerized, as he slowly, torturously leaned closer.

His breath ghosted across my lips. Just a whisper of contact. Not enough. Never enough.

"Tell me to stop," he murmured, but his hand was already sliding to cup the back of my neck, his fingers threading through my hair with devastating gentleness, careful to avoid the sore spot.

"No." The word was barely a breath, but it shattered whatever control he'd been clinging to.

For one suspended heartbeat, we hovered there, with his mouth a hairbreadth from mine, close enough that I could taste the promise of him. My whole body trembled with want.

"Sunshine," he breathed, reverent and destroyed.

And then his mouth was on mine.

The first contact was soft. Achingly, unexpectedly soft, like he was afraid I might break. But then I made a small, desperate sound against his lips, and something in him snapped. The kiss turned molten, years of pent-up longing pouring out in a rush that left me dizzy.

This wasn't like our fake kisses or the one meant to make Mathew jealous. No audience. No performance. Just raw, desperate hunger that had been building between us since the day we met.

He kissed me like he was trying to apologize and claim me, all at once, like I was precious and he was starving. His tongue swept against mine, and my whole body ignited, every nerve ending sparking to life. I gasped into his mouth, fingers tangling in his hair, pulling him closer, needing more. So much more.

He made a sound—half groan, half growl—that I felt everywhere, the vibration of it shooting straight through me like lightning. His hand ghosted down my jaw, and I went limp against him, surrendering to the storm we'd created.

We kissed like we fought, with everything we had, holding nothing back. Every sweep of his tongue was a challenge I met eagerly. Every nip of teeth was a dare. When I sucked lightly on his bottom lip, his whole body shuddered, and the power of it, of affecting him like this, was heavier than wine.

We couldn't stop. Couldn't pull away. Every time one of us tried to break for air, the other would chase their mouth back, desperate for another taste, another second of this perfect madness.

The car took a sharp turn, and we broke apart, breathing hard.

"Why?" I whispered, my lips still tingling. "Why did you keep it from me? Who were you engaged to?"

His whole body tensed. "Dakota, I ..."

The car stopped. Harsh hospital lights flooded through the windows.

"We're here, Mr. Pierce," the driver announced.

Axel's jaw clenched, that vulnerable moment evaporating like smoke. He shifted me carefully as the door opened, people already approaching with a wheelchair.

He pressed a kiss to my forehead, gentle but final. "Later, Sunshine. Let's get you treated. Make sure you're really okay."

But as they wheeled me through those automatic doors, his expression already shuttering closed, I wondered if later would ever come. Or if I'd just lost my only chance to understand the mystery that was Axel Pierce.

The man who'd just kissed me like I was the only thing keeping him alive.

44

PSA: SOME CONFESSIONS REQUIRE KISSING TO PROCESS PROPERLY. #EMERGENCYPROTOCOL

DAKOTA

The penthouse looked like a crime scene.

Blood streaked across marble. Shattered glass glittering by the dining table. The ghost of Mathew's fury still hanging in the air like smoke.

And Axel, standing in the middle of it all, looking like he wanted to tear the place apart with his bare hands.

"You shouldn't have gone outside." His voice could've frozen hell.

I stopped dead in my tracks. "Excuse me?"

"You heard me."

"Oh, we're doing this now?" I kicked off my heels with more force than necessary, ignoring the throb in my freshly stitched head. "After you kissed me senseless in the back of that car? After you told me I'm all that matters? Now you want to scold me like I'm a child?"

"You could have been killed."

"By a punch? Blake said—"

"I don't give a damn what Blake said." He spun toward me,

and the raw fury in his eyes made me step back. "Do you have any idea what seeing you covered in blood did to me?"

"Maybe if you'd told me about your secret fiancée, I wouldn't have needed to storm out for air."

Something dangerous flashed across his face. "You want to know about her? Fine."

He started pacing. Not the casual kind. The caged-predator kind that made my skin prickle with awareness.

"Her name was Cassandra. We worked together." He ran a hand through his already-disheveled hair. "And the only reason I ever touched her was because I couldn't stop thinking about *you*."

My heart stuttered. "What?"

"You heard me." He stopped pacing, pinning me with that steel gaze that always made my knees weak. "Everything I've done for years has been about not thinking about you. Not wanting you. Not having feelings for you."

The words hit harder than that punch to the head. Years?

"That day in the snow," he continued, voice rougher now, like gravel and whiskey. "Remember?"

How could I forget? The day everything changed between us. Back before Knox got arrested.

His voice dropped to something raw, almost broken. "You stole Knox's ridiculous parka. The one that was three sizes too big."

I remembered. The monstrosity that had swallowed me whole.

"You were tipsy on two beers. Declared the snow was ..." He stopped, his jaw working like the words physically hurt. " 'Too perfect to waste.' I followed you outside to make sure you didn't break your neck on the ice."

His hands clenched and unclenched at his sides, like he was fighting the memory itself.

"But then you started spinning." The words came out rougher now, his eyes locked on something far away. "Arms wide, catching snowflakes on your tongue like you were five years old. That silver dress under the parka catching the light."

I watched his throat bob as he swallowed hard.

"There was this one snowflake that landed right on your eyelash. Left one. You blinked it away and laughed at ... at nothing. At everything. And that laugh ..."

He cut himself off, turning away from me sharply. When he turned back, his eyes were wild, desperate.

"You grabbed my hands. Tried to make me dance with you in the fucking snow. Your fingers were freezing, but your eyes were so ..." He dragged a hand down his face. "Christ, Dakota. The way you looked at me."

The silence stretched taut between us before he continued, voice barely above a whisper.

"That's when I knew. Right then, with snow falling between us and your cold hands in mine. I was completely gone for you." A bitter smile escaped him. "Terrified the hell out of me. I dropped your hands like they were on fire. Left you out there, spinning alone."

He met my eyes then, and the pain there took my breath away.

"I've never looked at snow the same way since. Can't see a single snowflake without seeing you in that silver dress, without remembering how I knew I had to stay away or I'd destroy us both."

My stomach clenched. I never knew why he'd suddenly turned cold after that weekend. Started treating me like I was invisible, like I was something contaminated.

"I was falling in love with you." The confession ripped out of him, raw and bleeding. "And I couldn't have you, Dakota. Not just because Knox would've pummeled me into next week. But because I never wanted anyone in my life. Not after what I experienced, growing up. Relationships were doomed; love was fake. I refused to fall into the trap of thinking it could be real, just to end up like my parents."

He stopped in front of the window, his reflection a tortured shadow against the city lights.

"I certainly wasn't going to drag a child into that hell. By the time I met you, I was already broken." He turned back to me, and the vulnerability in his eyes stole my breath. "And you challenged everything I believed in. It terrified me, but even if I could've gotten past that fear, I wasn't going to infect you with my darkness."

"So, you pushed me away."

"I tried." His smile could've cut glass. "God, I tried. Figured if I was cold enough, cruel enough, you'd hate me. Problem solved."

"Clearly, that worked out brilliantly for you."

"It was torture." He moved closer, and I had to tilt my head back to maintain eye contact. "The longer it went on, the worse it got. Like I was starving and you were the only thing that could save me."

My breathing had gone shallow.

"It pissed me off actually." His muscle tightened the way it did when he was fighting for control. "I chose everything else in my life. My career, my friends, my women. But you?" He shook his head slowly. "You invaded every thought, every dream, every goddamn moment without my permission."

Every molecule between us felt magnetized, humming with years of suppressed want.

"So, when dating a different woman every week didn't work, I tried something more drastic." His voice dropped. "Cassandra pursued me. Hard and persistently. Eventually, I caved and dated her. Four weeks in, she started talking marriage. One night, after enough whiskey to drown my conscience, I was desperate enough to think maybe if I committed to someone else, I'd finally stop wanting you." He let out a deep breath. "Which was the most screwed-up logic, in hindsight. You were too precious to taint with me, but I was willing to do that to her." He shook his head.

"But you didn't go through with it."

"How could I?" He reached up slowly, as if fighting against

himself, and when his thumb finally grazed my jawline, my breath caught. The pad of his thumb was achingly gentle, tracing the curve of bone beneath my skin with a tenderness that made my chest tighten. "Every time I looked at her, I saw your face. Every time she laughed, I heard your voice."

His eyes followed the path of his thumb as it mapped the line of my jaw like he was memorizing it.

Heat spread down my neck, raising goose bumps along my arms.

"I was planning a future with one woman while being completely consumed by another."

I … didn't know what to say.

"Do you want to know how much you consumed me?" His voice dropped, raw with vulnerability. "I went to your college graduation."

My breath caught. "What?"

"I told myself I just wanted to be there because Knox couldn't be. But the minute I saw you in that orange dress, I knew it was a lie." His thumb traced along my cheek. "I wanted the excuse to see you. I wanted to be there for your big moments, even if you didn't know I was celebrating them with you, Sunshine."

The confession hit me like a warm sun on a winter day. My heart cracked wide open, spilling years of unspoken longing. Axel had been there. He'd traveled all those miles just to watch me walk across that stage, to silently celebrate what should have been one of the happiest days of my life. The weight of it stole my breath, knowing he'd wanted to be there for my big moments, that he'd cared enough to show up, even when I couldn't see him.

"You were there?"

"Back row, baseball cap pulled low. When you walked across that stage …" He swallowed hard. "You looked so proud, so radiant. But then I saw you scan the crowd, and I watched your face change when you remembered Knox was missing it."

My throat tightened. I remembered that moment. The sharp pang of loss when the reality hit that my brother wasn't there to see me graduate. But now, knowing Axel had been there, loving me through it, even from the shadows … it rewrote everything. Every lonely moment from that day suddenly felt less empty.

"I wanted to cross that entire auditorium and hold you," he continued, voice breaking. "Tell you that someone who loved you was there, cheering you on."

"Axel …" I whispered, my vision starting to blur with tears.

"And those parking tickets you kept getting when you visited Knox? The ones that mysteriously got dismissed?" His eyes never left mine. "That was me. Ryker had connections at the courthouse, and I asked him to help. I couldn't stand the thought of you getting punished for being a good sister."

The puzzle pieces were clicking into place, stealing my breath. "The tow truck …"

"Your car broke down after visiting Knox. I was …" He ran a hand through his hair, looking almost embarrassed. "I may have been keeping tabs on your visits. Making sure you were safe. When I saw you stranded there, I called the tow truck and paid for it."

"And the gardenias," I breathed, understanding flooding through me. "Every birthday."

He nodded, that vulnerability in his eyes deepening. "Your favorite flowers. I remembered from that conversation we had years ago when you visited Knox. I just … I needed you to know someone remembered. Someone cared about celebrating you, even if I couldn't be the one to do it openly."

Years of secret care. Years of him watching over me from the shadows while I thought he barely tolerated my existence.

"I secretly did something for you too." The words tumbled out before I could stop them. His eyebrows rose, and I felt heat creep up my neck. "I told myself I was crazy for it at the time, but I hated the way some people would come for you online. Calling you a playboy, making nasty comments about your dating life."

His expression shifted, surprise flickering across his features.

"Knowing algorithms became my profession, so when

someone would start to troll you, I knew exactly how to try and squash it." Too bad our PR crisis was too big to solve with the same strategy. I couldn't meet his eyes, focusing instead on the buttons of his shirt. "I had one anonymous alternate account I used for my business, for creative testing and whatnot. Used it to boost positive comments of you by engaging with them early—likes, replies, shares—knowing the algorithm would push them to the top while the negative ones got buried."

"Dakota ..."

"And when there was bad press about your dating life, I'd time my own viral posts to push your negative stories out of the trending cycle. I even created positive content that would rank higher in search results than the nasty articles." I finally looked up at him, vulnerability written all over my face. "I was consumed by you, too, even if I didn't want to be. I couldn't stand watching people tear you apart online when you'd always been there for my family."

His thumb traced my cheek, and something raw and wondering filled his expression. "You protected me."

"Like you protected me," I whispered. "We were both taking care of each other from the shadows, weren't we?"

He nodded, something fierce and tender crossing his face. "And I was too consumed by you to stay with her."

My throat felt tight. His thumb moved to trace my lower lip, and I fought not to lean into his touch.

"Staying with her would make me just as bad as my parents. Pretending to love someone, pretending to be happy. Living a lie."

"So, you ended it."

"The day before we were going to go public on social media." His hand dropped, and I immediately missed its warmth.

"Did the guys know?" Because, hello, even though he'd said no one knew, I thought they knew everything about each other.

He shook his head. "Should have been a red flag that I never wanted to tell them." He dragged both hands through his hair, leaving it perfectly messy. "First, it was because they'd give me shit about settling down. You know how I am—was—about commitment. Then, the longer I waited, the weirder it got. Like, how do you casually drop, *Oh, by the way, I've been dating someone, and now I'm engaged*, into poker night?"

Despite everything, I almost smiled at the mental image.

"Point is, I ended it with her. It wasn't fair to her to stay with someone who didn't love her. She deserved more." His expression darkened, storm clouds gathering. "She didn't take it well. Destroyed my business from the inside out. Stole clients, sabotaged deals. Left me scrambling to save everything I'd built."

"That's why you need these investors."

"Jace offered to help, but his capital was tied up in the acquisition of Scarlett's company." He waved a dismissive hand. "Besides, needed to fix my own mess."

Typical Axel. Too proud to accept help, even when drowning.

He studied my face with an intensity that made me want to squirm. "After that, I went into overtime, keeping every woman at a safe distance. But then I saw you that night you took the photo."

His voice went soft, reverent almost. "God, you looked so beautiful, Sunshine. I bet you didn't notice I was staring at you across the room the whole time, drowning my sorrows in whiskey. You looked ..." He paused, searching for words. "Lost. Like I felt. I wanted to come over and wrap my arms around you. I wanted to tell you it was you all along."

My chest constricted. All those times I'd felt his eyes on me across crowded rooms, convinced myself I was imagining it. All those moments I'd caught him staring, only to have him look away, cold and dismissive. He'd been drowning too. Fighting the same magnetic pull that had been slowly driving me insane for years. The thought that we'd both been suffering separately, unnecessarily, made me want to scream. Or cry. Or both.

"Why didn't you?"

"Because." He stepped closer, close enough that I had to press back against the wall. "If I finally confessed everything after all these years and you shut me down, there'd be no coming back from that. So, when that woman came up and started giving me attention ..."

"You went back to your playbook."

"I was desperate to feel something, anything, that wasn't you." His eyes closed for a moment. "I thought maybe if I could force myself to want someone else, even for just a moment, I could bury what I felt for you deep enough that I wouldn't do something stupid. But it was like trying to use a match to put out a wildfire."

We stood there for a moment, the weight of his confession settling between us like a living thing. Years of misunderstandings. Years of him pushing me away while pulling me closer in his mind. Years of unnecessary pain.

"Do you know what killed me most?" His voice darkened. "Watching you with Mathew. Seeing him have everything I wanted, but couldn't let myself have."

My breath caught. "Is that why you were such an ass about him?"

"Every single time." No hesitation. Pure honesty. "I wanted to be happy for you. Told myself you deserved someone good, someone whole. But every time I saw a photo of him ..." His hands clenched into fists. "I wanted to tear him apart."

The possessiveness in his voice should have scared me. Instead, it sent heat coursing through my veins.

"Axel ..."

"I'm done fighting this." His voice had gone rough, desperate, like something inside him was breaking free. "I'm done pretending I don't want you. That I don't need you like I need air."

The space hummed like the moment before a lightning strike. Every nerve in my body was screaming for him to close the distance, to finish what we'd started in that car.

"Tell me you don't feel this too," he challenged, bracing his hands on either side of my head, caging me in. The position should have felt threatening. Instead, it felt like coming home. "Tell me that kiss meant nothing."

"You know I can't."

"Then what are we doing, Sunshine?" His face was so close, I could feel his breath on my lips. "Why are we still pretending?"

My heart was racing so fast, I thought it might explode. "Because you're complicated and messy and probably going to break my heart."

"Probably?" That signature smirk appeared, but his eyes remained serious.

"Definitely." I lifted my chin, defiant. "But apparently, I'm a masochist."

His mouth was inches from mine now, his gaze dropping to my lips. "I'm trying to tell you that I'm in love with you. Have been for years. And if you don't stop me in the next three seconds, I'm going to show you exactly how much."

The challenge in his voice made something wild unfurl in my chest. I lifted my chin higher, meeting his intensity with my own.

"One."

His eyes darkened to molten silver.

"Two."

His hand slid into my hair, fingers tangling in the strands.

"Thr—"

He crashed his mouth to mine, and every coherent thought evaporated. This wasn't gentle or sweet or careful. This was years of pent-up desire exploding between us, consuming us both. His tongue swept into my mouth, and I moaned, shameless, fingers fisting in his shirt, pulling him impossibly closer.

When he lifted me against him, I wrapped my legs around his waist without hesitation, like my body had been waiting for this moment forever.

As he carried me down the hallway, his mouth never leaving mine, hands gripping me like I might disappear, one thought echoed through my mind.

I am completely, utterly, and irrevocably in love.
And I wouldn't have it any other way.

45

LET HIM GIVE YOU AN ORGASM IN A BUBBLE BATH. 🛁✨ #LIFEADVICE

DAKOTA

Axel's lips were soft, and this time, whatever he'd been holding back came completely undone. His fingers threaded through my hair gently, his eyes sweeping over the wound on my head to make sure he wouldn't hurt me.

I pulled back to whisper one loud declaration. "I love you too."

A moment. A beat of our hearts, and then Axel crashed his lips to mine.

The kiss took on a life of its own. Our bodies pressed together with all the unleashed passion we'd both been denying for years. I trailed my hands down his chest, feeling every ridge and dip of muscle that tightened with each movement of his body.

And with each movement, he ignited that familiar heat coiling in my lower belly, that throb between my thighs that made me want to feel these magnetic lips everywhere. Made me want to pull him on top of me and finally, finally ...

God, if only I didn't feel so dirty and gross right now. It was massively inconvenient—the dried blood streaked through my hair and down my neck, staining my dress. Equally inconvenient that instead of smelling like roses, the antiseptic scent of the hospital clung to my skin. Neither exactly the ingredients for a romantic encounter.

And not just any romantic encounter. *The* romantic encounter. The one I'd pretended I hadn't dreamed about for years. The one I'd fantasized about alone in my bed, in the quiet darkness of my room, pretending it was Axel's hands on my body.

Because looking back on it now, I realized that every step we'd taken over the last few years had been centered around each other.

The truth hit me like ice water in my veins, sharp and sudden and impossible to ignore. Mathew had once held my affection. But Axel?

Axel had always had my bones.

He lived in the marrow of me, in that primal place where logic went to die. Every cell in my body still turned toward him like a plant seeking sun, even after he'd learned to look through me as if I were made of glass. Even after he'd trained himself to grimace when I entered a room, as if my very presence burned.

I'd buried this want so deep, I'd almost convinced myself it was dead. Almost.

But all these years, he'd invaded my thoughts. I'd replayed that moment outside Knox's college home when some guy hit on me and Axel shoved him against the brick wall so hard, dust rained down. The sound of the impact, the way his knuckles went white, gripping the guy's collar. Not because Knox asked him to, but because something fierce and possessive had flashed in those eyes, turning them almost black.

How at that party Knox invited me to, Axel had stationed himself in the corner, nursing a beer, his gaze tracking me through the crowd like a laser. Every time some drunk frat boy got too close, Axel would somehow materialize nearby, his muscular presence alone enough to send them scurrying.

The time I'd tripped on that sidewalk crack, how he'd scooped me into his arms without hesitation, my body flush against his chest. I remembered the sharp intake of his breath, the way his arms had tightened around me for just a second too long, like it was the excuse he'd been waiting for his whole life.

And, God, how he'd held me that starlit night, looking down at me while his smile slowly faded, his heart hammering so hard, I could feel it against my ribs as his gaze dropped to my mouth. How his lips had parted and he'd drawn closer and closer, and I'd wanted his mouth on mine so badly, I could taste it. Until Knox's hand smacked Axel's shoulder, bursting our bubble like a pin to a balloon.

Yes. For years, I'd relived those moments, couldn't stop thinking about him, even when I desperately wanted to. Even as the years stretched on with no contact between us.

I'd asked myself why I found myself comparing every man to Axel. Why, even in the early days with Mathew, I'd wondered what it would feel like to have Axel's hands on me instead. Why the sound of his name could make my stomach flip.

Because it hadn't been just a crush, I realized. It had been recognition. Something my soul knew, even when my mind and heart fought against it. Even when it was a relationship that could never—would never—be real, some part of me had been reaching for him across every room, every year, every carefully constructed wall I'd built.

And now, finally, he was here. In my arms. Real and solid and mine.

Axel pulled back slightly, his gaze sweeping over the dried blood streaked across my skin.

"Let's get you cleaned up," he murmured, stroking my cheek with his thumb. His voice was gentle, but I could hear the barely restrained hunger beneath it, the desperate edge of a man who wanted to take me here and now but was fighting every instinct to do exactly that.

Chicago's biggest playboy could have had me in this moment. Hell, with any other woman, I bet he would have. But with me—

God, with me—he cared enough to put my needs first. To make sure I wasn't in pain. To ensure I felt clean and safe before we crossed this line we'd been dancing around for years.

He wanted to wash the stain of tonight's attack away so that when we finally came together, it wouldn't be in the shadow of violence and blood. So that one of the most important memories of my life could be exactly what it deserved to be: just us, finally us, with nothing ugly standing between what we felt.

"I'm going to draw you a bath." He kissed my forehead. A sweet, tender moment that lasted all of one second but penetrated straight through to my heart. With one last look into my eyes, checking to make sure I was okay, Axel set me down onto the bathroom floor.

Pressing my fingers to my lips, I couldn't stop the smile from spreading across my face as the sound of running water echoed against the tile.

"You have bubble bath?" I quirked an eyebrow.

"Came in one of those holiday gift baskets people always send." Axel rolled up his sleeves, exposing the long lines of his forearms, which were deliciously covered in tattoos.

"Do you like baths?" I wondered aloud, trailing my finger along the white bubbles floating in the deep tub.

"No." He shoved his hands into his pockets, tilting his head in a way that made me want to rip his clothes off right here and now. "I've never even drawn a bath before."

"Never?"

"Not once."

"Not even for another ... girlfriend?" I wasn't sure what to call his past non-relationships. The women he'd shared a bed with but nothing more, and after his confession about his ex-fiancée, I wasn't about to use that term either.

"No," Axel said simply, like it wasn't the biggest confession ever. To hear him doing this for me. Only me. He reached up to sweep my hair over my shoulder. "We need to get you out of this dress."

We. I could practically hear angels singing at that one word. Because the last thing I wanted was for Axel to leave right now.

"Can I stay?" he asked softly.

With those three words, I knew exactly what he was asking. He could leave me here to take this bath alone, or I could let him stay and help wash the darkness and violence off my skin.

I didn't even hesitate. "Yes."

With the water still running in the background, Axel stepped closer. Still wearing his button-down shirt and suit pants, he motioned for me to turn around. With my back to him, I swept my hair over one shoulder, feeling him there, hearing his breathing as his fingers gently grasped the zipper of my dress and slowly drew it down.

The fabric fell from my shoulders, down my arms, and caught on my hips. With my back bare, Axel delicately tugged the fabric over my hips and let it pool to the ground.

Wearing nothing but black lace panties, I turned. For a moment, his gaze met mine. Then it slowly wandered down my entire body. I could feel his stare everywhere: the heat of it on my collarbone, my breasts, my pebbled nipples, my abs, the space between my thighs. His breathing changed, grew deeper, and a look of pain crossed his features, like it took every ounce of restraint to keep his hands off me.

I eyed the tub, then made a decision and dropped my panties to the ground.

Axel's gaze snapped from mine to the space between my thighs. With his fingers twitching at his sides, he growled in a desperate command, "Dakota, get in the tub." Like I'd better hurry, before his control snapped.

I held back my smile but accepted his hand for balance as I stepped into the tub and sank into the bubbles. The water was warm, but not nearly as warm as the heat coming off Axel's eyes as he took a seat on the tub's edge, grabbed a soft white washcloth, dipped it beneath the water, and drew it along my neck.

When it came back coated in crimson, his body stilled.

"I'm sorry this happened to you."

"We don't know for sure it was some Mafia guy," I reminded him. "It could have been a random act of violence. Or an obsessed fan online that turned violent." The thought made me shudder. "Maybe I've been reckless with my online business. Dangerous."

He stilled, tilting my chin up to look at him. "Don't you dare do that. Do not blame yourself. This isn't on you, Dakota."

"I'm not blaming myself. I'm wondering if there could have been unintended consequences with always trying to look picture-perfect online."

"You're allowed to be exactly who you want to be."

I drew water over my arms, keeping my voice gentle. "Can we just pretend this whole attack thing didn't happen for right now?" Because, God, I had dreamed of a moment like this for so long; I didn't want whoever attacked me to steal even more from me than they already had.

It took him a second, but eventually, he nodded. He dipped the washcloth into the sudsy water, shut off the faucet so the tub didn't overflow, and proceeded to gently wash my face, my neck, my collarbone. My shoulders. Anywhere that had a drop of crimson was scrubbed completely clean. The whole time, he kept his eyes mostly fixed on mine, only letting them drift down when he absolutely needed to see what he was doing.

Every stroke of the cloth wound something tighter in my chest, a sweet ache that spread like honey through my limbs, and when I was completely clean of all my makeup, blood, and the grime of the evening, Axel didn't stop washing my skin.

Instead, he dipped the washcloth beneath the sudsy water and drew it to the hollow of my throat. He moved lower, slowly, until it grazed delicately over my left breast.

My nipples pebbled.

His eyes locked with mine as he dropped the cloth and traced the bud between his fingers.

Every cell in my body stood at attention, begging for their turn to be touched by him. He cupped my breast firmly, causing me to suck in a sharp breath, and then he knelt next to the tub so he could kiss me.

With his mouth on mine, he massaged my breasts, one at a time, like he wanted to memorize how they felt, every curve of them. He played with my nipples gently, but soon, our kiss deepened, and I threaded my wet fingers through his hair.

His hand began its descent from my breast, each inch a deliberate torture. Rough fingertips traced the curve of my ribs, explored the dip of my waist, and then his palm flattened against my abs, my muscles fluttering beneath his touch.

Lower.

My breath caught.

Lower still.

The anticipation coiled tight in my belly. Without conscious thought, my legs parted. An invitation. A plea. My sex throbbed with a need so acute, it bordered on pain while every nerve ending seemed to pulse in time with my racing heart.

His fingers hovered just above where I ached for him. Close enough that I could feel the heat radiating from his skin. Not close enough. Never close enough.

Then ...

His fingers slid over me with exquisite care, and my entire body trembled. The world narrowed to that single point of connection. To the way he touched me like I was precious. Like he had all the time in the world to learn every secret my body wanted to tell.

His mouth found my jaw. Teeth grazing. Lips soothing. He traced a path to my collarbone, tasting the water droplets that clung there. All the while, his fingers circled that bundle of nerves with maddening precision. Slow. Steady. Inevitable.

Something began to build inside me. Too fast. Too intense. Embarrassingly quickly, but I was past embarrassment. Past everything except the feel of Axel's hands and mouth and the promise of what was to come.

"I want to taste you," he said against my skin. Oh my God. "But you'd be cold out here."

I licked my lower lip. "I'll survive."

I could feel his lips curve into a smile. And then, much quicker than I was expecting, Axel lifted my body out of the tub, placing me on the tub's edge with a splash of water crashing against the floor's tile.

I thought he was going to grab a towel, dry me off, maybe carry me to his bed. But instead, he stood up, kicked off his shoes, stepped into the tub between my legs, and sank to his knees.

Fully clothed, a fresh wave of water splashing outside the tub's rim.

Holy crap. This is so hot.

Kissing my leg, he drew my right ankle up onto the side of the tub, followed by my left, until I was sitting there, spread open like an offering, my back pressed against the cool wall as he stared at my sex. Unbuttoning his shirt, he drew my nipple into his mouth, circling the bud with his tongue while that throb between my legs intensified. When he stripped his shirt off, it made me want him even more.

Axel Pierce was gorgeous. Covered in tattoos, his muscles flexed as he ran his hands over my abs, kissing a trail down them before pressing my thighs further apart.

With one last look that could have given me an orgasm with just his eyes, Axel lowered his mouth to me. The moment stretched between us, steam curling around our bodies, creating a sanctuary where only we existed.

The first touch of his tongue sent lightning through my veins. I jerked. Gasped. My fingers found the cool porcelain edge of the tub, gripping hard as he circled that perfect bundle of nerves. Over and over. My hips bucked of their own accord, my back arching as I threaded trembling fingers through his wet hair. Dark strands slipped between my knuckles. Water droplets traced paths down his neck, disappearing into the hollow of his throat.

I had never seen anything like this. My wet body with suds lingering on my toes, perched on the tub's edge. Axel Pierce on his knees before me, shirtless, his soaked pants clinging to powerful thighs. He touched me like I was something sacred. Something worth worshipping. The memory surfaced, unbidden: *"You deserve to feel worshipped, cherished, absolutely wrecked in the best possible way."*

His groan vibrated against my skin.

"You taste so good, Sunshine." His voice was rough velvet as he pulled back to look at me. One finger traced along my folds with maddening slowness. "Just like I knew you would."

He flattened his tongue. Pressed hard. The sound that escaped me was primal.

Good Lord. He wasn't kidding. Axel Pierce knew my body better than I knew it myself. He moved against my folds with the same intensity he'd shown when he'd slept on my floor, protective and unwavering. *"Go to sleep, Sunshine. I'll be right here."* But now that protective intensity had transformed into something darker. Hungrier.

He teased. Brought me to the edge. Those knowing eyes locked with mine before he retreated. When I moaned in agony, his lips curved into that familiar smirk. The same one he'd worn when he'd growled against my ear, *"You're telling me if I dip my fingers in your panties right now, they won't come back glistening?"*

"Trust me, Sunshine." His breath was hot against my sensitive flesh. "It's going to be so much better if I make you wait for it."

"Please." The word broke from my lips.

"Good girl." He licked around my sex while his hands gripped my thighs, anchoring me. Possessive. Like when he'd tangled his fingers in my hair. Like when he'd promised violence to anyone who dared hurt me. "When you shatter, it'll be my name on your tongue. You understand?"

I bit my lip. Nodded desperately. "Yes."

His mouth returned to the apex of my thighs with renewed focus. Swirling. Sucking. Building a climax that gathered like a storm in my core. His tongue moved with the same certainty he'd shown that day in the snow, when everything between us had shifted. *"I've never looked at snow the same way since."*

And suddenly, I understood. This wasn't just physical. This was Axel seeing me. Really seeing me. The way he'd noticed undercooked meat made me nauseous when no one else paid attention. The way he'd known I deserved passion that would leave marks on my soul.

I wasn't holding back anymore. Wasn't self-conscious about being spread before him. Wasn't wondering if my body was perfect. I had completely surrendered to the riptide of Axel, letting the current of desire pull me under. Into his ocean. Into him.

The climax built. Crested. When it crashed over me, I was brazen enough to hold his head in place. My fingers twisted in his hair. Our eyes locked as I screamed his name. No shame. No hesitation. Just pure, devastating release.

He watched my mouth part. Watched the moans escape. His tongue never stopped its rhythm as I quivered and trembled against him. Wave after wave of pleasure rolled through me until I thought I might come apart entirely.

This was what he'd promised. To make me forget my own name. To worship me until I saw stars.

And, God help me, he delivered.

"I love you," I said as he licked the last remnants of my orgasm into submission.

"Mmm ..." He kissed my inner thigh. "I love you too, Sunshine."

He stood up, water dripping from his pants, his erection pressing against the zipper so hard, I wondered if the metal would burst open. I leaned forward and grabbed his belt, pulling the leather from the buckle.

When a very unwanted sound interrupted us—the penthouse's version of a doorbell: a chime.

The one that alerted us that someone was on their way up, about to spill out into the penthouse. Not just anyone could come up; they had to check in with the front lobby, of course, which meant this was someone scheduled or preapproved.

Axel went completely still. His eyes widened as he looked toward the hallway, then slowly, painfully, back at me.

"No." He shook his head. "No, no, no ..."

Right. Ryker had graciously organized the detective to come *here* rather than us having to wait who knew how long at the ER for him to show.

"The police," I realized.

He dropped his forehead against mine, looking like a man who'd just been informed his birthday had been canceled. Forever.

"You've got to be kidding me." I let go of his belt.

Axel made a sound like a dying animal. "I'm deactivating that fucking elevator. And surrounding my place with a moat."

Looking like it literally tortured him, he stepped out of the tub and wrapped a fluffy towel around me with the careful, mournful movements of a man whose dreams had just been destroyed. He dried himself off quickly.

"Fucking hell." Axel stormed into the hallway, muttering, "Protect and serve ... more like interrupt and ruin ..."

With the towel securely fastened around my body, my plan was to dart into the bedroom and get dressed so I could give the police my statement. But right as Axel said, "The hell are you two doing here?" I froze.

Turned.

And saw that it wasn't the police who had interrupted us. It was Ryker and Faith.

Whose gaze had been busy taking in Axel's soaking wet pants (and probably his massive erection) before snapping to me, wearing nothing but a towel, caught sneaking toward his bedroom.

Faith smirked. "Well, looks like you're feeling better."

"What are you doing here?" Axel repeated angrily.

"The police are downstairs," Ryker said matter-of-factly.

"Remember how I arranged to have you give your statements here?"

"I thought they were showing up later," Axel said.

"It *is* later."

"Did you get"—Faith's eyes glided over Axel's godlike form—"distracted? Time run away from you?"

Axel shoved his hands down in front of his crotch.

Which only made Faith's smirk widen as she offered me a wink. "I can see what the appeal is. Congrats, girl."

"Faith!" I protested.

She shrugged. "If you have to be fake engaged to him, at least you're getting the real perks too. *Big* ones. Good for you."

Axel looked up at the heavens like he willed them to swallow him whole.

"Want us to reschedule?" Faith waggled her eyebrows. "I mean, we could always tell the police you were ... indisposed."

My cheeks incinerated. The idea of them all leaving, knowing we'd be having sex? I think not.

"No," I said quickly.

"We can't reschedule," Ryker chastised, ever the responsible one.

Okay, Axel could have made an effort to look less disappointed.

"What are you two doing *together*?" I wondered aloud.

Because looking closer, was it just me, or was Faith's hair a little mussed?

"Bumped into him downstairs," Faith explained. "I was coming here to check on you." She smirked. "Looks like you're feeling great though."

After a few seconds, Axel pinched the bridge of his nose, told them to sit in the living room, that he was going to change, and when he approached me, he leaned down and whispered, "Biggest case of blue balls I've ever had, Sunshine."

I chuckled. "At least now I know Faith approves of your ... assets."

"Jesus Christ," he muttered, but I caught the hint of a smile as he disappeared into his bedroom.

Faith called after us, "Take your time *getting dressed*! We'll just be out here … not thinking about what we just interrupted!"

"I'm never living this down," Axel groaned from the bedroom.

"Neither am I," I called back, but honestly, I was too blissed out to care.

46

PLOT TWIST: APPARENTLY, "I'LL FIND THEM FIRST" ISN'T WHAT DETECTIVES WANT TO HEAR. #LEGALADVICE

AXEL

"You're implying this was a good thing?" I snapped, my voice cutting through the room like a blade.

The detective's hardened eyes met mine.

"Axel," Ryker warned from his chair across the room.

I stood up, crossing my arms over my chest, glaring at the law enforcement officer in front of me. "No, he can explain himself. How my fiancée getting attacked is somehow a good thing. I'd like to hear this."

My eyes briefly locked with Dakota's, and using the word *fiancée* this time felt different than any other time I'd said it. There was more truth behind it now. Something real and raw that made my chest tight.

Her pupils dilated slightly, and I saw her breath catch. Even in the middle of this nightmare, that electric current between us was undeniable.

"What I said was"—the detective spoke his words slowly, like I was a child who couldn't comprehend—"he did this in a public area. There are multiple security cameras. We're already tracking them down and following his path. Identifying him will be much easier than—"

"We already know who's behind this," I reminded him, tension coiling tight between my shoulder blades.

"You suspect. You don't know for sure. And frankly, Mr. Pierce, your theory about organized crime might not align with the evidence. This looks more like random street violence. It's our job to find the actual perpetrator and lock them up."

"Random?" I laughed, but there was no humor in it. "Someone sends us threatening black roses, and then Dakota gets attacked? That's not random."

"Correlation isn't causation," the detective replied. "We see attacks like this all over Chicago. Young woman, alone at night, valuable jewelry. Could be a robbery gone wrong."

"Well, thank God for crimes against women. Otherwise, you wouldn't have a job."

"Axel!" Ryker snapped.

It was only the sharp tone of my friend that drew me out of my cloud of rage. I ran a hand over my face, the lingering dampness from the bath still clinging to parts of my hair where Dakota had run her fingers through it, reminding myself that this detective was supposed to be on our side. But, honest to God, when he started implying that this brutal attack against Dakota was somehow beneficial? How the hell was I supposed to react to that?

Dakota had been violently assaulted and could've been killed. How dare anyone suggest that was in any way good?

"I've got what I need for now." The detective stood up.

"That's it?" The disbelief in my voice was evident.

"For now."

I ground my molars together, tasting copper. "How quickly will you arrest him?"

"These things take time, Mr. Pierce."

"We don't have time!" I motioned toward the black roses still sitting on my kitchen counter, their thorns looking more menacing under the dim lighting. "Someone left us a threatening note—"

"Which you failed to report until now."

"And now they've escalated to physical violence."

"*Someone* attacked her," the detective corrected with maddening precision. "This is a big city, Mr. Pierce. Random violence happens every day. We can't assume every crime is connected to your ... celebrity status."

"Celebrity status. Like this was about fame and not about someone threatening the woman I ..."

The air in the room seemed to thicken, and I could feel Dakota's eyes on me, watching as every muscle in my body tensed like a coiled spring ready to snap.

"It's not random," I said, my voice dropping. "And you'd better catch whoever did this fast. Before I get to them first."

"Axel!" Ryker snapped.

The detective's expression hardened. "Mr. Pierce, I'd advise against making threats—"

"That wasn't a threat." I stepped closer, close enough that he had to tilt his head up to maintain eye contact. "That was a promise. Someone put their hands on her. Left bruises on her skin. Made her bleed." My voice cracked slightly on the last word. "So, you find them, Detective. Because if I find them first, you'll have a real crime scene to investigate."

47

WHEN YOU'RE ABOUT TO CHANGE YOUR LIFE FOREVER, JUST TAKE A DEEP BREATH. #NOTURNINGBACK

DAKOTA

"It's simple." Rebecca's voice crackled through the phone, her words as artificially sweet. "The brand reps have empathy for you having been attacked. Just go online, showcase some products, and show them you're still reliable. They'll be watching. Make it perfect, and you'll be home free."

Home free. As if *free* was a word that could ever describe the gilded cage I'd built around myself.

The truth was, this fake engagement with Axel was just the most recent and outrageous lie in a long catalog of deceptions. I'd been lying to my followers—hell, lying to myself—for so long, I sometimes couldn't remember what truth even felt like anymore.

My gaze swept across my studio in Axel's penthouse. The symphony of beauty lights, positioned at mathematically perfect angles. The expensive camera, mounted on its tripod. The rack, bursting with designer clothes I'd been "gifted" to showcase. My entire life, curated into a perfect, pore-less fantasy.

And I was so goddamn tired of it.

With trembling fingers, I grabbed the ring light and unceremoniously unplugged it. The shadows immediately crawled across my face in the mirror. Shadows I normally edited away with filters and strategic lighting. I dragged my phone holder to the other side of the room, where the unforgiving afternoon light would expose every imperfection.

This is it. No going back.

I activated the live camera on my social media app, heart hammering against my ribs like it was trying to escape. One deep breath. Then another. Before I could talk myself out of it, I pressed the blinking red button.

Live.

Immediately, notification pings erupted from my iPad with followers streaming in, curious about this unscheduled appearance from @DakotaFox. A cold sweat broke out across my back as the viewer count ticked upward.

"Hi," I said, my voice smaller than I intended. I cleared my throat and straightened my shoulders. "It's Dakota here. I have a major confession to make."

My iPad buzzed angrily on the nightstand. Undoubtedly our PR team already in panic mode.

"Trust me, it's not something you're going to want to miss," I continued, ignoring the vibrations. "But to do this right, I'm not going to stand here with my meticulous makeup in this outfit."

I backed away from the camera, gesturing to the designer dress clinging to my curves like a second skin.

"Let's talk about this outfit for a moment." My fingertips traced the intricate beadwork along the neckline. "This dress was donated by a top designer and then custom-tailored to fit every curve of my body. The fabric is high-end, the stitching is meticulous, and the tailoring enhances the shape of my body while hiding the imperfections."

I turned slowly, letting the light catch on the expensive material.

"Any one of you would look like a million dollars if you wore the same dress and it was tailored to fit you perfectly. But the truth is, this dress makes my body look a lot better than it does in real life, so I'm going to change. Stick with me, and I'll be right back."

I grabbed a pair of worn gray sweats and a plain white tank top from my drawer—clothes that never made appearances on my feed—and hurried down the hall. As I peeled off the designer dress, it felt like shedding a skin I'd outgrown. The soft cotton of the tank slid over my head, the familiar sweats loose around my hips. For the first time in months, I could breathe.

When I returned to the camera, the viewer count had exploded to 10,000. Comments bubbled frantically at the bottom of the screen, a chaotic stream of questions about Axel, about the "big confession," about a million things I couldn't focus on. I swiped the comments away with a flick of my finger.

"By now, you may have heard rumors that I've been faking an engagement to Axel." *Thanks, Mathew, for posting a smear campaign*. I'd decided I'd wanted to come clean on my own, but he'd beaten me to it. Ironically, most of my followers didn't believe him, so I could have easily denied it.

I grabbed a brush and began dismantling the perfect waves in my hair. Waves that had taken an hour to create this morning. With quick, almost-violent movements, I scraped my hair into a messy bun on top of my head, making no effort to fix the stray strands jutting out at odd angles.

"People have accused me of staging this public whirlwind engagement to save face from a mistake I made." I paused, meeting my own eyes in the phone screen. "I'm here to tell you ... it's absolutely true."

The viewer count skyrocketed as I gathered cotton pads and makeup remover from my dresser. My hands weren't shaking anymore. There was something almost freeing in finally saying it out loud.

Luckily, Axel's deal had already been inked. After the disaster at dinner, Frank and Carl had reached out to him. Not to back out, but to check on me after what happened. When Axel apologized for the evening, he'd apparently been completely honest about his feelings for me, how much he wanted this to work between us.

But then he'd shifted gears. He told them he understood if they had reservations about him personally, but that he'd never let the vulnerable people in the prison system down. This wasn't just business to him. The passion fueled everything he did, and something about his raw honesty in that moment convinced them the opportunity was too solid to pass up.

Especially when they went over the numbers again. Plus, they'd gotten an unsettling glimpse of Mathew that night. The way he'd baited Axel, that calculated malice in his smile. Oh, and let's not forget hiring a PI. Holy creepy. They'd started asking questions about their new employee, and apparently, they didn't love what they were hearing.

In any case, I didn't have to worry about sabotaging Axel's deal with what I was about to do. If not for that, I might not have the courage to do the right thing.

"I've been lying to everyone," I continued, dipping a pad in makeup remover and bringing it to my eye. The cold liquid seeped through my lashes. "I did it because the repercussions of my mistake weren't confined to me. They put my family in jeopardy, and I was willing to do whatever it took to protect them."

I dragged the cotton across my eyelid, watching as the expertly applied shadow transferred from my face to the white pad, now smeared with bronze and gold and black.

"But I went about it all wrong. What I should have done was simply come online, apologize, and accept whatever consequences came my way. You all deserved honesty, not a cover-up."

With one eye completely bare, I grabbed a fresh pad for the other. The asymmetry of my reflection was jarring: half the carefully constructed Dakota Fox, half the woman beneath.

The viewer count had surged to 55,000. My iPad pinged relentlessly.

"The truth is, I've known Axel for a long time." My voice softened at his name, an involuntary tell I hoped no one would notice. "The night I posted that picture of him online, I never meant to post it publicly. But that doesn't change that it was mean-spirited, fueled by alcohol and jealousy."

I swallowed hard, forcing myself to continue.

"I was jealous that Axel was giving that woman attention. I was jealous because I wanted to be that woman." The admission burned my throat like whiskey. "Rather than admit that to myself or my friends, it was easier and less painful to tell myself that he was a bad guy. A playboy with no heart."

My makeup-free eyes stared back at me from the screen, vulnerable and exposed.

"It was a narrative I'd told myself for longer than I can remember."

I grabbed the phone holder and brought it into the bathroom with me, propping it on the counter. The harsh angle of lighting was merciless, highlighting every pore, every freckle, every slight discoloration I normally concealed.

"If this public relations nightmare had only impacted me," I said, running water over a washcloth, "I'd like to tell you that I would've done the right thing, taken responsibility, and apologized."

The cloth turned warm in my hands as I worked soap into a lather. I pressed it against my face, feeling the weight of it against my skin.

"But the truth is, I don't know what I would've done," I admitted, my voice partially muffled by the cloth. "I've spent years creating this social media company, and I don't know if I would've had the courage to take responsibility if doing so jeopardized everything I'd built."

I scrubbed the skin around my lips, feeling the cool air against my wet skin like a baptism in honesty. Foundation transferred to the white cloth, staining it the artificial tan that I'd passed off as my natural complexion.

"Regardless, my mistake hurt Axel. It hurt my family. And it jeopardized their businesses." I met my increasingly bare face in the mirror, forcing myself not to flinch. "To all of my viewers, companies I've worked with, to Axel, to my family and friends, I sincerely apologize."

I moved the cloth down to my neck, where the line between my makeup and natural skin had always been carefully blended. Now, that separation was exposed, a literal line between truth and fiction.

"Once the lie started, others started building on top of it like a house of cards, and suddenly, I felt like there was no way out." My voice cracked, and I cleared my throat. "My family has been through a lot, and if my social media business failed, it would affect them." I wiped my face dry with a clean towel, patting gently at skin that felt raw and new. Moving my phone holder back to the dresser and the unforgiving light, I sat down, letting the shadows reveal the darker side of me I'd kept hidden.

"There's one more thing you don't know about me." I sucked in a breath, steeling myself, "My name isn't Dakota Fox. It's Dakota Blackwood. My brother is in prison for murder."

The comment notification sound became a constant drone, reactions flooding in like a ruptured dam, but I couldn't bring myself to look at them. My heart pounded in my ears, nearly drowning out my own voice.

"My brother's story is his own, but from early on, I assumed if people knew that about me, they'd never accept me." I dug crescents into my palms.

The words tumbled out faster now, as if the first confession had broken something open inside me and all the ugly truths I'd hoarded were spilling free. Each admission felt like peeling off another layer of armor I'd worn so long, it had fused to my skin.

"Regardless of where my fear started, it doesn't change what I did. It gives me no excuse. I should never have taken that picture of Axel to begin with. I was being snarky and mean."

I pushed a stray strand of hair from my face, tucking it behind my ear.

"Because that's the truth. I am nice and kind and giving, and I can also be flawed." The admission felt like setting down a weight I'd carried for years.

My eyes stung with unshed tears, but I refused to let them fall. This was my mess, and I had no right to feel sorry for myself right now. The people who had every right to be upset were the now 134,000 viewers witnessing this meltdown in real time.

"I guess I presumed early on in my social media life that folks don't like people who are flawed." I gestured vaguely at the expensive equipment surrounding me. "So, I started Photoshopping images to erase imperfections. When I recorded myself, I made sure my makeup was always flawless, my hair done perfectly. I started wearing clothing that enhanced my body. I used filters that made my skin look perfect."

I tilted my face at different angles, letting the shadows and light expose every pore, every tiny red mark and blackhead that normally never saw the light of day on my feed.

"I thought I had to be this perfect version of myself. And it seemed like once I started doing that, my views and followers skyrocketed." I exhaled slowly. "But the more I created this perfect persona, the less true to myself I became."

I moved to the floor, sitting cross-legged in front of the camera, no longer concerned with how the angle might emphasize my double chin or the way my stomach folded when I sat.

"The truth is, I'm just an ordinary girl. I'm nothing special. There's no difference between someone with ten followers versus me with millions."

I looked down at my fingers, twisting them nervously in my lap.

"Well, I suppose there's one big difference, isn't there?" A humorless smile escaped me. "The girl with ten followers is being authentic and honest. And I wasn't. I never deserved those millions of followers."

My chest felt tight, like something was pressing against it from the inside, demanding release.

"From the bottom of my heart, I'm really sorry. I lied to you. I misled you, long before I pretended to get engaged to Axel." The words tumbled out faster now. "To the brands that entrusted me with your sponsorships, I'm sorry. To my family, who never put the burden of keeping their lives financially afloat on me, I'm sorry."

I paused, my throat constricting as Axel's face flashed in my mind. Not the smirking playboy the public saw, but the man who'd held me when I cried about Knox, who'd seen me at my worst and still agreed to this ridiculous charade.

"And to Axel …" My voice broke, betraying me. I pinched the bridge of my nose, fighting for composure. "I'm really sorry for what I put you through. You all deserved better than what I've done."

Through the window behind me, the sun cast long shadows across the room. How fitting that darkness would soon fall as I finally stepped into the light.

"Social media has a dark side," I said softly. "You open it up, and you see the best five percent of someone's life. Or worse, a false version that makes everything look perfect and makes you feel even more imperfect than you already do."

The memories flooded back of endless nights of scrolling, comparing, despairing.

"They have a clean house, or they make perfect food, or they have a perfect body, or they have the best makeup or hair or clothes or friends or whatever. I swear, I used to open social media, and whatever insecurity I was feeling, it had this power to magnify that vulnerability and make me feel worse about myself."

I placed a hand flat against my chest, feeling my heartbeat beneath my palm.

"And I probably made you feel worse about yourself." The realization hit with fresh pain. How had I never thought of that before? "What I wish I would've done differently was be true to myself and be true to you. I mean, so what if my hair was messy? So what if I had a coffee stain on my shirt or dust on my desk when filming?"

A tear finally escaped, sliding down my cheek.

"Maybe if I would've had the courage to lean into that, maybe everything would've been different."

I paused.

"I thought being vulnerable made me weak. That revealing imperfections would lead to being rejected. I thought that the perfectly curated image I'd created was what people wanted, and sadly, that extended to my romantic relationships too. I thought anyone who saw the real me would leave. But my obsession with appearing perfect prevented me from having meaningful, genuine connections and made me less authentic with you, my audience. I've learned that in life, true intimacy and authenticity are about sharing both strengths and weaknesses. So"—I opened my arms wide, turning my face from side to side—"this is me. No makeup. No filter. No hairdo, and no beautiful outfit."

The words came easier now, a dam breaking. "The truth is, I'm a hot mess, just like many other people out there. The difference is, I let my insecurities lead my life while others were much braver than I was."

I leaned closer to the camera, as if I could somehow reach through the screen and connect with each person watching.

"Please know that social media isn't bad. It's actually a wonderful place. There's a whole world of people you get to meet. There's inspiration, joy, ideas, and camaraderie. And there are plenty of people being authentic and cheering each other on. I wish I had been one of those people."

My phone had stopped buzzing. Either my PR team had given up or they were watching in horrified silence like everyone else.

"I took all of that for granted when I agreed to this charade. Please know this whole thing is on me, not my family, who knew nothing about it. And it's not on Axel."

The memory of his eyes, dark with his profession of love, tightened my chest.

"Axel is ... he's a really good guy." My voice dropped to nearly a whisper. "I'm the one who dragged him into this, not the other way around."

More tears now, falling freely despite my best efforts to contain them. I swiped at them with the back of my hand.

"Anyway," I said, pulling in a shaky breath, "I just wanted to come on here and apologize and thank you for everything you've done for me."

I looked directly into the camera, letting them see the redness in my eyes, the blotchiness in my cheeks.

"With my last post, I wanted to show you who I really am. I'm a girl who has let her insecurities rule her life. I'm a girl who camouflaged those insecurities with images of perfection online. But that ends today. Today, I embrace my true self."

The setting sun cast its final golden rays across my bare face. I squared my shoulders, feeling both lighter and heavier than I had in years.

"Today I'm not signing off as Dakota Fox." My finger hovered over the end button. "I'm signing off as Dakota Blackwood."

As the screen went black, my phone immediately exploded with notifications, but I shifted my attention to the floor-length mirror.

I hadn't realized how much my obsession with perfectionism had chipped away at my self-esteem. By habitually editing every single image of myself, I had trained my mind to hunt for my imperfections.

And remove them.

The way my right eye was slightly bigger than my left, just like my grandmother's had been. God, I missed her so much, and I had the blessing of seeing her in the mirror every day through my eyes, yet I filtered them out? As if they were something to be ashamed of instead of treasured.

The freckles that dusted my skin. The ones that matched my beautiful mother's, the ones that linked me to my family's DNA, that proved I belonged to something bigger than myself. How could I have ever not been proud of them? How could I have seen them as anything but a gift?

The tiny lines around my eyes, the ones I'd been desperately smoothing out in every photo. Those weren't wrinkles; they were proof of joy, times I'd laughed so hard, the happiness was literally etched into my skin. Every line a memory of doubled-over laughter with friends, of moments so perfect that my face couldn't contain the smile. And I'd been erasing them like they were mistakes.

And that slight scar on my temple, barely visible, unless you knew where to look. The one I'd gotten when Dad was teaching me to ride a bike, his strong hands steadying me before letting go, trusting me to fly. That tiny mark was proof of his love, of a perfect Saturday afternoon when I was seven and brave. I should have wanted to frame it, not conceal it.

Somewhere along the way, I'd grown to hate these pieces of me, and I no longer looked at images of myself and saw beauty.

I saw flaws.

But they weren't flaws at all. They were love letters written on my body, proof of where I came from, evidence of being loved. And being unique.

Worse than that, somewhere along the way, I had fallen out of love with the girl that I was. I had let the girl in the mirror down. Convinced her that she needed to be fixed.

How could I have let this happen?

It wasn't until Axel stormed into my life and made me question all my editing decisions that I finally relooked at my image with a new lens. Seeing myself through a different filter.

Or maybe, for the first time, through no filter at all.

The biggest gift that Axel gave me was making me fall in love with myself again.

My heart broke for the girl staring back at me. The reflection of the woman I had convinced was broken somehow when the only thing that had ever been broken was the cruel voice inside her head: my voice, telling her she wasn't enough.

"You're perfect just the way you are. You're beautiful," I whispered to the girl in the mirror, "and I'm sorry for making you feel like you weren't."

Everyone on this planet was beautiful, if only they'd allow themselves to see it.

Suddenly, something in my peripheral vision grabbed my attention.

Axel.

48

PLOT TWIST: I DIDN'T EXPECT HIS REACTION TO INCLUDE BENDING ME OVER HIS DESK. #HOLYHOTNESS

DAKOTA

"You thought you weren't perfect?" Axel's voice cracked through the silence, raw and disbelieving. His anger radiated from him in waves. Not at me. Never at me. At the cruel voice in my head that had whispered lies for so long.

"I ..."

He didn't wait for me to finish before he pushed off the doorframe with barely contained fury. The muscles in his jaw clenched. Released. Clenched again.

But he didn't come to me. Not yet. Instead, he yanked the full-length mirror from its standing position in the corner, propped it against the wall behind the desk so harshly, the glass rattled in its frame. Only then did he reach down, his large hands gripping my arms, pulling me to standing, and as he did, his touch burned through my skin, leaving trails of heat in its wake.

"You were horrible to yourself." The words came out rough, broken. He looked at me the way he'd look at anyone who dared hurt me. Except the enemy this time was my own reflection. "How could you not see how perfect you are?"

His hands found the hem of my tank top. The fabric whispered against my skin as he pulled it over my head. Cool air kissed my bare shoulders. He repeated the motion with my sweats, then my panties, each piece of clothing falling away like old insecurities. Until I stood naked. Exposed. Vulnerable in a way that had nothing to do with lacking clothes.

"Look at yourself."

I swallowed hard and looked at the woman in the mirror. At the shirtless man behind her, his chest covered in intricate black ink that seemed to move with each breath. A phoenix wrapped around his ribs. Thorns and roses climbed his shoulder. All of it flexing with barely controlled need.

"This throat ..." Still standing behind me, Axel drew his fingertips up my neck. The touch was featherlight, tender. My pulse jumped beneath his fingers. "I've watched you throw your head back when you laugh. Watched it flush pink when you're shy." His breath warmed my ear. "This collarbone." His fingers traced its delicate line. "I've imagined kissing it a thousand times."

Goose bumps erupted across my skin and every nerve ending sparked to life, hungry for more.

His hand moved lower, cupping my breast. "These are perfect. The way they fit in my palms. The way your nipples harden just from my breath on your neck."

As if to prove his point, he exhaled slowly against my shoulder. My body responded instantly.

He squeezed my nipple between his fingers inciting a sharp pleasure-pain that made me gasp.

"How dare you not see them as perfect?"

His palm flattened against my stomach, the heat of it searing. "This stomach." His voice caught, just barely, and his fingers spread wider against my skin. The words that came next were quieter. "Beautiful. Perfect."

But he didn't move his hand. Not yet. His thumb traced a small, unconscious circle just below my navel, where a baby would grow if I ever became pregnant, and when I looked up at him, something flickered in his eyes. A question he wasn't ready to ask, maybe wasn't even aware of yet. The moment stretched between us, heavy with unspoken possibility.

Then he blinked, and his hand continued its journey while the ghost of that touch lingered, along with everything he hadn't said.

But coherent thought scattered as his hand traveled lower. His eyes never left mine in the mirror, dark and intense, as his fingers slipped between my folds. I was already wet. Already aching.

"Lift your leg." The command rumbled through his chest, where it pressed against my back. "Put your foot on the chair."

I obeyed, placing my foot on the chair to my right. The position left me completely exposed. Vulnerable. Open.

"Look how perfect and pink and glistening you are." His fingers traced my entrance slowly. Torturously. "Look at how wet you get for me. How your body knows exactly what it wants."

I'd never examined myself like this. Never had the courage. But through Axel's eyes, I saw something different. Something beautiful. The shame I'd carried for so long began to crack and fall away.

He pushed two fingers inside me. Slowly. Letting me feel every inch. My thigh quivered, and heat coiled tight in my belly, spreading outward like wildfire.

"Look at how you take me, Sunshine." His voice was pure gravel now. Pure need. "So tight. So warm. Like you were made for me."

He pushed deeper, curling his fingers to hit that spot that made stars explode behind my eyes. With his free hand, he cupped my breast, thumb circling my nipple, while his lips found my shoulder, his teeth grazing my skin between kisses.

"Say it," he commanded, pumping his fingers faster. "Say you're perfect."

My head fell back against his shoulder and my legs shook.

He stopped moving. Bit down on my shoulder hard enough to sting. "Say. It." He grabbed my chin with his free hand, forcing my gaze back to the mirror. "Watch yourself when you say it."

"I'm perfect," I whispered.

His eyes narrowed. "Not good enough, Sunshine."

He withdrew his fingers. My body clenched around nothing, aching with loss. But suddenly, he was on his knees in front of me. His mouth replaced his fingers, tongue circling that bundle of nerves before sucking hard.

I gasped., and when my hips bucked forward, he gripped my thighs, spreading them wider. From this angle, turned slightly toward the mirror, I could watch everything. His dark hair between my legs. The flex of his shoulders. His tongue disappearing inside me.

"Watch me make you come," he ordered against my flesh. The vibration of his words sent shock waves through me. "See what I see. How beautiful your face is when you shatter."

His tongue was relentless. Circling, flicking, sucking. My hands found his hair, thick and soft between my fingers, and when I tugged hard, he groaned against me, the sound traveling through my core.

He looked up, locked eyes with me, and thrust his tongue deep inside. In and out. Faster. Harder. The coil in my stomach wound tighter, my thighs trembled, and my breath came in short gasps.

Just as I reached the edge, he pulled back and stood in one fluid motion.

Before I could process the ache of having been so close, he spun me around and pushed my chest down against the desk. The wood was cool against my flushed skin. He kicked my legs wider apart, and I heard the rustle of fabric as his pants hit the floor.

"You look at that mirror. Now."

I turned my face to the right. Saw us both reflected there. Me, bent over like an offering. Him, standing behind me like a conquering god. The phoenix on his ribs seemed to spread its wings as he breathed, and his erection stood proud and thick, the head glistening.

"I've been tested." He rubbed himself along my entrance, the sensation making me whimper. "Haven't been with anyone since. Tell me you're on birth control."

"I am."

"Tell me you're perfect."

I hesitated.

His palm connected with my ass, the slap echoing through the room.

I yelped, but heat bloomed where he'd struck.

"Try that again, Sunshine." His palm soothed the stinging skin, circular motions that made me push back against him.

"I'm perfect."

Another slap. Harder. The pain melted into pleasure that made me moan.

"More convincing," he demanded.

"I'm. Perfect."

Slap. My skin burned deliciously.

"Louder."

"I'm perfect!" The words rang out clear and strong.

Bending over, he kissed my tender skin. "Good girl. Now give me your wrists."

He gathered them behind my back, pinning them with one large hand while he used the other to guide himself to my entrance. "Watch the mirror, Sunshine. Watch yourself swallow me."

He breached my entrance slightly, making me exhale a sharp breath of air. Reading my face carefully, putting my needs ahead of his own, Axel waited, letting my body adjust before he pushed in inch by careful inch, and as he sank deeper, his eyes never left mine until finally, with one last controlled thrust, he was all the way inside.

My body stretched around him, the fullness even better than I'd expected—perfect and overwhelming and exactly right.

"You feel incredible, Sunshine." Axel gave my body a few more seconds to adjust to him. "Like you were made for me."

I'd never felt so complete.

"You're so tight." His voice shook with restraint. "Look at how wet you are. See how I glisten when I pull out?"

He withdrew slightly, and I could see him coated with my arousal before he pushed back in. Deeper this time. The fullness was overwhelming, a mixture of perfect pain and perfect pleasure.

"You made me wait for this." He pulled out. Slammed back in hard enough to make the desk creak. "Wore that yoga outfit. Do you know what you looked like? Bent over in downward dog?" Thrust. "I wanted to take you right there on the mat." Thrust. "Make you scream my name in front of everyone. Teach you a lesson for teasing me."

"So, teach me," I moaned, pushing back to meet him.

His muscles tightened. In the mirror, I watched the roses on his shoulder ripple. "Oh, Sunshine. I'm going to claim every inch of your body. Going to make you come so many times, you forget your own name. Only remember mine."

"And I'll claim every inch of yours," I promised.

Something wild flashed in his eyes, and he released my wrists to grip my hips with both hands. He found his rhythm with deep, powerful strokes that hit that perfect spot every time, the sound of skin against skin filling the room, mixing with our gasps and moans.

"Why do you call me Sunshine?" I wondered breathlessly.

"Because my whole life was one dark storm," he explained between thrusts. "Until you came in like a beacon of light. My own personal sunshine."

I moaned when he slammed even harder into me.

"That's it, Sunshine. You take me. All of me. Every inch." His abs clenched and released with each thrust, while sweat made his skin gleam. "Watch in the mirror as you come around me. Watch how beautiful you are when you let go."

I watched. Watched him take me. Watched my face flush and contort with pleasure. Watched my body accept him over and over all while the coil wound impossibly tight and my inner walls began to flutter.

"Axel!" His name tore from my throat as I shattered. Wave after wave of pleasure crashed through me.

He worked me through it, extending the orgasm until I thought I might die from the intensity. Only then did he let himself go, slamming deep with a growl that seemed to come from his soul. I felt him pulse inside me. Felt his release fill me with warmth.

After, he stayed buried inside me for a moment. Both of us breathing hard. Then he kissed my spine tenderly. Each vertebra. A trail of worship.

"Say it again." Softer this time. Gentle.

"I'm perfect."

"You're perfect, Sunshine. Every inch. Every curve. Every part you see as a flaw is part of your story. And I love your story." He withdrew slowly, both of us hissing at the sensitivity. "If you ever talk bad about yourself again, I'll make your ass even redder."

I smiled. Somehow, it didn't surprise me that Axel would protect me from any bully. Even if that bully was me.

"Stay." He vanished for a moment, returning with a warm washcloth. The terry cloth was soft against my sensitive flesh as he cleaned me with impossible gentleness.

"I'm not done with you," he warned, already beginning to harden again. "Are you too sore for round two?"

Truth was, I was a little sore. But the good kind. The kind that made me want more.

"My turn," I said, taking the washcloth from him. I ran it along his length, cleaning away our combined release. He groaned as I stroked him, and he grew harder with each pass.

"Now you watch." I dropped to my knees. "Watch how perfect this looks."

I took him in my mouth, tasting both of us.

Axel's head fell back, and a groan rumbled from deep in his chest.

I pulled off with a pop. "I said, watch."

His lips quirked up with a flash of that cocky smile I loved.

But like a good boy, he obeyed, and his eyes fixed on where my mouth wrapped around him.

"Now hold the back of my head," I instructed. "Use my mouth. Show me how you've imagined it."

The tendons in his neck went taut as he fisted my hair. I relaxed my jaw as he pushed deeper, until he hit the back of my throat and I gagged slightly.

"Relax, baby. Breathe through your nose."

I nodded, taking a deep breath. He tried again, and this time, he went slow, patient, until, finally, my nose pressed against his pelvis. Until he filled my mouth and throat completely.

"Sunshine. Do. Not. Move."

He began to thrust. Shallow at first, then deeper. Finding his rhythm as he watched from above. Watched in the mirror from the side—our eyes locked in the reflection.

"You're so beautiful like this." His voice was wrecked. "On your knees for me. Taking me so well. Do you know how many times I've pictured this? Jerked off, thinking about your pretty mouth?"

He moved faster. Deeper. His grip in my hair tightened just enough to sting perfectly.

"I'm getting close." His thrusts grew erratic. "Do you want me to pull out?"

I shook my head, hollowed my cheeks, and sucked harder.

"Fuck!" He shouted.

I swallowed everything he gave me. Licked him clean as he trembled above me.

He pulled out gently, then hauled me to my feet, and Cupped my face in both hands.

"You're mine." He declared.

"I'm yours."

"Forever, Sunshine. This wasn't just sex. You know that, right? This was me claiming you. Showing you what you are to me."

I nodded, tears pricking my eyes. Happy tears.

"Good. Now let's get you in bed. Because round three is going to be slow. I'm going to worship every inch I was too impatient to properly appreciate."

As he led me to the bedroom, I caught sight of us in the mirror one more time. Flushed. Satisfied. His arm around my waist.

Perfect.

49

HE WENT FROM SPANKING ME TO KISSING EVERY INCH LIKE I'M MADE OF STARLIGHT. #SLOWBURNTOSLOWLOVE

DAKOTA

The walk to his bedroom wasn't urgent or desperate. Something softer. Something that made my chest ache with tenderness.

Axel's hand engulfed mine as he led me through the doorway, and moonlight spilled through the windows, painting silver streaks across his king-sized bed with its dark sheets.

He turned to face me, cupping my face in both hands. "You're still trembling."

I was. Not from cold or even from the aftermath of what we'd just shared. From the magnitude of what was happening between us. The walls we'd both demolished. The future stretching out before us, uncertain but somehow exactly right.

"Axel," I whispered, searching his eyes, "earlier, when you ... when you held my stomach, you looked at me like ..." I trailed off, unable to finish the thought. *Like you were imagining it swollen with your child.*

His thumb traced my cheekbone with infinite gentleness. The tough, commanding man from earlier had melted into something softer. Vulnerable.

"Like what?" His voice was careful, waiting.

"Like you were seeing something. A future maybe."

He was quiet for a long moment, his gaze holding mine. "I've never imagined my future the way I do when I think of you." The admission fell between us like a stone into still water. His palm found my stomach again, resting there with deliberate tenderness. "Never thought I'd want ... more."

His expression shifted into raw emotion that he didn't try to hide.

"And now?" The question barely made it past my lips.

His voice came out rough. Honest. "Now I see things I never let myself see before. A different life than the one I'd resigned myself to." He leaned his forehead against mine. "With you, I want ... God, Sunshine, I want everything. Things I was too scared to even name before."

The weight of what he wasn't quite saying, couldn't quite say yet, hung between us. But I understood. In the way his hand spread protectively over my stomach, in the wonder in his eyes, I understood perfectly.

He was opening the door to possibility between us. The possibility of kids.

Tears pricked my eyes. Happy tears that I didn't try to stop.

"Come here," he murmured, pulling me toward the bed. But not with the desperate hunger from before. This was something else entirely. Something that made my heart feel too big for my chest.

He sat on the edge of the bed, pulling me to stand between his knees.

"I want to memorize you," he said, his voice barely above a whisper. "Every inch. Every freckle. Every place that makes you sigh."

He pressed his lips to my stomach. Soft. Barely there. A whisper of a kiss that somehow felt more intimate than everything we'd already done.

"So beautiful," he murmured against my skin.

His hands skimmed down my sides. No grabbing or claiming

this time. Just gentle exploration, like he had all the time in the world. Like nothing existed outside this room, this moment, this slow unraveling of our souls.

"Lie down for me, Sunshine."

I crawled onto his bed, the sheets cool and soft against my skin. Smelling like his cologne. Like safety. Like home. The moonlight caught the edges of his tattoos, turning them into shadows and silver.

"You're staring," he said, the corner of his mouth lifting.

"You're worth staring at."

He joined me on the bed. But instead of covering me with his body, he lay beside me. Propped on one elbow. Looking down at me like I was some kind of miracle.

"What?" I whispered.

"Just thinking about how I almost lost this." His fingers traced my collarbone. Light as butterfly wings. "Almost let you walk away because I was too stubborn to admit what you meant to me."

"I'm here now."

"You are." He leaned down, pressing his lips to my shoulder. Then my collarbone. The hollow of my throat. Each kiss deliberate and tender. "And I'm going to spend the rest of my life making sure you know exactly how precious you are to me."

His mouth traveled lower. Not rushed or demanding. He kissed the swell of my breast, The valley between them, and then my ribs, one by one, like he was counting them. Treasuring them.

When his lips found my nipple, it wasn't the urgent sucking from before. He laved it gently with his tongue, worshipped it with soft pulls that sent lazy heat spiraling through me. Building slowly. Like honey warming in the sun.

"Axel ..." His name came out as a sigh.

He switched to the other breast, giving it the same patient attention while his hand stroked my side. My hip. The curve of my waist. Learning me. Mapping me. Claiming me in an entirely different way than before.

He pressed his lips to my belly button. To the curve of my hip. He kissed my thighs. My knees. Even my ankles received his careful attention.

"Turn over," he said softly.

I rolled onto my stomach, and he started again. Kissing up the backs of my legs. The sensitive spot behind my knees that made me shiver. My thighs. Higher.

When he kissed the small of my back, I felt tears slip down my cheeks. No one had ever touched me like this. Like I was precious. Sacred. Worth worshipping.

"Why are you crying, Sunshine?" He turned me gently onto my back again, concern etched across his features.

"Because you see me," I whispered. "Really see me. And you still think I'm worth all this tenderness."

"Oh, Sunshine." He kissed my tears away. First one cheek, then the other. "You're worth so much more than you know."

He settled between my thighs, but didn't push inside. Instead he kissed me deeply. Slowly. Our tongues dancing together in a rhythm that had nothing to do with urgency and everything to do with connection. I could taste myself on his lips from earlier. Could taste our combined desire and something sweeter. Something that tasted like forever.

"I need you," I whispered against his mouth.

"You have me." He positioned himself at my entrance. "You've had me since the day you walked into my life and turned everything upside down."

He pushed inside slowly, letting me feel every inch. Letting our bodies adjust to each other. When he was fully inside, he stopped and pressed his forehead to mine. We breathed together, hearts beating in sync.

"I love you," he said, the words falling between us like a vow.

"I love you too."

He began to move. Slow, deep strokes that built a different kind of fire. Not the inferno from before. This was molten gold.

Thick and sweet and all-consuming in a way that went beyond physical.

Our bodies moved together like we'd found our rhythm not just in bed, but in life, and as his hands linked with mine, pressing them into the mattress beside my head, I couldn't help but think how this position left me completely open to him. Vulnerable. Safe.

"Look at me," he whispered.

I opened my eyes, finding his gaze in the darkness. I'd never seen him look so open. So completely unguarded.

"You're mine," he said, but it wasn't a command this time. It was a promise. "And I'm yours. Completely. Whatever that means. Whatever you need."

The wave built slowly this time. Starting in my toes and traveling up my body in increments. Axel must have felt it in the way my breathing changed, the way my body began to tighten around him.

"That's it, Sunshine. Let go for me. Let me see you."

He kept the same steady rhythm. The same deep strokes that hit every perfect spot. The same locked gaze that made me feel seen down to my soul. The wave crested gently. Powerfully. Rolling through me in pulses that seemed to go on forever.

"Axel!"

He followed me over the edge, groaning my name as he buried his face in my neck. His body shuddered against mine, and we stayed locked together, breathing hard, hearts gradually slowing.

"Don't leave," I whispered, not sure if I meant *don't pull out* or *don't leave me* or *don't leave this bed* or maybe all of it at once.

"Never," he promised, understanding perfectly. "I'm never leaving you, Sunshine. You're stuck with me."

He rolled off onto his back, and I shifted to my side, resting my head on his damp chest. His arm wrapped around me like armor against the world.

Listening to his heartbeat, feeling his arms around me, I thought about how, sometimes, love doesn't arrive gently. Sometimes, it crashes into your life, disguised as conflict. Sometimes, it looks like a fake engagement that becomes the most real thing you've ever known.

"I love you," I whispered into the darkness.

His arms tightened around me, and even in sleep, he murmured back, "Love you too, Sunshine. I love every version of you. Every version that you want to be. The polished one in designer dresses. The messy one in sweatpants. The fierce one who stands up for what's right. The girl bent over my desk while I fuck her from behind." He kissed the top of my head. "Every beautiful, complicated piece of you, Sunshine. All of it. Always."

Tonight, in his bed, in his arms, with our bodies still connected and our hearts finally aligned, everything was perfect.

I was home.

50

2 FOLDERS + 1 CRYPTIC COMMENT = LEAST EXPECTED MOMENT IN HISTORY. 📁🤔 #UNEXPECTED

DAKOTA

"What the hell, Dakota?!" Our publicist slapped two folders down onto the dining room table, the sharp sound echoing through the otherwise silent room. Her perfectly manicured fingernails drummed against the manila surfaces. "What the hell were you thinking?"

I flinched, unable to meet her laser-focused glare. After the emotional purge of yesterday's live stream, I felt hollow, scraped raw, and completely unprepared for this confrontation.

"You didn't even give us a heads-up that you were about to do it," she continued, her voice rising with each accusation. "We could've gone about this in the right way. We could have scripted an apology!"

"Hey," Axel said, holding his palm up like a traffic cop. "Don't talk to her like that."

He stood beside me, our shoulders almost touching, his presence solid and unexpectedly comforting.

The publicist's eyes widened in disbelief. "Are you kidding me? Do you know how hard we worked to get you both out of this mess?" Her voice rose with each word. "And she has the audacity to go online and not just deviate from our script, but blow the whole thing up with a grenade?"

Something sparked inside me. Not anger exactly, but a flicker of the same resolve that had pushed me to go live in the first place.

"I was just trying to be honest," I said, my voice quiet but steady. "I wouldn't have wanted to do this from a script. I just wanted to be true for once." I leaned forward, hands splayed on the table. "I'm sure that I said things wrong, and I'm sure that I went about it all wrong, but that's the whole problem: overthinking everything I do online. It's not healthy."

The publicist opened her mouth to object, but I pressed on.

"If I was going to apologize to my followers, they deserved that apology to come from the heart, not some script that my public relations company handed me."

"You hired us," she pointed out.

"I know. And I'm sorry that I didn't give you a heads-up." I met her gaze squarely. "It wouldn't have changed what I did, and it wouldn't have changed how I went about it, but after everything you've done for us, you deserved to be in the loop."

"Your damn right I did!"

"Hey!" Axel snapped. "I told you. Do NOT talk to her like that."

The publicist leered at Axel. "I'm surprised I have to explain to you how reckless this was," she hissed. "And I'm even more surprised you're defending her."

Axel leaned forward, his palms resting on the table, eyes never leaving the publicist's face. "And I'm surprised I have to explain to you that someone giving a public apology from the bottom of her heart is never the wrong thing to do."

"Her heart was in the right place? Seriously?"

"Is this why you came here? To berate her?" Axel jerked his thumb toward the elevator. "Because if so, there's the door."

My gaze snapped to Axel. He had every right to be furious with me, and yet here he was, having my back, even when, one could argue, I'd made yet another impulsive mistake.

"She's right," I said softly, finding my voice again. "I should've at least given you guys a heads-up that I was going to do that."

"You think?" the publicist snapped, nostrils flaring.

"Last warning," Axel snarled.

My eyes burned with the threat of tears. Ride or die, it seemed, Axel was in my corner.

Axel gestured toward the files, clearly attempting to redirect the conversation. "What's in the folders?"

The publicist pressed her fingertips down on the files, as if afraid they might fly away. It looked like it took her serious effort —and I do mean, serious—to let go of the verbal lashing she was giving me and answer his question.

"I had my assistant compile and print some of the comments and reactions to that godforsaken live event. I've categorized them into two folders. One contains responses from people raising their pitchforks and hating you both."

She flipped open the first folder, and I immediately wished she hadn't. The top comment made my heart chill.

@BlushBabe123: You ruined everything. You were perfect, and you DESTROYED it. Years of watching you, supporting you. You were supposed to stay beautiful and flawless. Now you're just another broken girl, crying on camera. I'm disgusted. You've betrayed everyone who believed in you.

My stomach twisted. BlushBabe123 had been my most devoted follower for years. Always first to comment, always showing up with heart-eye emojis and gushing praise. I'd actually started to find her constant presence a little ... intense. But seeing her turn on me so viciously? It stung.

"Jesus," Axel muttered, reading over my shoulder. "That's not criticism. That's ... unhinged."

Seriously. Something about BlushBabe123's fury felt different. Personal. Like I'd betrayed her specifically.

The publicist quickly flipped the folder closed. "There are more like that, many also directed at Axel."

Oh God. "One of my *main* goals was to not let Axel take a

hit," I said, regret bubbling. Maybe I should have gone about it another way. "Is he going to suffer because of this?"

Her shoulders drew back as she took a deep breath, and in my opinion, she looked like she hated what she was about to say. "His follower count increased."

Oh. She didn't want to be wrong.

Hope took flight in my ribs. "That's a good sign, right? He was shielded from harm?"

But Axel didn't seem to care about himself. He pointed to the second fatter file on the desk, getting back to the comments and reactions.

"And the other folder?" Axel demanded.

The publicist's hesitation was slight but noticeable. "The other, it seems, is full of people that found her apology sincere. That evidently see her as a human being, making mistakes and doing it publicly. They're showing empathy for her." The admission clearly cost her. "They found her raw honesty ... refreshing."

"That makes no sense," I said, blinking in confusion. "I assumed all people would hate me by now."

At this, her lips thinned further, and something told me that what this woman hated more than my "reckless" apology was being incorrect in guessing how people would respond to it.

"Many of your followers were upset," she explained, her professional tone returning like a mask sliding back into place. "Very upset. They felt lied to and manipulated and conned by you."

"Because they were," I said, running a hand through my still-disheveled hair. "My whole life online has been some flavor of untruth."

The publicist sighed, a fraction of tension leaving her shoulders. "Yeah, well, there's one more thing about online culture. It's, at times, unpredictable."

"Meaning?" Axel prompted, coming closer until his shoulder touched mine.

She tapped the second folder. "Meaning, by every account,

what Dakota did yesterday should have been the end of her social media business." A note of reluctant admiration crept into her voice. "But it seems many followers were touched by her honesty and vulnerability."

I blinked rapidly, trying to process this information. "I'm not following."

The woman could not let go of that resting angry face, the one where she was, at least partly, wrong.

"Have you checked your social media accounts?" she asked.

The memory of my phone exploding with notifications after the live stream made me wince. "No. I didn't want to subject myself to the hateful comments."

"Well, your follower count did go down." She crossed her arms, looking genuinely pissed off that she had to deliver good news when it went against everything she'd advised. "And trust me, there were a lot of hateful comments. But it seems the majority consensus is that they loved what you did. They expressed disappointment in your decisions, but by and large, they were touched by your sincerity and candor." She spread some of the papers open on the table. "It seems even influencers found your post to be, and I quote, 'the tipping point our society needs to peel back the layers of what we hide from everyone and be brave enough to show our true selves, even when doing so could cost us everything.' "

I leaned forward, scanning the comments with thousands of likes and replies:

I felt your pain so deeply. Thank you for being brave enough to show us it's okay to not be perfect.

I've never commented before, but I had to tell you, this post just saved me. I was so lost in comparing myself to everyone else's highlight reel. You just reminded me we're all fighting the same battle.

I've never felt pretty enough, smart enough, good enough. Seeing you without all the filters made me realize I'm not alone.

I've been crying for 20 minutes. Every morning, I look at Insta-

gram before getting my kids ready and feel like I'm failing at everything. This is the first time someone showed me I'm not.

I've missed so many pool days with my kids because I was ashamed of my body. You just gave me permission to stop stealing joy from myself.

Thank you for stripping bare for us. I needed to see that people online aren't as perfect as they seem. I thought I was the only imperfect one.

You are beautiful just the way you are, Dakota Fox/Blackwood. Thank you for showing us that real is better than perfect.

My vision blurred as tears gathered in my eyes. One slipped down my cheek, then another. It wasn't the acceptance of strangers that had me crying, though that meant more than I could have imagined. It was that my moment of vulnerability had apparently given others permission to be vulnerable too.

Maybe, in the wake of everything I'd screwed up, some good had actually come out of it.

"It would seem," Rebecca said, "that your unpredictable, unplanned post ironically generated more authentic engagement from your followers than anything else you've carefully crafted."

"They felt like they saw me," I realized. "The real me."

Axel smiled, adoration and pride gleaming from his eyes. "Sometimes, the bravest thing you can do is let them see the real you, Sunshine."

Rebecca's eyebrows lifted meaningfully. "They want to see more of that."

"More of that?" I shook my head in disbelief. "I intended for that to be my last post. Honestly, I need to brush up my résumé and thank my lucky stars that I have a degree to fall back on."

"It can be your last post if you want it to be," she said, her tone surprisingly gentle now, the anger apparently burned out. "But ..." Rebecca said, her voice softer now.

She pulled something else from the folder and placed it in front of me. My breath caught.

"My brand deal?" I lifted the contract, scanning the terms.

The same deal I thought I'd lost forever when I posted that video. "But I thought they'd drop me for sure."

"Apparently," Rebecca said, and now she actually looked pleased, "they want to partner with you specifically because of your authenticity. They're pivoting their entire campaign to *Real Beauty*. No filters, no fake perfection. They want you as the face of it."

Axel's hand squeezed my shoulder, and when I looked up at him, his eyes were warm with pride.

"The contract is actually better than the original," Rebecca continued. "Higher pay, more creative control, and—this is the kicker—they want you to do a whole series about being real online. Showing your actual morning routine, your bad-skin days, everything."

I stared at the papers, hardly believing what I was reading. "They want to pay me ... to be myself?"

"Revolutionary concept, right?" Rebecca said dryly, but she was almost smiling now. "Who knew that in a world full of perfectly curated lies, the truth would be so ... marketable?"

I laughed through my tears, the sound a little hysterical. "I can't believe this is real. I've got a new opportunity here," I realized aloud, the idea taking shape as I spoke. "To be myself and to be honest. No filters, no scripts, just ... me."

Axel's hand found mine, the simple gesture steadying me.

The publicist studied me for a long moment, her expression unreadable. Finally, she nodded. "You do."

She gathered the folders, sliding them across the table toward me. "Take a look. Process the feedback. Then decide what you want to do next." Her gaze shifted to include Axel. "What you both want to do next."

As she stood to leave, she paused, smoothing her immaculate blazer. "For what it's worth," she said, not quite meeting my eyes, "it was brave. Stupid, but brave."

I smiled.

"Oh, and one more thing," Rebecca said, throwing her purse

over her shoulder as she prepared to leave. "There's a detective downstairs who wants to talk to you both."

The way she said it, with a little smile playing at the corners of her mouth, suggested it was good news.

And with that cryptic comment, she was gone, leaving me staring at a contract that proved sometimes the scariest thing you can do, showing the world who you really are, turns out to be exactly what the world was waiting for.

But I think the most shocking thing that would happen today came with what the detective was about to say ...

51

OKAY, I FEEL BAD THAT I FEEL RELIEVED ABOUT A DEADLY PLANE CRASH … #GOINGTOHELL

AXEL

"They're dead?" I repeated, my hands clenching and unclenching in my lap.

Dakota's hand landed on my thigh as we sat across from Detective Reeves in my living room, her touch the only thing keeping me grounded. It was kind of Ryker to pull some strings and get him here so quickly. Based on the detective's change of demeanor, Ryker must have also finally convinced him to be less skeptical about the danger the Romano family might've posed to us.

"How?" she asked.

"Private plane crash," Reeves explained, pulling out his tablet. "Senator Stephen Webb and his wife, Victoria, were flying to a retreat in Colorado. Plane went down about forty miles outside Denver." He turned the screen toward us, showing a news article with the headline: *TRAGIC LOSS: Presidential Hopeful and Wife Die in Plane Crash.*

"Jesus," I breathed, studying the photos of the wreckage.

"Both died on impact," Reeves continued. "No survivors."

"Was it ..." Dakota started. "Was the crash an accident?"

"Investigation is underway. But an informant is claiming it was a power move by another crime family."

Dakota glanced at me. "Is this our fault? Are they dead because of us? Because we accidentally outed their fake marriage?"

"Highly unlikely," the guy said quickly. "There's been a power struggle between two crime families for a while. Looks like one finally made the first official act of war. Or the crash truly was an accident."

Dakota shifted beside me. "But ... but this changes everything, doesn't it? I mean, if Senator Webb and Victoria are dead ..."

I could hear the hope creeping into her voice, fragile and desperate.

"There's nothing to be gained by killing us," I realized. "Have you brought in Romano?" I pressed. "Because he's the real threat here. He has to be the one who sent us those flowers."

"We looked into it," Reeves said. "Found no ties to the flowers and him or his associates. Same with the attack on Dakota."

Still, both had to be from him. Right? Who else would have done that?

"Besides, here's the thing," the detective continued. "With Senator Webb dead, Romano has much bigger problems than two social media stars. His path to the White House just crumbled overnight. And with that plane crash, two crime family organizations are now under official investigation. Including his. And officially at war. So, he has bigger fish to fry."

I exchanged glances with Dakota, then Ryker, before turning back to the detective.

"You're saying we're *safe*?" Dakota leaned forward.

"The last thing Tony Romano wants is more attention from law enforcement," Reeves said. "Going after you two now would destroy everything for him."

Dakota looked at me, then back to Reeves. "So, what happens now? Does someone else in the Romano family take over their vendetta against us?"

Reeves exchanged a look with Ryker that made my stomach tighten.

"From what our organized crime unit tells me, the Romano family is in full damage control mode. They're liquidating assets, cutting ties, trying to disappear before the Feds connect the dots between Webb's campaign and their operations."

Holy shit.

"Are you saying ..." Dakota could barely let herself voice it. "Are you saying the threat is actually gone? Forever?"

"What's left of their operation has much bigger problems than some influencer couple who accidentally exposed a flirtatious picture," Reeves said. "They're trying to avoid federal prison right now. Every soldier, every lieutenant ... they're either fleeing the country or focused on covering their tracks."

"It's over?" she asked.

"It's over." Detective Reeves left no doubt in his tone.

The silence that followed was deafening. I felt like I'd been holding my breath for weeks and could finally exhale. That crushing weight I'd been carrying—the constant fear that something would happen to Dakota, that I'd lose her before we even had a real chance—suddenly lifted from my chest.

Dakota's hand squeezed my thigh, and when I looked at her, I saw tears in her eyes. Relief, pure and overwhelming.

"We can actually"—she swallowed hard—"have a normal life?"

"You can have whatever life you want," Reeves said, standing to leave. "As for the Romano crime family, the threat is eliminated."

After he left, Dakota and I sat in stunned silence for a long moment. Then she launched herself into my arms, and I held her tight, breathing in the scent of her hair, feeling her heartbeat against my chest.

"It's really over," she whispered against my neck.

"It's over," I repeated.

For the first time in weeks, Dakota felt safe in my arms. For the first time since this nightmare started, we could think about the future instead of just surviving the present.

It felt almost too good to be true ...

52

WHEN YOUR EX SHOWS UP AND YOUR FAKE FIANCÉ IS INSIDE OF YOU. #OMGHISREACTION

DAKOTA

Axel's thumb circled that sensitive bundle of nerves between my thighs as he stared right into my eyes, his other hand cupping my breast.

"You know how gorgeous you are, Sunshine?"

Making love to him on my couch, with me straddling him, wasn't the plan. The plan had been simple: come here, grab the last of my belongings, and move them into his penthouse. Close this chapter of my life for good.

But we couldn't seem to keep our hands off each other. We'd made love everywhere in his penthouse. And I mean, everywhere. His kitchen counter. The dining room table. The shower. His office desk. Virtually every surface had been claimed by our desperate need for each other. So, when we came here to retrieve my things, I guess I should've seen this coming.

No pun intended.

I grabbed his tattooed shoulders and leaned down, nipping his bottom lip with my teeth. Hard enough to make him growl.

He responded by delivering a sharp slap to my ass, making me yelp at the delicious bite of pain, chased by pure pleasure.

"Every day," he growled, jerking his hips up to thrust deeply into me hard, fast, and claiming. "I need you every single day of my life, Sunshine."

"That sounds a lot like a proposal, Mr. Pierce." I slammed my hips down on him this time, reveling in this push and pull we had going, this intoxicating exchange of control.

"I miss my ring on your finger," he admitted with another devastating thrust, pinching my nipple between his fingers just hard enough to make me gasp.

"It was just a loaner," I reminded him.

"Still, I liked seeing it on you; I want everyone to know you're *mine.*"

Mine. The word echoed through every chamber of my heart, planting seeds that took immediate root. Growing vines through my chest and spreading throughout my entire body.

Making the wave building inside me rise even higher.

"I'm yours," I assured him breathlessly. "Always."

A sudden, sharp knock made me jerk to a stop.

"Dakota?" a familiar voice called from the other side of my front door.

Mathew. My ex. You'd think the man who'd once broken my heart would have better things to do than keep trying to contact me. But evidently, when his texts and calls went unanswered, he resorted to showing up here.

Disappointment flooded my system as I stilled, staring down at Axel. We'd been so close to sharing another earth-shattering climax, only to have it interrupted by the last person I wanted to deal with.

"I should—"

Axel's large hand clamped over my mouth, cutting off my words. His eyes blazed with something primal and possessive as he shook his head in a silent command. *We are not stopping.*

I nipped at his finger, earning a wicked smirk as he slowly drew his hand away.

"He's right on the other side of that door," I whispered, nodding toward the entrance that was mere fifteen feet from where Axel was buried deep inside me.

Arching one dark eyebrow, Axel thrust his hips up in one sharp, claiming motion. Burying himself so deep, I saw stars.

I sucked in a ragged breath, my nails digging into his shoulders.

Then I glared at him. Axel was playing dirty, and he knew it.

"Dakota?" Mathew knocked again, more insistently this time. "I saw your car in the parking lot."

Thrust.

Axel cocked his head with that irritatingly sexy arrogance I'd come to crave, returning his thumb to circle that bundle of nerves with devastating precision.

"I know you're home. Please open the door. We need to talk."

Thrust. Deeper this time.

It took me several seconds to find my voice, what with his thumb working magic and him sinking impossibly deeper into me with each movement. "He's not going to go away," I managed to whisper.

Thrust.

Gasp.

Axel continued those maddening circles, instantly reclaiming the climax exactly where it had left off: right on the precipice of falling over the edge. My body throbbed around him, drawing him deeper, claiming him as thoroughly as he was claiming me.

When his lips found my nipple and sucked hard, I gave up fighting this. My fingers threaded through his dark hair as our bodies moved together in perfect rhythm, climbing higher and higher toward oblivion.

"Dakota, please." Mathew's voice grew desperate through the door.

The irony wasn't lost on me. Here was the man who'd left me while I was currently being worshipped by a man who was everything Mathew could never be. Stronger. More passionate. More devoted to my pleasure than his own.

Thrust.

Axel pinched my nipple so hard, I had to bite my lip to keep from crying out.

"You're terrible," I whimpered, trying desperately to hold back my approaching climax. "I don't want him to hear—"

Axel clamped his hand over my mouth again, his eyes burning with possessive fire, as if to say, *You will come, Sunshine.*

Thrust. He rocked his hips up to meet my pace, and all the while, those intense eyes watched my face for the telltale signs that I was about to tip over the edge.

"Dakota, please!" Mathew pounded harder on the door.

But I barely heard his begging. Because I was too busy crashing, shattering completely with a moan that would've made a saint blush.

The problem? Axel pulled his hand away at the last possible second, letting my cry of ecstasy echo through the entire apartment.

When we were both spent, trembling from the intensity of our releases, I glared down at him through my postorgasmic haze.

"You did that on purpose," I accused.

Axel didn't look even slightly guilty. Instead, he cupped my breast with tender possession. "You're mine, Sunshine. And I want him to know exactly what he lost."

His explanation should have angered me. Should have made me feel used or embarrassed. But it didn't. His proclamation was primal, raw, claiming what was his for all the world, including my pathetic ex, to hear.

And, dear Lord, did that turn me on.

"Dakota?" Mathew's voice had changed, uncertainty creeping in. The pounding had stopped. "Are you ... are you okay in there?"

Axel's nostrils flared with irritation, but there was satisfaction gleaming in his dark eyes.

"Stay here," I commanded, slipping off him and reaching for my clothes, tossing his onto his crotch to cover him. "Don't you dare move."

As I hastily dressed, I caught sight of myself in the mirror across the room. Hair mussed. Lips swollen. Skin flushed with satisfaction, with a sheen of sweat. I looked like a woman who'd been thoroughly ravaged.

I had a choice: Spend several minutes cleaning myself up, pretending I hadn't just been gloriously taken by the man I loved. Hide the truth, or just be me. Unfiltered and unapologetic.

As if reading my mind, Axel's voice was low as he said, "Let him see exactly what he gave up. Let him realize that while he was out there playing games, you found a man who worships you."

Okay, that's not what I meant; I didn't want to hurt Mathew.

"Dakota?" Mathew barked.

I opened the door.

Mathew's face shifted through a symphony of emotions: relief, surprise, then slow, dawning realization. His gaze swept over the flush painting my cheeks, the dewiness at the base of my throat, my thoroughly mussed hair.

Any lingering doubt about what he'd interrupted evaporated when hurt flashed across his features, followed immediately by something darker.

For a split second, I almost felt bad for him. *Almost*. But watching him take in my satisfied glow, seeing the exact moment he realized another man had just claimed me completely?

God, it felt empowering after Mathew had tried to emotionally cut me off at the knees.

"Mathew." I kept my voice steady. "Did you need something?"

He pushed the hurt aside and swallowed hard, shoving his hands deep into his pockets. "I wanted to apologize. And I thought …" His voice trailed off as his eyes tracked over my appearance again. "I really thought this whole engagement thing was just for show. For the cameras."

"There's no need—"

"But you're really with him." It wasn't a question. The realization seemed to hit him like a hammer to his chest. "This is real."

I felt a flicker of something. Pity maybe? "Mathew—"

"Dakota, I love you." His attention dropped to my bare ring finger, and hope flickered desperately in his eyes. "I made a mistake. The biggest mistake of my life."

"We've been over this," I said, this time not hiding my irritation. "It's over. I love Axel."

The words came out easier than I'd expected. Clear. Definitive. Real. I loved Axel.

He studied my face, searching for any crack in my resolve. When he found none, his jaw ticced.

"First the live stream." His voice went flat and cold. "Now this."

Wait, what? Why did he care about the live stream? Something niggled in my mind, something I couldn't place.

"I moved halfway around the world for you."

"You also called me worthless," I reminded him.

"Just give me one chance. Let me prove—"

"He called you worthless?" Axel materialized beside me like an avenging angel. Shirtless, his tattooed torso still glistening with a fine sheen of sweat from our lovemaking. Every inch of him radiated dangerous masculinity and absolute possession.

The contrast was devastating. Mathew in his perfectly pressed business casual, and Axel, raw, powerful, unapologetically male, with the satisfied air of a man who'd just thoroughly claimed his woman.

Mathew's body almost vibrated with disbelief as he took in Axel's state of undress. "I'm talking to her, not you."

Axel took an aggressive step closer to him.

"You called her worthless?" Holy shit. Axel's voice was like a razer, sharp and cutting. Ominously dripping with warning.

"Couples argue," Mathew retorted.

When I put my hand on Axel's shoulder, he spared me a quick glance, then snapped his attention to my ex.

"Only reason you still have an unbroken nose is because I promised Dakota I would try to control my rage. Do yourself a favor and leave before I lose that battle."

Mathew stared at Axel's arm around me, then narrowed his eyes. "I thought you loved me, Dakota."

"You're really going to play the victim card now?" Axel's eyebrows rose in disbelief. "If you want to blame someone, blame yourself. You walked away from the best thing that ever happened to you. Your loss became my greatest gift."

"Axel—"

Mathew shoved Axel hard enough to dislodge his arm from my shoulder.

Big mistake.

Axel moved like lightning, pinning Mathew against the outside wall with a muscled forearm pressed to his throat. Every tattoo on his torso seemed to come alive as his muscles flexed and coiled with power.

"Axel!"

"You ever show up at her door uninvited again, and we're going to have a very different conversation," Axel said, his voice deadly calm. "Dakota told you no. That means no. Accept that it's over and move on."

For a moment, I thought Mathew might actually apologize. But I knew how his mind worked, how his father's bullying had twisted him into someone who saw every challenge as a threat to his masculinity.

When Axel released him with a look of disgust, Mathew straightened his rumpled shirt, his gaze bouncing between Axel and me with something cold and calculating.

"You made the wrong choice, Dakota," he said quietly, his tone sending an unexpected chill down my spine.

Then he turned and walked away.

"You shouldn't have done that," I said once he was gone.

"You don't deserve to have to keep telling him that it's over."

True. I hated that things had to end this way with Mathew, but at least there was no way he'd misunderstand this anymore. At least now, he knew it was truly over.

And he'd move on ...

53

BREAKING: MAN WHO PHOTOSHOPPED ROMANCE NOVEL COVERS, NOW LIVING IN ONE. #IRONICTWIST

AXEL

Dakota and I locked eyes as she stood next to the other bridesmaids, sharing an intimate moment that belonged only to us before the collective gasp of the crowd cascaded through the audience.

Everyone rose to their feet.

Tessa glided forward, ethereal in white silk that pooled behind her in an endless train. She didn't acknowledge the hundreds of guests watching her with hushed awe. Didn't notice every meticulous detail she'd obsessed over in her planning: the archway of white roses and peonies, the cascades of ivy draping the stone walls, the hundreds of flickering candles casting everything in golden light.

The only thing she saw was Blake.

He stood at the front of the altar, looking like he was about to cry and trying desperately not to. The expression on his face hit me square in the chest. Something I never would've understood a few months ago, but now felt in every fiber of my being.

It was the look of a man who'd found his purpose. His soul's other half. His reason for existing.

And standing here, watching as one of my closest friends was about to marry the love of his life, I knew with absolute certainty that I would make Dakota my bride. That pathetic "proposal" she'd called me out on when we'd been making love hadn't been a proposal at all. She deserved something magnificent. Something worthy of her. Complete with a brand-new ring, created just for her.

Ryker stood as the best man on Blake's side, lips curved in the slightest smile. Which was as close to emotional as the criminal lawyer ever got. Then, second, stood me. And then third, Jace, looking annoyingly dignified in his tux.

I'd been calling him Number Three all day, and he fucking hated it.

Worth it.

The fourth groomsman spot remained empty. I worried that Knox's absence at the wedding might be hard on Dakota. But either she was handling it well or choosing to focus on the positive: two of our closest friends were getting married today.

And that was worth celebrating.

Scarlett, Dakota, and Faith were dressed in matching colors of peach, but I only had eyes for Dakota.

Christ, she was breathtaking. I didn't want her to upstage the bride, but Dakota was hands down the most beautiful woman in this room. On this planet. Her hair was swept up in some elegant style that left her neck exposed, and that dress hugged every curve I'd memorized with my hands.

The old me would've gagged at this whole production. Would've checked my watch every five minutes, mentally calculating how long until I could escape to the bar. Would've made sarcastic comments about the over-the-top flower arrangements and the string quartet playing sappy love songs.

But as the ceremony progressed—listening to Blake and Tessa exchange vows they'd written themselves, watching them slide rings onto trembling fingers, feeling the pure love radiating from them like heat from a fire—I found myself completely captivated.

More than that, I was eager for this. Desperate for the day I'd get to watch Dakota walk down an aisle toward me.

Because this woman had changed me. Forever and always. She'd reached deep into my soul, pulled out every dark fear I'd buried there, and crushed them to dust in her capable hands.

Never before had I felt so free. Never before had I been this excited about the future. Because every single day of it would have her in it.

And someday, with little kids that looked just like her.

When Blake finally kissed his bride and the crowd erupted in cheers, I caught Dakota wiping tears from her eyes. She was glowing with happiness, and something in my chest tightened with the overwhelming need to be the one to put that expression on her face every day for the rest of our lives.

The ceremony was beautiful, but it was the reception I'd been looking forward to most. Because now Dakota was finally in my arms, and I could stop pretending to pay attention to anything else.

"Tessa did such an incredible job, planning this." Dakota beamed, practically bouncing on her toes. "Did you hear where they're going for their honeymoon?" Her eyes lit up like Christmas morning.

"Italy." Blake had only mentioned it about fifty times today. The guy had chartered a private jet and booked some exclusive villa right on the Mediterranean. "He's taking her to tour the vineyards in Tuscany."

"Can you even imagine?" Dakota's smile was infectious. "Going all the way to Italy? Seeing all that beauty? The history, the art, the food ..."

"Would you like to do that?"

She wrapped her arms around my neck, pulling herself closer.

"I want to see everything." Her eyes sparkled with dreams. "Italy and Paris. I want to see Rome and the Eiffel Tower. I want to swim with the dolphins, visit every single national park in this country, and watch the sunrise from Machu Picchu."

I swept my thumb along her lower lip, marveling at how soft she was. "Make a list. We'll start working on it tomorrow."

She arched one perfect eyebrow. "You know, I never thought I'd see the day that Axel Pierce became a bit of a golden retriever, ready to fetch whatever I want."

"I didn't just bend to your will, Sunshine." I pulled her closer. "I broke completely. I'm yours. And from this point forward, I want to spend every minute of my life making you happy."

Her eyes widened, shimmering with tears of joy.

Something shifted in that moment: a realization that hit me right in the sternum. This incredible woman had never been anyone's priority. Not really. Her family loved her, sure, but between Knox's imprisonment and her parents' struggle to cope with their shattered world, Dakota's needs had somehow gotten lost in the chaos.

She'd handled it the way she handled everything: with strength and grace and endless love for everyone around her. But no one had ever put her first. Not even close.

So help me, I would put her first every single moment of every single day forever.

Starting right now.

"Dude." Jace glided over, spinning Scarlett in some elaborate twirl that was way too smooth for a guy who used to think romance was a line item in his quarterly reports. "You look like a lovesick puppy who just found his favorite tennis ball."

I shot him a death glare. "That's rich, coming from Mr. I Bought Her Entire Company Because I Had a Crush."

"I bought her company *before* I knew she worked—"

Scarlett immediately smacked Jace's chest. "Quiet. He's happy and in love."

"Oh, I'm sorry," Jace said. "Are we forgetting that this is the same guy who Photoshopped my picture onto a romance novel cover called *Douchebag Cowboy*, book one of the Men Who Surrendered Their Balls Series, and had it delivered to my office?

On a six-by-nine-foot corkboard? You think I'm not going to give you complete shit now that you're the one whipped?"

My grin stretched wider. "That was art, my friend. Pure art."

"Leave him alone," Scarlett demanded, but she was fighting a smile.

"You heard the boss." I arched an eyebrow at Jace, daring him to challenge the fact that Scarlett owned his ass completely. Because she absolutely did. And honestly, I loved it. Jace had been nothing but an uptight billionaire workaholic before Scarlett came along and loosened him up into something resembling a human being.

"We should all go on a trip together!" Dakota suddenly squealed, bouncing on her toes.

"Oh my God, yes!" Scarlett clapped her hands.

"I already spend enough time with these idiots," I muttered. "Now you want me to vacation with them too?"

"Well, get used to it," Scarlett shot back, "because we're going to be spending tons of time together now." She actually clapped. Like full-on seal clapping.

Dakota nodded enthusiastically. "Let's talk to Tessa when she gets back from the honeymoon. Maybe we could plan something for spring?"

Speaking of the happy couple, Blake and Tessa were lost in their own world on the dance floor, gazing into each other's eyes like they'd forgotten the other three hundred guests existed.

"Look at those two," I said. "Blake's probably already calculating how many hours until he can get her alone."

We all danced near each other for a few more songs, lost in love and all that.

"Let's grab drinks," Scarlett said, tugging on Dakota's hand.

I smirked, shoving my hands in my pockets as Jace and I dutifully followed our women toward the bar. "They're plotting something."

"They have a plan," Jace agreed, then nodded toward the bar.

"Speaking of plans, look who's doing his best impression of a stalker."

Ryker stood about twenty feet away from Faith, nursing a whiskey and staring at her like she was evidence in a case he was dying to examine more thoroughly.

"Someone needs to put that poor bastard out of his misery," Jace muttered.

We approached our self-appointed brother.

"Dude," I said, clapping him on the shoulder. "If this is you trying to be subtle, you need to work on those googly eyes. You're about as covert as a neon sign."

"Shut up, Axel."

"What's stopping you from asking her to dance?" Jace asked.

"It's not just ..." Ryker stopped. Was it just me, or did he smirk a little, as if hiding a secret, only to swallow it? "What if she says no?"

I threw my arm around his shoulders in mock sympathy. "Aww, don't worry, buddy. I heard from Jessica, who heard from Stacy, who heard from Kevin that Faith totally likes you and wants you to ask her to the spring formal. Maybe you two can share a milkshake after!"

"Fuck off." Ryker shoved me away while I snickered.

"Either make a move or stop staring," Jace said with typical CEO bluntness. "You're making the rest of us uncomfortable."

"Spoken like a true executive," I said. "What's next, a PowerPoint presentation on Effective Dating Strategies?"

Jace shrugged. "I've got another piece of advice: shit or get off the pot."

Ryker glared at him. "Your romantic wisdom is truly inspiring."

"What's your actual holdup here?" I pressed. "You're a criminal defense lawyer. You've stared down murderers without flinching. One tiny woman shouldn't be this terrifying."

Ryker rubbed the back of his neck. "Blake may have given me

a warning that involved the precision of surgical scalpels if I hurt his sister in, and I quote, 'any way, shape, or form.' "

I burst out laughing. "That's pretty ironic, considering he just married *your* sister."

"Right?" Ryker sighed heavily. "His hypocrisy is stunning."

"Blake's all bark," Jace claimed. But we knew better. "Besides, what's he going to do? Stitch you back together wrong?"

"Don't give him ideas," Ryker muttered.

"Look," I said, getting serious for exactly three seconds. "You're overthinking this. Just ask her to dance. Worst-case scenario: she says no, and you go back to your corner to brood some more."

"Thanks for the pep talk, Coach."

Ryker continued gawking at the bar behind me and then said, "I'll ask her out." Ryker straightened his shoulders. "But not tonight. I don't want to risk ruining Blake and Tessa's wedding if she shoots me down in flames."

"Smart man." Jace nodded approvingly. "Always have an exit strategy."

"Plus, look how much fun she's having." Ryker added, watching the girls behind me. "I'm not about to interrupt that."

"When did we all become so ..." I searched for the word.

"Whipped?" Jace supplied helpfully.

"I was going to say *considerate*, but yeah. Whipped works."

We stood there for a moment, guys who used to think relationships were for suckers, now completely gone for our respective women.

"This is pathetic," Ryker said.

"Absolutely," Jace agreed.

"Completely," I added.

We clinked our glasses together.

"To being pathetic," I toasted.

"To being happy," Jace finished, and somehow, that felt exactly right.

I turned to look at our women, expecting to see them laughing at the bar. Instead, I found Scarlett and Faith on the dance floor, spinning each other around like teenagers. Tessa was still locked in Blake's arms, lost in newlywed bliss.

And Dakota was ...

Where the hell was Dakota?

54

PSA: DON'T GO TO THE LADIES' ROOM DURING A WEDDING RECEPTION. #LESSONLEARNED

DAKOTA

"I'm going to the ladies' room." I squeezed Scarlett's arm.

I glanced back at Axel, who was completely absorbed in a conversation with Jace and Ryker, cracking up. God, I loved seeing him like this: relaxed, surrounded by his chosen family, that gorgeous smile lighting up his entire face.

I couldn't believe how lucky I was to have found him. To discover that the love of your life had been there all along, just waiting for you to finally open the door and step into the happiest room you'd ever been in. Life didn't get any better than this. A perfect night, celebrating two of our friends marrying each other.

And, as if that weren't amazing enough, Tessa let it slip why she'd had such a short engagement. At thirty-three, she wanted a family and didn't want to spend a year and a half waiting for the official wedding to start. Besides, when you plan weddings for a living, it's surprising how efficiently you can pull together a stunning celebration like this ...

A baby. Wow, they were going to try for a baby. I smiled.

The ladies' room was quiet, except for the muffled sounds of the reception bleeding through the walls. Only one stall door was closed. As I walked past it toward the sinks, I heard the lock unclick.

I turned with a polite smile ready for whoever was emerging, but my heart stopped.

It wasn't a woman.

It was a man. A man I knew, his face twisted with rage and something darker, something that made every instinct I had shout, *Run*.

"Hello, Dakota."

I opened my mouth to scream, but a wet cloth clamped over my nose and mouth before I could make a sound. The chemical smell burned my nostrils, sharp and medicinal and wrong.

No, no, no.

I clawed at his hands, tried to shove him away, but he was so much bigger than me. So much stronger. My nails raked across his wrists, drawing blood, but his grip only tightened.

"Stop fighting," he hissed against my ear. "This is your fault. All of it."

I held my breath until my lungs burned, but I couldn't hold it forever. When I finally gasped for air, the chemical flooded my system, the room tilted sideways, and my legs turned to water.

Axel, I thought desperately as darkness crept in from the edges of my vision.

My muscles went limp, arms dropping uselessly to my sides. He caught me as I collapsed, throwing me over his shoulder in a fireman's carry like I weighed nothing.

"Excuse me," he said cheerfully to someone as we passed through the door. I could hear the smile in his voice, the perfect act of concern. "She had a little too much champagne. Better get her home."

I tried to lift my head, tried to wave my hand, tried to do anything to signal for help. But my body had betrayed me completely. I was nothing but dead weight in his arms.

The last thing I heard was the emergency exit door clicking

shut behind us, cutting me off from the warmth and laughter and safety of the reception.

Cutting me off from Axel.

The cool night air hit my face as I realized with growing horror that no one had seen us leave.

No one was coming to save me.

55

AXEL

A flicker of unease sparked in my chest. A nagging feeling when something's slightly off. She'd probably just gone to talk to someone else or something. But as my eyes swept the crowd again, that flicker grew brighter.

My feet started moving toward the restrooms. Casually at first, just checking.

"Excuse me," I said to an elderly woman emerging from the ladies' room. "Is there a woman in there? One of the bridesmaids?"

She looked puzzled. "Oh, no, dear. It's completely empty."

Empty.

The unease in my chest shifted, hardening into something sharper. I pushed open the door myself, ignoring the scandalized gasp from a passing guest. Seven stalls, all open. All vacant.

The wariness was spreading now, creeping up my spine like cold weeds.

She was probably getting a drink. Maybe I'd missed her in the crowd; three hundred people made it easy to lose someone. Right?

So, why were the hairs on the back of my neck standing up?

"What's wrong?" Jace asked.

He and Ryker appeared at my side when I returned, all traces of our earlier banter evaporated.

"I can't find Dakota."

They caught the edge in my voice immediately. Jace's expression shifted from casual concern to sharp focus.

"There are three hundred people here," he said, but his tone was already shifting from reassurance to strategy. "She's probably just socializing somewhere."

Probably. But that cold feeling was spreading through my chest like spilled ice water.

"I'll take the east side," Ryker said, his lawyer brain already cataloging exit points.

"West side," Jace confirmed.

I was already moving toward the dance floor, that chill now racing through my bloodstream. When I reached Scarlett and Faith, still laughing and twirling, their smiles died the second they saw my face.

"Where's Dakota?" The question cut through their joy like an axe.

"What?" Faith's brow furrowed.

"Dakota," I snapped, crueler than I meant to be. "Did she tell you where she was going?"

The girls exchanged a look that made my stomach drop.

"She said she was going to the ladies' room."

Fuck.

My heart was hammering now, beating with copper and fear.

I spun around, and suddenly, the entire reception had shifted. The warm golden lighting felt harsh and glaring. The laughter around me turned warped and distant, like hearing sound underwater, and every face in the crowd looked wrong. Too many strangers, too many people I didn't know or trust.

This beautiful fairy-tale wedding had just crashed into black and white with a record screech.

"What's going on?" Blake appeared at my elbow, abandoning his bride mid-dance.

"Dakota." I was moving through the crowd now, pushing past guests with growing desperation. "I can't find Dakota anywhere."

He fell into step beside me. "When did you last see her?"

"Five minutes ago. Maybe ten?" I ran a hand through my hair. How had I not been watching her? "She was at the bar with the girls." I found Jace near the exit, his face grim. "Any luck?"

"Nothing. Tried calling her. Straight to voicemail."

The fear was a living thing now, clawing its way up my throat.

"Ryker?" I called out as he approached.

"Nothing," he said, but his lawyer's mask had slipped. I could see the worry etched in the lines around his eyes. "She's not anywhere in the venue, as far as I can tell. Even checked the bridal suite."

"... not anywhere in the venue."

The words hit me like a sword to my sternum. All our friends had gathered around me now: Scarlett, Faith gripping Blake's arm, Tessa looking between us with growing alarm. Everyone was trying to keep their voices calm, their expressions hopeful.

But none of us could say out loud what I knew with sick certainty in the pit of my stomach.

Dakota wasn't lost in the crowd.

Dakota was gone.

"Call the police," I said, my voice barely recognizable. "Call them now."

56

DAKOTA

Pieces of consciousness came back to me in fragments. Dark shapes at first, all still, not moving. My chest burned from whatever I had inhaled. My throat was raw.

The first thing I realized was that I couldn't move my arms. They were twisted behind my back, something biting into my wrists whenever I tried to move. My back pressed against something hard. I was seated, I realized. In a room. A dark room. Small room.

In the darkness, it was difficult to make out what was in front of me. It looked like a series of sticks of some sort, propped up on the ground. Something round protruded from one, and a square protruded from another. All of them taking the form of silhouettes with the faintest artificial light streaming through the window. City lights? Streetlights? That familiar amber color that used to stream into my old apartment—

Wait.

That shadowy dent in the wall. That specific crack in the plaster that looked like a lightning bolt. I'd stared at it a thousand times while filming, always meaning to patch it, but never getting around to—

Holy shit.

I'm in my apartment.

My old studio room, to be exact. The room where I'd built my empire, one perfectly curated post at a time. Everything had been moved, relocated to Axel's penthouse. But somehow, this man had gotten in. Copied my key when I wasn't looking? Broken in? Did it matter?

Movement flickered in my peripheral vision just before lights exploded like a bomb going off. Stadium bright. Interrogation-room bright.

I squeezed my eyes shut from the assault.

"Good. You're awake." Mathew's voice drifted from across the room, casual, as if we'd bumped into each other at Starbucks.

I forced my eyes open, blinking through the burn until the room came into focus.

He stood behind what I now recognized as a professional setup he must have brought himself: tripods loaded with cameras, angled beauty lights, positioned with surgical precision. One circular, one square. He'd even set up a bounce board against the far wall, the kind that made your skin look porcelain perfect and erased every flaw.

All of it aimed directly at me.

A quick scan revealed the rest of his twisted vision: my old dresses—the ones I'd been searching for, the ones that had somehow disappeared shortly before we broke up—now hung in shredded ribbons across the back of my chair like confetti from hell. And covering every inch of the wall behind me were photos. Hundreds of them.

All of me.

Screenshots from my videos, candid shots I'd never posed for, images where I was smiling that perfect influencer smile. Every single one showed me looking like the epitome of success and beauty.

What in the ever-loving hell is this?

"What ..." My voice cracked, thanks to whatever chemical cocktail he'd used to knock me out. How long had I been out? Hours? Days? "What are you doing?"

Mathew ignored me completely, fingers dancing across multiple cell phones and camera controls. Over half a dozen devices, all blinking red, like hungry little eyes.

"Time for your live stream," he said, not bothering to look at me. His tone was conversational. Friendly even. Which somehow made it ten times more terrifying.

He's about to go live, I realized. Probably on all *my* platforms.

"Want to know what I'm calling it?"

The cameras beeped in sequence with a digital countdown to disaster. My follower notifications were probably exploding right now. Thousands of people tuning in, expecting another slice of my life.

"Dakota Fox's Final Live Stream."

The word hit me like a sledgehammer to the chest.

Final.

Oh God.

57

AXEL

"There has to be more we can do!" I snapped, my hands clenched into fists.

"I'll call my PI," Jace offered.

"That's too slow!"

"Sir, you need to calm down," the short officer with the too-thick mustache drawled, like he was discussing the weather instead of the missing love of my life.

Jace put a hand on my shoulder, but I shrugged it off. I didn't need comfort. I needed him to join Blake in hunting the premises again. I needed someone to actually do something. *I* needed to do something.

"Someone's taken her," I shot back, desperation bleeding through every syllable.

"You don't know that." The cop couldn't have sounded more bored if he'd tried. His lazy eyes swept over me like I was some hysterical boyfriend crying wolf.

Are you fucking kidding me?

"Did you not hear a word we said?" I snapped, pacing the

parking lot like a caged animal. Bits of gravel crunched under my dress shoes with each sharp turn. "No one can find her!"

"Yet," the officer said.

I stepped forward, ready to grab this useless piece of ... but Ryker blocked my path. His hand pressed against my sternum. Hard.

"Easy," Ryker warned. "You won't do her any good behind bars."

He was right. Damn it, he was right.

Breathe. Think. Dakota needs you thinking, not fighting.

"Look," I growled at the cop, forcing my voice lower. "Fucking LOOK for her! That's your job, isn't it? What you get paid to do?"

The officer's spine straightened two inches. "You're lucky I'm taking a report at all," he clapped back. "Only reason I'm doing that is because he pulled in a favor." He jerked a thumb toward Ryker. "Normal protocol is, you wait at least twenty-four hours to file a missing person's report for an adult—"

"Are you going to do anything or not?" I stopped pacing, pinning him with a glare.

"Let's go over your statement again."

Jesus Christ.

"The cameras." I motioned toward the security system mounted on the building. "Review them!"

"No one here saw her leave."

"Which is exactly why the cameras are so helpful!" My voice cracked with frustration. "She couldn't have vanished into thin air. Surely, the cameras caught something."

God, this was like pulling teeth. I would've been better off barging into the security room myself and knocking the guard unconscious just to get my hands on the footage.

At the pace this guy was going, Dakota might be dead long before he even finished taking his damn statement. Because they must have been wrong. The Romano family must have very much wanted revenge after all.

"I'm going to check her phone again," I muttered, pulling out my cell.

"No one found it," he reminded me, like I hadn't been there when they'd searched.

"No shit." I pulled up the Find My Phone app and was once again punched in the gut with the reality that her phone was still off. I knew it was a long shot, but this app was my only tether to her, the only way I could—

Ding.

My social media app lit up with a notification.

Dakota Fox is live!

My blood turned to ice. "What the fuck?"

I clicked on the link with shaking fingers, and cold dread flooded my limbs like poison. The image that filled my screen made my knees nearly buckle.

Dakota. Half conscious. Tied to a chair.

No. No, no, no.

58

DAKOTA

Mathew slipped on a ski mask and came over to me. Instinctively, I recoiled away from him, but he merely chuckled.

"So dramatic," he muttered, sweeping some fallen hair back into position.

"What are you doing, Ma—"

The blur of his hand registered a millisecond before pain exploded across my cheek. Hard. So hard, my head whipped to the left, and stars danced behind my eyelids.

"If you want the privilege of continuing to have a tongue, you'll be careful with your words."

My cheekbone throbbed like a drum, but I pushed through the pain and turned back to him. Oh. He was trying to keep his identity hidden. For the cameras.

Like anyone watching won't figure out it's my unstable ex-boyfriend.

"What are you doing?" I managed.

"You thought you could just push me away? After everything I've done for you?" His voice cracked with hurt and rage. A dangerous combination.

My mind scrambled to understand. "What are you talking about?"

"I made you, Dakota. I was your first fan. First person who believed in you when you were nothing."

I blinked away the shock swimming in my vision.

"Username BlushBabe123 ring a bell?" He asked.

My jaw fell open, horror swirling in my chest like a warning siren sounding far too late. "*You* are BlushBabe123?"

I could hear his smirk beneath the mask. "The one and only."

No. No, no, no.

My stomach dropped to my feet. I thought that person was some girl who appreciated my makeup tutorials and hair product reviews. But after a while, BlushBabe123 started to creep me out. I'd post a video, and fifteen seconds later, there would be a comment, like they were just sitting there watching my account, waiting for me to post something. I told myself I was being paranoid, that the girl probably just had alerts set up on her phone. Plus, that was what I wanted, wasn't it? Engagement?

God, I was so stupid.

Now I replayed all of that through this new lens. That had been Mathew the entire time? Long before we ever "met"? And when we did meet, he'd claimed he'd never seen my online account.

"I was your biggest supporter before anyone else cared. I saw your potential when you were nobody."

He leaned down, bringing those dark eyes—and, Jesus, the black had spread through them like ink, like the Devil himself had drained away all the color—closer to mine.

"I helped cultivate your rise." His tone dripped with ownership. "I created a hundred usernames to comment on your posts. The algorithms love that kind of engagement."

A hundred different accounts? It was a full-time job for me to keep up with just one. That wasn't support.

It was obsession.

"I gave you your first expensive studio light. I gave you the stage. I built the woman they adore. I'm the one who encouraged you to always look your best."

Which I had interpreted as encouragement from a supportive boyfriend. Not manipulation from an online stalker who'd been pulling my strings from day one.

"I became your fantasy ideal," I realized.

"And you ruined it!" His voice cracked like a whip. "You ruined everything! You were perfect, Dakota. My perfect creation. And then you destroyed yourself on that live stream. You showed them the broken, pathetic girl underneath all the beauty I built."

Looking at the pictures taped behind me again, I realized with growing horror that Mathew wasn't just a jilted ex-boyfriend. He was an obsessed fan who'd lost his favorite toy.

"But you left me," I said, grasping for logic in this nightmare. "Months ago, you left me for another job."

I braced for him to catch my mistake, to deflect or punish me for nearly exposing his identity. After all, anyone close to me would know *who* had left me for another job. But he was too far gone in his rage to even notice what he was revealing.

"You were supposed to come with me!" he snapped, and I could see his hands shaking with rage. He was hemorrhaging tells now, leaving breadcrumbs that would lead straight back to him. But he was spiraling too fast to realize it, lost in whatever twisted narrative he'd built in his head.

I replayed what happened with a new light. At the time, I had been so devastated at the obvious end of our relationship because there was no way I would move across the world from my family. I thought Mathew knew that. But looking back, that's exactly what he expected. And by the time he realized I wasn't going to do it, too many things had been set into motion. Hell, if I remembered correctly, the furniture had already been shipped overseas when he'd finally gotten the message.

And when he moved and I didn't follow, that's why he wouldn't stop texting and calling me. Not because he loved me.

Because he still thought he could manipulate me into following him. When that didn't work, he came back.

"It wasn't a coincidence that you showed up at the restaurant that night, was it?" I accused. The night Axel and I made our first public appearance together.

Axel and I were basically finished with dinner when Mathew had arrived with his brother and future sister-in-law. They'd just sat down to eat. He must've convinced them to come with him so it wouldn't look so obvious.

"You were monitoring my social media posts. Following those influencers who were reposting real-time updates of my dinner with Axel. Including the location."

"I moved halfway across the world for you." The venom in his voice carried the promise of retribution. "And then there you were, in the arms of another man. After everything I sacrificed! After everything I built for you! You threw it all away for him."

Something else niggled in the back of my mind. His jealousy, his possessiveness. "You're the one behind the threats, aren't you?"

Mathew stood up, satisfaction radiating from his posture.

"You're the one who sent those flowers." The memory hit me like ice water. Had he been following me too?

"You should have left Axel Pierce then."

"You wanted me to be afraid to date him. Like we'd be in danger."

"He hit on a woman whose family has ties to suspected organized crime. He *is* a threat to you, Dakota."

Jesus. Of course Mathew would've seen my accidental post that started the PR nightmare. With his level of obsession, he probably would've researched Axel Pierce immediately, figured out exactly who that woman was and what kind of people she was connected to.

"You're behind my assault too," I realized, the pieces clicking together with sickening clarity.

"All I did was hire a guy to hit you. *Once*. Didn't it strike you as odd that he didn't rob you or do anything else? I wasn't going to let you get killed, Dakota."

I was going to be sick. Actually throw up right here on live stream.

"You led a violent criminal right to me!"

"The flowers didn't work, so you needed another push to leave him. I was trying to save you from yourself, Dakota. You were making all the wrong choices. First destroying your perfect image online, then choosing him over me. Me! The person who made you everything you are!"

Oh my God. "You're deranged," I said, staring at this stranger wearing my ex-boyfriend's eyes. "You can't claim to love someone and send a violent criminal to hurt them at the same time."

I thought back to how Mathew acted that night I'd been hit. He'd been crouching by my side, almost as if ... as if he expected I'd seek refuge in his arms?

"Love?" He laughed, a sound like broken glass. "This stopped being about love the moment you betrayed everything I built. You were supposed to be grateful. You were supposed to choose me. Instead, you spat in my face."

That's what set him over the edge, I realized. Coming to my apartment. Finally hearing me profess my love for Axel, seeing the evidence we'd just made love in the dew on my skin.

Mathew walked to the other side of the cameras again, adjusting the lighting to get it just right. Professional to the end. And then, to my horror, he picked up something from the floor, gesturing around the room with it.

"You want to know what this is really about, Dakota?" He turned back to me, his voice turning cold and methodical. "First, I'm going to destroy what's left of your pathetic online image. Show everyone who you really are underneath all the makeup and filters. The broken, ugly truth."

I'd already revealed my makeup-free self to my followers, so something told me whatever he had planned to show who I "really" was, would be much more ominous.

"Mathew—"

"Then, when I'm done humiliating you the way you humiliated me ..." His voice dropped to a whisper that somehow felt more terrifying than his shouting. "Well, if I can't have you, no one can. Especially not him."

The implication hit me like a sledgehammer. He was going to kill me. On camera. For everyone to see.

"Enough talking." He walked closer to me, and that's when the studio lights reflected off something in his hand.

Something that gleamed like a promise.

A knife.

59

AXEL

The police officer, Ryker, and Jace crowded next to me, staring at my screen in stunned silence.

"He has her." The words came out flat, final. "This isn't the Romano family. It's Mathew."

I'm going to kill him.

"I'm calling backup," the officer said, suddenly all business now that he had proof.

Too late for that.

God, she looked so vulnerable. Right behind the cold dread of realization came boiling hot fury that burned through my veins like acid. He'd taken her. He'd done this to her. I needed to get to her. Now.

But where? Where the hell was she?

I scrutinized the video feed, searching for any clue, any detail that could tell me her location. A lone wall stood behind her, wall-papered with photos of Dakota, like some sick shrine. I pushed down the bile of disgust, realizing this was so much more than a jilted ex-lover.

This is pure, deranged obsession.

Wait.

That door.

"What is it?" Jace asked, noticing my sudden focus.

"I think I recognize that door." My heart hammered against my ribs.

"How?"

"When I was moving Dakota's camera equipment out, I smacked it with one of the tripods. Put a little hole in the door, just like that." I pointed to the screen, to the tiny puncture in the wood that I'd made. "She freaked out because she thought it would cost her the security deposit and ..."

The only way I'd gotten her to calm down was by kissing her.

"He took her to her old apartment."

"What's the address?" Ryker demanded.

I rattled it off: apartment number, building code, everything.

"Can you get backup there now?" Ryker pressed the deputy.

"Calling it in."

"I'll make a call too," Jace insisted.

The officer was already on his radio, but I was done waiting. Done with protocols and procedures while Dakota was—

"Axel, wait," Ryker pleaded as I started running. "Where are you going?"

"I'm not waiting."

"You're never going to beat the cops there," Jace reasoned, jogging to keep up with me.

He was right. Traffic would be hell, and even if I floored it, sirens moved faster than civilian cars.

Unless ...

I spotted a kid leaving the venue, early twenties by the looks of it. Probably a waiter. But most importantly, he had just swung his leg over a motorcycle.

Perfect.

"I need to borrow your bike." I approached him with my hands up in a nonthreatening gesture.

The kid furrowed his eyebrows at me, waiting for the punch line. "Yeah, that's not gonna happen, man."

"Listen to me." My voice was steel. "There's a woman in danger. I need to get to her right now. Your bike is the only way I can get through this traffic fast enough."

"Dude, I'm not loaning my motorcycle to some random stranger." He started putting his helmet on, dismissing me entirely.

Fuck it.

I contemplated punching him in the throat, knocking him unconscious, and stealing his bike, but with my luck, I'd end up in a jail cell instead of saving Dakota.

"I'll give you a hundred thousand dollars." Jace appeared next to me, phone already in hand like some kind of miracle.

The kid pulled his helmet off slowly, his eyes rounding. "Wait ... are you Jace Lockwood?"

"I am."

"Dude, I'm in business school. I've seen your articles in *Fortune* magazine and—"

"A hundred grand," Jace cut him off, all business. "But only if you give him the motorcycle right now. He'll return it when he's done. Tell me your favorite money transfer app, and I'll wire it immediately. If you know my name, you know I'm good for it."

The kid looked between Jace and me, probably calculating whether this was real or some elaborate prank.

"Dude, for a hundred grand, you can keep the bike." He slammed the helmet into my chest. "Keys are in it."

"Thank you," I said to my billionaire friend, who gave me a sharp nod.

I didn't waste time putting the helmet on. Instead, I hopped on the bike, and as Jace and the kid started fumbling with transfer apps behind me, I peeled out of the parking lot so fast, the scent of burned rubber filled my nose.

"I'm coming, Sunshine," I shouted into the wind, the engine

roaring beneath me as I wove through traffic like my life depended on it.

Because hers does.

"Hold on."

60

DAKOTA

"You were always meant to be mine. Perfect, poised, polished. For me." Mathew's voice carried the weight of years of delusion. "But now you're flaunting your flaws and calling it bravery?"

He held out a piece of paper in front of me, covered in scribbled writing. In his other hand, he twisted the knife handle like a nervous habit.

I jerked against my restraints, trying to break free, but that's when I realized my legs were bound to the chair too. The binds scratched against my ankles. With my arms bound behind me, legs trapped, there was no escape.

Think, Dakota. There has to be a way out of this.

I started wiggling my wrists, trying to work them free from what felt like zip ties that bit deeper into my flesh with every movement. The plastic edges drew blood, warm and sticky against my skin.

"Read this."

"Screw you."

"Read this."

The blade kissed my throat, cold as winter, my pulse hammering against the sharp edge.

"*I lied to all of—*"

"Louder!" Mathew barked.

"*I lied to you all. I'm not brave. I'm a fraud. I need the filters. I'm nothing without your approval.*"

He lowered the paper and, to my immense relief, set the knife on the floor. But then he retrieved something else: a cloth and a small bottle full of liquid.

Oh, hell no.

I began squirming and thrashing, trying to kick, trying to knock myself over, anything to prevent another round of chemicals, and as I did, the chair creaked ominously under my struggles.

"Stop," Mathew said, dripping liquid onto the cloth and drawing it closer to my face.

I tried to jerk away. *What if it's acid? What if he's done playing games and this time, this chemical will kill me?*

"No!" I cried, pulling away from the cloth every chance I got, but within seconds, he had it pressed against my cheek.

He wasn't holding it over my mouth or nose though, and it didn't burn.

When he continued wiping my face, the cloth coming back tinted tan and pink, understanding hit me like a slap.

Makeup remover.

"Stop moving." He grabbed my jaw, his fingers digging into my cheeks as he scrubbed the cloth so harshly against my skin, it burned. The makeup remover stung my eyes, making tears stream down my face as he methodically removed every trace of foundation, mascara, lipstick. The cloth grew darker with each swipe.

He's deconstructing me. Taking apart the perfect image piece by piece. He wanted to strip away the fantasy girl and show everyone what was underneath. Show them that I was just ... human.

I'd already done that on my own, but this was different.

He wanted to degrade me. Humiliate me in front of however many people were watching.

I stared into the cameras, wondering how many feeds might still be live. Surely, the major social media platforms would've flagged this content by now and shut it down, but he had multiple cameras, some I could only assume were connected to darker corners of the internet.

He needs his stage. His audience.

Which gave me an opportunity, didn't it? I needed to get a message to anyone who was watching. I needed to tell them where I was before it was too late. It was a long shot, but maybe someone could save me before Mathew did something there was no coming back from.

"Please help me. I'm at 41—"

His hand clamped my mouth shut before I could read off the rest of my address.

"Now." Mathew grabbed the knife again, testing its edge against his thumb. A thin line of red appeared, and I could smell the copper scent of blood, mixing with the lingering chemical odor in the air. "You're really not going to like this part."

61

AXEL

A river of taillights stretched before me like a blood-red warning, and wind rushed through my hair, across my skin, the violent rumble of the engine vibrating through my entire body until my bones hummed with it.

Move. Faster.

With my heart racing, I wove through traffic at dangerous speeds, running another red light. Horns blared behind me as the city around me blurred into a kaleidoscope of streetlights and headlights piercing through the darkness.

Hold on, Sunshine. Just hold on.

Taking a sharp left, the bike nearly tipped over and the world tilted sickeningly before I corrected, with adrenaline flooding my system. A split-second reminder that if I crashed, I was no good to her.

But I can't slow down. Not now.

I picked up speed, swerving right around a white sedan, left around a black pickup truck, leaning into every turn until the asphalt felt inches from my knee. Skyscrapers flew past me in towering blurs of glass and steel.

I should've seen this coming.

Mathew's obsession. The threats. The flowers. All of it had been building to this, and I'd been too focused on our fake engagement, too caught up in falling for her to see the real danger lurking in the shadows.

I should've protected her.

My knuckles were white on the handlebars, heart pounding so hard, I could hear it, even over the engine's roar. The speedometer climbed higher. Sixty, seventy, eighty through city streets that weren't meant for this kind of speed.

What if he's already—

No. I couldn't think like that. Dakota was strong. She'd fight him. She'd find a way to survive until I got there.

She had to.

The familiar streets of her neighborhood came into view, and I leaned hard into the final turn. Rubber squealed against asphalt, the smell of burning tire once again filling my nose.

Almost there.

Please don't let me be too late.

62

DAKOTA

I tried two more times to scream my address, my location, and his identity for police, but Mathew clamped my mouth each time until finally, he threatened me.

"I'll stuff your mouth with cloth," he warned. "But you might choke to death on it."

My heart stilled. I couldn't risk choking. I had to keep him talking, keep dragging this out, looking for an opportunity to escape or pray to hell the cops would show up in time.

"You're never going to get away with this." I thrashed around, trying to escape the knife.

"If you don't hold still, you're likely to really get hurt, Dakota. You wouldn't want that, would you?" His voice was sickeningly patient, like he was talking to a child.

"You're about to slash my throat."

"Not yet, Dakota. Not yet." The promise in those words made my blood turn to ice.

Mathew's free hand moved to my hair, fingers threading through the strands until he found the clip that held it up. He unfastened it, then removed all the bobby pins one by one, each metal piece falling to the floor like tiny metal countdowns to my demise.

What in the creepy clown hell is he doing?

"You stripped yourself down for the world. So, let me help." His breath was hot against my ear. "Let me show them who you really are."

He grabbed a fistful of my hair and used the knife to start slicing through it. The blade whispered through each lock, chunks of strawberry-blonde falling to the floor like dying leaves.

This can't be happening.

After everything Axel and I had been through, I thought we'd finally gotten our happily ever after. I thought the worst was behind us.

Thinking of Axel sent a fresh wave of agony crashing through me. When he found out what happened, when they found my body, Axel would never forgive himself. I could only hope Mathew would be in prison or dead because if he wasn't, Axel would hunt Mathew to the ends of the earth and kill him.

That's the depth of protectiveness he had for me. Axel would never let it go.

Ever.

But that wouldn't change anything right now. As much as I thrashed around, I couldn't escape these bindings. I couldn't escape this chair, and I couldn't escape this stage of horror. And even if someone somehow recognized where I was, it would be too late to save me by the time they got here.

I would never get to hold Axel again. Never get to kiss him and tell him I loved him. I wished I'd told him just one more time before I left the wedding.

"Do they still love you when you cry like this?" Mathew taunted, cutting through the last lock of hair. "Or do they finally see you the way I do now: pathetic and broken?"

Tears streamed down my face, but I swallowed back the sobs building in my chest.

I really hope Axel isn't watching this.

But this live stream was my only connection to the outside world. Mathew might kill me, but I wouldn't let him get away with it. And I sure as hell wouldn't let him control the narrative.

I looked directly into one of the cameras, hoping it was still live.

"This is what happens when a man thinks he owns you. When you stop being his fantasy and become a woman with a voice."

Mathew's slap came fierce and hard, the crack echoing through the small room. "You don't like it when I use your platform against you, do you?"

I spat blood onto the floor.

Mathew put the knife to my throat again, but I looked at the camera one more time.

"This is what obsessive control looks like. This is—"

Pain exploded against my jaw. At first, I thought I'd been stabbed, especially because I was suddenly on the floor, the chair having toppled with me under the impact of Mathew's fist. The full force hit my jaw so hard, I tasted copper and feared something was cracked.

But his attack had an unintended side effect: when I fell, my left leg's tie had slipped off the chair leg. And with one fast kick, I got my right foot free as well.

Oh my God. My legs are free. I'm free of the chair.

My right shoulder screamed in pain from the landing, but with adrenaline flooding my system, I rolled up onto my knees.

Run.

Run, Dakota.

Get to the front door.

"Help!" I screamed, praying a neighbor would hear me through these thin apartment walls. "HELP ME!"

Another blow caught me in the ribs, sending me sprawling again. Blood dripped from my nose onto the floor, right near—

The knife!

In our struggle, one of the cameras had been knocked over, too, its red recording light still blinking frantically.

"Goddammit," Mathew snapped, pressing his finger to his split lip and drawing it back to reveal blood. "You're a pain in the ass—you know that?"

I rolled my body over the knife before he could see it, the blade's handle digging into my back as Mathew stood up to fix one of the cameras.

Come on, come on.

As Mathew spat out a stream of curses, picking up the tripod and adjusting the lighting that had been disrupted in our struggle, I rolled onto my side and began sawing at my bindings. Fast. Furious.

Snap.

I heard the slight pop at the precise moment my wrists freed themselves, circulation rushing back into my hands like fire.

"Now." Mathew stalked closer to me, his mask slightly askew. "Time for the finale."

I rolled onto my side and jumped to my feet, holding the knife out in front of me with trembling hands. "Stay back!"

He froze. Those dark eyes, the only thing visible beneath that mask, narrowed with fury.

My lips quirked up in the first genuine smile I'd felt in hours. "Oops. You dropped your knife, MATHEW."

His chest heaved.

"Mathew Ashford," I announced to the cameras, my voice stronger now. "He's my ex-boyfriend and evidently an obsessed stalker."

"You're a lying little bitch."

Mathew lunged for me. I tried to stab him in the gut, but he was faster, grabbing my wrist and twisting it behind my back, spinning me around so my back was pressed against his chest. My arm burned where he'd wrenched it, the knife trapped between our bodies.

“That was a very stupid move, Dakota.” His breath was hot against my neck.

With my one free hand, I reached up behind me and grabbed the edge of his ski mask.

And ripped it off.

Exposing Mathew’s face for all the world to see.

63

AXEL

There it is.

My eyes burned with relief at the sight of Dakota's apartment building. In the distance, I could hear police sirens wailing through the night. They were close. But not close enough.

Not yet.

I screeched up onto the sidewalk in front of the building and dropped the bike right there. Didn't even bother turning it off. The engine continued its angry rumble as I sprinted toward the entrance.

Slamming the front door open so hard that it bounced off the wall behind it, I made my way to the stairwell, taking steps three at a time. My dress shoes slipped on the worn concrete, but I caught myself on the railing and kept climbing.

Please, Dakota. Please be okay.

The familiar smell of the building hit me: old carpet, cooking oil, the faint mustiness of too many people living too close together. Smells that might've meant home had I been visiting her on another occasion. Now they just meant desperation.

I glanced down at my phone screen during the rush up the stairs, and my blood turned to ice.

The live stream on her primary platform had ended. Or been shut off due to violence?

Oh God.

What if I'm too late?

Images flashed through my mind: Mathew with that knife, Dakota's terrified face, the way she'd looked so small, tied to that chair. What if the last thing I'd see of her was through a phone screen?

I charged up the stairs even faster, my lungs burning, and finally bolted down the hallway toward her apartment door.

Please don't be too late. Please, please, please.

The hallway stretched endlessly in front of me, each step echoing off the walls like gunshots. Her door was just ahead: 3B. A place that had been her sanctuary.

Now it was her prison.

I reached for the handle.

Locked.

64

DAKOTA

Mathew shoved me to the ground.

I fell to my knees, the impact jarring through my bones, but quickly spun around. In a heartbeat that felt like the expanse of eternity, I registered the pure fury rippling across his face. His lips curled back, revealing teeth like a snarling animal, and one of his hands was balled into such a tight fist that his knuckles had gone white while the other gripped the knife like a lifeline.

He grabbed me by my much shorter hair.

With a yelp, I tried to fight him off, clawing at his arms, but he was stronger. So much stronger. His rage seemed to fuel him, making him superhuman as he held me with one hand and used his knife-yielding one to prop the chair back upright.

Then he slammed me back down onto it.

The breath whooshed out of my lungs as my spine hit the hard wood.

"You want to show your authentic self?" he snarled, moving into position behind me. The blade of the knife kissed my jugular, and I could feel my pulse hammering against the sharp steel. It was the only thing that kept me perfectly still now. One wrong move, one twist in the wrong direction, and I would bleed out on live stream. "Let's show them the real you. Scared, helpless, not the strong, independent woman you pretend to be."

This is it. This is how I die.

"Mathew, please." My voice cracked, barely a whisper.

"You wanted raw? You wanted real?" His breath was hot against my ear, and I could smell the metallic scent of blood, mixed with his sweat. "This is as real as it gets, baby."

Tears cascaded down my cheeks, hot and unstoppable. The salt stung the raw patches where he'd scrubbed away my makeup. With the cameras still rolling, recording every second of my humiliation, the knife pressed deeper into my skin. I felt the sharp bite of metal, felt a warm trickle slide down my neck.

The social media empire I built. The thing I was so proud of.

It had attracted this. A deranged man who'd fallen in love with a fantasy. A man who believed he was responsible for all my success. A man who believed he owned me.

And now it would cost me everything.

Axel, I'm so sorry. I love you.

Mathew's grip tightened in my hair, and the blade pressed deeper.

"Say goodbye, Dakota."

65

AXEL

I slammed my heel against the door, sending it flying open with a deafening crack of splintered wood. The frame exploded inward as I ran into her apartment and straight into the room that had been her studio.

It was there that Mathew held Dakota with a knife to her throat.

He must've heard the front door crack open because now, rather than facing the cameras, he had spun her around so she was facing me. Like some sick show-and-tell.

One look at the terror in her eyes was all it took to shatter me completely. I quickly assessed her body for injuries, cataloging each horror: her beautiful hair chopped short and uneven; red marks circling her wrists, where she'd clearly been bound; little pinpricks on her neck, where the knife tip had already drawn blood. Fresh tears streaked down her makeup-free face.

What did he do to you?

And still, the blade pressed against her jugular.

I put my palms up in surrender. "Let her go."

Mathew licked his lower lip, savoring the moment. "You're too late to be the hero, Pierce."

"Take me instead." The words came out steady, final. I meant every syllable.

"Take another step, and she'll bleed out faster than an ambulance can reach her."

I ground my jaw, tasting copper where I'd bitten my tongue.

"Tell me what you want." I forced my voice to stay calm. "My business? My money? All of it can be yours if you just let her go."

"Axel ..." Dakota's voice cracked, and she gasped when the knife pressed harder into her throat. A thin line of red appeared.

Don't you dare.

"She was mine first," Mathew sneered into her ear, his breath hot against her skin. "The only reason you want her is because of what I made her into."

Made her into? I had no idea what the hell he was talking about, but it didn't matter. Nothing mattered except getting that blade away from her neck.

"Put the knife down."

Instead, he trailed it along her throat, playing games. Relishing the control he had over both of us. The sick bastard was getting off on this.

I took one careful step forward.

Mathew snickered. "You think you can save her? Look at her." He grabbed her hair with his free hand, twisting her head to the side. "She's ruined."

"She's not a doll. She's a woman." My voice dropped to a growl. "And no matter what you do to her, you can never break her."

Dakota locked eyes with me and I watched her fear retreat behind a wall of pure determination. The same look she'd worn when she'd decided to fight for us.

That's my girl.

She gave me the slightest nod, and then she brought her knee up and stomped her heel down on his foot with everything she had.

Mathew jerked with a yelp of pain.

I lunged forward, using his moment of distraction to barrel into him. We went down hard, crashing into the tripods and sending cameras flying. I landed three solid punches to his temple, the impact reverberating up my knuckles, and then I wrapped my hands around his throat.

Squeezing the life out of him felt like justice. Mathew's eyes bulged as he clawed at my hands. He tried bucking me off, but I was straddling him with all my weight, and I had the angle.

Die, you sick fuck.

Unfortunately, he still had the knife.

He managed to slash it across my forearm, the sudden pain making me jerk back just enough for him to throw me off. We both scrambled to our feet, circling each other like wild animals, blood dripping from my arm.

Mathew lunged at me with the blade. I caught his wrist, but he was desperate now, fighting with the fury of a cornered animal. We grappled, spinning and crashing into the wall.

Suddenly, he twisted free and drove the knife forward.

The blade plunged into my side between my ribs with a burning explosion of pain that seared through my entire body. I staggered backward, gasping as the world tilted.

Shit.

The blade was still lodged in my side, hot blood soaking through my shirt. My chest felt like it was filled with concrete.

My lung is punctured.

But something far more horrifying took shape in my blurring vision: Mathew grabbing Dakota and slamming her up against the far wall, wrapping his hands around her throat.

I pushed forward, determination overriding the agony. Three steps. That was all I managed before my legs betrayed me and I crashed to one knee.

My brave girl fought him with everything she had. She tried to knee him in the groin, but he twisted away. She clawed at his arms, punched at his chest and face, but his grip was unrelenting.

As I heaved for air that wouldn't fill my lungs, she and I locked eyes across the chaos.

Both of us realizing we were going to die together.

66

DAKOTA

Blackness crept into my vision, and my focus blurred until everything became soft around the edges. My muscles weakened so that every kick, every punch, every desperate scratch lost its battle for strength.

This is it. This is how it ends.

I locked eyes with Axel across the chaos, wishing he could hear what I was trying to say rather than just see me mouth the words.

"I love you," I tried to squeak out.

But Mathew's hands were clamped too tightly around my throat, his fingers digging into my windpipe like a vise. The blackness encroached further, swallowing everything except Axel's face.

At least the last thing I'll see is him.

This was it. Axel was dying, too, blood pooling beneath him on the floor.

As my final breaths were withheld, I found myself grateful that my last thoughts were of love instead of fear. I was glad that I had found Axel. That I'd found true love. Something had awakened inside of me that many people never got to experience in their lifetime. The feeling of being truly alive and free and full of joy. The feeling of being someone's number one priority, being desired, being loved, being adored.

And being 100% my authentic self.

At least I got to experience it for a little while.

Goodbye, my love.

I will love you for all of eternity, I thought.

And then everything went dark as I slumped to the ground.

For a second, I thought I had died. But then I heard this inhuman wheezing sound, and I realized it was me. My lungs were sucking in deep gulps of oxygen so violently, it sounded animalistic, like I was drowning. My vision was returning, too, the blackness dissolving into light and blurry shapes.

I'm alive. How am I alive?

A figure moved in front of me, and through my tears, I saw him.

Axel.

"Dakota." He cupped my cheek with a trembling hand, his thumb brushing away the tears I didn't realize were falling.

Confusion swirled through me as consciousness fully returned. That's when I spotted Mathew lying motionless on the floor, a pool of blood streaming from his head. Lying next to him was a tripod with one of the cameras that, moments ago, had been recording our nightmare. It, too, was smeared with blood.

"You're safe now. I'm here. I've got you," Axel said, his voice rough with pain and relief. "Just breathe."

So, I did. Deep and slow, surrounded by the man I loved, feeling his heartbeat beneath my palm.

"Your side," I wheezed, noticing the knife still protruding from between his ribs. Blood soaked through his dress shirt, turning it crimson.

Axel looked down at the blade sticking out of his body, his own breathing labored and shallow. It was like his injuries were an afterthought compared to my safety.

"I'm fine," he claimed.

"You shouldn't have come." My voice was barely a whisper. "You could have been killed."

Axel's knuckles swept along my jaw, so gentle after all the violence. "Dakota, if you weren't breathing on this planet, I wouldn't want to breathe either."

Fresh tears flooded my eyes. Not from fear this time, but from overwhelming love.

He swiped a fallen tear from my cheek with his thumb. "Let's get you to the hospital."

Sirens grew louder outside, and a minute later, the room flooded with police officers and paramedics rushing toward us.

The live stream was over.

And our real life was just beginning.

I pressed my face into his chest, careful to avoid his wound, and Axel held me like he would never let me go. Like nothing in this world could ever tear us apart again.

67

LIVE FROM THE TIRE SLASHER VS. FLAT-TIRE VICTIM GROUP CHAT

AXEL

I eyed the name of the group chat, wondering why none of them had changed it back yet. But then I understood. This wasn't just about a name anymore. It was about officially putting this nightmare behind us. And that honor belonged to me.

Me: I need a favor.

Jace: Need another kitten mobile? I'm on it. [Sends GIF of a man running.]

Jace: Wait. I almost forgot. Made something for you:

Jace sent a picture of me in that cat convertible. He'd Photoshopped it into a romance book cover with the title: *Duke of the Dashboard Whiskers*. Book one in the Big Boys, Tiny Cars Series.

I smiled, grateful my friends were back to goading me. If they treated Dakota and me like victims, it would have bothered me extensively.

Me: Original. Do I need to pull up that picture of you on horseback again? I can make 50 romance covers and blast it online.

Blake: I just got home from my honeymoon. Don't give me a minute to catch my breath or anything. But sure, what can I do for you, lover boy?

Me: The favor's not for me, jackasses.

*Blake: Care to be more cryptic? *bored emoji* Use your words like a big boy.*

Jace: Let me guess. Dakota needs something?

Blake: Our fake boyfriend is officially whipped. Shocking development.

Ryker: "It's not for me" is code for "Dakota has me wrapped around her finger."

Me: Are you free on Saturday?

Jace: I'm not helping anyone move again. Drawing the line. My back has a restraining order against cardboard boxes.

Me: Relax, you pretentious billionaire. It's not moving. But it is manual labor ...

Jace: Pass.

Me: [Sends a picture of Jace on a horse with the title The Cowboy Who Couldn't Get His Fingernails Dirty, *book one in The CEO Who Cried Ew While Pretending to Be Rugged Series.]*

Jace: You're a jackass.

Me: [Sends a picture of Jace on a horse with the title From Boardroom to Barn: A Coward's Journey.*]*

Blake: Tessa would buy that in a heartbeat.

Me: I got twenty more ready to go. I'll send them to your office. Again.

Jace: You suck.

Ryker: So, what's the manual labor? Building Dakota a gazebo? Planting her a garden?

Blake: Installing a swing set for future fake babies? Scarlett let it slip that you changed your mind about future children, by the way.

Jace: Should we get matching I Survived Axel's Fake Relationship T-shirts?

Me: I'll take that as a yes. I'll send the address. See you Saturday. Bring work gloves. And your dignity, if you can find it.

Me: [Renames the group chat to Sinners and Saints.]

68

UPDATE: I THINK MY MOM HAS THE HOTS FOR AXEL. #MOMAPPROVAL

DAKOTA

I navigated the streets of the suburb with a smile on my face, feeling so grateful for everything.

I was grateful that Mathew was dead. Maybe that made me a horrible person, but the thought of someone that dangerous ever entering society again or somehow escaping prison would've kept me up at night for the rest of my life. I was grateful that Axel was okay after his stint in the hospital. I was grateful that I was okay too.

But today, I was most grateful for love. The love that Axel and I shared was like a new heartbeat in my soul, pumping joy and optimism through every breath. And I was grateful for the love of my parents.

Today, we had a longer to-do list on the house. We were going to tackle replacing the kitchen faucet, the rotted wood around the garage door, the exterior light fixture that had broken, and we were going to prep the front of the house for the new ramp I'd ordered. It would arrive next weekend, so we had to get everything ready.

It would be a long day, but I was looking forward to it. Next weekend, we'd move on to the gutters.

In the hospital, Jace had once again offered to hire an entire crew to handle this. Axel did too. Which was really sweet. But they didn't know my mom and dad. They were hardworking people, and financial handouts weren't in their comfort zone. It was hard enough for them to accept the help I was offering with my endorsement money.

Plus, I didn't mind the hard work. It gave us something to accomplish together.

I just wished we could get through the list faster. Because every repair that wasn't done was something hindering Mom and Dad's ability to live comfortably. A faucet without hot water, obstacles preventing Mom from moving around certain areas of the house with ease.

I turned the corner, and my smile fell, replaced with confusion.

"Oh no."

There were a handful of people on my parents' front lawn.

Did Jace not listen to me? I knew he probably would never understand, but Mom and Dad would be so upset if...

Wait.

Those weren't contractors.

The mixture of men and women all looked familiar.

As I pulled into the driveway, I threw the car in park and got out, my heart swelling.

"Told you she'd cry," Faith said with a grin.

"What are you all doing here?" I managed, looking at the people before me. Axel, Jace. Ryker, and Blake were dressed in jeans, T-shirts, and steel-toed boots, looking every part the construction workers rather than the billionaire, CEO, lawyer, and emergency room doctor that they were.

"Axel said if we didn't show up to help, he'd post our most embarrassing college photos on Instagram," Jace started.

Scarlett smacked his abs to shut him up. "I think what he's

trying to say is that Axel mentioned you guys could use some help."

Jace smirked, rubbing his stomach. "I'm just saying, phone calls are a lot easier than hammering nails."

"You're so spoiled," Scarlett said, trailing a finger down his chest. "It'll do you good to get your hands dirty. Besides, I'm loving seeing you in this construction gear."

"Jesus," Ryker muttered, adjusting his tool belt. "Can you two stop eye-fucking each other for like five seconds? You're as bad as Tessa and Blake with the PDA."

"Hey, we're still newlyweds," Tessa protested. "We get to have massive PDA for at least a year."

Blake grabbed her ass, and she squealed with delight.

Ryker leveled him with his best death glare. "I know you're her husband now, but for your dear brother-in-law's sake, can you keep your hands off my sister when I'm within a fifty-foot radius?"

"My husband can touch me anywhere, anytime," Tessa said, staring defiantly at her brother.

"And I will," Blake added with a wicked grin, pulling her closer.

Ryker made an exaggerated gagging sound. "Dakota, I'm happy to help, but if those two keep fondling each other, I'm out."

I smirked, wiping a tear off my cheek. "Fair enough."

"Well, while they're busy being gross ..." Jace said, patting his pockets. "Scarlett, where's my phone? You said I'd get it back once I could no longer replace us with paid contractors."

I smirked, imagining her snatching that thing from him.

"Come and get it," she challenged, backing away with a mischievous smile.

"Oh, you're asking for it now." Jace stalked toward her.

"Am I?" Scarlett took off running toward the backyard.

Jace immediately gave chase. "You're going to pay for that!"

Their laughter echoed as they disappeared around the corner, followed by a loud squeal that told us he'd caught her.

"Can you believe that dude runs a billion-dollar empire?" Axel shook his head.

"He's in love," I said, wrapping my arms around Axel, careful of his side. "Anyone in love is stripped down to their most basic instincts."

"You mean acting like horny teenagers?" Blake interjected.

"Children," Axel corrected. "She's calling them children."

I smacked his chest. "I am not!"

"Dakota!" Mom's voice rang out as she rolled down her bumpy ramp, Dad appearing behind her.

"Mom!" I jogged over and threw my arms around her. She'd visited me in the hospital, but I no longer took any of these moments for granted. I now understood that each time I saw someone I loved could be the last.

"Where's all this help coming from?" Dad asked, eyeing the group with amused suspicion.

"Axel called in reinforcements," I explained.

"We weren't expecting so much help," Mom said, her eyes bright with excitement. "I only bought snacks for four people."

"Don't worry about snacks, Mom."

Jace reappeared from the backyard, Scarlett thrown over his shoulder. "I can have any snacks you want delivered within the hour. What do you need? Sandwiches? Pizza? I can have Swiss chocolate air-dropped into the backyard—"

"Put me down, you caveman!" Scarlett laughed, pounding on his back.

"Give me my phone first."

"Never!"

Faith watched the chaos with an amused smile, and I caught Ryker sneaking glances at her when he thought no one was looking. She was wearing fitted jeans and a fitted shirt that showed off her toned arms. As such, Ryker seemed to be having trouble focusing on his tool belt.

"All right, all right," Dad interrupted, clapping his hands together. "Before someone gets hurt, let's get organized. Axel, son, where would you like us to start?"

Son. My heart melted.

Axel looked at my mom. "Mrs. Blackwood, this is your house. You're the boss."

Mom beamed and shot me a knowing look. "I really like your boyfriend, honey."

"Knox wasn't too thrilled," I reminded her.

"Your brother's cranky. When he gets out of prison, he'll come around. Now, follow me. I think we should start in the kitchen."

As everyone started discussing the day's tasks, Axel took my hand and paused for one last moment before we all got started.

"I love you, Sunshine." He kissed me raw, deep, and apparently without caring about our audience.

"Get a room!" Ryker called out, but I noticed he was still stealing glances at Faith, who was pretending not to notice.

"You know, I remember a time when you barely ever cried." He smirked, wiping away a tear.

"Well, that was before you made me go all soft and mushy."

He laughed. "Come on, Sunshine."

A fresh squeal from Scarlett came from the side of the house. Apparently, Jace wasn't done with his revenge. Blake and Tessa were sharing another quick kiss by the front steps. And Faith was asking Ryker to help her carry some supplies, their hands brushing as they reached for the same box.

Definitely interesting.

Axel walked me by the hand toward my parents' home. Into my future. Surrounded by friends who felt like family—actual family—and, most of all, love.

The kind of love that made even the hardest work feel like play and every ordinary moment feel like magic.

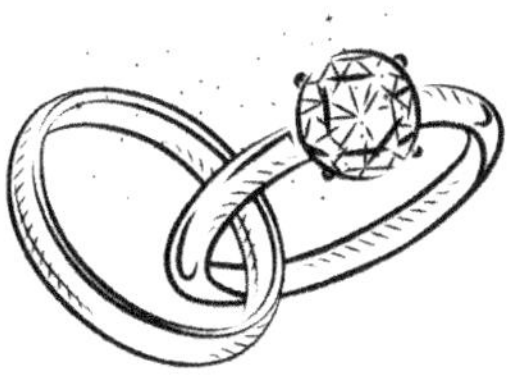

EPILOGUE

RYKER

"As I live and breathe, I cannot believe Axel Pierce has settled down with a woman." Blake shuffled the deck in the mansion's living room.

I snorted, tossing back my whiskey.

"The apocalypse must be approaching," Jace agreed.

Axel's trademark smirk surfaced. "We need to find Ryker a woman."

I reached for my drink. "I'm focused on getting Knox out of prison. And building my new firm."

Knox's absence sat at our table like a tangible weight, the empty chair sitting where we always left it for him.

"It's not your fault he's been denied parole," Blake said quietly.

I squeezed my cards until the edges bit into my palm. Years of law school with a near-perfect record, and I couldn't get my friend out. But I would. So help me, this was the year I would. "Let's just talk about something else."

"How's your new firm?" Jace asked, graciously changing subjects.

"Good. We only defend the innocent—that's our entire brand." I set down my cards. "Turn down anyone who's guilty, no matter what they pay. My entire career now depends on that principle."

We settled into familiar betting and bluffing until Axel leaned back with an unusual genuine smile. One that warned me he was about to stir the pot.

"So, how long have you been interested in Faith?"

Blake's eyes snapped to me, suddenly dangerous. "What?"

I couldn't help my smile. Blake's sister, Faith, had started coming around recently, and she was ... devastating. Not just beautiful either. It was the way she listened, like words actually mattered. It was the mysterious sadness in her eyes that made me want to know every story she'd never told.

For the first time in my life, I found myself actually wanting someone. Not just for a night. I wanted to know her. All of her.

I found myself looking for excuses to be wherever she was. Lying awake, wondering what made her feel safe, what her story really was beneath that carefully constructed surface. She was the first woman who'd ever made me reconsider my stance on relationships.

"Dude, that's my sister," Blake snarled.

"You're married to mine," I reminded him. "You don't have the moral high ground here."

"Go find someone else," Blake growled. "Faith's been through enough."

The little I'd learned about her—how she'd been brutally assaulted by a foster father and Blake had saved her life by killing him—made me grow only more intoxicatingly curious to know her. Every story, every scar, every truth she kept buried. How could a woman who'd been through so much be so effervescently full of light?

But that light had dimmed the last time I'd seen her. She'd seemed distracted. Almost afraid. I'd asked if she was okay, and she'd smiled, but it hadn't reached her eyes. I should have pushed harder.

I would push harder, the next time I saw her.

"The guy who fell for my sister against my explicit wishes has no right to complain," I said.

"She's still healing. The last thing she needs is someone breaking her heart."

"Who says I'd break it?"

Blake glared. "Stay away from her."

If he only knew.

Faith and I already had our secrets. Stolen moments, quiet confessions, a tension I pretended not to feel. Things Blake didn't know about. Not yet.

I wasn't sure how to even begin to tell him. Would I start with what happened in the elevator that day we caught Axel and Dakota in a compromising position? Or what really happened at his wedding, before Dakota had gone missing?

Before I could decide, the front door burst open with such force that we all jerked toward the sound, conversation forgotten, as a figure emerged in the mansion's living room.

Blood was splattered across her chest, down her legs, turning her white outfit into a macabre canvas of crimson. Her hair was wild, tangled, with something dark matting sections together.

Faith.

Everything in me went cold, then blazing hot. The room tilted sideways and my pulse detonated in my ears. I'd seen blood before —plenty of it in crime scene photos—but never on *her*. Never on the woman who'd somehow become the first crack in my armor.

She was shaking violently, breath coming in short gasps.

That's when I noticed the object in her hand. A serrated blade, slick with wet crimson.

No.

No.

I never defend killers. My entire firm—the one I built with every dollar I had—was founded on that principle. My reputation. My career. Everything I'd worked for.

And the only woman I'd ever wanted was holding what I was pretty sure was a murder weapon.

Faith's wide, terrified eyes snapped to mine. Not Blake's.

Mine.

Her lips trembled. "Ryker..."

Hearing my name in her broken, desperate voice, nearly brought me to my knees.

Then she whispered four words that changed everything:

"I need a lawyer."

Don't miss Faith and Ryker's story in DOUBT—an explosive forbidden romance where secrets, forced proximity, and a single impossible choice could tear the Sinners & Saints apart.

Craving more of Axel and Dakota? Get an exclusive bonus scene you won't find anywhere else by scanning the code below.

bitly

If you loved the enemies-to-lovers energy in **BOUND**, you'll devour, **FATAL CURE**—where a DEA agent hunts the kingpin who destroyed her family... only to discover he's the man she's fallen in love with...

Or, if you're craving more of Jace and the Lockwood brothers, jump into **SECRET VENDETTA** next.

ACKNOWLEDGMENTS

I'd like to thank you, the reader. Your time is limited, and I can't tell you how grateful I am that you chose to spend it in the Lockheart Universe! From the bottom of my heart, THANK YOU.

I want to thank Skye Warren and all the presenters and contributors to Romance Author Mastermind. I attended my first conference in 2024 and I've never experienced anything like it. Everyone there wanted to share with each other and help each other grow. There was a sense of camaraderie and support that was overwhelming and beautiful. It was at this conference that I discovered the next stepping stones of my career, and I can truly say I learned so much as an author. Thank you for sharing everything you learn with others!

I also want to specifically thank Jill Ramsower and Hannah Shield. I cannot express how much I appreciate you going above and beyond to share best practices with me, encourage me, and help educate me. Your support, encouragement, and wisdom have helped me grow as both an author and an entrepreneur. Thank you!

To my friends and family: your love and encouragement are something I feel grateful for every single day of my life. I love you more than any words I could ever write on a page.

Thank you to Susan Staudinger. Your developmental and content editing made this book far better than it ever would have been without you.

To Kristen, my formal beta reader. Thank you for helping make this story even better.

To Valentine and the entire staff at Valentine PR! This book wouldn't be what it is without you. Thank you!

To my editor Jovana, your attention to detail polished this story and made it the best it could be! To my cover artists, Hang Le and Sherri with Wild Love Designs, for bringing such beauty to this novel!

To all the authors who came before me—your success paves the road for new writers to do what they love. Thank you.

~ *Kathy*

LET'S CONNECT!

The easiest way to connect with me is to go to my website, www.KathyLockheart.com, and find my social media links. I interact with readers, so don't be surprised if you see me reply to your post or invite you to join a reader team!

Xoxo

Kathy

amazon.com/Kathy-Lockheart/e/B08XY5F2XG
bookbub.com/profile/kathy-lockheart
facebook.com/KathyLockheartAuthor
tiktok.com/@kathylockheart_author
instagram.com/kathy_lockheart
x.com/Kathy_Lockheart
pinterest.com/kathylockheart

Printed in Dunstable, United Kingdom

81403163R00262